N. O. K.

BRUCE BALLISTER

This is a work of fiction. All of the characters, names, incidents, organizations, and dialogue in this novel are either the products of the author's imagination or are used fictitiously. No person, living or dead is represented by the characters in this book. Some locations do exist and are used fictitiously. We make no representations of real persons who may use, reside, or control these locations, or the suitability of these actual locations.

N. O. K.
Copyright © Ballister Books 2021
Direct inquiries to: www.ballisterbooks.com

Cover Photo composite, the Author
Author Photo: Christine Chiricos
all rights reserved.

ISBN-13: 978-1733257121 Hardcover
ISBN-13: 978-1733257176 Softcover Trade
ISBN-13: 978-1733257114 ebook
LCCN: 2021907243

Printed in the United States of America

Dedicated to my wife and best friend, Christine.

I owe a special thank you to my pre-readers Sandra and Suzanne who were the inspiration for this special friend group and were my own high school friends. Thank you too, Betty Webb for the insight into the locale. I know of this part of Florida as a frequent visitor, she knows it as her home. I'm thankful too, for my editor, Christine Chiricos, for her diligence and persistence on top of her full-time obligations. And finally, Claire Matturro, for your insights and last-minute volunteered editing advice, thanks.

Other works by the author:

Dreamland Diaries and its follow-up **Orion's Light** follow Brad Hitchens from his discovery of an alien artifact in the Florida pinewoods behind his rural home through a journey that transforms human understanding of its place in the cosmos. He must battle federal agents who would hide the truth of its origins. He's had to leave home, hide with distant relatives, suffer loneliness and the relentless pursuit of the Feds. *Orion's Light* takes up the story, and to say more would spoil the fun. Who likes spoilers? Right?

Room for Tomorrow takes a fresh look at Cli-Fi, or Climate Fiction with a Sci-Fi twist. The book takes a hard look at where the climatological trend lines go. It's horrific to say the least. In *Room for Tomorrow*, Parker Parrish gets a look at that horror show in a small farmhouse bedroom in the hill country of Southern California. That room and its secrets may hold the key to our global salvation. The plot line progresses on two parallel timelines spaced one-hundred-ninety-four-years apart.

Ballister's foray into non-fiction includes **Welcome to the Zipper Club**, an account of his experience with heart disease, triple by-pass surgery, and the road to recovery. It is a short, fast, and personal account meant to inform and advise those who are anticipating a coronary artery bypass graft, or CABG, and the consequences of open chest surgery. The ebook is especially accessible, if you need this book in a hurry for yourself or a loved one.

Find your copies at Amazon books or ask for them
at your local bookseller.

Reader Reviews

"As a long-time fan of his other works, I couldn't wait to read Ballister's *N. O. K.*. With a unique voice set in one of the few remaining slices of 'Old Florida,' the novel opens with an immediately engaging protagonist where the action quickly escalates. Unlike most peoples' perceptions of touristy Florida, Apalachicola is the perfect setting for a tense thriller where young lives hang in the balance. Ballister skillfully weaves his way through many unpredictable turns in the action, as main character Jayson Saylor works to solve a missing person case that has life-altering implications for him, all while crafting a novel-within-a novel too! For a fast-paced story filled with believable characters, *N.O.K.* can hold its own with works by Edna Buchannan, Randy Wayne White, and Tim Dorsey. I highly recommend this first entry in what I hope will be a continuing series of crime fiction set in my favorite fishing village."

VernaLynn Swanson Brock, retired librarian

"Bruce Ballister might well be poised to do for the Forgotten Coast of North Florida what John D. MacDonald and Edna Buchanan did for South Florida—that is, put the region on the map for fans of suspense, mystery, and crime thrillers with a strong sense of place. Ballister spins a compelling, high stakes tale of a big city journalist who returns home to the Florida panhandle to write a novel only to be swept up into a missing-persons case involving a lovely young woman. Jason Saylor, hometown boy and fledgling author, becomes the lead person of interest in the case due his chance meeting with Lindsey Lawrence, the missing woman. But his connection to Lindsey goes far deeper than anyone—including Jason himself—could suspect. With criminal elements that cross the plot like newspaper headlines, questions of who-is-who and who can be trusted dig the mysteries deeper. The pacing, plot, danger, and characters are stellar and often steal the show, yet don't overlook the writing itself. Ballister knows how to put words together for dramatic and emotional impact. His frequently lyrical and beautifully descriptive phrases will bring the waters and coastlines of North Florida home for the readers."

Claire Matturro, author of *The Smuggler's Daughter* and associated editor of The Southern Literary Review.

With *N.O.K.*, police shorthand for "Next of Kin," author Bruce Ballister tells a taut mystery set against the watery wonderland of the Northwest Florida coast. He reels in the reader as expertly as an old-time Florida fisherman lures a trophy red. Folding in a developing romance, Ballister lands an exhilarating mystery with as many twists and turns as the Apalachicola River on its way to a surprise ending his readers might not see coming around the bend.

M R Street, Managing Editor, Turtle Cove Press

N. O. K.

BRUCE BALLISTER

1

Line Up

Jason Saylor noticed the police car in his rear-view mirror before the light bar lit up. His pulse had already elevated, pupils dilated, his focus shifted to ninety percent cop in the mirror and less than ten on the road ahead. He quickly glanced at the dials and noted thirty-seven miles per hour. The old school Garmin glued to his dash showed a thirty-five-mile-per-hour zone. The light bar flashed in alternating bursts of cop blue and emergency red. *Crap!* He did a mental inventory of anything possibly wrong. *Taillights? Registration should be good till his birthday, ten months out. Where is the receipt for insurance? Glove box, I think.* He glanced up at the mirror. It was a Franklin County Sheriff's patrol, not the City of Apalachicola.

He knew not to lean for the glove box until the officer was actually beside him. They'd think he might be going for a concealed weapon. Saylor had done ride-a-longs on his newspaper's cop beat too many times. *High beams? What the hell?* It hadn't been more than a moment, and he had only taken his foot off the gas. *There's an empty parking lot.* He flicked a finger to his right turn signal. At the same time, headlights again flashed impatiently from behind. Retina searing high beams in the mirror added to the migraine-inducing flashes of colors pulsing in his car.

Saylor pulled his aging Prius into one of the white rectangles. The patrol car pulled up diagonally behind him while, to his astonishment, a second patrol car pulled up in front, boxing his car. *Damn, two patrol cars? Is it a slow day in the off-season? Breaking News in Backwater! Two patrol cars respond to a broken tail light.*

Bruce Ballister

Saylor's mind, usually responding to new stimuli with plot or scene possibilities, was trying to continue the news flash idea when he heard the rap on his side window. He startled back to the current unreality and toggled the button to lower the passenger window. He noted that both front doors on the patrol car in front had opened, and two uniforms had gotten out.

"Sir, please put your hands where I can see them." The patrol officer's voice, polite as it was, left no option.

He put both hands at the ten and two position on the steering wheel. "Certainly. Officer is there a..., can I ask—"

"Sir, is this your vehicle?"

He looked up at the RayBan'd officer. "Why yes, I've had it since it was, since uh, about eight years now." He flashed back to the dealer and the deal and the surprise purchase of the—.

"Would you mind stepping out of the car, sir?" The officer stepped back a few feet and opened an arm as if to ward off a shoved door.

Or maybe just to invite his presence outside his Prius. Jason's mind was whirling, *not a tail light. What?*

"Sir?" A little more strident this time.

"Yes, of course. You've got me a little confused. Can I ask what the problem is?"

"Yes, but please step out of the car."

Saylor opened the door, got out, and stood, arms loose at his side. "Don't you want my license and registration?" The officer told him to reach in and get them. By this time, three officers stood around his car, a navy-blue Prius on its second battery pack. A junior officer with no rank insignia had his right hand on the black service holster on his hip. *Jesus, Mary, and Joseph!* He stood again and offered the registration, then pulled at his wallet for ID.

The first officer, unsmiling as before, twitched on seeing the driver's license. "Mr. Jason Saylor?"

"Yes."

"You're from Texas?" Saylor squinted from sunglassed uniform to sunglassed uniform. Officer One looked up from the license, from behind his shades. In the bright morning light, Jason could see through the heavy tint on his sunglasses. Sunlight reflecting off the bronzed name tag rendered it illegible.

2

Saylor answered inelegantly, "Uhm, yes, lately that is. Actually, I'm from here. I went to high school here, that is, class of 2001. Moved off to Tallahassee to go to college, then the army, more college, coupla jobs and, well, I'm back for a while."

"I see." The officer tapped the license on the fingertips of his left hand and having come to some conclusion, said, "Mr. Saylor, I'd like to ask you to come for a ride with us if you don't mind. You can lock up your car. It won't take too long. But we'd appreciate your cooperation." Officer One stepped aside a half step, signaling a now opened rear door to his cruiser.

"What?" Saylor stretched his imagination for anything he'd done or even imagined doing lately that could have initiated police interest. Hell, he hadn't even smoked in over ten years. "Am I under arrest? Can I ask why I need to go with you?"

"You especially busy? Need to make a call? We need you to come to the station for a small chat. We can probably clear things up. Your car will be fine here. Lock it up. Keep the keys."

Saylor stood his ground, but with his arms raised in surrender. "Why exactly do I need to go with you. I've done my share of ride-a-longs with law enforcement while on the job. I get to at least know." He waited, as the three officers exchanged sunglassed looks. "Right?"

Officer One said. "You are middle-aged, dark hair, dark car, and you're not from here." He tilted his head as if this were enough. "You do ride-a-longs you know what a BOLO is."

"Sure, 'be on the lookout.'"

The officer put a hand out as if encompassing the totality of what he was seeing. "That's you."

In a surreal sequence, he was guided to the back of a green and white and assisted into the rear seat, a palm on his head as he'd seen various criminals escorted away on TV. He noted that the two other officers both circled his car, one talking into a recorder as he peered into the back seat and passenger compartment. The ride to the sheriff's compound was short, only a few minutes. In those few minutes, Officer One said little. He'd only offered some reassurances that he'd probably be back to his morning in less than an hour.

An hour? What could take an hour? And nobody had mentioned Miranda. No cuffs. Everyone's polite but clam tight. No hint of the cause of the traffic stop. A young female officer ushered Saylor into a small room with a few other civilians who, if anything, looked as bewildered by their presence in the sheriff's office as he felt. He had been instructed to say nothing to the others and was sure they had been told to be silent as well, but the group communicated enough by shrugs, raised eyebrows, and wagged heads for all to understand that none of the others knew why they were there.

Officer Two, the driver of the second patrol car, entered, followed by Officer Three, who told the small group to follow him. They were each given a small card with a number and led into a line-up booth that he immediately recognized from several crime dramas— a white backdrop, with thin black lines marking height at six-inch intervals from four-foot-six to six-foot-six. Jason then realized that he and the others were all white males of about six feet in height, dark hair in varying stages of receding hairlines, and varying waistlines. Looking left and right, he saw that the youngest was maybe late twenties, the oldest was probably pushing fifty.

"Please stand still, and face forward." A voice directed through a tired speaker with more squawk than anything manufactured since the 1970s. "Please hold your number card up." Jason looked down, reversed his, and realized he held number two, but his location was in the three out of five position. He exchanged a glance with the guy to his right, then immediately knew that he didn't know from which direction they would have counted one.

"Number two? Eyes front, please." He stared forward at his reflection in a two-way mirror. He squelched a temptation to reach up and smooth his hair. He'd remembered in afterthought that as he had been first standing beside his Prius that a sea breeze had stirred his thinning hair, and he'd not thought to press it back into place. *No matter, I've just been caught up in a BOLO, and I resembled someone's description of a suspect.*

The squawk box demanded, "Please turn to your right. Left shoulder against the wall, please."

He shuffled to the right. He leaned against the wall, then noticed that the three in front of him were standing erect. He shifted his weight back to center. He took a deep breath, wanting to scratch an itch that announced an untimely need for a scratch on his left elbow.

He resisted that and noted he could smell his sweat. Or was that the guy in front of him, another slightly balding thirty-something.

"To the front again." They all shifted again, back to the mirror. "Please look down and to the right." Most of them did so. "To the RIGHT." Amazing choreography, he thought. Five guys picked up at random, and now we're practicing our manners in a syncopated sweat-stained line-up. *What the god-damned hell?*

The speaker squawked again. "OK, stand straight and turn to your left."

They turned, more or less in unison. He could see beads of sweat forming on number four's neckline, despite the air conditioning.

Saylor heard the creak of a door to his right but didn't look until spoken to. A young woman in uniform said. "Thank you, please exit to the right, and thank you for your cooperation." Her smile was genuine, her uniform was county issue, her crossed-arm stance said don't even think about it. She directed them into another small room with no chairs.

Officer Three, Mallory by his nameplate, said. "Gentlemen, I know this has been unsettling, but we are working a missing person case, a possible kidnapping. A person described as being young to middle-aged, dark hair, dark-colored car, and not from here is all we had to work with."

The twenty-something from the line-up spoke up first. "The Hell you say?" He hocked up a spit, realized he was still in a police station, and swallowed. "You pull me off'n the fishing pier to come stand in your line-up, don't tell me a god-damned thing, scare the living bejeezus out of me? Hell, all of us. And you just say, thank you?" Several more raised their questions and complaints. Jason just stood, took it in, absorbed the details, the other guys' facial hair. It might make for a good scene in the work-in-progress.

Saylor had only seen the line-up sequence from the point of view of a witness in numerous cop shows and movies. He'd never seen it produced from the point of view inside the line-up. The real thing was what? *The real damn thing!* The bright lights, the mirror. You stood looking at your own hopefully innocent face. The closet-sized viewing room was small enough that he could have reached out and touched that reflected face. Not enough time to conjure up why the deputies pulled him over, but if he had been the guilty party? What would

THAT guy have been thinking, staring at his reflection? Each of them smelling each other's sweat. Was it the sweat of a warm Florida morning, or nervous sweat, or guilty sweat?

He stepped out into bright April sunlight, thinking about how to put the details in his next novel, or maybe its sequel. He squinted against the glare coming off a crushed shell parking lot and let Mallory guide him to one of the patrol cars. As it pulled out, Mallory spoke, with an edge of civility that had been missing before. "Mr. Saylor, I'm sure you are a little confused or pissed. It happens. Please accept our apologies. The sheriff said not to give any explanation going in. We had a mic on in that ready room to see if we might pick up some grumblings."

"Did you? I mean, did any of those guys say anything to help you?"

"I really can't say."

"Oh, right. Even if you had, you couldn't tell me. Right?"

"Yes, Sir. It would have been material to the case."

"Who is missing? You don't mind if I ask, do you?"

"Local girl, trouble in the family, but a good kid. She's been missing three days now. We're probably going to have to call in the FBI missing persons if something doesn't break soon."

"But the line-up, what info did you have that would have led you to pick me up? It couldn't have been my car. That one kid said he you guys picked him up on the pier."

"I'm sorry, Mr. Saylor. That would be material," Mallory added after a pause, "too." This as he pulled into the parking lot where his Prius waited.

Saylor reached for the door handle and noticed there wasn't one in the back of the cruiser. Officer One was out of the driver's seat and at the door before he had a chance to panic. Looking up, Mallory was actually smiling beneath his Ray-Bans. *Too little, too late,* he thought. *Way to ruin a day!*

But later, as he drove back to the campground, he had to admit, the experience, out of the blue like it was, had been full of snapshots of realism that he could jot down for later inclusion in his thriller. He just had to find a way to get his hero in trouble with local law enforcement.

Being a writer is a lonely occupation for most in the trade. By natural law, it is an endeavor done in private with only the company of the characters he/she invented. True, he'd admit after a few drinks, you do identify with them. Cheer 'em on. Get them in danger to the brink of hopelessness before you toss a lifeline. They even talked back occasionally as you typed them into a corner or steered a bad plot mechanism into something that worked better. He would share that bit of tradecraft or craziness with anyone, no matter how many drinks.

His separation and eventual divorce the previous fall had made life even lonelier. Even his old group of writers had become tiresome. His critique group had been his only avenue of occasional cordial interaction, support, and valuable criticism, tips on style and structure. He had two published novels under his belt. The first, an espionage slash coming of age story, was a self-pub. The second, a cold war thriller, had been picked up by a real publisher. But he had still been working then and only been able to attend regional book signings and promotional events the publisher set up. A national tour to major markets and events had been out of the question while still working the Harris County crime beat. That second book had sold only four thousand copies, still three thousand more than the self-published effort.

Jason approached the campground in a funk. The funk arose from knowing that he was burning to tell someone about the BOLO, and there was no one around to talk about the experience. He'd been back for three weeks and hadn't taken the time to look up any of his old friends. Turning in, he saw the silver Airstream that, although smaller than most campground denizens, still blocked the water view. The old man in the Airstream had the annoying habit of digging deep for some tale that always seemed a lame attempt to go one better than the one being told. Weird old man. Most of the others in the campground were weeklies. They'd be gone in a few days, or maybe in another week. Then there was Mr. Montana, Dwayne Biggs.

Saylor noted the return of a long gray interstate bus conversion. Dwayne Biggs, the owner of the Class A cross-country land yacht, was little better than Mr. Airstream. Kicked out of his house by his third wife, Dwayne was trying hard to drink himself to death and usually was only capable of a rational discussion before 11 a.m. and that was if he was even up by eleven. Everyone else he'd met was a weekly.

Saylor pulled up to his Class-C twenty-four-footer that sported a single red strip horizontal at driver's window height. He looked up at it from the car. *At least it's bigger than a tiny house.* Stepping up the two-step ladder he thought, *but not much bigger.*

He settled in at the dinette that converted into the base for a kid-sized bed and turned on his battered newspaper-issued laptop. An hour later, he had a draft of a new scene in which the hero was apprehended by the Mannheim Polizei, questioned, presented to a hostile witness in a line-up with four of Europe's worst, and picked by the unseen accuser beyond the mirror. He tapped a triumphant period to end the paragraph that described said hero being tossed unceremoniously into a cold cement-walled cell. He ended the section with the loud clang of the cell's heavy steel door. He momentarily debated if it should get an exclamation.

2

First Interview

Dawn was a rare sight. Jason Saylor told friends back in Houston that he'd be camping out on the beaches of sunny Florida, catching the sun rises with freshly brewed coffee and a beach chair. A post-coffee swim would be just the thing to get the juices flowing in the morning. He'd hoped to get five to six thousand words down in a week. Three months max per book in a planned series of five, maybe six. He planned to write the next Euro-spy masterpiece, with a twist, part Ludlum, and part DeSilva, with some Dan Brownian mysticism to spice things up. Political research might take some of the books into three or more weeks of on-the-ground research to clarify and verify real places and document local history. The kind of on-the-ground verification needed would require a trip to Europe. He had hoped the major opus would be ready for an editor in four months. That *had been* the plan.

Reality found him up late with diversions, binge-watching Netflix, video games, and the occasional extra few hundred words, maybe some edits on the day's earlier efforts. A good eight thousand words a week was his best effort so far. Sleep usually came between 2 a.m. to 4 a.m., and he missed the sunrises most days.

The morning after his adventure at the Franklin County Sheriff's HQ was no different with respect to dawn. The knocking on his aluminum door was an unwelcome addition. He glanced at his watch and decided against yesterday's socks. Seven-thirty. Ugh. Somehow to Saylor, wearing a robe and socks was slightly more acceptable than a robe and bare feet. Rummaging through a sock drawer for a pair, he decided that matching was essential and found two reasonably close shades of brown. Robed and socked, and hair quickly brushed, he opened the door to two officers in sheriff's deputy gray.

He smiled down at Officer Mallory and another officer. Saylor squinted against the bright morning light of 7:35 and read Arnett on the uniform he recognized as Officer Two from the previous day. "Officer Arnett, would you and Officer Mallory like some coffee? The pot is ready. I just have to push the button. Care to come in?"

Officer Arnett stepped back a half step as Officer Mallory took the lead. "Mr. Saylor, I'm afraid we're going to have to ask you to come down to the station one more time." Arnett coughed quietly into his fist. Mallory corrected. "At least one more time. There are some questions the sheriff would like to go over with you."

And so it was that Jason Saylor came up with the plot twist that might get his hero, Andy Jackson, out of deepening trouble with both Germany's BND and Israel's Mossad. But that would not occur to him until much later. He blinked twice, absorbed the request, and acquiesced. "Sure, give me two minutes to get dressed."

In another twenty, he was in the plainly furnished and over-air-conditioned office of Sheriff Stanley Pierson. Officer Mallory took a seat in a wooden chair to his left. Arnett held a small bunch of files, and Sheriff Pierson was offering coffee from his personal pot. Pierson was well known for his casual style and his results. He'd been re-elected five times. Pierson said. "Mr. Taylor, thank you for coming down. I understand from Tommy," he nodded toward Arnett, "that this is early for you. Care for some coffee?"

"Yes, thanks, and that's Saylor. I'm Jason Saylor. It's spelled like Taylor, only with the S." He noticed Mallory turning toward the coffee pot. "That's one cream, two sweeteners. Please."

"Unusual name, Saylor. Where's that from?"

"England. I looked it up in college. An alteration of sailor with a 'Y,' often an occupational name for real sailors from the fifteenth or so century. Germanic origin, if I remember right. Had to do with ropes, both the guilds that made rope and the men who went to sea and worked the boats." He looked up as Mallory set down a thick porcelain mug steaming with black coffee. Black wasn't usually his style, but he sniffed and took a cautious pull.

Sheriff Pierson blew on the edge of his steaming cup and took a sip. He seemed to be appraising the answer. Saylor hoped the explanation actually sounded as if he'd earned that master's degree in English Lit. This morning, unshaven and dressed in a wrinkled tee and faded denim, he looked much more like a failed anything rather than a man on a quest to write his personal best.

"Saylor, I'm going to cut to the chase with you. I understand you went through the line-up process yesterday with very little understanding of why you were called in."

"Yes, Sir." He reached for the offered cup, took a cautious sip. It really needed sweetener and cream, a lot of both. "They were polite, I suppose, business-like. But from hello to goodbye, I was never given much more than an explanation than a girl is missing."

Pierson leaned forward as Arnett approached. "And that is absolutely the truth—a girl is missing." Arnett handed Pierson a brown folder from the top of his pile. It was so thin Saylor wondered if there could be anything in it. The sheriff opened the folder and turned it so its contents were readable to Saylor. He then flipped to a second page in the binder with two four-by-fives of a young girl, a brunette with a great smile and braces. He figured aged fourteen or so in the first one, the second, maybe eighteen. It appeared to be an enlargement of a yearbook photo. "Does this girl look familiar to you? Ever seen her before?"

Saylor's initial shock at recognition led immediately to a deeper sense of dread. He knew the missing girl. He stumbled out, "I, uhm, yes. I do know her. At least, I've met her, Lindy? Libby?"

"Lindsey, Lindsey Lawrence."

"Yeah, Lindsey. I don't think I got her last name." He looked up from the pictures. "She's the missing girl?" He looked down at them again.

"She's been missing for goin' on four days now." All friendliness disappeared from Pierson's face. "Can you fill us in please on the last time you might have run into her; any details at all will be helpful."

Saylor took a deep breath. This was going to be more than strange. He had written this chapter over a week ago.

◊ ◊ ◊ ◊ ◊

"Andy Jackson looked up from his French onion soup and paused, his spoon millimeters from his lips. Anyone would have thought he was blowing on the hot soup before sipping. But he had spied from his two-seater low-top table an extraordinarily beautiful young woman seated at an umbrellaed table outside the franchised patisserie. He'd become captivated by her smile, her natural beauty with no or little makeup apparent, and the glow of the afternoon sun on her auburn hair. In the early evening's low angled rays, the sun illuminated a golden halo of errant strands the slight breeze pulled loose. They were face on, maybe eight meters apart, and he could see outdoors perfectly well. He doubted she could see him inside the restaurant against the reflecting glare from outside light.

If she could, she was certainly unmindful of his study. And he did study her. Jackson thought at that moment that any man would, any male over fifteen would be caught short by such a natural beauty. Proving his point, a middle-aged couple walked past him, exited the restaurant, and continued along the sidewalk. The woman seemed preoccupied with her purse, perhaps digging for car keys, the man's head pivoted in unabashed study as they walked past the young woman. Jackson, still in the restaurant, smiled, vindicated.

He saw now that she was preoccupied with editing or sorting a small stack of photographs. She had a few laid out on her table. The rest slowly appeared in order from the envelope with evident drug store labeling. He wondered if she had sent digital files for printing or if she was an old-school purist who could capture an afternoon in thirty-six exposures: the limit of 35mm film cameras. He assumed from her apparent youth that she must have sent digital files. Few her age would have put up with the inconvenience of chemical photography.

Thinking about it, he knew there was a 35mm Asahi Pentax somewhere in storage. Still worked. Probably needed a battery now to run the exposure meter. Soup spilled from his spoon. He looked down at the splatters on the paper-lined plastic tray and then around to see if anyone had noticed. No one was paying any attention to a fortyish guy in cargo shorts, boat shoes, and a T-shirt adorned with a tri-color heart. His usual costume in Marseille's eight months of summer allowed for temperature swings from comfortable high sixties in the morning to a sweltering, go-find-air-conditioning nineties by late afternoon. Today he was in that heat shedding garb and was actually a little uncomfortable in the restaurant's artificial chill.

The girl was looking up now, unfocused on anything in the material world. Her line of sight was either the clear sky, or perhaps distant clouds, or infinity itself. But the enigmatic smile had persisted. Maybe, he thought, she was lost in some memory. Or perhaps a construct of a future meeting. From a distance and angle, he couldn't tell what the pictures were of and could only conjecture. Was it a boyfriend? A pet? Family or friends? He decided that if she was still there when he left, he would at least peek as he walked by.

He had no thought of any meeting, or even more preposterous, a liaison with the girl. She was probably close to half his age or less. But his eyes had been drawn by the deep vee of her partially unbuttoned blouse to the less tanned flesh at the upper hint of cleavage. No harm in looking. His dad had always said that God's gift to aging men was the fresh issue of nineteen-year-olds to admire every summer. Was she even nineteen? He couldn't tell. In this metropolitan center, he could no longer tell if a counter girl was in finishing school or grad school. He had guessed wrong so often he rarely tried anymore. But she was a stunning beauty, that was certain, no matter her age.

He looked down at the now cold bowl of soup, sighed against the lonely evening he'd face after the meet. But agency protocol insisted that he travel alone, leave few tracks, make the assigned contact, neutralize said contact, and move on. Sometimes he'd pass on new information immediately. Sometimes, he'd have to transcribe tapes. At least he'd play them into a computer's audio file for transmission back to Langley, and then only on a secure line. He could never trust a telephone, cell or landline, in his line of work. The agency didn't, and he didn't. His life depended on security. When he looked up, she was gone."

◇ ◇ ◇ ◇ ◇　

With mounting annoyance, Saylor recounted the scene as closely as possible to the scene he'd written the evening after the encounter. He answered enough questions, he thought, to give both credence to his account of the chance encounter and the differences in his retelling in the scene. "Yes, it actually did happen. No, it was not in a patisserie in Marseilles. It was at a Panera coffee shop in Tallahassee. NO, I'm not in the CIA. I'm a writer—I take scenes from real life occasionally because of the ring of truth." He thought he'd done rather well and that having taken the time to relate the chance sighting to Pierson was enhanced by his having written it down.

Sheriff Pierson nodded, glanced at the elapsed time indicator on his recorder, and made a note in his notebook. He looked up at Saylor. "That was the first time you met her, right?"

"Well, like I said, I didn't actually meet her. I just saw her through the restaurant's window." Saylor squirmed a little, the hard wooden chair was biting into a butt cheek, and he needed to shift weight. At that movement, the sheriff wrote something down. Did he think that was a tell? *Jesus, this chair is just freaking uncomfortable.*

"So, you're telling me you found her very attractive. That right?"

"Yes, of course. I think the word I used was extraordinary. Anyone would by acclimation. She was a beautiful girl, like I said."

"And you didn't act on that in any way?"

"No, hell no. Like I just said, I was finishing my sandwich and soup when I looked up, she was gone."

"You didn't follow her out? Maybe see which way she went, what color car she may have gotten into."

"No." The word came out too shrill, like a denial with exceptions. "Well, yes. I did leave the restaurant after she left her seat, but no, I didn't see where she went. I'm not sure if I actively scanned for her." Saylor thought back to the moment. "Sheriff Pierson, she was just pretty scenery, that's all. Much prettier to look at while I ate my meal than the cheesy art on their walls."

He'd found himself sitting too stiffly upright. *Try to relax, man. You haven't done anything. They're just asking questions.* He leaned into the back support.

Pierson pressed on, "Afterwards, at any time after that encounter at the Panera in Tallahassee, have you seen her anywhere else? You did say you didn't get her last name, but you did know her first name, approximately."

Saylor noted a dimple puckered and relaxed in the sheriff's left cheek. A poker tell! The man had something more. *Was he going for the second meeting? That's probably why I've been called back in after yesterday's line-up.* He suppressed a yawn. He hadn't had a chance to get breakfast, and he'd only gotten four or five hours of sleep. His mounting desire to actually drink more of the sheriff's coffee was arguing with an overriding and growing fear that he was being lined up for a possible murder if this girl didn't turn up.

He evaluated his own appearance to the man across the desk. Disheveled, unshaven, sunken tired eyes. *Could he possibly be so stupid? Of course! He would not have been called back in if they didn't know about the other meeting.*

14

As if sharing a mind meld, Pierson set down his coffee mug and leaned forward on his elbows. "Listen, Mr. Saylor, I've got to ask—"

Saylor interrupted. "There were more occasions, that is, other times." He looked around as if proper wording might be written on the wall.

"Other times? Plural? Which other times, Mr. Saylor?"

"Well, and I was completely surprised, but I was at the Fish House last, uhm, last Wednesday or Thursday, I think it was. I saw her there."

"The Fish House here? On St. George—?"

"On the Island. Yeah, the Fish House." Saylor paused, in mounting discomfort. He hadn't divulged this encounter, and in fact had detailed a previous, alleged first, meeting with Lindsey the sheriff probably hadn't known about.

Pierson let the silence drag as he pulled a pack of cigarettes from the drawer. He shook the pack letting three filtered tips slide out of the opening. He offered one across the desk to Saylor. "Do you smoke? Care for one?"

Saylor looked around the small office. One small black frame held a diploma from Florida State in Criminology, going back a couple of decades. A few others boasted other career milestones or awards. Most of the other wall space was given to glossy green paint, that thin green favored by the Air Force in five-gallon cans. Saylor wondered if it was surplus from Tyndall. He realized he hadn't answered. "Can I smoke in here?"

"Sure. Go ahead." Pierson reached into a drawer and came up with a square glass ashtray that shouted military surplus or Huddle House and pushed it across the desk.

"Believe I will." Saylor knew it was the sheriff putting on his good cop act. Hoping to get him to relax and tell all. It had been a few years, but he thought now was as good a time as any to light one up. He leaned across the desk to accept the offered light.

"Please continue," Pierson prodded, "You were at the Fish House, for dinner?"

"I was early. I'd taken a break from writing and had driven into town for a few groceries and decided to eat first. I don't like to shop hungry." An awkward smile played on Saylor's lips. "I diverted out to the Island because I wanted to see if the Fish House was, in fact, still

15

there. It had been a while. I was eating alone, as usual, out on the deck. One of the wait staff came out with a busboy tray and began to prepare setups for the evening crowd."

"Setups?" Saylor knew that Pierson knew perfectly well what setups were. It was productive to encourage a suspect, or a witness, or a source to keep talking. Sometimes, sometimes you'd get lucky.

"You know, silverware wrapped in napkins. Only at the Fish House, it's a plastic knife and fork wrapped in a folded paper towel."

Pierson lit a cigarette, said nothing to fill the silence.

Saylor continued. "She was sitting facing the front desk. I only saw the side of her face, but she turned her head watching a family go by and made eye contact with the family's little boy. They smiled at each other, and it hit me that she was the same girl I'd seen up in Tallahassee."

"So that was it? You just saw her working a pile of setups?"

"No, after I ate, I was getting up, and I caught her eye and nodded, she said something about did I enjoy the meal. So I stopped and said yes, thank you, or something. But I decided to ask if she had been in Tallahassee the week before. She looked surprised, you know, eyebrows raised, head back a little. I didn't want to freak her out, so I told her that I had noticed her at the Panera when she was looking at some photographs. That I thought she was a very pretty young lady."

"That pick-up line work for you often?"

"What, no. I mean, no, I don't really have a pick-up line. Just divorced a few months back, not really looking yet, if you know what I mean. The wife took me for almost everything except half the house equity. That's mostly what I'm living on." Saylor leaned back in the perp chair. He was beginning to feel ill. It had been too many years since he'd last had a cigarette. Making it worse, Pierson let a lungful of spent Marlboro drift close to his face. He waved a feckless hand at the blue cloud, irritated, but he didn't say anything more.

Pierson persisted "That was it? So you went on your way?"

"No, she told me she had just gotten a series of pictures taken on a trip out to Little St. George. I was a little impressed, not many get to go to that island."

"Well, anyone else with a boat?"

"Yeah, that's what she said. That she and her mom had motored over there, landed on the state lands side of the cut, and walked across the island to get the waves crashing on the rocks. I'm not sure when, but I sat down to talk to her. Told her I was a writer and all. Didn't faze her a bit."

"Should it have?"

"Some people say oh what do you write or ask my name to see if I was famous or anything. Occasionally, I hand out a business card, sometimes that turns into a sale and a new reader." He managed a wan smile. "We deal in volume if we want to make a living, but each personal sale is a new fan."

"She wasn't impressed?"

"No, well, how should I know? She was bored wrapping plastic tableware in paper towels, and I hadn't had a real conversation with a human in a few weeks. I saw she was getting near the end of her supply of plastic forks, so I got up to leave. That was it." Saylor flicked the ash off his cigarette then decided to kill it in the bottom of the resin-stained ashtray.

"That was it? You're sure?"

"Well, you know, the pleasantries."

"I don't know. How pleasant?"

"Jeez, don't quote me, something like, 'nice to meet you' or 'see you around,' that kind of thing. I really don't remember."

Pierson snuffed out his own cigarette and dumped both of them into a waste basket, waved at the remnants of the smoke cloud, and put the ashtray back in the desk drawer. He picked at something paper-clipped to the folder's edge. He tossed a business card in front of Saylor with the skill of a blackjack dealer. "Recognize this?"

He did. It was one of his business cards with the front cover of his first novel, *Lost in Dreamland*. If it were flipped over, the reader would get his email, and website information as well as a hook phrase to provoke interest. His was, "There's a reason some dreams are called nightmares."

His mouth started to drop open, but he gulped and clamped his jaw tight. "Yes, but. I really don't remember handing her that card. Slipped my mind. I do hand out a lot of them."

Pierson just nodded and said, "Uh, huh. Spectacularly pretty young lady, and you don't remember giving her your card?"

This time Saylor's mouth did flop open, closed, opened, ready to speak "but...Sheriff, honestly, I don't remember handing her the card. Like I said, I do it a lot, to cashiers, etc." He stopped talking, didn't know what else he could or should say.

Pierson picked at the bottom of one of the sheets in the brown case file and looked at the next sheet down. After absorbing its content, he looked up at Saylor again and leaned forward on his elbows, his fingers woven together. "So, that was it. You stared at her over dinner without her knowing it up in Tallahassee, and you had a brief, what, maybe two- or three-minute conversation down here at the Fish House. That about it?"

"That's all I can remember."

Then he did remember.

3

Disappearance

There was the scene. Written just a few nights ago. His hero, now cast as a female, is off assignment on two weeks leave before going back to the international thug-of-the-day manhunt job. Her partner, line-of-duty dead, rating a new star on the wall at Langley. How much of the scene was inspiration? He'd visualized the girl in the scene, but...he recalled his typed effort:

Beyond the glow of the beach hut's tiki bar, two figures were barely discernible in the gloom, one stationary, cross-legged just above the surf's reach. Her features impenetrable in the darkness. An observer wouldn't have been able to tell calm meditation from an earnest searching of the horizon.

The other stumbling, struggling against probability to remain erect and only roughly on course meandered toward her. Gravity's pull complicated the slopes and dips on the beach. Any observer would quickly conclude advanced inebriation. Jackson's curving track neared the seated girl who called out. "Hey. You OK?"

"Ss, sorru." A shallow burp and a sniff. "Sorry. I think I probably had one too many. I started out with just shweet tea but ended up with a Long Island Tea, or two. I'm not supposed to drink anymore."

"For real? You doing the twelve steps?"

Jackson sat down in a clumsy heap and righted herself. The voice in the dark was friendly and female and her partner of five years had just been buried with a hole in his chest. She needed a voice in the dark. She looked out to where the other was looking, nothing but the crashing surf. Farther offshore, winked white lights of the working boats. Tomorrow's seafood harvest was being scooped up as she watched. Jackson looked over at the other girl. "Ss, sorry to innerrupt your thoughts. Juss, glad to see someone out here. Feelin' kinda shitty."

The girl looked askance in Jackson's direction. "It's that kind of a night I guess."

"You lose someone," a pause, "too?" Jackson tried to turn in the girl's direction, but balance proved precarious, even sitting down.

Now the other girl turned to fully face Jackson. "Yeah, I did and it does feel kind of shitty. Got you on that." She turned to study the incoming waves. The surf that washed up just beyond her feet glowed a bio-luminescent green.

Jackson loved when it did that, an ethereal aquatic aurora, when the weather and the ocean were warm enough, reminding her of some long-lost evenings. When she looked back to the other girl, she was standing, brushing sand off her legs and butt. She called out to her in the dark. "Be careful..."

"Thanks, just gotta go for a drive." The girl looked back at her, waved with a toss of her hand.

"OK, be really careful."

Jackson felt gravity become irrelevant. Felt the coolness of sand on her cheek. Hoped vaguely that it was already high tide, then let sleep and the too-strong cocktails wash away her grief.

Saylor realized that he'd been silent for maybe thirty seconds, had it been longer? Would that be seen as guilt for something? "Look, Sheriff Pierson. Here's the thing. I wrote a scene a week ago that could have some elements of truth in it. Like I said earlier, I often draw on things that happen in RL and put them in the books."

"RL?"

"Sorry, Real Life. That's gamer speak for real life as opposed to VR for virtual reality in the immersive world of gaming."

"OK, So this scene—"

"Yeah, I have to admit that I was on the beach, the same night I had that little chat with Libby, I mean, Lindsey. But I'd had a few too many. I got to thinking about my last couple of months, closing down my cubicle at the paper in Houston, buying this little Class C camper, and coming home. What a frikkin' homecoming! I've been gone most of twenty years. Did pretty well for a while, made a name in the business, some big papers were aware that I'd be available and were interested. And I wrote a couple of books on the side that did OK for a newbie. Then my wife goes and fucks our neighbor and claims irreconcilable differences. So, summing up, in the last half-year, my life's been circling the toilet."

Pierson eyed him, thinking about the revelation. "This makes you angry?"

"Angry?" Saylor stared back, resolute. "Fuckin' A it made me angry. Just because she couldn't make babies, she figured her little honey pot could be shared around. 'Why not have all the fun it can have before it dried up?' She actually said that. Of course, she was drunk and screaming at the time, but damn, if it didn't ring true!"

"This kind of anger extend to all females?" The sheriff's head tilted slightly to the left. Through lips that barely moved he followed up, "You get any counseling for this kind of angry?"

Saylor deflated. "No, you don't get it. Not at all. Yes, I was angry as hell at my wife. But I never strayed beyond imaginary wanderings. Then I find out our marriage contract isn't any better than a temporary lease."

"OK, so this scene. Your heroine is inebriated and, on the beach, and meets up with a stranger who will listen to her sorry tale." There was a flicker of a smirk that vanished immediately. "How much of that is R-L?"

"God, I wish I knew, Sheriff. Like I said, I was pretty tanked." *That much is true.* "Whether Lindsey was there too or not, or wishful thinking, or what. I don't know. I, for God's honest truth, don't know. I woke up on the beach. It was about an hour after sunrise, getting hot."

"You spent the night on the beach in front of the Fish House?"

"Actually, it was a bit farther down the beach, nearer the lighthouse park. Some silver-haired lady in a ponytail. I think she was

21

with the Turtle Patrol. She had a loggerhead patch on her jersey. She woke me up."

Pierson nodded as if he knew who that was. Made a note in his pad. Saylor could read 'turtle lady' upside down. "Look Sheriff, beyond some weird circumstances, I don't know this girl from Adam's apple. She inspired some decent writing once, and some questionable writing a second time. I don't know her. I'm sorry as all hell that she's turned up missing. I don't even remember her family. You said her last name was Lawrence?"

"That's right. Lindsey Hardin Lawrence"

"Look, I know you came here from somewhere else, but I'm from here. Born at Weems Hospital, thirty-eight years ago. Stayed here for the next eighteen years. Never met any Lawrences I remember. I guess they're good people. I don't know them or know of 'em. I only heard about Lindy or Lindsey being missing and that she was a Lawrence, from you people."

The sheriff leaned back in his chair as if re-appraising him.

Saylor continued. "Look, I was an investigative reporter for years in San Antonio, then Houston. I've got some chops with any wified computer. If there's any way I can help look for this kid, I'll be happy to help. But listen, I haven't had anything today but this really terrible coffee and your stale Marlboro. I'd like to go home and get some breakfast." The sheriff just nodded slowly. Saylor stood, brushing imaginary cooties from his pants. "You apparently know where to find me, so...can I go?"

Pierson's face, unreadable as ever, pinned him to the floor. "I know you might think you've got sleuthing skills, as a reporter, that is. Please, leave that to us, if you don't mind. Just stay out of it. I don't want you mucking around in my investigation, y'hear?" Then he nodded and gestured at the door. "Sure. For now, you're free to go."

4

Back at the Campground

Saylor took the short drive from the sheriff's compound down to the Coastal Highway slowly. He'd brushed off the first encounter with some equanimity, the result of a BOLO. Be on the lookout for anyone looking like me? It could happen to anyone. This second visit, the rousing from bed and subsequent interrogation, was a lot more to worry about. The bright blue rectangle of the bay grew larger ahead and he slowed for the stop sign. This was a no-fooling stop sign. If you ignored it, you could either pick a tree to ram or go swimming. Well, he thought, maybe wading. Beyond the drop-off of maybe eight feet, water depth in that part of the bay varied from zero to two feet, depending on the tides. He slowed to a stop, watched an Airstream followed by five impatient tourists and one seafood truck heading East towards Carrabelle, Tallahassee, or Jacksonville and points south? Conscious of the proximity to the sheriff's office, he tapped his right blinker and headed home.

The Coastal Paradise Campground was only a thousand yards west. The campground had been clear-cut prior to development and being relatively recent, had no shade to speak of. A few developer trees, struggling in the sandy soil, would create meaningful shade in maybe ten years. If the owners would let a tree get to any height. The property was totally exposed to whatever tropical force winds a storm might throw at them. It had the minor protection of the barrier island chain. Dog Island, St. George Island, and Little St. George, created by a man-made navigation channel, and St. Vincent's were strung like a pearl necklace along Franklin County's coastline. They took the full force and fury of hurricanes. Except for increasingly expensive repairs, the Coastal Highway rimming the mainland usually remained open. The highway and a stone revetment of Georgia granite were all that separated the campground from saltwater.

His camper was parked in the second row. He'd been promised front row and an unobstructed view when the snowbirds left. Usually, most of them would have been gone by early April. He was hopeful as he stood outside. From the vantage of his patio area, his view took in the back end of a forty-two-foot land yacht. The silver-gray monster had three times his floor space and storage. His view had improved, he noted, the Airstream was gone. There was a wider slice of bay view, broken in the immediate foreground by a multi-colored beach umbrella, portable fire pit, folding chairs, and a Yeti cooler. He sighed, soon. Soon, he could move across the narrow RV park road to a front-row bay-view site.

Saylor pulled out his keys, unlocked, and entered. Sighed again. Home sweet home. His eyes quickly found the coffee pot in the dim shuttered light and tapped its brew button. *How the hell could the sheriff survive on that crap?* Overhead, the AC unit mounted on the roof kicked in with a resonant hum that rattled the sheet metal skin as it got up to speed. He thought about the last part of the conversation with Pierson. *Did he really have an encounter with Lindsey on the beach?* When he wrote the embellished scene, he'd wondered then if it had been imagination, dream, or alcohol-sodden memory. He opened the laptop, listening to the sounds of the coffee pot brewing its morning magic as the machine booted.

The work in progress, or WIP as most writers referred to them, was up and centered. He'd been up the night before getting his hero into more trouble in eastern Europe. He scanned the chapter headings on the left margin. There were two scenes labeled beach. One was in the sequence, the other in the trash folder. He opened the trashed file and read.

Saylor looked at the text as if someone else had written it. It was quite different from the version he'd kept. It was a relic from before he changed the hero's gender. He read on.

◇ ◇ ◇ ◇ ◇

She spoke again, out of the darkness. In that darkness, he told this perfect stranger more about the horrible day that had resulted in his partner's death than he'd told anyone. He looked back over to see her more clearly. Her profile black against the lights of the tiki bar beyond. She said, "You'd better move up. You're gonna get soaked down there."

"Too late." His admission carried the tone of drunken humor tinged with embarrassment. "I'm soaked," he laughed, "inside and out." He watched another set of waves crashing on the nearshore sandbar and calculated its run. On a combination of hands, elbows, heels, and butt, he scooted another few yards to the top of the slope and felt dry sand beneath his elbows. The white foam edged to a stop two feet below his soaked sandals.

Before he could stop himself, he heard his slurred voice get out the barroom standard. "You come here often?" After an answering laugh, he slurred. "Sorry, shtupid thing to say."

"Hey," the bright voice sounded. "You certainly aren't the first." Then, "I think I recognize you. You the guy that sat down while I was folding set-ups?"

He had to think what that meant, measuring out each word through a filter. Putting them in order. As the silence grew, the voice in the dark tried again. "Wrapping plastic forks and knives in paper towels. Before dinner."

It rang true. "Yeah, that waas mee." He heard himself— another sorry drunk. "I'm sorry. Like I said. I'm not supposed to drink. One-eighth Indian." Now he laughed, "and seven-eights drunk. The agency would be pissed to know I fell off the wagon." He turned to her dark profile. Put his finger to his lips. "Sssshhh. You can't tell anyone I was too drunker to walk. They might pull my—" He almost said clearance.

"Hey mister, no problem. I am the picture of discretion."

"From what I remember, you are quite a picture." The alcohol took the next step toward stupidity. "Prettiest girl I've seen or had the good fortune to share conversation with in too long a time." Hearing himself, he thought, *shit, shit, shit.* "I'm sorry— that wasss stupid of me. I'm not trying to put the make on you. I jus' had one too many of those Long Island Teas." A hiccup. "In honor of my recently deceased partner."

"Happens all the time, mister. Don't you even worry a bit about it."

He opened his eyes, hoping a horizon fix would stop the world from tilting sideways. "I guess we should be formally introduced. I'm Andy, Andy Jackson. Fucking ironic, isn't it? A fucking Indian named after Andrew Jackson?" He turned toward the girl extending a sand-covered hand, realized he was a few yards away and couldn't reach, or get up to shorten the distance. Against the glare of lights, he held up his hand to try to make out her face.

She simply waved at him. He could make out the movement and had to blink and turn away from the deck lights. Several waves crashed and sloshed up the beach before she spoke again. "Sorry to hear about your partner. You a cop?"

"A cop? No, I—" How do you tell a stranger that you are hired by the government to kill bad guys without trial, without a hearing, based on evidence in a government written dossier that justifies their removal from the human race? How do you do that when you aren't sure yourself why you do it? Why do you keep losing friends, wives? *Shit.* "No, I'm not a cop. I work high-stakes security kinda. Can't really share much more."

"Well, Andy. I hope you feel better in the morning. Chances are, this will fade. Most things do. Time heals and all that."

"Thank you, uh. What waass your name? Did we do that?"

"No," her laugh was like music floating on the sea breeze. "We didn't do that. I'm Lindsey."

He tried to register it. He used to be good at names. But lately...

"Well, I think I'll be moving on. It's about high tide. Think I'll go for a drive."

"Ok." The two thoughts didn't make sense in the same sentence. But hey, he was drunk enough to know it. "OK, Lindy. Drive careful." He opened his eyes again to see the beach before him tilting. Then the side of his face felt cool sand. Then he felt nothing.

He hadn't remembered that it was written from his point of view *with* Lindsey. He'd remembered it as a first draft, then re-written it from the point of view of his main character, Andy Jackson. It was more of a life sketch and probably more accurate than the version of the incident retained in his draft.

Saylor leaned back against the cabinetry that framed the small dinette table that converted to a third bunk. *Damn, that's not bad writing for a drunk. How much of that was Lindsey, and how much of that was me filling in blanks?* The next day, he'd changed Andy Jackson to Andie Jackson, a female. He knew the statistics well; women outnumber male readers five to three. If you are writing for chicks, make the superhero a chick! Don't have to sink to the level of chic-lit to do it.

Just suppose there was something to it. That he'd written about that night on the following morning, putting his hero in his sorry ass shoes. Yes, he'd had some drinks at the Fish House. No, he didn't drink Long Island Iced Teas. He preferred rum and coke, or if hardcore was needed, a Manhattan.

Right now, he needed coffee!

5

Patrick

He made the two steps from the dinette to the kitchen, pulled down a mug, and prepared to fill it. From outside his door, he heard tires on sandy gravel. He pulled down one of the one-inch mini blinds shading the round window in the door to see a black and white from the Apalachicola Police pulling up to a camper in the row behind his. Still weirded out by his interview with the sheriff, he stood, empty coffee cup in one hand, while the other maintained the slit in the blinds. He watched as an officer knocked on his neighbor's door and had a brief conversation. He nearly dropped the mug when a hand extended from the darkness of that camper and pointed directly at him. The officer's sunglasses turned just as he released the blind with a metallic snap.

"Dammit!" He hadn't even had breakfast yet. Or the coffee. In a rush for caffeine, he tore open the two required packets of sweetener, flipped open the refrigerator, and managed to splash in an ounce or so of creamer before he heard the five rapid raps on his door. He took a sip, "Dammit!" and then another.

"Police, please open up."

He did and looked down into the smiling Ray-Banned face of his old high school quarterback, Patrick Wills.

"Patrick. Son of a bitch! Somehow I never pictured you wearing the uniform."

"That's OK, and somehow I never expected you'd be in a line-up over at the sheriff's shed. You do know there's a jail right behind his office. You can go from 'I fucked up' to serving time in a heartbeat."

"Yeah, I got the idea from the concertina wire on top of the fence. I figured there was a jail in the backyard. Come on in, how the hell are you?" Then, studying his friend's face, "Does everyone have to wear Ray Bans?"

Patrick Wills smiled, "Yeah, it's a thing around here." Fifteen pounds heavier than his high school weight but still solidly trim, he grasped the grab bar by the door and pulled himself up and into the camper.

He took off the service cap revealing an unruly batch of yellow to white thatch. Removing the dark green sunglasses, he peered around at his friend's humble digs. "Looks nicer than I'd a thought from the outside."

"Yes, I did luck out. It's old but low miles. It spent most of its life under a shed roof. It needed a mechanic's TLC and some fresh rubber, hoses, and belts, but it only had twelve thousand original miles. Here, let me get you a cup. It's fresh. Just finished brewing. Have a seat, get comfy, and I'll get your mug." Saylor pulled down another cup and stopped filling an inch short of the rim. "You take creamer?"

"Nope, stopped with that sissy stuff in the service."

"Service? You signed up?"

"Semper Fi, motherfucker!"

"Son of a bitch! Seriously?"

Patrick beamed back at Saylor. "Seriously."

"Man, that's a trip. You go to the sandbox?"

"Yup, no fun. No women, bootleg booze."

"Bummer," Saylor rubbed his stubble, "I think I had an easier time of it."

"You go in?"

"Army Engineers. Let's see—Fort Benning, then Canal Zone picked up *un poco Español*, then Ft. Meade."

"Spy school?"

"Nah, but I'm not at liberty to say—either." He smiled as enigmatically as he could.

"I'm guessing it was a sight nicer than Kabul."

Saylor simply nodded. There were probably things in both of their military careers that should go unmentioned. The two of them had been inseparable in class, usually in adjacent rows. After school, usually in the same skiff, trawler, or junk mobile. They formed a quarterback-receiver team on the gridiron that took the Wildcats to regional playoffs and state semi-finals before going down to one of the

29

Bruce Ballister

triple-A teams. Patrick went to the Corps, and Afghanistan, and cop school. Saylor went to the Army then college and never looked back.

"Like I said, son of a bitch." Saylor pushed the laptop out of the way, and they settled into opposite sides of the tiny dinette. "Good to see you, man. What brings you here?"

"Yeah, well, first off. Good to see you're back in town. I heard you were here to write the next great American novel."

Saylor's high school snorky laugh returned subconsciously. "Great American novel. Hah! That's actually a marketable title. THE GREAT AMERICAN NOVEL," he said in an announcer's basso profundo voice. "I wish. The one I'm working on now is probably too pedestrian. I'll have to see if my agent likes anything. I'm about to send in some of the rough first chapters and an outline for the end."

"Cool, what's it about?"

"International spy thriller. A middle-aged agent is on leave after the death of her partner from hostile fire. The investigation is ongoing as to whether her negligence was involved. Her best friend is a dead hero, and she's the agency's newest fuck-up unless she gets cleared of all questions." He grinned across the table at his old friend. "I hope you don't mind. He kind of looks like you."

"The dead guy?" Patrick adopted a mock horror look.

"Uhm, yeah, the dead guy. You were a natural for the chick's best friend. My hero, well, she kind of looks like I imagined Suzanne would look by now."

They shared a smile, and the memories began to flood across the table. They spent an hour over two cups of coffee catching up with two careers, Patrick's model family, his own marriages. His rise to stardom at the Chronicle after his breaking coverage of undercover work broke a massive human trafficking ring in Houston's Fourth Ward. The loss of his first wife after her two miscarriages and finally cancer. The heartache over his second wife's betrayals.

The downer moment following led to a moment's quiet reflection. "Listen, Jason." Patrick changed the subject gently. "This is a small county. Almost everyone knows almost everything. What's going on with the Lawrence girl?"

"Jesus, Pat. Hell if I know. Yesterday." *Was it really just yesterday?* "Yeah, yesterday I'm coming back from getting groceries in Apalach, and a County Mounty pulls me over. I pulled into the furniture store parking lot and found I'm blocked fore and aft by two patrols. I get the back seat drive over to the sheriff's to stand in the line-up. Quite the operation!" He thought better of saying anything more. It was a small town, and the police and sheriff's forces were probably pretty close.

"Then this morning. I get shaken out of bed to go down for an interview with Pierson. The High Sheriff himself. Probably only thirty or forty minutes, but it felt like a coupla hours. Hell, if I knew anything, I'd be glad to help." He picked up his mug to find it empty and set it down again. "Pat? What do you know about her? I was fairly good at the ole who, what, why, where, and when thing as a reporter. Maybe I could help dig. I mean, it's not like I actually knew the kid, but she was pretty enough to be a target. If you know what I mean."

Patrick tilted his head, lips pursed. "I probably shouldn't man." He tilted his head away for a moment then turned back to Saylor. "But I know a little. Her family's not old Apalach. Moved here when she was an infant, just after she was born. Not sure. I guess that would be about seventeen or eighteen years ago. They set up one of those shops on Commerce Street and sold beachwear, shells, and crap made in China to the tourists, and decorations to all the out-of-towners furnishing beach rentals for the weeklies."

Saylor was well aware of the kind of business. Once an offshore timber plot, St. George Island had transformed from the mid-1960s into a multi-billion-dollar real estate development with hundreds of beachfront and second- and third-tier beach view properties ninety-five percent rental market. Maintaining that rental market, its upkeep and repairs, custodial services, pool cleaners, HVAC and electrical techs, carpenters, and roofers worked year-round making good enough money that the Franklin County housing industry was doing all right.

"So," Patrick continued, "the family isn't deep in history, but they've been here a while. "And she was born here?" Saylor got up to refill his mug.

"That's one of the weird things, Jase." Patrick scratched his chin, squinting. The Chief checked for a birth certificate at the Health Department, didn't find one. We figured she must have been a newborn when the family moved in. Bummer though. Her father died a few years back when she was a kid. Boating accident and her mother died a just few months ago. Breast cancer."

"Pisser, I suppose for the girl and the mom." Saylor thought back to the afternoon in Tallahassee. Lindsey was looking through pictures. He'd only seen the blank backs of the photographs as she looked through them. *Old family fun times?*

"What about the store? With the mom dead...?"

"Lindsey and a friend had kept the shop open, not sure how. Oh yeah, actually, it was her mother's employee who first asked about posting a missing person."

"Did she wait the twenty-four hours to report a missing person?"

"No, she called us and then the sheriff the next morning. Said Lindsey would never not come home, at least, hadn't pulled an all-nighter before, not without telling her roomie. Especially, you know. Damn teenagers! Hook up with some friends, boyfriends. One thing leads to another." He smirked, knowing he and Jason both had similar histories in that department. "Kid comes home for a late breakfast, all grown up, no longer a virgin." Patrick took a long pull on his coffee mug, looked at it, appreciating the taste. "Damn good coffee, Bud."

"I try. So she waited?"

"She had to. We told her she had to go to the sheriff's office, report it there, but to wait for the official twenty-four hours before doing a formal missing person report, and that we'd notify patrol to keep an eye out."

"Yeah, well. I guess she went to report it to the sheriff that evening. What was that, two days ago?"

"No, three nights ago."

"So, she's been gone four days?"

"Yes."

"Crap, that does put it the night after I saw her at the Fish House. No wonder Pierson has me on his shit list."

"Don't be too creeped out about it, Jase. You're not the only one on the list."

Saylor frowned. "I sure felt like I was Mr. Special sitting across from him."

"Like I said, he's got a lot of fish in that barrel. He was just shooting at you this morning."

"How'd you hear about it over in Apalach?"

"Magic of radio, my friend. Only one 911 dispatch for the county. Anyone works for sheriff, fire, EMTs, police, even the ER at Weems Hospital. Anyone that would remember your name from the waybacks would know about you."

"Hmm, your chief sent you over? I don't remember the guy or the name. Was he a local or an import?"

"Chief Hammons? No, not a local. He got pretty high on the list up in Tallahassee but knew he'd never make chief in that town. Besides, he likes to go out and drop long lines for big fish." Patrick chuckled to himself. "In the long days of summer, he'll finish his eight-to-five, hop in his boat, and be on the other side of the island before most of us have got dinner organized." Patrick' eyes sparkled with a wink. "How many cop shop refrigerators you know with snapper steaks in the freezer?"

Saylor took it in, figured there was a good operation in the City of Apalachicola. Probably too, the sheriff's job was secure. *Could he help? Should he help? If Lindsey Lawrence was in danger and not off on a lark.* "Do you know if there'd been any friction between the Lawrence girl and any family? He consciously used the last name to put a little distance between himself and Lindsey.

"There isn't any other family. Like I said, her dad's been gone," Patrick scratched his head, "about eight or so years. Lost at sea. And her mom died late last year. Everything else seems clean too. Her last boyfriend has alibied up. It checked out. She wasn't in any current relationships we know about. She graduated last year, a year ago. Did one semester up at FSU and came back to help run the store after her mom got the bad news last summer. She decided to wait for more college when she knew what she really wanted. Street says she wasn't going to put the store up for sale. She'd ride that for a while, then go back and get her degree if she liked business."

"That sounds like a mature stance for someone her age."

"Well, I'm not sure. Speculating here, but there might have been money issues too. Maybe mom couldn't help with the tuition. Cancer's expensive. And there was the store, sitting there needing help."

Saylor rubbed at the bridge of his nose, thinking. "Any idea of a motive?"

"If she was kidnapped, there's a motive there for mayhem for sure. She was bathing suit model pretty. And then, Chief Hammons said there's some money in the family properties. But with no known next of kin, who knows what the disposition of the estate is? I heard she was given a trust in her mom's will for as long as she remained at school. Don't know much about that, hearsay at best."

"Patrick, did you know her? Personally, know her by face and name? She have any run-ins with the law you know about?"

"I knew her, mostly knew of her." He shook his head in the negative. "No, no real trouble I can remember. I can check. I should check. You know, just as a follow-up to see if any new angles show up. Good idea, Jase. Guess you were a top reporter out west."

"I did alright." Saylor's thumb tapped, a nervous tic, on the back edge of his coffee cup as he thought. "She have a car? Could she just have up and booked out of here?"

"There's a BOLO posted on her five-year-old silver Civic. But damn, I might as well be looking for sand on a beach. They're everywhere. You can't pop your flashers every time you see one, you'd never make it across town. And, before you ask, no response. Her car's MIA too. Here mom's old Dodge pickup has been parked at the house since she died. I guess Lindsey couldn't bring herself to sit in it. Mom, smell and all."

Saylor nodded understanding, then pulled his laptop over and started making notes. "OK, nineteen, one year college, silver Civic. What else?"

"Weirdness, her boat's missing too." He raised an eyebrow, "Don't see how you can drive a boat and a car at the same time when the trailer's sitting in the yard."

"Trailerable? So, fishing or sailing? What kind of boat?"

"Boston Whaler."

He chuffed a laugh. "Not the worn-out POC like we had. They're a little nicer these days."

"Neighbors say when the boat went missing?"

"Friday, that was a Friday night you saw her at the Fish House."

"Right, last seen on Friday." He looked across the table, spaced out for a moment on the view out the back of the camper. "I kind of lose track of days of the week down here. It's like an early retirement."

"You want to hire on at the paper?"

34

Saylor just laughed at the offer, went back to the subject at hand. "So, Chief Hammons gave up jurisdiction to Sheriff Pierson. The Lawrences live in the city or the county?"

"County, she and her employee shared a house up the river. Off Bluff Road." He waited while Saylor typed. He tilted his head back, his eyes closed, pulling up memory. "The roommate's name is Belle, Belle Tellerson, no, uhm, Tellefson. Belle had been the cheap local hired help at the store and did a pretty damn good job keeping the place going. As El got sicker, that's for Eleanor, seems everyone called her El. As El got sicker, Belle took over the books, orders, and all that, so it was at least limping along when Lindsey decided to drop the winter semester and stay home."

Saylor shook his head. "That's a lot of shit to go down when you think you are off to school, out of here. Who knows, maybe forever. Career, marriage, life. Then it all comes crashing down."

Patrick' eyes narrowed. "I guess you know about that, outta here, off to school, never going back kind of thing?"

"Look, Pat. I don't know that I ever really thought about it that way. I did six in the Army, declined a promotion to Captain to go back to school. Got a second BS in journalism, knew there was no way I would blow that on a weekly paper in Apalach. After graduation, I took the first offer that came, made a modest name in Austin, then got hired at the Houston Chronicle. Except for luck with wives, I was doing all right. It's not that I consciously wanted to leave and never come back. Life got busy. Mom and Dad weren't here."

"We did have a twentieth reunion last year. Thought you might have shown up."

"I got your note. Sorry, I was in the middle of a major story then, they can take over your life. Lots of issues. It just wasn't a good time."

Patrick nodded, frowning. "OK, I get it. So now you're working on a novel?"

"I thought so, but I'm not terrifically inspired. I might go poking around here, though, to see if any stone hasn't been turned over. For Lindsey." Saylor shrugged, palms up as if offering— something.

"Whoa, Jase. Sheriff Pierson's pretty damn good, and the Chief is no slouch. I'm thinking they might turn their focus back on you if you go poking around."

"OK, OK, I'll keep it to the internet. See if I find anything that looks suspicious. I do, I'll call. You can do what you want with it."

Patrick looked into the empty bottom of his coffee mug and looked up. "That sounds good. Listen, I need to get back to it. I'm out of my jurisdiction here in Eastpoint. I told Chief that I'd come to see you, see what the story was. I'll tell him you're all right."

Saylor watched the black and white pull out of the park entrance and make a right turn back to Apalachicola, not left toward the sheriff's compound at the jail. Good.

Then he thought about all the things they had not talked about. *Dammit, I should have asked more about Suzanne and the kids.* His sigh carried real regret. Patrick had been a close friend and confidant through high school. He considered his own, currently lonesome condition and wondered how all those relationships from the past had been so easily let go.

6

The Shop

Eleanor Lawrence's shop was on Commerce Street, downtown Apalachicola, shortened to Apalach by its natives and frequent visitors. The History House - Decor and More was not in the best location, but meandering tourists eventually found it. Commerce was shadier than the more crowded Market or Water Streets. Market had to service Hwy 98 through traffic and wasn't car- or pedestrian-friendly. Water Street served the marinas and seafood restaurants and a few shops and was one of the most photographed and painted of the local streets. Commerce Street was often overlooked by all but the serious curio shopper.

The building's shell was a holdover from the reconstruction era with dark red brick walls, a glass front, and a half glass green door. The show window was lined with a string of crab trap floats and filled with a random menagerie of cast-off maritime junk, salvaged running lights, and manufactured-for-the-trade facsimiles of marine brass hardware. The door slapped a small silver bell as he entered, its peel announcing a potential customer. As he scanned the entry, he noted a bookshelf to one side filled with local histories, fishing guides, pictorials, all with local interest. The rest of the store was floor-to-ceiling furnishings and accents with fishing, sailing, marine or marine life, and beach themes.

"Hi, can I help you?" The clerk came out of a backroom, a pencil eraser sticking out of straight light brown hair. The longish pixie cut showed more golden streaks from salt and sun bleaching. A tan work apron, stained and worn at the edges, hung on a frayed loop around her thin neck. At first glance, she was what he'd have called "almost pretty." The kind of attractive young woman whose flash of youthful beauty would require very little help later as she aged. Standing a few feet into the larger display area, she reached into an apron pocket for

37

a notepad and then pulled the pencil from her ear. Over a tired but welcoming smile, her eyebrows raised in question. "Are you looking for anything in particular?"

"Uhm, just browsing. It's been a long time since I walked around downtown," he said, "this used to be a rotting old shell of a building. Looks like it's been put to good use."

She eyed him more closely, interpreting. "Long time since you visited here last?"

"No, actually, I'm from here. I left quite a while ago. It's about twenty years now since I've been home."

"Home? You're from here? You're actually *from* Apalach?"

He flopped his arms, feeling embarrassed as if he were confessing a secret past. "Yeah, I'm a homie."

"Glad you're back?" A pair of dimples formed as her smile widened.

He looked at her, connecting a little, he thought. She was older than he'd expected. He thought a housemate, 'roomie' was what Patrick had said, would be in the same age range—early twenty-ish. She appeared to be on the other side of the twenties.

"You know?" He said, surprised at his own answer, "I think I am glad to be back." He'd been feeling melancholy, reluctant to reach out to his old world. But today—actually talking to people who weren't visitors in the campground, or law enforcement, he began to feel more 'at home.'

She extended a welcoming hand to shake. "I'm Belle. I'm from here too!" Belle's grip was firm, no-nonsense. Her smile radiated genuine warmth as her face lit up with an open, friendly welcome. *Very attractive*, he reconsidered. Toned arms extended from a yellow silk blouse over a just long enough white skirt. Shedding her apron, she'd stand out anywhere. He remembered an observation of a college roommate. The pretty girls always stick together. He could have thought of several counterexamples, but it was true often enough. He wondered about Lindsey's friend group, who else might have known her.

"Thank you." He looked around at the walls of the large front room, possibly twenty feet side to side and half again over that in depth. "I'm glad this place is being put to good use. And I'm Jason, glad to meet you."

Her smile faded a shade. "Well, to be honest, Jason, it's not *that* hard keeping a place like this up." She looked around at her familiar surroundings as if taking stock of its totality. "The owner and I, well..." she paused. Something unsaid. She gulped in a full breath, held it with her fist over her mouth. "I'm sorry." She let it out in a huff. "We've had a string of bad luck here." When she looked up at him again, she was blinking away an incipient tear.

He didn't say anything, thinking more might come if he waited, and perhaps she needed to get control of her voice.

"Actually, I wasn't sure I was going to be open today." She visibly deflated. "So, if you're not just browsing the streets and want something, I might be able to make you a deal off the asking."

"Business off? It looked like Market Street was pretty full of cars, tourists from all over as usual." He let the narrative hang out there.

She looked up at him, decided something, and closed up. "There've been some personal problems with the owner." She was still standing a handshake's distance. She backed away a step and waved a hand around. "Feel free to look the place over."

"Sure, sure. I was just enjoying the air out over by the wharf. Started walking around."

Belle pointed to a rotating rack by a window. "We have a new designer line just in. Dolphins, sailboats, anemones." Her eyes bespoke another radiant smile. "Even shark jaws!" Her cheeks raised as she snarled a mock shark mouth.

He concluded that he liked her. "Thanks, I guess I'll just look around for now."

"Ok, suit yourself." She turned and disappeared into the back room. He couldn't help noticing her figure retreating. *Nice!* Runner's calves. Soon, the sound of fingers dancing on a ten-key punctuated by the hand crank of an aging adding machine could be heard amid the softer sounds of shuffling paper.

Nothing in the shop led to anything specific. It held the same collections of shells imported from the south seas, aging crab trap floats, plein aire paintings of shrimp boats, anchored, or working, or sunk at their docks, carved fish, snow globes with sand flecks instead of snow. A wall section was covered in mermaids ready for mounting at a beach house. Another, tropical motif cards, and the usual miscellany he could find at the many competing shops over on Market

Street that paid more for the square footage. He found a pair of sturdy leather and hi-tech plastic sandals in his size and called out. "Belle? I think I've found something."

She popped back into view with an energy level that made him jealous. "Good, let me ring that up for you." She took the sandals from him, "Oh, you're gonna like these. Last for dang ever." That smile again. Not a put-on.

Unlike the ancient adding machine in the back, her point-of-sale equipment was up to date. Saylor tapped his card on the card reader. He offered an opening line again. "I've heard about the, um, string of bad luck." *That's putting a real shine on a heap of troubles.* "You're a champ for hanging in here with the store."

Belle looked up at him from behind the counter, appraising this new customer. She asked, "You going to stay around for a while? Or just back visiting family?" Then, "Who's your family? In this town, you know, almost everyone knows almost everyone." Her eyes were shining again. Her initial vendor/customer distance had vanished, replaced by genuine interest.

"Family's gone. I've got a brother in New York. Dad died. Mom moved to Texas. I'm back for a while, camped out over in Eastpoint until I see if I'm really going to sink roots or not." He found his eyes wandering to a rack of Tupelo honey jars next to the counter. He picked up a small bottle, nostalgic for the unique flavor. "Add this too." She reached for the bottle, but he'd turned it over to read the back label. "Special to the History House, Decor and More." He met her gaze. "That's here? You have your own house blend?"

"Long story. But yeah. We do." Her eyes told nothing more than that. Although a slight crease at her eyes spoke of some tension.

"Well, I'll be looking forward to it." He immediately realized he'd never used the small oven in the camper and wondered if he could make biscuits worthy of the Tupelo honey.

Her dimples were back. "You have some of that each morning and it might help you decide on whether you're puttin' down roots."

"Thanks, Belle. It's been nice chatting." He thought it would be nice to drop in again soon. As he stepped off the curb, he thought that somewhere between the door's bell ringing and the slam of the door closer, he'd heard her call out, "Come on back now, y'hear?"

7

Long Shot

Twenty-five minutes and two bridges later, Jason Saylor was back on the beach near the reconstructed St. George lighthouse. In a few more minutes, he'd unfurled his umbrella and settled into his beach chair to listen to the surf. An eight- to ten-knot east wind had been blowing all day, and a respectable surf was breaking across the bars. His perch near the end of the public boardwalk across the dune line was, he guessed, about two football fields away from the Fish House.

Saylor was grateful that its music was being carried away from him by the breezes. He settled into the straps of the chair and closed his eyes. He needed to get his mind off the local scene for a while and consider the plot of his work in progress.

His agent had expressed some initial interest, but he would need to concentrate and get an outline of the back half of the book to her to see if she thought she could or would market it. Having only one top 100 to his credit, he wasn't a sure thing anywhere.

His eyes closed. Countless waves lined up behind one another to meet their fate on his share of the beach. The wind-driven waves came in from the east. Was it simply the day's worth of easterlies that had kicked up these waves? A cross swell, longer period, was piling in from the southwest. Their crash and tumble fifty feet away did their job, lulled his thoughts. He imagined what stretch of ocean out there might have had a late afternoon squall to kick up that southwest swell. Was there a low-pressure system offshore, pulling obliquely at his piece of atmosphere to pull on his wind? He remembered from a particularly good science professor back in school that most winds in the semi-tropics don't blow, they suck, pulled toward areas of low pressure. It was all interconnected.

His thoughts ran to his work in progress. Andie Jackson? *Was that too hokey?* To have his hero be the namesake of one of the most despised presidents of the pre-civil war era by the new sensibilities of the modern era. Might want to keep her a one-eighth Indian.

Cherokee. Her dead partner was Billy Harrison. The two of them had been nicknamed the dead presidents. *Yeah, maybe that was too hokey to pull off as serious literature.* But then, international intrigue was rarely serious lit. And serious international intrigue, like *Tinker, Tailor, Soldier, Spy* was just so damn labyrinthine and boring. Why not liven it up with some humor? Something Will Smith might partner in. Someone with an occasional good laugh. Or someone with some serious history but a good heart. Hmm, should the hero be black? Can I write Black? Maybe, but I *can* write her as a female lead. He tried to imagine Zoe Kravitz as the main character. Hmm... He saw some of his opening plotlines fraying into loose ends. But then, the loose ends take care of themselves, make for the odd red herring or two to blend in with the real clues.

For a moment, the breeze backed off, permitting the beach music perpetually piped from the tiki bar to make it upwind. *Changes in Latitude* drifted by. *Well, not latitude, but I've got changes in longitude going on, guess I really need a change in attitude.* He thought of the morning chat with Patrick Wills. Officer Wills. Lieutenant Wills. Probably next in line to be Chief of Police Wills. Local boy made good, becomes the chief. Another local boy, a premier anti-crime reporter from Houston, crashes and burns in ignominy in an RV park in Eastpoint. His introspection was broken by the realization that the right sides of his ankles were burning. The sun had moved. Had he been asleep?

Saylor shifted his feet, sat up, and looked around. The day-trippers who usually came to the first beach they saw were mostly gone. Another straggler lay on her stomach, a Frisbee toss to the left. She was going to need serious skincare. He thought about waking her up but knew, present circumstances being as they were, he probably should not be seen approaching girls, women, half his age. He slipped his sun-dried feet into his new sandals and pulled up camp. He found the local seafood trailer hadn't closed yet and picked up a half-pound of headed and deveined shrimp for dinner. He had just enough cooking skills to max out the capabilities of the camper's micro kitchen.

Fortified by a nearly remembered recipe for shrimp and grits and kitchen cleaned, he sat at his laptop intending to outline Andie Jackson's next mission. He'd need an introduction and some backstory for the new partner. For the partner role, he'd thought first of a rookie male. Age difference conflicts, new school theory maybe a prep school type vs. field experience. His ivy league criminology background vs. Andie's street smarts and state university degrees in forensics.

When the laptop came out of sleep state, the document front and center was a Word doc with the notes he'd jotted down that morning with Patrick Wills. Lieutenant Wills. *Had the chief sent him on a fishing expedition? Was it a friendly visit?* He'd probably never know. The document displayed his earlier notes:

eighteen, nineteen?
1 year, FSU
Silver Civic, 5yrs old
Runabout, Boston whaler
Last seen friday nite,
County jurisd, bluff rd. North of Apalach
Belle Tellefson - roomie store clerk.
House on Bluff Rd

Thoughts of Andie Jackson's new partner dropped to the literary back burner. Saylor fixed the typos in the rapidly typed list. He mentally reviewed the morning's conversation. She must be almost nineteen, could have been a child prodigy. *Didn't Patrick say she'd finished high school a year early? That would have put her in Tallahassee as a seventeen-year-old? Or eighteen? When was her birthday? Need to look up a birth certificate, Franklin County Courthouse.* Leaning back, eyes closed, he reassembled the conversation. Patrick's face across the table, coffee mugs almost touching. Yes, she'd taken advanced placement classes, graduated a year early.

He added: minor at FSU, 18 years old. Probably a dorm. Roommate? Check with university housing?

Would that lead anywhere?

What else, Belle. Current roommate, but she was hired by momma Lawrence. He added: Belle, older. Follow up, local girl, to the entry.

Anything else at all? His thumb began vibrating on its own again, lightly tapping the space bar.

Going for a drive. Lindsey said she was "going for a drive." One of the last things heard before she left him on the beach. "I'm going for a drive." He added: off for a drive after dark to his list, selected the whole thing, and added bullets. Glancing at the mini blinds over the window adjacent to the dinette, only the ultra-white light of the campground's solar-powered LED lights shone.

Damn, too dark to drive up to Bluff Road tonight. OK, who the heck are you, Lindsey Lawrence?

He had some paid-up database subscriptions from his desk account at the Chronicle and began going through his list. White Pages confirmed her address on a loop off of Bluff Road, Apalachicola, FL. No other hits came up on the listing. Google Earth's street view showed her neighborhood to be behind steel privacy gates. She and Mother Lawrence, first name Eleanor, had been there for over ten years. No indication yet of Eleanor's deceased status. No record of a birth certificate for Lindsey Lawrence in Franklin County. He did hit on a book and page record address for a Lawrence family trust, but the record wouldn't open. Further digging found that the original hadn't been scanned.

He went to Intellius and TruthFinder, two crime report listing services. The first drew a blank 404 error, something expunged, possibly because she had been a minor. The second, a citation for excessive speed in a slow wake zone by Florida Fish & Wildlife. He opened the record. The vessel was an twenty-two-foot Boston Whaler. That was two years ago, before heading off for college. His dancing thumb accidentally tapped too hard on the space bar, and a second record appeared. Speeding violation, sheriff's department, Liberty County. Only an hour or so from Apalach, depending on where in Liberty County. He let a small grin spread to the side of his mouth. The girl liked to speed. Typical, he thought. Teenagers. It's a wonder they survive to become slow and cautious, conscientious parents. He back-buttoned to the previous record. The Whaler was listed as being owned by Eleanor Lawrence, Bluff Rd.

He decided to go for a drive tomorrow. A drive up the river, been wanting to get another boat anyway. Something lightweight that wouldn't kill the Prius. It would be a long shot, but what else did he have to do?

Oh, yeah. Andie Jackson's new partner.

Saylor opened his writing app, scrolled down to the character list, and added Amos Freeman. In his blank record, he typed: Amos Freeman, 28. Not apropos naming due to mixed Euro-Asian features. Small frame, muscularly fit. Short black hair. Military sidewall cut. Nondescript eye color changed with ambient light from gray to gray-green. HS in Orange County, FL. Still carried a hint of a southern accent when more than lightly inebriated. Undergrad Magna Cum Laude Princeton Sociology, Pre-Law, also Princeton. MS Summa Cum Laude, Criminology, U Penn. Recruited to the Farm at graduation. Recent graduate, field school at Langley based on a white paper on sociopathy.

He tapped open Andie Jackson's profile. Junior college certificate in criminology, six years in blue as a patrol officer. Changed her BA in criminology from UGA to Wake Forest. *Hmm, let her have an internship on the Cherokee reservation, get down on her Native American roots.* Then, accepted at Langley on her second try. *That ought to make for some fun scenes.* Scanning Amos Freeman's brief description again, he realized he had the makings of a good yin-yang partnership. Good, he thought, different enough from my thirty-eight-year-old Andie.

He slapped the laptop shut, plugged it in for the night's charge, and moved over to his thinly cushioned couch. The campground's basic cable was basic—no movie channels without commercials. Drowsy now, he found himself drifting off with ideas of buying a used runabout. Or a sailboat, no, a runabout. It's a long shot...but where is the Lawrences' runabout?

8

River

Saylor's morning was consumed by haggling sticker prices and buying a used twenty-two-foot aluminum V-hull, center console design, with a modest refurbished Yamaha 75. He wondered about the light horsepower until he took it for a test drive. The electric starter worked on first try. The aluminum hull offered little or no resistance to the powerful motor. It was up on plane and flying in less than ten seconds. He'd promptly turned around, grinning like a kid with a new bike, and closed the deal. Back inside the boat store for life jackets, a spare gas can, fenders, lines, and a fish finder.

By lunchtime, he was over five thousand dollars poorer. At least the dealer took care of the title and tag for the trailer and transferred the hull ID over to him as well. He enjoyed a basket of fried oysters at a wharf-side restaurant and decided he should go for a drive, as Lindsey had said. But was it as she meant it? Had she taken her car or boat? He knew well from his own youth that there's magic on the water at night if the moon cooperates. He also knew there was plenty of danger for the incautious.

Scipio Creek runs into the mouth of the Apalachicola River just above the high bridge that permits the offshore trawler fleet access to safe harbor. Compared to the river, the creek is a narrow muddy channel that fronts most of the real estate north of the city. It is separated from the river proper by acres of sawgrass. Bluff Road bypasses this impenetrable wetland for three miles upriver. It provides access to riverfront lots for the lucky and prosperous. Beyond these few houses, the Abercrombie public boat ramp is the last sign of real civilization on the river for almost fifty miles of untamed wilderness.

He plugged the Lawrence's street address into his phone's map app and took a slow cruise up the river. He zeroed in on their property just beyond an old railroad crossing that didn't look like it had been used since he was in high school. Examining the map image, he noted that the property was maybe a half-mile downstream from the junction of the river and the inland waterway. The waterway allowed barges and cruising motor sailors an inland passage from Apalachicola to Panama City via East Bay and onward to Pensacola behind barrier islands. He knew from his years in Apalach as a youngster on the water that hundreds of big money pleasure boats made this trip every year.

He reached into his carry-all duffel for his army surplus 7x50 binoculars. The contents of his small duffel, no bigger than a gym rat's bag, could light fires, chop trees, truss small animals or bad guys, keep him warm if needed, and feed him for three days. Today, he used the binoculars to fake bird watching in the trees lining the shoreline of most of the lots. As he approached the property indicated by the phone's GPS, he slowed the motor to idle. The Lawrence family, now only the younger Lawrence, was doing OK from appearances. That is, he thought, if she was still alive and well.

The house was elevated on concrete pilings, protected from storm surges. He guessed it would survey at over 2,400sf, not including the ample two-level decks facing the river. A short dock sported a floating extension that could rise and fall with the tides. A pickup was parked in one of the bays beneath the house, its shine diminished by a thin layer of dust. He saw no sign of a silver Honda Civic. An enclosed room with windows, perhaps twice the size of his camper, was beneath the main house.

He continued his charade of bird watching for a few more minutes, letting his engine quietly motor against the current. Shifting his view to the eastern shoreline and just beyond a broad sandbar where three boatloads of partiers were taking the sun, fishing, and drinking. He turned right at the junction with the inland waterway to go farther up the main river channel. The familiar shores, lined with water-loving cypress, sweetgum, willows, and black tupelo, extended north a hundred miles to a dam on the Georgia state line. Saylor had no interest in that trip today. He turned off the motor and drifted, thinking. Back at the Lawrence homestead, there had been no Civic, no boat at the dock, and no Lindsey. If she were in either of them, she could be anywhere. A standard five-gallon fuel tank and one spare tank could make the hundred-mile trip upstream against the current, or almost twice that to the west. If she'd gone in the car. Well, hell, she was gone. Why? Where?

He picked up the binocs again and began to scan the shoreline once again as his drifting boat glided past the western shoreline of the river. The current pushed him along faster now—he supposed a dropping tide was emptying the bay, adding unstoppable power to the river's current. The westering sun sparkled at the water's edge, but his wandering eye picked up colors as he passed below a public boat ramp. He pointed the glasses down and focused on small circles of oil spreading on the surface. He shook his head in disgust. Most of the fisherman he knew would be careful of the health of the waters they fished. Just one spent can of oil fallen or thoughtlessly tossed could dribble oil droplets for days.

He throttled up and headed for the public boat landing in Apalach. As he cruised south, hair blowing back, sun on his face, a broad grin spread across his face. He remembered why he loved this place and couldn't think of any good reason for never coming home to visit.

9

Suzanne

Five raps on his door brought Saylor immediately awake. *Holy crap, not again!* He sat up, stretched, took a deep breath, and scratched at his stubble. He pulled on last night's jeans, grabbed a fresh T-shirt from the laundry basket, shook it twice for wrinkles, and tossed it over his head. Expecting to see a patrol car in either sheriff's green and white or Apalachicola Police's black and white, his squint through the door's mini-blinds revealed no law enforcement in sight. He lowered his scan down and saw the RV park's resident manager's ragged hair and rounded red shoulders. She looked up about to knock again and presented a thin smile as he opened the door.

"Mr. Saylor, hope I didn't rouse you out of bed?" His late-night writing habit was known to his immediate neighbors and well known to Helen Faircloth.

"Good morning, Helen." He stifled a yawn with his fist. "What's up? You finally gonna let me have first tier?" He said it in jest, but there was always hope.

Faircloth shielded her eyes from the morning sun's reflection on his camper's siding. "Matter of fac', I am." She pointed at Monty Montana's gray behemoth across the drive. He noted that the usual array of lawn furniture was gone. Except for some loose gravel, the brick-paved apron beside the big diesel rig was clean. "He's heading out for Biloxi right after lunch. You still want it? Site #5, end of the row."

Uhm, moving up in the world means the forty-foot shift from Site#10 to #5. The thought of moving fought with the reality of moving. Normally, packing up to move would require a lot of stowed gear, a few hours. "Yes?" He realized it sounded like a question. "Yes, Helen. Damn, I'll change my busy schedule." He thought about his laughably not busy schedule: re-read the previous two days' work, consider any changes in the moving target that was his outline, a little light editing on earlier chapters for continuity's sake. "When do I need to move."

She lowered her arms, crossing them under the crest of her bosom. At just shy of six feet, sporting forty or so extra pounds, legs apart, and foursquare, she'd be a formidable blocking tackle. "Just as soon as you can put this thing in reverse and move over to that space. When you hear those diesels rumbling, start your engines."

"Helen? I had a few plans for the morning. Any particular reason for being that johnny-on-the-spot?"

"Sure do Mr. Saylor, about forty of 'em." She unhinged one forearm from her blocking stance and swiveled it and a pointing forefinger around in a loose arc. "Just about everyone else in here not in the first row, will be banging on my door as soon as they hear Monty Montana there hit his ignition. So, if you wanna be the johnny on that spot, you jes' be ready, ya hear?"

Monty Montana's nickname didn't match the man at all, but it fit the land yacht. The swirling graphics on its side framing mountain vistas behind two bison in the foreground were decidedly out of place on the Gulf coast. "Thank you, I'll be getting ready to move." He squinted at the mid-level sun angle. "It nine o'clock yet?"

"Just barely. Might want to get a move on in there. And be careful with your hoses. I don't want to be spraying down, no dribbling shits."

Faircloth was nothing if not blunt. "Will do, Helen, and thanks again." She had already turned away and waved one sunburned wrist in the air in parting. "Say, Helen?"

She stopped, turned her bulk back toward him, "Say what?"

"You mind if I back in, on the other side of the apron? I like to look out the back window as I work and enjoy the view."

She glanced over the area. There was ample room on the other side of the last parking spot in the row for him to fit and not drive into the ditch at the edge of the property. "Sure, but if'n you end up in the ditch, it's on you." She moved on without waiting for a thank you.

He mouthed a silent one anyway and began to detach his home from the grid.

He heard the diesel in warm-up mode at 12:30 and was out the door moving his outside furniture to the new site by 12:32. A few minutes later, as it belched its farewell cloud of black smoke, he was already in reverse. A few S-turn maneuvers later, and he was parked ready to crank down the stabilizers by 12:35. He checked his watch, grinned. *Thank you, Helen!* He went to the rear of his camper, looked out across Hwy 98, appreciating the sun-sparkled bay beyond and took in a deep breath of satisfaction. *It's going to be a great day.*

By 1:40 p.m., connections had been reconnected. His mobile estate was again anchored, stabilized, and plugged into the grid. As a plus, at his new location, the outside apron was on the east side of his camper's parking area. His unfolded beach chair could be positioned easily in the afternoon shade of the camper. He sat down to enjoy the view he'd been wishing for since he'd pulled in weeks ago. The only drawback to this site was its proximity to the coastal highway. A semi blew by at well over the speed limit, sucking behind it a brief blizzard of fine-grained sand. Wiping grit from his eyelids, he decided to pull the chair back another fifteen feet. He looked across his dominion, a paver-block outdoor use pad larger than the concrete patio behind the Houston home he'd left behind. Then another ten, maybe twelve feet to a vacant fifth wheel camper that didn't seem to have anyone ever in residence. His mind backed up to his former Houston house. He was never going back to that particular home, not even out of curiosity.

He thought back to yesterday's surveillance of the Lawrence's homestead and wondered under what circumstances he could innocently peruse the property. Without violating the sheriff's warning, that is.

Between the official message from Sheriff Pierson to stay out of it and Patrick's informal advice to keep a low profile, he had pretty much laid low. No, that wasn't it. Patrick had said "to not go poking around." Concluding that some people just do go missing, he had about exhausted his personal local and Internet search for foul play when he unfolded the thin Thursday edition of the Times. The local weekly was thinner than he remembered due to lowered levels of advertising and not much to report other than the usual squabbles at the City or County Commissions. A teaser paragraph on the lower front page led him to A3 where, above a half-page ad for the IGA, he read the follow-up article from last week's news. *Missing Girl's Disappearance Still A Mystery*. He read it through carefully twice and only learned that he had been one of thirteen men rounded up for questioning. The BOLO had been based on a tip phoned in describing a man she'd been seen talking to on St. George Island as she was filling her car at the Blue Store. The public was asked to be aware of a late thirties Caucasian male, balding in front, brown to black hair, thin beard.

He scratched at his three-day growth. *Is that a thin beard?* Saylor planned to shave more often, but knew he hadn't filled up at the island gas station and he wasn't balding in front. The back maybe, but his hairline in front was holding its ground. Just to check, he went inside to the micro-mirror on the wall over the bathroom sink. Nope, not balding yet. At least not much. More importantly, not enough for a casual witness to describe him as balding. He'd left the camper's door open to do this spot check of his hairline and was surprised to hear a tentative tap on the metal siding and, "Jase? Is that you?"

He turned to look out of his tiny bathroom across the minuscule hallway and focused on the woman at his doorway. It was still bright outside and her face was in the comparative dark.

She helped him out. "It's Suzanne, Suzanne Daniels."

"Yeah, I know, only, wow! Come on in, let me get a look at you!" She did, and she looked great. Only a little middle-aged padding over the youthful trim he remembered. Suzanne made looking pale in the tropics look good. Her skin had never been favored by too much sunshine. Even now, in late Spring, with afternoon temps in the upper eighties, she wore long sleeves, a loose white cotton thing with an exaggerated bow, but wide billowing sleeves that tapered to oversized cuffs. When she had been standing outside his door, the white blouse rippled in the breeze, allowing it to fold over her contours in all the right places. As she stepped into the camper, he said, "My God, Suzanne, you look great." And she did. Below the white blouse she wore a simple navy skirt and navy flats. Her raven hair framed a thin pale face, punctuated by bright blue eyes, a camera-perfect nose, and he remembered from high school, very kissable lips. If she wore makeup, it was understated and simply augmented her natural beauty.

He patted his own tummy. "I, on the other hand, do appear to have aged." They had been close, so he didn't think she would mind the scanning. "Hard to believe, twenty years later, and you look like you could be your kid's twin."

Her brow closed in question. "You've met Hannah?"

"No, no. I saw her picture in the Times. High school cheer squad, did that bake sale thing for the EMS and firefighters a week ago."

"Yeah, she's a great go-getter." She grinned.

"Come on in, set a spell." With a half bow, he waved expansively at his modest camper's interior.

She took it in from the walk-through access to the driver's seat to the undersized double bed at the back, which still held his laundry basket. It was flanked by a short pile of folded T-shirts and a tangled wad of something that might be underwear and socks. She sat at the dinette. "Patrick said you were over here." She glanced down at her clear-glossed fingernails, then nailed him with a soulful, almost wistful gaze. "Listen, I really can't stay too long, but I saw you as I was driving by. Sitting out by the street. You may be twenty years older, but you're not doing so shabby yourself."

Saylor sat opposite, wondering where to start. They truly did have a lot of history behind them. "So, I met Patrick. I suppose he told you." Her smile thinned a notch. Something in her eyes darkened. "Are you two OK?" Her smile disappeared entirely, screwing tight. He felt like he'd stepped on a wound. "I'm sorry, not prying. I just realized Patrick hadn't mentioned our old crowd when he was here. What, I guess it was about a week ago? I lose track of days of the week."

"Pat and I are separated. A few years now."

"Married still?"

"Yes, but it's one of those married-in-name-only things." Her face appeared to be on the edge of crumbling. "We don't share domestic duties, you might say."

"Jeez, Suzanne. I'm so sorry. You and Sandra, Pat and me. Seemed like we'd never be apart. Till..."

"Yeah." Her smile returned, but it was not one of genuine well-being.

She was a beautiful woman on the runway approach to forty. He figured if she put herself out there, it wouldn't take long back on the singles market. "How's Sandra? God, it's been forever since I thought about some of our exploits. You remember when we took the jet skis over to Little St. George? Pat's tiny scrapings of pot had gotten wet from salt spray. How bad that shit tasted?"

Her eyes widened, then narrowed, as her mouth slowly opened. "Christ, Jason. You don't know?"

"Know what?" Noting her reaction, he wasn't sure he wanted to know. "Is she OK? Sick? What?"

She reached across the narrow table and placed a pale, ringless left hand on his. "God, I hate to be the one."

"Shit, what? For crying out loud, Suzanne."

"Sandra has been dead for almost," she paused, "I don't know how many years. Hell, it was the same year you left. You'd just finished your freshman year at FSU. Came home to work a few weeks with your dad over on the Island. Sandra and I had just graduated. And I didn't even get to see you then..." A silence opened up, a gulf in time and distance. Her eyes spoke volumes of hurt and loss. "It's been so long, Jason." Her lower lip began to shake. She blinked at tears. "I loved that girl like my sister. Then you two, you two got together finally, that summer. When she left for UWF, that left Pat and me, well we were all that was left, and it felt like it was a natural thing."

She began to pull her hand away. He reached for it, held it in his. "I didn't know, Suzanne. I just didn't know. How come no one told me?"

"You two had gotten together, but you also broke up. After that last night."

"It wasn't like that, Suz. I really only came home for a few weeks to pack up my stuff because mom was moving to Austin. You were out of town, we went out for some drinks, we uh, hooked up" His slumped shoulders and downward glance betrayed simple embarrassment.

Saylor recovered from the shock of the news, looked back up. "I stayed another week and, well, we enjoyed each other's company, but we both went on to our separate schools. If we'd had cell phones in those days, we might have stayed in touch." Nothing could fill the growing pain in his chest. The news was a shock, an exploding bomb that left a vacuum behind the pressure wave. "Sandra's gone, all these years. Jesus, I guess I was going to look you guys up eventually, then this thing with the sheriff took over one of the front burners." He ran out of meaningless explanations.

Memories, locked away, shut away. Events rarely remembered came flooding back. The brief few weeks with Sandra had blossomed into the first real full-bodied love affair of his life. The weeks he's planned for Suzanne spent with Sandra instead. Then Sandra's parents' wholehearted disapproval of the relationship. A glorious reunion full of hope and promise had come crashing to the ground. Sitting across from Suzanne now, he remembered the terrible hurt he'd felt as a young man losing his first true love. Thinking about it, that loss probably hurt worse at nineteen than his last breakup in Houston at almost forty. He squeezed Suzanne's hand. "I would have liked to have known."

She nodded, emotions played across her face, indecision, loss, questions. "I should have called you, even as mad as I was at you. I should have gone to Tallahassee to find you. Like I said. At the time, I was angry."

"Did Sandra want to get back together with me? I was findable? Seemed like her parents were pretty firm." He mimicked Sandra's dad's voice. "That kid is not going to be with my daughter. You need to find someone with a real future." Saylor let out a harsh, hard laugh. "Huh! That's why I was out of here in the first place, to get a future. I didn't want anything to do with my dad's business. And after that episode with Sandra's mom and dad? That's why I was in school in the first place, to get out of here, to be something else than this." He blinked, "You were angry? How—?"

She shot right back at him. "How was I angry? I thought we were going to be the item. You, Jason, and me! Between the four of us, it was always you and me and Sandra and Pat."

Her eyebrows pulled together in a hard stare. "Yeah, she and I were a year behind you guys, but graduation had come and gone. We had our dreams too. But that summer, I was in the mountains with Mom and Dad. And I was waiting for you." Her face was contorted in a reflection of that long ago anger and loss. "But you never came back, Jason. You just never came back *to me*." Dry-eyed still, she drove in the nail. "Try to imagine how *I* felt when I found out. Christ Jason! You were always the oblivious one. How'd you get to be a reporter? Doesn't that take empathy skills?"

He didn't have an answer. He looked down at his hand on hers. His was gnarled and sunbaked, even though his primary workplace tools for more than a decade had been a telephone and a keyboard. Suzanne's hand was white, a little worn by housework, but soft and well-tended. He noticed for the first time that her nails were a polished dark red. Same as always. He looked up slowly. "How did she die?"

"She was in Pensacola, first year of college. She went a little wild after you left. We talked a lot on the phone, and it seemed she was enjoying college life maybe a little too much. She got pregnant, died in premature labor. Sepsis, I think. Not sure that I remember that right now, but that sounds right."

Saylor's throat locked up. He couldn't swallow, had a hard time breathing. "How could all of that happen and I didn't know?"

"I'm sorry to be the one to tell you. I guess we just thought you might have heard." She sniffed. "Whew, this is not at all where I thought this conversation would go today. Patrick said you were over here. Then I thought I saw you as I was driving by, and bam. This." She looked into his hurt. "I'm sorry, Jase. Sandra changed. Then the pregnancy. She was going to give the child up at Sacred Heart, but it never had a chance either."

His eyes were dry, but only through sheer willpower and actively blinking tears away. She had a single wet track of a tear on her left cheek. He gave her hand a squeeze. But not as hard a squeeze as the pressure he felt on his chest. He'd thought about Sandra just a few days ago. Thought about Suzanne too, especially after Patrick's visit. He'd wondered whether to drop by her parent's B & B or do a White Pages search. His mind flashed to the city cemetery. He had to make himself breathe. "Suz, I'll give you a call. We can catch up on some better times. For now, I think I need to process this."

10

Catching Up

Life had begun to get simple again for Jason Saylor. His day of fishing up the river and in Lake Wimico had brought home supper with spare fresh fish to make Helen Faircloth and her partner happy. Good to keep making positive points with the park's management, and in part, to thank her for the move to the front tier. It also helped that he'd hinted that he would probably be there through the summer. He knew it would probably be at least that long before he was through with the current work in progress and its planned sequel.

There were enough problem areas in world politics at any given time that he felt sure he could get Andie Jackson and her new partner into trouble and eventually into bed. His agent had been pretty convincing that the majority market of fiction readers was women, sixty-five to seventy percent. Shoot for that market and decorate the plot with a decent sprinkling of sex that wasn't overly blatant. Changing gender on his hero turned heroine had taken a while, but he warmed to the task. Putting his point of view in the female perspective had been a fun exercise.

He wondered, though, about getting it right. Could he be that presumptuous? Could he write from the POV of a female? Should he put in any details about the monthly visitor? It just didn't come up in any literature he'd seen. He'd never read any significant amount of chic lit and wasn't about to start. He had almost picked up the phone to see if Suzanne would be an advance draft reader when it buzzed on its charging pad.

He noted the caller ID was blocked. Picked up.

"Hello?"

"Jase, Patrick here."

"Hey, Pat. What's up?" He knew what was up. Suzanne was up. She'd left with old wounds freshly scraped open. Even if not living together, they talked if they had joint custody. Patrick would be upset that Suzanne was upset. Or maybe the news that he hadn't heard about Sandra was up.

"Listen, Jason," Patrick said, "you mind if I drop in? We really didn't get a chance to catch up on my last visit. I'd like to come over. I can bring a sixer, we can share war stories. What are you drinking these days?"

"It would be good to do some catching up, but I don't need a drink. Me and brother Al are not good for each other. Last time I drank, I ended up having four too many, fell asleep on the beach, and you lost a reliable witness to a possible last sighting of Lindsey Lawrence." *Had he just said too much?*

"No probs, brother. I'll be across the bridge in a few. I'm off duty."

"See ya. Oh, and I'm on the front row now. You'll see my rig from the road as you get close."

"OK, see you soon."

That's good, Saylor thought. We really didn't get into any old histories last time. I was Suspect Number 2. He straightened up a little, not much to clean up in the small space, but its minor assets made anything out of place look like a mess. He wasn't punctilious, but he hated disorder. As promised, Patrick Wills' pickup pulled up about fifteen minutes later. Good time for the ten miles from downtown Apalach and the posted speed limits. But then, Patrick had the ultimate get-out-of-jail-free card. His own blue light dash flasher. And, he thought, being a cop gets you a blocked number.

He opened the door, "Come on up. I've got some queso warmed up and some chips."

Patrick set down a six-pack of Coronas. "If you change your mind, I think you used to like these."

"We'll see. Crack one of those open for you, I'll grab a coke, and we can sit down on my veranda."

They settled into beach chairs on the brick patio just outside. Late afternoon shade and a good shore breeze made for a comfortable setting. "I suppose Suzanne told you about running into me. Or actually, seeing me and dropping in."

"Yeah, she did." Patrick settled his athletic frame into the chair, testing its dubious support. "She seemed split on whether it was good to see you again or not."

"I understand. There were good times, mostly. And I'm the asshole for disappearing and not keeping up. For that, I can't say I'm sorry enough. Especially for not even knowing about Sandra. That was tough to hear about." He cracked open the plastic cap of his diet Coke and turned to Patrick, offering up the drink for a tap. "Here's to the good times in the past, and good times in the future."

They sat and talked about old exploits as the sun settled beyond the tree line. They recounted some of the more famous crucial plays from their notable high school football career. Patrick now had a twelve-year-old son entering middle school on the football squad and a daughter on the high school cheer squad. Not everything was perfect, he admitted, but he was hopeful he and Suzanne could pull things together.

No, Jason hadn't heard lately from his six-year-older brother. Last news was that he was a commodities trader with a home office in Manhattan with few goals besides creating personal wealth and keeping his ex from touching it. Jason's mother remarried, was in Austin selling real estate, and praying for the East Texas bubble not to burst.

Sandra's folks were still around, her little sister had gone to the University of South Florida, in St. Pete, and was rarely in town except for occasional holidays. As their talks drifted, cloud tops offshore took on the orange tint of the lower sun angle. Patrick set down his third Corona on the concrete. "Hey, I need to use the head. Do you mind?"

Saylor nodded at the door to the camper. "In there, can't miss it." He looked back out across the bay, considering motoring across the gap between St. George Island and Dog Island. In the right tides, there was good fishing at either point, but there was no driving access to Dog Island so a better chance of a private beach. Clattering noise turned his head toward his camper.

Patrick came to the door, looking sheepish. "Sorry, I knocked your shaving kit off the sink." He took one step down, nearly missed the second, but recovered without falling.

"Careful, this is a hard landing zone." They shared a laugh. It felt like old times, even if he wasn't drinking. He gave a momentary thought about getting back in the program then came back to the present. "Not to worry about the shaving kit, man. That bathroom is so small that, well, hell, it's just too damn small." They shared a laugh again. "I'm glad you came back by, Pat. I really am." He got up and looked at his old best friend, who was still holding on to the aluminum handle next to the door. Something about Patrick Wills didn't look right. "You OK? You can drive, right?"

"Sure, sure. I'm good. Only three beers. You keep the other three."

"No man, like I said. I'm off it for a while. It doesn't help the muse."

"The moose?"

"No, the muse, m - u - s - e. My writing inspiration." He knew it wasn't easy to explain to a non-writer that nothing got written when the muse wasn't there. Ideas were hard to come by and the characters were silent. They needed to talk to him, and he needed to be able to listen as fast as his fingers could type. He closed the two steps between them and embraced his friend. The man hug felt good. "Listen, tell Suzanne I'm sorry if I upset her the other night. You and Suz are really all I have around here. I tried to call Tommy Lassiter and found he'd died in Iraq. Sissy Miller's married and gone." He shrugged. "You two are about it for who I'd like to look up."

Patrick returned a genuine smile. "You know it. I'll ask her when's a good time for you to come over for dinner to meet the kids." He laughed a shrug, "Maybe she'll let me eat too." They exchanged email addresses and cell phone numbers and said their goodbyes. Saylor watched as Patrick's pickup turned onto the highway and sped into the dusk toward the Apalachicola Bay bridge. Patrick had been and could be a good friend. If only the past could stay past.

11

Records Search

Two mornings later, Saylor was working on a plot outline for the sequel. The first novel was nearing an end, and it couldn't hurt to leave some easter eggs for future readers that might foreshadow the next in a series. He'd always admired the construction of Michael Connelly's Harry Bosch series. That detective's career had been covered from early days on the LAPD well into post-retirement working cold cases. He could only hope that someday Andie Jackson would be a name that avid crime readers would know well. It would also beat working for a living, even with the grind of a book tour every year. If this third novel hit the ground with the reader base he'd gotten from his second, he might be able to garner a few days on the top ten Amazon list or, better yet, a five-star review in the Times.

Saylor's phone, usually used as a game platform to kill odd moments, buzzed. He normally kept the ringer off. In the confines of his eight by twenty-four living, dining, bedroom, kitchen, and bath, it was never more than a few steps away. Caller ID announced MC. Margaret Campbell was a former between-the-wives swing and a miss. He was glad he'd stayed on good terms as she was a terrific legal clerk and a terrific dumpster diver into online databases. She knew more arcane law citations than most lawyers. She could interrupt his day any time she called.

He picked up. "Saylor."

"Jason, it's Margaret Campbell. I have news."

"Oh great, and is it good news, or should I be moving on?"

"Well, I don't know, but it's interesting, certainly puts a twist on your missing girlfriend."

He was confused, then. "No, she was not a girlfriend. Just a girl I met a few days or hours before she went missing. I'd almost forgotten about her."

"You're too busy to keep your ass out of jail?"

"The local cops haven't bothered me in a few days, just don't seem interested anymore." He hoped so anyway. "What did you find out?"

"Did you know she was wealthy?"

"Don't know that I did. Does it matter?" He pulled the laptop near, opened a new document, and set the phone down on speaker. "Go ahead. I can take notes."

Margaret began at a speed she knew he could keep up with on a keypad. "Lindsey Lawrence, daughter of Eleanor Sands Lawrence, is the beneficiary of a trust to be valid at age seventeen. The trust is specific for use for room and board, tuition, and was good through age twenty-five." There was a brief pause, which he appreciated as he typed. "I guess that would allow for grad school. Eight years is a long time."

"Especially since she graduated from high school early and had most of her first year done as AP classes." He paused to take a hit of cold coffee. "She was damn near finished with her first year when she left for college."

Campbell asked, "You know that how?"

"I'm a reporter, Marge. Give me a break. I have skills." Saylor shook his head in mock disgust as if she could see him from her desk in Houston. It helped that he remembered the brief bio in the local paper added to the missing persons copy. "So, how much was this trust worth?"

"Jason, it gets better." Sounds of rustling paper. "The trust was worth $600,000. That's good for seventy-five grand a year for eight years."

"Maybe they made allowances for something besides a public university. If Lindsey opted for Miami or Rice or really almost anywhere out of state. It could easily get that expensive."

"True, but remember, she left school, went back home."

"Were there termination clauses?"

"I looked for that before I called you. I can't find any in this contract for trust unless there were riders I can't find."

"Well, maybe it wasn't an issue. She was home helping her mom with the family store. Mom was sick. But breast cancer is survivable." He thought about the little he knew. "Quite possible, the turn for the worse was pretty quick, and it just never occurred to anyone to revise the trust. There'd have been a lot of psychic trauma to deal with. An only child, mom dying, all that." He couldn't imagine, began to feel sorry for the kid he really didn't know all over again. "Marge, can you tell from what you've dug up if the account has been drawn on and where?"

"No, not from this. It's a scan from a public record at the courthouse. Looks like your locals are finally beyond microfiche because it's an excellent copy."

"It's in the Franklin County Courthouse?"

"Where else?"

"Just checking, Marge." He grinned as he made notes. *I do need to get down there myself. Sheesh!* "Did I ever tell you I love you?"

He heard laughter on the other end. "There was that one time, Fourth of July? I'm pretty sure you were drunk. I didn't hold you to it."

"I remember holding on to you pretty hard. I think I remember you liked being held."

"I think I was holding you up, so you wouldn't fall down. And past is past, Jason."

"Past could be prologue."

"Not from seven hundred miles away."

"Alright, alright. Hey, did you look that up? Gonna come see me?"

There was a break in the conversation. Their light patter had hit a speed bump. She finally filled the silence. "I'll just say that I briefly considered delivering the news. In person."

He considered that. A brief relationship. Hot at the time but cooled by time and distance. Had the absent heart grown fonder? "Margie, my dear. Should you ever want to make that trip, you'd be very welcome, but we might want to get something more comfortable than my current accommodations." He scanned his micro-estate, grimaced at the thought. "And it's I-10 all the way to Exit 142."

Again, laughter on the other end. "Same ole, same ole, Jason."

"I'm just saying that if the spirit moved you, it's faster to drive from Houston to this little semi-tropical paradise than anything to do with airplanes."

"You make it sound so attractive."

He looked up to take in the brilliant clear blue sky, emerald to brown waters in the bay. A squadron of brown pelicans in vee formation was heading into the wind scanning the water as they passed. "It does have its charms. But they don't hold a candle to yours."

"Enough, cowboy." It sounded like she'd had enough flirting. "I'll call you if anything else turns up."

"Thanks, Marge. Seriously. This may lead to something." They exchanged cursory goodbyes and the phone went dark. He blew out a sigh. Suddenly, the camper felt smaller, lonelier.

His view to the bay dissolved into memories of a Fourth of July celebration in Houston's downtown park. Bray's Bayou Park, a grassed or landscaped flood plain adjacent to the downtown high-rise district, was the city's prime spot for fireworks and celebrations. Saylor and Margaret had decided to enjoy the festivities after a long evening in the press room and drinks at the revolving bar on top of the Tenneco Building. Casual kissing in the dark evolved into a late-night stay-over at the downtown Hilton and another two or three weeks finding out that they really were not compatible. They parted friends before feelings got hurt and before they needed to tell the Chronicle's HR department that they were an announced couple.

Driving over the bridge to Apalachicola, he found himself thinking about Margaret. Thinking about Margaret led to thinking of his recent divorce and of Caroline. He realized he missed Caroline. They had been together six years and had some good times. He missed Houston the way they had shared it. Picnics on Brays Bayou Park, hiking in the San Jacinto preserve, beach trips to Galveston, and day sailing on Galveston Bay.

Some days he felt like a lone dried pea rattling around in a can. His melancholy mood found him driving around downtown looking for parking near the courthouse. At least he could find out what might be in the Lawrence family trust and dig to find out if there were any other pertinent family documents recorded in the period around its recording. Or, if he got lucky, maybe the clerks could help him with a name search in the records. So many counties, so many different ways to cross-reference records. He had long ago learned to be as friendly as possible with the locals.

Frustrated, he'd been around the courthouse parking area twice. A possible commission meeting had filled the few parking spaces available on that side of the bay bridge's ramp. On Commerce Street, he found a spot across the street from History House – Decor and More. Not totally in charge of where his feet went, he found himself at the door and then jumping again in surprise as the silver bell overhead announced his entrance.

"Just a sec. Feel free to look around—I'll be out in a jiff." Belle's voice sang out from the back room. He cocked his head for sounds of her racking the ten-key adding machine but heard nothing. He found himself looking absently through a vee-shaped display of mounted but unframed artwork. Most were from the plein-aire school that descended on the city every spring and fall. Some were by a few of the painters who lived in town year-round. If you wanted a one-off painting of a shrimp trawler or a whole line of them in the same style, there was a wide selection.

At movement, he turned. Belle stopped short on seeing him. She smiled and pulled off her stained denim apron. "Run out of honey already?"

"No, I was cruising for a parking space near the courthouse and found myself here again."

She nodded toward the rack of paintings. "Did you see anything in there you like? If not, there's another batch in the back on consignment." She pointed at the display near him. "Those we bought outright, to help the artists out." After a brief pause. "The owner did that. She liked to help out like that."

He knew a lot more about the situation than she knew he did, so he opened carefully and lied. "I do need a bigger jar of that Tupelo honey. Seems I've been putting it in my coffee, on my toast." He shrugged helplessly. He couldn't think of another use immediately. "It'll be gone soon."

"I gotcha completely. I just LOVE it on my oatmeal. Oh man, and on a warm buttered biscuit? Whoa. Hold me back."

He found himself grinning from ear to ear at her enthusiasm. In light of the fact that he'd probably do anything this young sprite asked, he answered honestly, "Sounds good. I'll have to cook up some biscuits."

"Well now, Jason Saylor, right? The reporter and novelist?"

Surprised, "Yes, I am Jason Saylor, and I have written a novel or two. Fact is, I'm back in town, taking some time to see if I'm worth writing a few more. They say everyone has one good story in them, but only a few can do anything with the information or the inspiration." He found his hands and arms loose, dangly. He crossed them. "How'd you know that? OH! I guess you got the name from my card. Have you read the book?" He felt foolish that there was just that one book that went sort of big time. Did one of the few thousand copies make it to a bookstore in Apalachicola?

"Well, no." She looked at the door behind him, then back up into his eyes. Searching for something. "Scuse me." She slipped between him and a rack of postcards and flicked the ancient brass lock shut. She flipped the Open sign to display Closed to the outside world, then slid past him again and turned back to face him. "Would you mind stepping into the back room for a minute?"

Before he could get over her abrupt movements, she twirled on her heels and walked into the back room out of sight. Overhead, the interior lights to the salesroom went dim. He followed her into the brightly illuminated catastrophe of a back office. Boxes of inventory were stacked against two walls. Some lay opened on a massive wooden work counter, others lay in rows below it. A hand truck stood blocking a back door, wedged at an angle to keep the door from being opened from the outside. A mail station's scale and a roll of brown packaging paper were just visible under a loose pile of shipping envelopes and a spray of small FedEx boxes.

She sat at the desk chair and offered him a spot in the only other chair. "I hope you don't mind. I bet you've got questions."

"Well—" He was cut off before he could decide what to tell her.

"I sure do." Belle laid her arms on the gray padded arms of an office chair so old the faux leather was worn off its backing fabric at too many places. She tucked an ankle under the opposite leg and pushed her small frame into the back padding. Comfortable now, she said, "I think I need your help."

To Saylor, she seemed to have shrunk a few sizes. He was silent for at least thirty seconds. He realized he would like to know more about Lindsey's immediate past, and being honest, he'd like to learn more about Belle. He hadn't expected this.

He extended the fingers of his left hand and began counting them off with the index finger of his right hand. "First of all, you barely know me. What makes me Mr. Trustworthy? Second, does this have anything to do with the disappearance of Lindsey Lawrence? Three, do you know anything at all that would tell you whether she's alive or dead? Four, do you have any knowledge at all that would point to her whereabouts if she is still alive?"

He closed his eyes, thinking. His right hand's thumb began rhythmically tapping on the countertop. "Did you know that Lindsey was the beneficiary of a Trust fund if she was in school?"

Her eyes widened at the last question. "I don't know if I'll get all of those out in order."

"Give it a shot." He lifted a shoulder in a half shrug. "I was dropping in today, because well, I'm not sure. I think I just wanted to chat, and yes, I was here before because, and I think you know this, because the police and sheriff's office had me listed as a person of interest for a while. But that doesn't explain why the first thing you say is 'I need your help.' Why me, specifically."

"So, the honey jar excuse was BS?"

"Got me."

Her expression was tight, lips pursed, eyes narrow. Her hand gripped the arms of her chair with what might have been desperation. When she answered, it came out in a fierce torrent.

"One, because that piece of shit Patrick Wills was in here asking if I knew you, he had a picture. I said yes, but not well; that you'd come in and bought some honey. That's it. I asked about you. He said you were old buds, and he was just trying to make sure you were clean. But he also said you might come prying because you were an investigating reporter back in Texas. And to tell him if you come back. That's about it for number one. And bonus answer, that's why I looked you up. You do seem to be a good investigator."

"Two. Yes hell, I'm concerned about Lindsey's disappearance! I'm worried sick about her. She owns the place since her mom died. Actually, I think it's in probate or soon will be, but it will go to her if she's alive. Probate will shut it down in a month or two if she stays missing. That's not that long and I'll need a job and a house real quick.

"Three, Jesus! No idea where she might be, and I hope to God she's alive. Four, I have no god-damned idea. If I did, I'd go to the sheriff, not that piece of shit prick, Wills."

"What was five? Oh yeah, Trust fund?" She barked out a hard humorless laugh. "No, I did not. But I did find some deposits to the bank account, but they don't jive with the sales records. If the money is coming from that, fabulous. As long as it doesn't get her in trouble." Belle looked down into her lap, sighed. She looked up. The momentary flash of anger had lapsed. "Without those whatever-they-were deposits, this place would be broke. We'd have had to shut the doors two months ago."

Saylor relaxed and shifted sideways, resting his arm against a counter full of boxes of postcards. "How big were those extra deposits?"

"The ones that don't come from the daily receipts. Six and a quarter thousand a month, a real lifeline."

"Is that what you were working on when I was in here last time? I heard you going to town on that ten-key."

She looked somewhere inward as if correlating her bootleg accounting on the paper tape and his earlier visit. "Yes, that was probably it."

"I've got to ask because Patrick Wills and I do go back to better times. And so, for "that piece of shit prick Wills" to be your frame of reference. You can see there's a conflict there."

She softened. "I'm sorry but listen. Almost any single girl in this town and probably half the married ones will tell you that he can't keep his dick in his pants. He hit on me for weeks before I finally had to tell him, no thanks, please leave me some space. When Lin came home from school, he started in on her. Even knowing that Eleanor was sick and getting sicker, the little shit kept it up. She's half his age. Made me sick. If you were a friend of his, I'm sorry." Her mouth screwed into a tight O again. "So, will you help me?"

"What exactly do you mean by helping? The sheriff told me in clear terms to stay out of it. Patrick gave me the same message."

"Ever think that they were a little nervous about your skillset?"

"What do you mean?"

"I looked you up. You covered some pretty serious stuff back in Texas. State House scandals in Austin. You were all over the front pages, did some TV stuff. Subpoenaed for not providing sources to the DA. Then Houston, you did some undercover with a chic reporter and blew open a migrant trafficking ring. Some nasty dudes went to jail." She paused for breath. "And the pollution thing in Pasadena. I thought Pasadena was in California."

He nodded, assessing her in a new light. "Pasadena, Texas is a chemical shithole southeast of downtown Houston. Makes the Love Canal look like a field of lavender." He calculated that she wasn't old enough to understand the significance of the Love Canal environmental disaster. "Whatever, just another case of big money trying to save nickels by poisoning the groundwater beneath low-income housing." He waved a hand in an off-hand who cares motion. "Pisses me off, but that's just me, apparently. The paper buckled and decided to let me voluntarily go on leave."

"Whatever, it seemed like you might be the kind of guy who could find someone. No one around here is going to look all that hard for a missing girl." She shook her head in dismissal. "Probably waiting for the Panama City police to call to have someone come get her."

"Look, Belle. I see that you're coming up to a time limit here. Not sure what specifically I can do, but I was about to go to the courthouse to look up some public records on the Lawrences. If I find something interesting, you want me to drop back by?"

"Wanna get some oysters when you come back?" She glanced up at a twelve-inch school regulator clock on the wall. "Think it will take long?"

He followed her glance. "11:15 Probably not a good idea. Too small a town. Not sure if I should be seen with you. And at the courthouse, I don't know if they'll shoo me out to shut down for lunch or not. If not, I'll probably have to spend a little time there. I'll give you a call later, when and if I find anything interesting."

"Thanks." She looked down at her hands, folded with interlocking fingers. He couldn't tell if her reaction was disappointment, or maybe he should have said yes. She looked back, and softly and husky with near-the-surface emotion. "Really, thanks, Mr. Saylor. My job, this store, where I'll be living, are nearing some kind of endpoint, and I haven't a clue what to do next."

"Please, just Jason." Was she getting misty on him? Then he thought about Patrick. "You're OK? Patrick isn't harassing you, is he?"

69

Bruce Ballister

"No, not in a while. Good luck with the search."

"Thanks, who knows." He smoothed back his hair with both hands, gave her a smile, and turned to go. "Later." He stopped at the door, not having pulled it all the way open, and looked back. "Promise you this, I will give you a call, whatever I find." As he stepped out onto the sidewalk, he found himself looking left and right along Commerce Street, not looking for traffic. That was easy enough to rule out based on the quiet. He was checking for patrol cars. He looked back at the storefront before stepping away. Something about Belle's fragility. He reached for the crystal doorknob and, turning it just past the click of release, leaned toward the opening, and cracked it an inch.

"If you need me, I'm at the Coastal Paradise Campground in Eastpoint. I'm right on the highway. A white camper with a Dodge front end poking out from under a cab-over sleeper. Twelve-inch red racing stripe down the sides. It's old and ugly, hard to miss." He didn't hear anything but quiet from the back room.

He was about to poke his head in and repeat it when she responded. "Got it, red stripe. Thanks."

The records search was filled with all the pitfalls of searching in a new county for the first time. Searching by name and type of record gave him book and page numbers for legal papers. His search for property records provided book and page numbers in another set of books. He just had to pull the log for that year and month and then do an electronic search for the book and page if those years had been completely digitized. Tapping drop-down menus and left and right arrows on the document retrieval screen for records filed at the approximate time of the Trust filing yielded absolutely nothing.

He found the recorded transfer records moving all the properties from Lawrences' joint ownership to a Florida LLC, with Eleanor Lawrence as sole proprietor. Odd, nothing at all on his death certificate, but a newspaper clipping was in that batch briefly outlining details of Jeremy Lawrence's sailboat found dismasted and drifting with no sign of the owner. *Did that serve as death notice in lieu of an MA's report?* Paper records it seemed, were not as universally digitized as property records. These were, after all, the

70

main search category for the title clerks and agents involved in the high turn-over real estate business in the county.

Saylor's next efforts in the title books were more successful. It seemed Eleanor Sands Lawrence and Jeremy Stanley Lawrence were pretty good at real estate investments. They owned several properties on St. George Island with purchases ranging back fifteen years. They were all listed as lot and block properties in the attachments, but the addresses were also listed on the title transfer documents. A few had been bare earth properties when purchased and two of the island properties had structures. He also found the title to a house north of town on the river. The store was in the name of JEL LLC. Easy enough, he thought, Jeremy and Eleanor Lawrence became JEL, a Florida limited liability corporation.

He looked up a loudly ticking wall clock and saw that he'd worked through any lunch hour and was deep into the afternoon. He got water to satisfy his grumbling stomach and dug back in. His search found a simple will for Jeremy Lawrence that transferred all community property assets to the sole ownership of Eleanor Sands Lawrence, and in the case of her demise, to daughter Lindsey. He pulled copies for them all and paid the required dollar per copy. He looked up to see that it was already after three in the afternoon. He walked down the hall toward the property appraiser's office, noted the blue-uniformed security guard at the metal detector guarded entrance to the courthouse, and decided he could finish the next phase of the search at home.

12

For Whom the Belle Tolls

Saylor leaned back from his takeout lunch in the blessed cool darkness of his camper. The late April temps outside were already steaming well into the upper 80s. He pulled up the property appraiser's website and began tabulating the results. All five island properties now had rental properties on them. Two of them custom-built for Jeremy and Eleanor's corporate entity, JEL LLC. They ranged in taxable value from just under half a million for a third-tier house, the first property acquired, to one at one point one million on the beach. The second most valuable was only slightly less. The river property, located behind gates off Bluff Road, came in at three hundred-fifty thousand. Quick figuring brought the book value of the Lawrences' real estate holdings to a shade under four million dollars. He looked at the number on his spreadsheet, then tapped the menu item to boldface the font. He then added another column to the sheet. Real Value.

He pulled up his old quick-and-dirty real estate research friend, Zillow. He added these figures to his table that seemed to be about twenty-five percent higher than the taxable values. The new total was five and a half million dollars. Yes, they were primarily rentals, but in one of the many off weeks when one sat empty, the Lawrences would have had their pick of beachfront homes with a pool and elevator. They might also select a much more modest one-story three-bedroom beachfront. All would have maintenance contracts with the rental management companies. He figured these were the people actually making good money off the sandcastle industry in Franklin County.

He retrieved a flip phone from its long-term storage in one of the suitcases stored in the cab-over bunk. The bunk was designed for kids, kids who didn't mind sleeping on a four-inch cotton pad. His own bunk had the added comfort of an eggshell foam mattress pad but still would have to be classed as extra firm. The phone was old, its main purpose was research. Its area code from Austin had assisted in many searches in Harris County, Texas as an out-of-town listing. Here on the Florida panhandle, he had absolute assurance that it wasn't traceable back to him.

A search for the rental agencies verified that all were handled by the same company, one whose name he remembered from his high school days. Old money, he thought. Pillars of the community, major influencers who were behind the curtain when any hint of a policy change affected St. George Island. A search of Eleanor Lawrence's rental listings found that the highest valued house on the list rented for fourteen thousand a week from late May through Labor Day week. In the cool to cold month of January, it would still get ninety-five hundred. Still, like most of these rentals, they'd be empty for the majority of winter months. Obviously, if you put serious money down for the property and could handle Florida's punishing insurance policies over the long term, they would make money, and they would appreciate far better than any bank account.

He went back to the first property they'd purchased, a three-bedroom third-tier unit. They'd bought it in 2009 during hard times for St. George Island. The '08 crash and its refracting aftermath. Its sale price then was seventy-three thousand. Its Zillow market price now was four-eighty. He whistled. That's somewhere near a six hundred percent increase over eleven years. A glance up and out the camper's rear window caught the first hint of orange on high stratus clouds—time for a swim.

The Coastal Highway, US 98, had suffered extensively from hurricane storm surges over the last several decades. The State of Florida had never seriously considered relocating the artery back into the national forest and dutifully added more armoring after each event. Saylor had marked a route with clumps of seagrass on the stable chunks of Georgia granite that lined the embankment to get down to the water. Beyond the hard rock armoring, shallows extended for a few hundred yards such that he could wade in knee-deep to waist-deep water out for two hundred yards at mid-tide. When his personal water line crept past his waistband to tickle his abdomen, he took the plunge. His typical afternoon swim took him out beyond neck-deep for several underwater forays, scanning the scant seagrass beds for rare starfish, more common sand dollars, occasional scallops, and for the sheer joy of weightless cruising in the shallows.

He'd pulled along one underwater run of perhaps thirty yards and came up for air with a five-inch sand dollar. Extending to touch bottom, he found he was over his head and began to fan his arms to stay above water. Turning to get a fix on the shoreline, he was out further than he was comfortable. He dropped the sand dollar into his bathing suit pocket and headed for shore. On reaching chest-deep water, he contemplated liberating the sand dollar. Feeling for it in his pocket, its several hundred legs were exploring their new surroundings, brainless activity attempting to burrow out of the way of danger. He carefully pulled it out, watched the feet swivel and squirm, and tossed it a few feet away. He ducked under and began an alternating surfaced and submerged return to shore.

He was near the base of the granite embankment and scanning for his safe path up the rocks when he saw a car pulling into the campground. A Subaru from the profile. He didn't remember one from the few residents in the park, but then, the neighbors changed out frequently, usually a near-complete turnover from month to month. Some were annoyingly chatty, wanting to share their road warrior experiences, horrid campgrounds, gorgeous scenery, or the weather. Some stayed inside, watched TV, and drank. It took all kinds.

He hauled himself up the rock embankment hand over hand, carefully ensuring that each five-hundred-pound boulder was securely stable, found his flip flops at the edge of the grass line, and stepped cautiously through the high grasses loaded with early-season sand spurs. The spiked seed heads were debilitatingly painful underfoot and worthy of caution. Rounding the back corner of his camper, he found the olive-green Subaru parked beside his Prius hybrid. Closer examination revealed the profile of an occupant in the driver's seat. He approached, flip flops slapping at his heels. The noise brought the driver's head up.

Belle got out of the car and leaned on the upper frame of the open door. "Hey, hope you don't mind. You did provide excellent directions."

"I don't mind. I was just thinking of you."

"Oh, good things, I hope."

"Yes, I was thinking about supplying your store with genuine sun-dried St. George Sound sand dollars. I just tossed one back that was, oh, yea big." He circled thumbs and forefingers, approximating the five-inch diameter of the lucky throw-back.

"I wouldn't be able to pay you much. No way to make a living. I buy them bulk online for so cheap I feel sorry for the little guys."

"What about the little gals? Feel sorry for them too?"

"Especially them, but I'm not sure if anyone knows how to tell the difference."

He smiled at her. "I'm sure I don't. You going to stand there, or you want to come over, maybe have a seat on my bay view porch."

"Just a sec." She turned to get access to the back seat for a package. She came out with a sixpack of longnecks and approached. Gone was the stylish clothing of the mid-to-upscale souvenir retailer. She wore a Springsteen concert tour t-shirt over denim cutoffs. Her small feet wore child-sized gold sandals with a pair of mermaids attached above the toe strap.

When he saw the brand of beer she was carrying, he broke out laughing. "Really, Red Stripe?"

"The idea came to me as soon as you tossed back those directions. I love this stuff."

He found himself salivating at the thought but conflicted with the idea of having at least half of them versus reconsidering his recent quest for abstinence. His feet were moving toward the camper before his brain decided. "Let me get an opener. I'll be right out."

In a few minutes, he'd fished a second folding chair from his luggage compartment, and they were side-by-side, comparing notes on the purpling clouds on the far horizon. He'd set Belle's chair down two feet from his, she'd moved it closer, almost elbow to elbow before she sat.

He thought that's good. We might want to keep our voices down if we discuss my findings at the courthouse. He said, raising the long neck bottle, "The beer is good. Good choice."

She raised hers in a mock toast. "Best export Jamaica has to offer. Well, maybe the second-best export." Her grin was infectious.

He returned it and clicked bottles. "And the best export is...?"

She pinched thumb and forefinger and mimed taking a hit on a joint.

75

"Oh, the devil weed itself. Let's hear it for Ganja Nation!"

He laughed at himself. Shaking his head, he said, "It's been a while." He had to think back. *Thirty-fifth birthday party? Some random office party?* "Yes, long enough ago that I don't know when."

"Not to worry, the shit does make you forgetful."

He looked back at her. Her eyes were dancing across the cloud tops, now purple on orange as the sun angle left the lower ones in shadow. Only the upper-level atmosphere behind them held on to the last rays. The first traces of alcohol were dancing around his forebrain. They felt good, familiar. "So, you're not in any immediate danger? Back at the store, I think I said something about 'if you need help' before I gave you those directions."

"You said, and I quote. "If you need me, I'm at the Coastal Paradise Campground. I'm right on the highway. A white camper with a Dodge front end poking out from under a cab-over sleeper. Twelve-inch red racing stripe down the sides. It's old and ugly. It's hard to miss." She looked over at him, her grin mischievous in its certainty. "That about right?"

"Uhm, sounds pretty much verbatim." He squinted. "You blessed with eidetic memory?"

"No, shorthand. I excelled at it in high school and found it was indispensable in college lecture classes. Everyone else was transcribing from recordings full of shuffling paper sounds and inaudible lecture content. I could already read my notes. I used to transcribe mine and sell them." Her grin, lopsided now, full of confidence and achievement.

He found he liked her a lot and wanted to know more, specifically, if their apparent age gap was surmountable. "Belle, as I age, I find that I have a real difficulty age-dating younger woman. I know Lindsey was an advanced year freshman, maybe eighteen, nineteen tops. I don't think the sheriff really said. You're her roomie. How old are you?"

"This for your research?" Her eyebrows, eight shades darker than her hair, pulled together beneath her sun-lightened bangs, a slight crease forming at the top of her nose.

"Not exactly. I just wanted to know, for reference, you know?"

"Yes, we're roomies. That's because her mom, Eleanor, let me rent the bottom floor bungalow at their house in exchange for slave labor wages at the store. When El..." her throat hitched with emotion. "When she got really sick, Lindsey came home to help. I stayed on." She got control of her emotions and her voice. "Later, after the funeral, Lindsey offered me one of the upstairs bedrooms and we became roomies. Just so you know, I'm ten years older than her. I'm twenty-nine. Almost old."

"Ouch, so over thirty is old?" He set his bottle down on the brick pavers. "That's a mean thing to say. I wasn't planning to call myself old until at least fifty." He found that they had been staring into each other's eyes for the past few minutes. "And I'm still many, many moons away from fifty."

Impishly, she asked, "I told you mine, you tell me yours." Her right eyebrow lifted in question.

"My birthday is next October, so I get to be thirty-eight for half a year." He stretched his hands out full, "A long, long way from forty." He pulled them back to about a foot apart. "A lot further than twenty-nine is from thirty."

"Tell me about it." She slumped back into her chair seat. She looked up as if seeking salvation from a horrible fate. Beyond the darkening sky, Venus and Betelgeuse signaled approaching night. She turned her attention back to him. "Actually, tell me about your research. What did you find out about the Lawrence family holdings at the courthouse?"

13

River House

Belle's eyes rounded. "Wow, five and a half million bucks." Thin white light from one of the RV park's LED street lamps had overtaken the fading skylight.

"That's only the real estate. There may be other holdings in other investments. Papa Jeremy seemed to be good at making money grow. Momma Eleanor did alright too. They weren't hurting financially. Lindsey would have been well cared for." He instantly regretted the past tense.

"We don't know that she's dead!" Belle's voice was hard, almost guttural.

"I'm sorry, Belle. I wasn't careful there. I didn't mean to put her in the past tense. You're right. But it's been well over a week now. What? Ten days?"

She leaned back against the folding chair's straps and looked up. Stars were becoming more numerous, deep cerulean faded to black overhead. "Eleven days today." She folded forward, looking down at nothing but away from the moment that was developing. Her head turned up to look out over the darkened bay. "I'm sorry for barking at you. She was a friend."

"I know it's been tough. You want another beer?" He reached behind him for the small cooler that held the others and just enough ice from his mini-fridge. This would be a stretch. He hadn't had a drink for eleven days now. Just have to know enough to stop. He looked down and noticed four empties between them. *How did that happen?*

"Sure. You want to get something to eat?" Her mood had flipped, her tone lighter.

"I'd offer to cook something, but the cupboard is pretty bare. I was going to get a bite out, probably Mexican." Even in the dim light

78

from the overhead park lights, he could see she'd damped down tears. Clearly, she was upset about Lindsey's unknown status. Clearly, she was not a suspect.

She turned back to him, leaning on her elbow, the smile was back. "I can do me some Mexican." He had some questions for her that had been building, but they could wait.

They took her Forester and headed into Eastpoint to the new location of one of the best regional chains of TexMex in the panhandle of Florida. He elected not to have another beer and asked for an iced tea at the restaurant. The weekday crowd was thin, and they found privacy in a row of booths with no other diners nearby. His usual order, *huevos rancheros*, was perfect. She picked apart her chorizo-stuffed pepper with a fork, stirred in some frijoles, then rolled the whole mess into a specially requested large flour tortilla. She ate this recombination with relish with her fingers.

Belle was licking at her fingers, not conscious of the effect on Saylor. He was thinking he'd like to suck on those petite fingers himself. He knew in his big head that it would be too soon. But his little head was still a little high on the two Red Stripes. "Belle?" he paused, looking around. Everyone was in deep conversation and eating dinner. No one, not even the wait staff, appeared to be looking at or slightly interested in them. He continued in quiet tones anyway, just understandable over the Latin soundtrack. "Did you have any idea at all that Lindsey's family was worth that much?"

"No, not really. I mean the Lawrences seemed to be able to do what they wanted to do. Lindsey and El took vacations to the islands, Europe. Lindsey told me they'd even been to South Africa once back when her dad was alive."

Saylor nodded. "I swear I'll never tell. This is solely in the spirit of trying to find out any reason for her to leave on her own, against the possibility that some psychopath abducted her." He paused, then asked, "Have you ever gone into Eleanor's room or looked over her things? Did Lindsey move into the master bedroom?"

She stared back at him, put the last few bites of the tortilla down, and scanned the room as he had done. "No, I'm not a dumb ass. I know that fingers leave prints. That if someone finally sends in a note demanding ransom, then the Feds will be over every inch of that house. I don't need my lovely rat-brown locks ending up in her closet or an evidence bag."

He thought, not rat-brown. She's looking pretty good right now. He said, "OK, and that's good. I just wondered if you'd done any sleuthing, you know, as the worried friend."

"Well, I *am* a worried friend."

"What would you say to a studiously clean examination of first Lindsey's room, then her mother's room. If nothing turns up, then the attic space, a shed, anywhere else we can think of."

"Studiously clean?"

"Gloves, hairnets. Take some before pictures on my phone so we can put things back if we disturb anything. That kind of studious."

"You sure you're not agency?"

"I promise, I'm not with any agency." He thought of his enforced leave of absence from the Chronicle. "Currently, I'm not with anything. 'Cept with you, enjoying these beans and rice." He pushed the last of those onto a fork with a chip and shoveled them in.

On the way over to the Lawrence house near the end of Bluff Road, he explained that he had earlier checked out the place from the river. This elicited a soft 'oh' from her as she drove.

"You do enjoy a sleuthing problem, though. Don't you? Must be from all those years working stories, chasing leads, even bad guys."

"I do. I guess it's in the genes. You have 'em, and there are a lot of careers that can put them to good use: local law, the feds, agency law enforcement—and the papers." He paused, thinking of examples. "Bernstein and Woodward, for instance. Contacts, informants, and a lot of additional investigation were needed to confirm their conclusions long before they went public. Knowing who to ask the right questions. I don't chase the bad guys. That's for the uniforms."

"Yeah," she said, peering into the cone of light ahead. "But you get into their heads, right?"

"As best I can."

Bluff Road at night is unlit except for the rare glow of area lights and blue flickering from living rooms set back in the pines. There are places where trees overhanging the narrow-shouldered road appear to lean in with menace. She seemed to be used to it.

He looked out into the passing shadows. "The more I got into their heads, the more I wanted to be able to go to press with information that will lead to arrests. There are some real degenerate people out there." He blew a frustrated breath out, billowing a steam cloud on the window. "That's probably why I'm here now. Why my generalized wish to get another boat congealed so fast, why I went up the river, why we're going to check deeper into the Lawrences' back story. To find Lindsey." He turned to her dash-illuminated profile. "Because now, I have no way at all to get into anyone's head. There's no starting point."

He thought about the formal investigation. "What kinds of questions did the sheriff ask you?"

She glanced over. "Not much, really. When did I see her last? Who with? What was she wearing? Did she have any plans she'd mentioned? Was she unhappy? Seem depressed? A lot of questions on those lines. Let's see, not much else. The next morning, I drove over to officially file the missing person's report. It asked the same questions. They wouldn't process it until she'd been officially missing for twenty-four hours."

"Sounds about normal."

"Listen, Jason. She would not have offed herself. No way, you'd have to have known her."

They rode on in silence as they crossed the railroad tracks to the last bit of civilization along the riverfront. As they pulled up to then parked under the elevated house, her headlights flashed across the empty boat trailer and a dusty dodge pickup.

"Belle, another question. And I promise, there'll be a lot more."

She turned off the ignition. They listened to the heat of her engine ticking softly into the darkness.

He asked a question that had been bothering him since his trip up the river. "How is it that both Lindsey's car and boat are missing?"

"That's a poser for sure, Jason." She nodded ahead and toward a small utility shed. In the dim glow of the neighbor's barnyard light, a galvanized trailer poked through a season's worth of shin-high grass. She said, "That thing? Hasn't moved in a year that I noticed. Boat's not on the dock?"

"Nope."

"Son of a bitch."

"I guess I should have noticed."

The door sounds of getting out of the car triggered the ad hoc burglar alarm. A dog barked next door, another picked it up a few lots farther away. The neighborhood watch committee was no doubt activated. She shouted out, "Sugar! Sugar. It's me. We're good!" There was an answering desultory woof. She shouted out into the darkness. "SUGAR!" The dog, a snow-white German Shepard, remained silent but watchful on its side of the hog wire fence. Its stare fixed, but the tail wagged. "One of these days I'll have to take you over, let her sniff you, learn your voice."

Saylor scanned the house as motion sensor actuated lights came on when they approached the stairs. An enclosed and finished-out room took up about a fourth of the area under the house. He pointed to it. "The afore-mentioned bungalow?"

"Yeah, cozy but lonely. Designed to flood if you get the furniture out in time."

He nodded understanding. The ground floor was definitely flood plain. The main entrance at the top of the stairs was a simple landing wrapped in wooden lattice. Opening the unlocked door, she walked in, dropping her shoulder bag on a kitchen bar stool, and turned to a panel of light switches.

"Do you always leave the door unlocked?"

She turned, recognized her foolishness, "Ah, not anymore?"

He took in the plan of the lower floor. Southern chic, with a splash of fishing motifs and a few more boating references. Comfortable in its dated wood paneling. Pine or pecan was his first assessment, stained a honey gold. Plush furniture placed for easy movement while maintaining the view of the river from the kitchen and great room. A short hall at the back led to two bedrooms and a Jack and Jill bath. Stairs led up to the master bedroom and its en suite bath. A motorized dumb waiter located beneath the stairs allowed for hauling up groceries and small packages from the parking area below the house. Easy, comfortable living, he surmised. But so many unhappy people live in well-furnished luxury and go to bed with their dark thoughts.

"Belle, did Lindsey mention if her parents were happy people?"

"Whoa. That's out of left field."

"Sorry, just a vibe. Probably wrong."

She went to the stainless side-by-side refrigerator. Hauling open the left side, she announced. "I'm getting ice cream. Want some?"

This is why he had huevos rancheros for dinner, one of the lighter meals available, so moments like this didn't need to pass him by. "Absolutely, unless it's pistachio. Can't do green ice cream. There ought to be a law."

She brought two bowls of cookies and cream out to the great room, handed him one, and curled into a cross-legged pile on one side of the couch facing the near-total darkness outside. The neighbor's barn light lit one tulip poplar at the river's edge. Beyond that, a blackness full of bullfrog grunts and alligator's cold orange eyes that said, stay inside. He sat down opposite, curled one leg under a thigh. "Just one bowl, I have my limits."

"No problem, Jason." She took a spoonful of ice cream, let it slowly melt, and turned to study him. "What do they call you, Jason? Jace, Jay. JJ?

"Mostly Jason or Jace." He poked at the still-frozen ice cream, softening it. "What's Belle for? Belladonna, Isabelle? No," he grimaced, "not Jezebel."

"Uh, no. Not Jezebel, and wrong on the other two as well."

His face wrinkled, trying to think of another idea. "Not Belle Star!"

"Nope no outlaws in my roots, pilots. Granddad was in the Air Force. He flew all-nighters in a Stratofortress over the arctic circle just in case we needed to blow Russia off the map before they did the same to us."

"So which Belle?"

"The Memphis Belle. You know, Hiroshima?"

"Yeah, makes you some kind of dangerous?"

"Nah. I'm a real pussy cat." She smiled, drawing matching dimples on each cheek. "Just be careful when the claws come out."

He looked around at the house—simple, elegant furnishings in a country setting. Looking more closely now, he realized the paneling was cypress. *Money!*

"Do you know how dad got started in business? Where they got the cash to start buying those sandcastles on the beach?"

"Not real sure, you know? Lots of us grew up around here, families just getting by while we watched the rich get richer. Lots of them had their own rich bitch clubs. The good ole boy network is alive and well, so is built-in but casual racism. Blacks help the blacks. Whites help the whites. It's a friendly kind of exclusivity. Don't mean any harm by it, just neighbors helping neighbors, same as it ever was." She played with the Velcro strap on a sandal, finally ripped it loose, and let the sandal fall. She recrossed her legs, loosened then kicked off the second sandal.

"But that's not what you asked. I don't know. The shop was just another of the tourist shops until I needed another j-o-b. Ms. Lawrence, El, was really nice to me. I never really knew her until I started working there. I think he was an officer, ex-military, retired early. That set them up. She was a hospital administrator over in Pensacola. Maybe they make good money."

"I might be able to trace military in Pensacola. Navy training base there." He thought back to the newspaper clipping, yellowed when it had been scanned. He didn't remember the year. "Did you tell me when he died?"

"Don't remember. Don't know..." She looked inward for a casual memory, half-forgotten. "I think I remember her saying she was in third grade, so she'd have been maybe eight? So, probably ten years ago, there' bouts, maybe less."

"And they'd been here since she was born. If he was military..." He glanced up at plastic airplane models on a shelf. He recognized a C-130, and what he thought to be an F-15. "He might have been rifted out about 2000, maybe a year or two sooner." He noted her questioning look. "Rifted, periodically, some desk driver in DC decides a force reduction is required to save the budget, so they start cutting salaries. Officers cost more than grunts. Talented or otherwise, people are cut loose. Adrift. I don't think that's the origin of the word, though."

She said, after a moment of silence. "Usually, it's the poorest who get the shaft. I guess the military is an equal opportunity offender."

He just smiled at the quip. The girl had issues. He asked, "And Momma Lawrence was a hospital administrator? Pensacola? Can't be too many places to look. But that could take a little while."

She set her emptied bowl down. "Speaking of taking a while, I need to be on the job in the morning. If we're going to be super sleuths, we better get at it."

"You got it." He reached to the side table at his elbow and rifled in the shopping bag they'd picked up. Ripping open the packaging, he tossed her a pair of latex gloves and a hair net. "Here, make yourself beautiful."

14

Upstairs

Heading up the stairs to the master suite, Saylor stopped and put a hand back to warn Belle off further progress. Leaning down to get the advantage of side-lighting on the polished wood steps, he noted two sets of footprints in the dust on the treads. One up, one down, same footprint. Sneakers with a squiggle line tread pattern. Boat shoes. Turning to Belle, "Looks like only one set of tracks up and down in a very long time. We'll need to dust these steps when we've finished."

She looked down at the tracks. "Looks like Lindsay made at least one trip up here since Momma Eleanor died."

Reaching the top floor, the setting reinforced the impression that serious money had been expended inside the modest home to make the space comfortable. Refined, dignified, and comfortable, the room took up more than half of the floor plan. The landside of the floor had three doors leading to two walk-in closets flanking a beautifully up-to-date bath with a step-in shower behind a six-foot glass wall. The king-sized bed sat five feet from that back wall, seeming to float above a pedestal base. Between it and the glass wall facing riverside, a white leather sofa and easy chairs had seating room for, he guessed, six or eight. Unusual for a bedroom. A wet bar protruded from one corner. Bookshelves occupied the opposite corner.

He walked over to the sliding doors that led to the private deck and turned around. The back of the room was filled with closets and a bath and no side windows. The only daylight in was from the riverside. *Absolute privacy. Nice!* "Belle, you notice the windows?"

She quickly scanned the paneled side walls, then the wall of glass facing the deck and the river. "No, I didn't. Why?"

"No one would know we were up here because there's no side light coming out of this room. I'd been a little worried about that."

"Again, why?"

"Call me paranoid. Say, did the sheriff come by here? Do any searching?"

"Not that I know of." But then, I'm at the shop all day." She looked at him sheepishly. "I don't always lock up. We're kind of a trusting neighborhood. You know, a dog barks, and all the neighbors know your business."

He looked at her. Finally, the day was getting to her. Even in a cheap hair net, make-up around the eyes smeared at one corner, her smile could lite up his world. Damn, she looked good. *Business boy, keep your mind on business.* "Belle, you seem to be on top of things at the shop. What did you do before you needed that j-o-b?"

"I taught third grade. I was pretty good at it too." She shrugged. "At least, according to the moms." A broad smile broke out of the tired face. "And the kids, the kids are what it's about, and I loved my kids."

"So, why—"

"Let's just save that one for another day when we've got time to talk it through."

"OK, just wondered is all." He pointed toward the stairwell. "I'll start downstairs with his gun cabinet, you might want to start in one of those closets." She dutifully turned and headed for the nearest closet.

Downstairs, he moved toward the gun cabinet, noting anew that it was a fine piece of furniture. The guns inside were, he supposed, beautiful pieces of craftsmanship and expensive, but he didn't really know guns. Beyond having a small-bore bird gun as a kid, his basic military training with an aging carbine, and his familiarization training with an officer's side-arm automatic pistol, he was just above ignorant, and he'd never seen combat. The Army had given him other challenges, but not combat.

The cabinet held slots for eight long guns. Five were filled with two shotguns and three rifles. Saylor pulled a pump shotgun out, pulled the slide to note that its chamber was empty, and returned it to its felt-lined slot. Beside it a 410 over and under, a small-bore bird gun. Among the rifles, one was a camo special with scope. Another looked to be a target special—a decent collection for any enthusiast. A horizontal drop-down door turned into a work surface at seated height. He guessed for oiling and cleaning. This was verified by the tools and supplies needed for that purpose and the increased smell of gun oils.

Two drawers below the working surface contained ammo boxes, holsters, and vests with pouches and slots for shotgun shells. An array of ammo boxes was arranged in a row at the front of the cabinet. As he read the labels, they were in the same order as the rifles and guns above. The lower drawer also contained two pistol boxes: one heavy, one light. The light one opened to reveal the indent for what looked like the profile of an automatic pistol. Turning the box, the underside label said, Glock, and in fine print: Deutsch-Wagram, Austria. He put them carefully back in their original positions. The heavier one held a lady's gun. A short barrel .38 revolver. Chromed with a pearl handle. Definitely hers. Small enough to fit in a purse, but deadly stopping force at less than ten feet.

Before finishing at the gun cabinet, he opened the two glass doors to the long guns again. The felt lining the upper slot of one of the empty gun positions seemed to be a bit shinier than the other two. *Is there a rifle missing too?* As he stepped back from the cabinet, he noted the glass was, if anything, greasy enough to indicate lack of use and neglect. *So, he was the shooter. She couldn't care less.*

He stepped in front of the bookshelf. Three were full side-to-side with novels—some well-known works and a few traditional novels that aroused no curiosity. The non-fiction, if the collection reflected Eleanor's tastes, indicated that she was a Democrat with a liberal slant. He noticed two recent books that came out just before the last election: one from Michael Beschloss, the other from David Plouffe. He smiled at that. Good for her. She appreciated a free press. Below these, scrapbooks. The oldest, from its binder's apparent age and its contents, was from Eleanor's childhood. Starting with black and whites in front of a white clapboard farmhouse framed with winter naked trees, to Eleanor and girlfriends sitting in a convertible. One of the girls wore an Emory sweatshirt, but he found no other evidence of her schooling.

The second confirmed her schooling at Emory on Atlanta's east side. Graduation pictures and poses of girlfriends, different guys, and finally, as a bookend, a wedding announcement for the betrothal of

Eleanor Elizabeth Sands to Jeremy Paulson Lawrence. The third, predictably now, began with wedding pictures, a honeymoon on an unknown island resort, possibly in the Caribbean, as the hired help in the backgrounds were very dark. A house, gardens. Vacation pics. Meaningless histories without narration. One poignant picture of Eleanor in a hospital, a tiny newborn, eyes closed, bundled beneath her chin. She'd been crying. Her chin was dimpled. *Not the happiest new mom picture in the world.* But then, he'd never pushed a baby into the world.

He pulled the picture from the two confining corner tabs. Baby Janet and 3/7/98. *Older than Lindsey, and—who is Janet?* He tucked it back into place. Few pictures followed. More scenes on a beach, smiling on the high side of a sailboat underway. Leaning back, looking terrified with an unknown female friend on a guardrail at the Grand Canyon. Then, baby scenes. One with a grimacing Jeremy up to his elbows in baby poop at a changing table. Other sections depicted a family's journey. Many were on a sailboat or at the Apalachicola public marina. Halfway through, there were no more pictures of Jeremy. The family adventures continued but as an apparently close and loving mother-daughter partnership. Eleanor had not remarried. He put the album back, noticed a black line between two of the novels.

Inching it out between the two hardcovers, it was a nine by twelve picture frame. He blew the dust off and began to read slowly through what Spanish he could make out. *Cruz de la Fuerza Aérea al Mérito Aeronáutico.* A lot of gold and filigree surrounding, more Spanish he couldn't translate. And in clear sans serif font, Captain Jeremy Lawrence, USN. *Son of a bitch, the guy's a hero to the Columbian Air Force.*

He pulled his phone and took a picture. A real translation could wait, but he knew just enough to infer an Air Force cross of merit had been bestowed on Capt. Lawrence. The detailed silver work on the ornate cross was impressive. He'd certainly made a good impression in Columbia. He remembered the long reach of his investigations in Houston. Columbians had a habit of playing both sides of the game.

He stood back from the shelves not much else to speak of. His examination of the wet bar proved nothing more than that Ms. Lawrence liked expensive gin. "Belle, how's it going?" Climbing to the top of the stairs, he saw that she'd already cleared one closet and moved on.

"I'm good but look at this." The walk-ins were a designer's deluxe installation. This one must have been his. The hanging racks were empty. Cardboard moving boxes lined the lower back wall, and beneath a row of neatly folded linens on hangers, dust on the white-on-white brocade indicating out-of-use curtains, a portable fire-proof vault. Belle was cross-legged, staring at the numbered dials that could provide access. A set of five numbered tumblers with knurled edges.

He said, "Jackpot."

"Maybe." She looked up at him. A dust smudge darkened her left temple. She looked tired.

"How many numbers on each wheel?" She looked blank, then down at the safe, rolled one silently through its range, put it back to its original numeral six. "Eight."

"Way too many combinations to experiment." He pursed his lips in thought. "I'm not sure I even remember how to calculate that."

"Should we take it with us?"

"Take it where? You live here."

"Right." She shoved the thing back into the footprint squashed into the carpet and started to get up. He offered a hand. She took it and ended up standing awfully close. She smelled good. God knows home many hours since this girl has hit the showers, and she smells good. Saylor stepped back and allowed her to exit the closet's confined space. He only hoped he didn't still reek of St. George Sound's brackish brew. He checked his watch. 1:13.

Turning, she caught his raised eyebrows. "What time is it?"

He told her.

"Shit, shit, shit!"

"Right, guess we ought to call it a night." Then he realized she'd driven to dinner. They'd made the one stop at the CVS for gloves and hair bonnets and come on to the house.

She was ahead of him. "Can you stay here?' Her eyes looked up into his, betraying a long day and fatigue nearing exhaustion. "I mean, if I take you back, it'll be three before I can even think about a shower and bed." She blew out a puff that momentarily gave her Louis Armstrong cheeks. She opened her arms, palms up. "So...?"

His hesitation must have transmitted his conflict, but he responded with the honorable solution. "Sure, the couch downstairs looks fine."

"What will that do to our super-sleuthing strategy? Hair, skin particles, *et cetera*?" Her voice was almost sing-song, finishing the Latin phrase syllable by syllable.

"It will totally screw it up. I'm sorry, but it's a really long walk home."

To his surprise, she reached up, pulled his head down to her level, and whispered softly. "If you are a gentleman, you can sleep in my bed. I'll toss the sheets in the machine in the morning."

The tension that comes from attraction had been building all evening. From his first recognition that Belle was in the green Forester through their shared bottles of Red Stripe and dinner, he'd felt an undeserved closeness. Growing familiarity engendered fondness as he learned more of her backstory, felt more of her straightforward blunt honesty. Examining how he felt, he recognized a shade of protection rather than intimacy in response to her morning request for help. Had that only been this morning? Yes, it's possible to share a bed with a very bed-able female, but damn, could he tell his body not to respond? To be the gentleman?

"Well?"

He recognized he'd let the question hang too long. "I think that's the best bet. You need to sleep. I need to sleep." He smiled. "Win-win."

Despite his reservations, indecision on making some overt advance, he found sleep came quickly. Her soft snoring beside him had started up almost immediately. The long day took its toll, and dawn arrived far too soon. He awoke to soft shower sounds and decided that coffee was the next best move. Dressed and foundering in a kitchen several times larger than his campers', he fist-pumped a yes when he found the single-serve coffee packets and prepared his own mug. As he heard Belle's footfalls on the staircase, he tapped the button to start hers.

Her head and body were wrapped in a white cloud of terrycloth. She approached in a hair wrap made of the same material as the luxury hotel variety over-sized robe that hung to her ankles. "Uhm, thanks for getting the coffee, and my brand too."

"It's your kitchen." Over the gasp and sputter of the machine, he said, "have a seat, I'll bring it to you. What do you want in it?"

"One blue packet, a splash of half-and-half." She moved to the window wall, opened the slider, and stepped out onto the deck. From the kitchen, he watched her remove the hair wrap and wipe morning dew from two Adirondack chairs and the matching table between them. Nice digs, he thought. Uncertain future and all, this house was a nice place to have to face that uncertainty. At the coffee maker's last gasp, he poured the morning elixir into her mug that already had the fixings and joined her.

"I hope this tastes right."

She sipped, "Good enough."

The morning sun was still dragging mist out of the woodlands beyond the sawgrass. The brown river below them flowed on with the authority of eternity on its side. All seemed right with the world. Mentally, he heard the scratch of needle on record. No, not right. Lindsey is still missing. Belle is calmly waiting to find out if she has a place to be in days or weeks from now.

"Belle, you're from here. You must know people. What happens if Lindsey's situation doesn't change? Do you have any idea how long you can stay here?"

"Got no other place to be. I wouldn't go home. That jackass my mom married is too effing creepy. Like he'd like to slip in and roll me over some night." She shivered. "He gives me the willies. Every time he looks at me, I've got to check to make sure I put clothes on." She drew a deep breath, puckered, and with her cheeks fully puffed, slowly let it out. "Legally? I have no idea how long I can stay here. I guess I should check with the family attorney and find out. Far as I know? There aren't any Lawrence relatives knocking on the door. I don't have any contract or anything. It was verbal with Eleanor. Lindsey was thankful, both for the help at the store and for someone to talk to."

She looked over at him, shading her eyes from the sun. "The store's an issue too. I'm basically running it, have been for six months now since Eleanor got too sick to come in more than once a week. Most of the locals know the story. But you know? There's something weird about the books. I was trying to reconcile them, and I've got to get a handle on them. Come to think of it, I might need to file for temporary power of attorney. The store does alright, but it can't pay the mortgage on this place. It's supported by other income, the properties I imagine." She relaxed into the slats of the chair back. "I can't legally write a check on Eleanor Lawrence's check book to pay the bills on this." She waved an all-inclusive hand in a circle.

"So, unless someone comes to say otherwise, you're good here?"

"Hell if I know. Yes, I guess."

"You mentioned the family attorney. You ought to check in with him, explain the store's situation, see if he can file for limited temporary power of attorney. For the sake of the business. See if he, as their chosen attorney, can set up payments from their personal bank account to make sure the mortgage and utilities get paid."

She turned to him, again, staring while shifting her weight to an elbow. "Damn. I'm so glad I've got you on my team. That's frickin' obvious, but I just haven't been thinking about those details. IF that can happen, that's a small victory."

It was his turn for humble. "I try." He tried not to let his heart stop as she dead-eyed him. *Change the subject.*

"We didn't find much last night," he said. "I think I know a little bit more about Lindsey's family, but no reasons to suspect foul play or imminent danger. What have you found in her room?"

"I haven't been in her room." She gave a half snort, half laugh. "That's not entirely true. When she didn't come into the store, and then didn't come home, I did go in. Looking for any sign of why. You know, a note that she should have left on the kitchen counter, missing toothbrush, that kind of thing. Not one blessed clue."

"So, no note saying I've got to get back to school or anything?"

"I wish." She squinted up at the sun as if measuring the time. "Listen Jason, I'll give her room a once-over when I get off work. For now, I've got to get ready for work and I have to get you home first."

He tried hard not to notice the long expanse of tanned thigh as she ejected herself out of the chair and turned to go in. "Call me when you get through, OK?"

"Sure thing. If not sooner." She pivoted and moved beside his chair, leaned over, and planted a light kiss on his balding spot. "Thanks!"

"For?" He turned in his chair to look up.

"For everything, for last night." A half smile raised a dimple he hadn't noticed before. "For being a gentleman." She made a gesture with both hands, thumbs pointing at her heart, her pinkies pointing at him. "Trust, you know. It's earned." And she turned for the door. As she disappeared into the house, he heard, "Let's talk tonight after I've had a chance to get lawyered up."

15

Tap Water?

Jason Saylor had split his day three ways. Not productively, he concluded, as he stirred dinner on the two-burner stovetop. One of his favorite quick-n-dirties that used to piss off his first wife for its culinary simplicity and its dubious nutrition; canned beef stew over noodles du jour. The stand-in vegetable for the overcooked carrots and peas in the can was an apple. The first part of his day was spent unsuccessfully fishing on the flats just across the road, hence the canned dinner. But it suited his solitary nature and provided time to think about plot lines while he worked the fishing lines. He'd mentally framed the opening chapters of novel number three.

The second part of the day was spent typing that up as fast as he could remember it. A content draft of novel number two had been sent off to his editor/agent. If she could stand his stream of consciousness writing and still think the plot could sell, he'd be a lot more interested in working further on number three. A check had arrived at his P.O. Box indicating that sales of number one were dwindling to smaller numbers per week. Not a good sign.

The third portion of his day had been spent considering the Lindsey – Belle dilemmas. Belle had phoned. She'd gone home for lunch and hadn't found anything in Lindsey's room pointing to her disappearance. *And Belle, whew! What to think about Belle?* Yes, there seemed to be a mutual attraction. Yes, last night had been difficult; waking to hear her soft breathing in the dark. Falling asleep at almost 2:00 a.m. hadn't been hard, getting back to sleep at 5:30 had been.

She was supposed to call again after work. A quick glance outside said she was either working late, or...he couldn't fill in the blanks. He'd spent exactly one evening with the girl and couldn't honestly say he had any claim on her time. *She* had asked *him* for help, though.

Lindsey was still the big outstanding problem. He'd put in a call to Sheriff Pierson, left an unanswered message. He'd been tempted to call Patrick Wills and decided not to, based on Belle's updated character reference. But the question remained—if Lindsey had been abducted for monetary gain—he couldn't figure the angle. Who would benefit from her estate if there were no further beneficiaries to the Lawrence's considerable assets? If not an abduction for ransom or a quest for control of her estate, there was the simple motive of sexual attraction, rape, and very possibly, murder. She had been an extraordinarily pretty young woman.

The aromas of the warming stew rose, brought back memories of college dinners for one. Stirring the pot, he was immediately sorry for having framed her in the past tense. She had left no note, a possible indicator of her going missing against her will. Nothing Belle had said about Lindsey would point to reckless, thoughtless behavior, to her leaving without notice.

Belle's search of Lindsey's room, although brief, didn't find any stack of illuminating papers that would explain all, or even a scribbled note. They left it as they found it, bed made, laundry and closet in reasonably good order. Typical for an atypically Type-A kid. Young woman? Kid, he decided. He was twice her age. Steam had begun to rise from the stew pot and the noodles needed draining when he heard the skritch of tires on gravel swerve onto his parking space and come to a stop outside. He flicked both burners off and went to the door. Always suspecting law enforcement, he was relieved to see a green Subaru outside.

He opened the door as Belle was about to knock. "Come on in. See how a bachelor eats. I'd offer to share, but…"

Sniffing the aromas in the steam-dampened kitchenette, she said. "Oh, hey I could eat that. We used to eat that stuff all the time in college."

To his tired eyes, she was a welcome addition to what would have been a lonely meal. She was still in work clothes, minus the apron. A starched white men's business shirt, two buttons open - cuffs rolled back, over khaki capri pants that fit very well.

"Hard to disguise the smell," he said. "You haven't eaten?"

"No, I was going to suggest gumbo, Lynn's place is practically the only place still on the water in Eastpoint that survived Dennis and Michael." He nodded, understanding that Hurricane Dennis had destroyed most of the waterfront commercial buildings save one or two. New building codes affecting rebuilding from hurricane damage had introduced a decade of rot-in-place decay.

"Gumbo sounds good. Better than this." He waved his spoon over the pot as bubbles began to throw up tiny globules of the brown sauce.

"Sorry, it's closed for dinner now. I shouldn't have mentioned it. It was on my mind as I drove over, but the place looked dark." She looked at the pots on the stove, sniffed, and nodded approval. "That stuff still smells edible." Together, and in each other's elbow-bumping way, they drained water from the noodles and wicked excess grease off the stew mix and sat down to eat.

He summarized his thinking on Lindsey's absence, fearing abduction with the intent of physical harm or worse. She nodded in grim agreement. "I spent the day hoping for the best. Hoping for a phone call from Lindsey, or that each ring of the bell would be her. It didn't happen."

"Did you get a chance to talk to the lawyer?"

Her face brightened. "I was just going to tell you. That's why it took so long to get over here. I had to close a little early to meet his last appointment slot, but it went well."

"That's great. And...?"

"He's seen the paper, knows she was reported missing, but didn't know it was reported by me. And before you ask, no one has contacted him about a ransom. He's been their lawyer for over ten years and didn't make the connection that with Lindsey missing, there might be an end to the line. He agreed that their holdings could be in jeopardy for lack of attention." She stopped talking to take and enjoy another mouthful.

"He was helpful though." She pulled a spiral-bound flip pad from her purse. He saw a bulleted list, but the shorthand notes on each line were indecipherable. "Full power of attorney. Might be hard to get because I'm not a relative. Limited power of attorney for the purposes of running the store's business interest only, easier since I'm a townie in good standing. No issues with the law."

She slowed to take a bite and begin chewing. "He said, I would not believe how rare that is. Imagine, a citizen with no, nada, zero, issues with the law! I think he was either trying to be funny or hitting on me. Anyway, he's going to try, going to consult with the judge. Probably going to be good because, it turns out Daddy Jeremy used to be a golf and sailing buddy with the judge." She swallowed, flashed him a grin. "Cool, huh?"

"Coupla rounds of golf with the right folks never hurts. OK, what else."

"He's going to set up a trust account with the bank. Eleanor had moved all banking accounts to one branch, and it should be easy to get the real estate payments and fees all working on one account while I work out of another that I use for store business. He called a friend at the bank and found there's plenty of balance on hand if the real estate market slows." Her face brightened several wattage levels. "And so, probably by tomorrow night, I'll have signature authority for the store's operations and the house will be taken care of." She took another bite, and chewing, let a worry pass across her forehead, then looked up apparently happy with the outcome.

"What was that hesitation? Something didn't go right, or you got a bad piece of gristle."

"It's just that something...something he seemed about to say, it didn't get said. He was talking about Eleanor and Jeremy and he just stopped, like he caught himself about to say something he shouldn't say."

"Sounds lawyerly to me. They are extremely careful of what they say to whom. True, you were in to see him on behalf of the estate, little-e. But he is the attorney of record for the Estate, capital E. You, in his legal frame of reference, are a friend of the estate, as far as he can tell. But he's doing his job if he has to withhold certain information. His client is the Lawrence girl, Lindsey, or for the time being, her estate. Does that make sense?"

"Yeah, I guess."

"What were you discussing when he clammed up?"

"Of all things, boats. Did I tell you Jeremy died in a boating accident?"

"Nope, not that I remember. I did see a newspaper clipping in the research. It was attached to the paperwork that transferred all of the joint holdings into her new LLC."

"Is that helpful?" Her response was garbled with a cheek full of noodles.

"Probably not, loose ends though, always tie up loose ends. It just leaves you with fewer places to look. One parent gone as a kid, another as a young adult, and no sibs. It makes it hard to figure any motive for kidnap. I don't know if I've heard of it before, having an estate lawyer be the responsible party for posting a ransom. And as far as we know, no one has asked for a ransom."

She screwed her mouth sideways, sucking in a cheek. "Huh! So, what else can we do? Where else do we look? If ransom isn't a motivation, that kind of makes her case a little more desperate, doesn't it?" There was a sadness in her face that he found compelling. Not quite a lonely puppy sadness, but something close. The kind of innate emotional appeal that crosses boundaries, destroys inhibitions. He seriously considered getting up, pulling her to her feet, and hugging it away. He'd heard somewhere, possibly a Facebook post or some other social media fountain of general information, that a twenty-second hug per day can add years to your life.

He let the urge slide. "I don't know, it doesn't help," his eyes brightened, "but you did good today. You stabilized a mess that could have become really bad really fast. You needed to get the bills paid on all those properties, to the extent that whatever can be done has been done to take care of it." He raised an eyebrow in emphasis. "You did real good today! We can figure out tomorrow, tomorrow."

His phone buzzed behind him. The short staccato bzz bzz bzz of an incoming message.

"Well, well, it's Sheriff Pierson." He read out the message. [Mr. Saylor, sorry to get back to you so late. Can you drop by tomorrow morning?] He returned Belle's wide-eyed look. "You asked. The Sheriff answered."

"Do you think he knows of our snooping around?"

"This small a town, I'd be surprised if he didn't. A clerk at the courthouse, somebody at the restaurant could have seen us together. Probably the only thing they don't know is that we were both at your house last night. I left a message for him; said I'd found some interesting things at the courthouse. I don't think he wants to share what *he* knows."

"Are you going in?"

"Of course, and I can ask if there's been any sign of a ransom." He had second-guessed his outreach to the Sheriff and now felt resigned to it. Now, it was no longer a choice. "It's not exactly a summons to appear, but since I asked first, I'm sure if I don't answer, there'll be a friendly officer here tomorrow morning to collect me."

He typed back; [Sure, is 10 OK?] and tapped send.

The reply was immediate. [10:30 better. see you then]. "So, till tomorrow." He hoisted his tumbler of iced tea as a toast.

She wiped at some errant gravy at the edge of her mouth with a napkin. "That was as good as I remember it."

"And not any better either." He pushed away his unfinished bowl.

"Well, it's good to have company instead of eating it out of a hot pot in a dorm."

"True that." Their eyes locked, questions sent but unanswered in both directions.

She broke the silence. "I guess I should be going." She slid out of the dinette's bench seating and stood, looking up. She was a full head shorter. The lost puppy look returned but she said nothing.

It started with a hand on her shoulder, a reassuring 'I'm on your side' gentle pressure. She reached up and held it in place. He had intended to lean over and give her a reassuring hug but found her yielding, sliding into his reach. Her arms pulled him in as his closed behind her. This time when she looked up, her eyes were darting between eyes and lips. He raised his hands to cup her head and pulled her lips to his. The first kiss with any new lover is always memorable. This one was broken by a hiccup.

Belle giggled, dropped her head. She pulled in, holding him close. Burrowing her head into his chest. He bent his head over, smelled her hair. "Umm."

"What?" Her voice was almost not there, tentative.

"Whatever you use for conditioner, don't change it. Your head smells great."

"Tap water usually, I rinse with city tap water."

"Even better, *you* smell great."

Her hands slid down, then up inside his shirt. He felt her splayed fingers pressing into his back, locking together across the lumps of his vertebrae.

Whatever had been holding him back, melted. The bond of attraction had been building, but always with a sense of 'this could be too important to screw up. Don't rush.' The tension he'd felt in her presence since the first meeting in her store lifted. She pulled back; her hands moved quickly to his chest. As she began to work at the buttons on his shirt, he reached and turned out the lights. They made furious, all-consuming love the first time. The second was slower, exploratory. What do you like, what do I like? Skin. They reveled in skin. Fingers, lips, tongues, noses, eyebrows, skin. Exhausted, they slept, spooned, legs entwined.

In the wee hours, a waxing moon lit his view to the south, painting a dancing white moonlit pathway to the barrier island. A check of the time, an ancient blue LED display left by the prior owners, showed a few hours still before sunrise. He untangled an arm from beneath Belle's neck. Slipping on shorts, he moved back to his dinette after first pulling the privacy curtain to the camper's "master suite." He pulled open the laptop and began a new document. He put up a throwaway title "Lost Child." The document grew as he threw in the details. The list, mostly phrases or short sentences, detailed everything he knew about Lindsey Lawrence. He hoped that if he started to outline it as a series of actions, historical footnotes, he could look at it as a plot, a storyline; wishing in the darkness that sense would come out of it. Who might benefit from her abduction if it had to do with control of the financial assets, and who might be involved if it was a bodily harm abduction? He had learned more about Lindsey's family, but little about her.

In an hour, he stopped. Completely at a loss. The easy exercise hadn't jelled toward any particular pathway forward. He looked above the glowing rectangle of the laptop to see that the moon had slid out of view to the west and a brightening glow to the east was edging higher. He slipped back under the sheets, feeling the warmth of a shared bed for the first time in nearly a year. It felt good.

16

Sheriff Pierson Ups the Game

Pierson looked up at the wall clock when Saylor tapped at the door frame. "10:30 on the dot. I like that."

Saylor put on his best greeting smile. "Good morning, Sheriff. What can I do for you?" He felt apprehensive but hopeful. He had called after all. Maybe the sheriff would be receptive to his inputs.

"Saylor," the man's stare was piercing, not hostile, but sure to make contact with your inner demons and angels. "I'm not sure what to do with you. It's damned interesting that you called me."

"I just wanted to follow up. Our first meeting got my attention. I did do some poking around." He put his hands up in mock surrender. "I know, you said to stay out of it." Saylor waited, not wanting to make an opening when it seemed the sheriff had his own agenda for the meeting. Pierson motioned to the chair opposite his desk. Saylor sat and waited.

Pierson's smile, if that was what it was, would have to be considered neutral. It neither looked happy, conveyed satisfaction, or gave warning. Saylor concluded that Pierson had the perfect definition of an enigmatic smile. He'd have to figure out how to describe it on one of Andie Jackson's adversaries.

Pierson finally spoke. "Mr. Saylor, I have a shrinking list of people that merit more questions. It's down to two actually, there's an old boyfriend from her high school days that was, according to our reports, an unhappy boy at the time. Jilted, abandoned in the midst of his unrequited love affair. You can imagine the feelings of a teenager in love. Right?"

At this moment, having just recently left a warm bed, he could. "Yes, I imagine if he felt slighted, but those usually fall away, someone else comes along. It's the old circle game. You win some, lose some, keep trying. We all grow out of it."

"This guy didn't. She blocked him from her Snapchat page, according to her classmates." He thought, Snapchat, damn! No wonder she wasn't on Facebook. He said, "So, this guy. You've been following up on him? Did he have any history with you, the Law?"

"In fact, he does. Seems he was fond of square mullet. You know what that is?"

Saylor tried to suppress a laugh. Couldn't help it. "Back in the day, yes. I guess it still means the same thing." Pierson didn't add anything but a slight twitch of his mouth. "If one of the offshore hookups between the cigarette boats and the trawler fleet went bad, or the Coast Guard moved in, they'd dump their cargo and try to get out of the neighborhood. They'd leave behind hundreds of cellophane-wrapped bricks of pot floating with the tide. Some of those bricks ended up in fishing nets or even the beach. They'd find their way into the side hallways of good ole Franklin County High. So, if that's what it still means, then yes, I know about square mullet."

"Interesting wording, 'you know *about* square mullet.'"

"I liked beer. When we could get it. It was our high of choice. But I think the statute of limitations is out on my underage possession."

"So, no history with the evil weed?"

"I'd be crazy to deny it. Somebody somewhere will remember the time or two it passed my way. We didn't seek it out, didn't say no if someone passed a roach. We were kids. Kids whose biggest challenge was to find someone who'd buy us a twelve pack." Pierson just nodded in the affirmative. Saylor understood that the sheriff already knew this. "Does pot in any way figure in your investigation? Smuggling? Surely she wasn't involved in smuggling."

"Why do you say that?"

"Lindsey had only been home a few months. Her mom was dying of cancer and she was trying to learn the management ropes at the family store. Doesn't sound like the profile of someone who's going to ditch college to come home and get involved in running dope."

"You seem to know a lot. I seem to remember specifically asking you to stay out of it."

Saylor raised his hands in surrender. "Got me. You did. But you got my attention the first time your boys set me down in the back seat. It's the kind of thing that takes hold of a curious mind." There was no reaction. "And I have a curious mind." Pierson was waiting for more. "So, I visited the store, didn't find anything out."

"But then a day later, I've got you at the courthouse, pulling records relating to the Lawrence's holdings?" He leaned forward, transferring weight to his crossed arms on the front of the calendar blotter. "That's the part of 'stay out of it' I asked you not to do."

That gave Saylor pause, could the sheriff be in on this? Ten million is a lot of money, serious money. He let that thought slide. *Get back on defense.* He crossed his arms, adopting a defensive posture. "Sheriff Pierson, my whole career has been investigative journalism. I'm not trying to research the great American crime story or anything. I've actually got two active plots I'm working. But after the first visit to the store, the History House, their hired help asked me to help. Hey, she's cute. I'm a softy for cute, and large pleading brown eyes are a world changer. I started doing what little I could to see if there was some angle that someone might benefit from taking her."

"Get anywhere?"

"Jeez, I wish. I made a few summary notes this morning trying to pull together some of the loose strings. Zilch. I can't think of any reason why anyone could profit from an abduction for ransom. I was beginning to think the worst."

"That being..."

"Abduction, rape, or worse." Saylor let out a sigh, a lot of thought had gone into the early morning brainstorming, and he'd gotten nowhere. He leaned forward, not precisely mimicking the sheriff's posture but getting closer, hoping for some overt expression of sincere interest. "I'd be happy to send over the file. It's not much. I'd be happy to help in any way."

Pierson's expression might as well have been carved in rock. "What line were you following?"

"The Lawrences' estate. It's modest, but in a county that's ten percent doing really well, as in real estate well, and the other ninety percent that's dirt poor, oyster raking poor, shrimp dragging poor, five and a half million is a lot of money. And I'd be looking around in that ten percent for anyone who could benefit."

"Why do you say that?"

"Because there's no next of kin. No heirs. Her dad died ten or so years ago, the mom died a few months ago, leaving Lindsey. There was one other kid, I forget the name right now, apparently still-born. No, wait, Janet. It seems the Lawrences had a still-born girl they named Janet. Then there's Lindsey? I haven't found any record there. With Lindsey gone, the estate is up for grabs."

He eyed Pierson, whose smile, if it could be called one, was razor-thin. "Sheriff, do you know of anyone seeking a ransom for Lindsey?"

"No, I suppose if one was to come in, it would go to the family attorney, they'd never call me."

"Yeah, I guess not. So, if it's not for some move on the estate, then I'd be thinking of mayhem. A physical assault, battery potentially, rape probably, after some time, or maybe only thirty minutes, murder."

The razor-thin smile vanished as Pierson appeared to be chewing on his inner cheek. "Jason, mind if I call you Jason?"

"Sure, no problems. What?"

"Jason," Pierson's head took a slight lean to his left. "What do you know about genealogy?"

"X's and Y's. Mendel's research in peas, not a whole lot about that. A few hundred years later, DNA is getting a lot of wrongfully convicted people out of jail, because the Innocence Project is working through the rape kits."

"So you do have a working knowledge. You ever check in with Ancestry.com? 123 and Me? Either of those?"

"No. No need. Sheriff, you're kind of new here, but my folks go way back, like turn of the last century back. My people built one of the early electric sawmills after the war, world war one. He cut cypress and yellow pine, ran a lumber and hardware store. After he busted in the depression, Grandpa crewed on a trawler, pulled seine nets for mullet, and finally signed on with the Merchant Marine. His ship got sunk by a Japanese sub in the Gulf of Mexico shortly after he got grams pregnant. He showed up later, he'd been rescued by a trawler out of Mississippi. Gramps did a lot of this and that in the war like a lot of folks. After the war though, he was changed, wasn't terribly ambitious. They did manage one kid, my mother."

"Mom did all right. Learned to sell real estate on the island. Dad, when he wasn't drinking, envisioned a life as a custom builder of sandcastles. I was junior in college when he drove his truck into an oncoming car on the old bridge. So, life sucks, right. Growing up, we had a little place back behind the cemetery, convenient for my brother and me because it was close to the old high school. I lived in that schoolyard and on the docks. It's a small town and it's flat. I could go anywhere on a bike. I grew up, saw that I didn't want to sell or build sand castles, and I really didn't want to catch, clean, cook, or serve seafood, so I left. So, I know my own story, and no. I never sent spit to Ancestry."

Pierson leaned back in his brown leather chair. "Follow me here. OK? We were thinking along the same lines as you were. Who would likely benefit from an estate worth over ten million dollars—"

"Ten! What did they have besides real estate?"

Pierson actually broke his face and grinned. "We have subpoena powers, Mr. Sleuth Reporter. Bank records and a search of their lockbox indicate substantial investments. Not to mention, liquid cash. The Lawrences had more than one bank account according to their attorney. One here in town. Two in Jacksonville, another on Grand Cayman."

Saylor sat back, mouth dropping.

"That surprises you, Jason?"

"Holy shit. Sorry. Yes, that surprises the hell out of me." Then. "So, you're looking to see if there are other relatives out there." Saylor slapped the desk enthusiastically. "That's right, they're new money. They don't have history here." Saylor mulled that over. He actually had thought about a genealogy database search. Still, there was no way to get a spit sample from a missing person.

Saylor remembered the sheriff's earlier introduction. "You said there were two people on your shortening list. You got a hit? Who's the other one?"

Pierson's eyebrows lifted. "You."

17

Genealogy

"Me? What the fuck!" He recovered. "I'm sorry. Me?" His mind roiled, he had no kids. His wife couldn't after trying and trying. Their marriage knot unraveled, and the heartbreaking divorce had left him aloof and alone. A newsroom friendship blossomed in the aftermath with Caroline, and HR policy or not, their dating led to her firing and a marriage born out of guilt. It wasn't the strongest reason for getting married and it ended by mutual consent. It also ended because he'd caught her coming out of the neighbor's garage at three in the morning. He realized he'd been silent, searching for who, what, when.

"Seriously, you can't think of anybody?"

"What? Am I a third cousin or something?" Saylor was foundering on the surprise connection. He said, "Search me, I can't think of anybody. Come to think of it, you did search me. How did you come by my DNA?"

"You know Patrick Wills?"

"Patrick? Of course, he's a good friend. He—"

"He was on my auxiliary for years before he got full time at the City. He did me a favor."

Saylor remembered Patrick's last visit. A quiet chat by the highway, taking in the sunset. "Ah, he made a piss call. Came out apologizing for knocking over my shaving kit." *Son of a bitch.* He said, "I guess you can't always depend on your friends." His mind was still buzzing trying to make connections.

Pierson said. "I had a long chat with Officer Wills the other day." He let that thought hang out there, sails in the wind. "You might want to re-evaluate that relationship. I understand there was a lot of history."

"Yeah, we were buds, jocks in a jock world. BMOCs, even if it was a very small campus. I was wide receiver for his quarterbacking.

That boy had a mean throwing arm." Saylor absent-mindedly rubbed at ribs. "I'd get bruises below the pads from catching his bullets." He stopped musing. "And we hung around a lot. We were good friends."

"And you left." To Saylor's surprise, Pierson mocked a line from an old Beatles song. "Now we've hit the big time." Saylor flinched. "And you never looked back. Ever wonder how that affected your best bud?"

"No. Like you said. I never looked back. Well, once. I came back the next summer before my sophomore year. But after college, the Army. Damn, it does broaden one's horizons."

"You came back that one summer. That summer was just about twenty years ago, right?"

"Yeah, oh!" Memories began crashing into his present. He felt the room shimmer. Pierson became a disembodied face. One with a razor-thin smile.

The face asked, "You get chummy with anyone that summer?"

Saylor felt a cold sweat forming. "Christ!" His vision narrowed to a swirling mass. Pierson's face went sideways just before Saylor hit the floor. His last thought, before the desk filling his vision faded to black: "Sandra."

His head hurt. Apparently, he'd hit his head on the edge of Pierson's desk on the way down. The EMT said not to worry, syncope on hearing startling news is common. The uniformed first responder asked him about his heart, had he had breakfast, had he been keeping hydrated? He answered in a surreal world where everything about him was being redefined. No heart problems I know of. Yes, coffee. Does that count? He didn't mention it was a wonderfully simple sunrise breakfast on the patio with Belle. And no, probably not fully hydrated.

"OK, then. We're going to let you go. You sign here and you're outta here."

Saylor looked around, remembered his last location, but a lot had changed. "Where am I? Weems Hospital?" Saylor asked. He glanced at the man's shirt. Corso, and a Franklin County EMT patch.

He regarded the paramedic, huge; defensive lineman huge, and black as they come in the rural south. A huge smile, with whitened teeth.

In a resonant base that recalled Samuel Jackson, Corso said. "No, you were only out for a few minutes. We're at the Emergency Response HQ, attached to the Sheriff's office. How are you feeling now?" Corso's peering stare spoke of serious concern. "You might want to see a cardiologist; most people just don't feint out like that." He smiled, flashing those bright pearly whites. "It probably would have been only moments if you hadn't hit your head."

Saylor reached up and felt the square bandage taped over his left temple. He pulled his hand back as it made light contact. *That hurt!*

Corso stood back, observing. "You sure you're feeling OK? It's only been a few minutes. I just happened to be here with my rig. Lucky you!"

"Yeah," he was tempted to touch his head again, reconsidered. "Lucky me."

"High Sheriff said he wanted to talk to you a bit more when you came to." EMT Corso finished putting gauze, scissors, and tape away, closed his bag. "He's just down the hall. Here, drink this. It'll help."

Saylor took an offered bottle of orange Gatorade and downed half of it."

"Good. See, just keep hydrated. Here, stand for me. I want to see that you've got your balance back." Saylor did so, didn't feel unsteady. Corso added, "You don't need any more bumps on that head, right?"

"Right," he took another short swig. "Hey, thanks. Glad you were here."

Corso smiled and waved as he slid away out of sight.

Saylor looked briefly for the cap to the bottle, didn't see one, and decided to take it with him. Pierson's office door was open. He tapped tentatively.

"Come on in. Sit over there if you would." Saylor looked and saw that a cheap leatherette couch, previously covered in file boxes had been cleared. He moved to it and sat.

"Sandra?" Pierson took the lead with little ceremony.

Saylor nodded, took in a deep breath. No need to let his oxygen levels plummet again. "Sandra Hardin, one of our group. She and a girlfriend, Suzanne were running mates with Patrick and me. Pretty much an inseparable group in my senior year. The girls were a year behind us." He remembered where the conversation had left off. "Last time I was back here. I'd just finished a year at FSU, came down here and we were all grown up then. Felt like it, anyway. All the affection of years as good friends turned, well, you get the picture. We had sex a couple of times. We parted friends. I went back to FSU. She went to UWF in Pensacola."

"That it, another burned bridge?"

"What? No, not intentionally. Look it was casual, it was great, but we knew we both had other plans. If she'd gone to Tallahassee instead of Pensacola, who knows? I might have married the love of my life and we'd have been happy ever after." He looked down at his sandals. The import was beginning to weigh in. The elephant in the room beginning to raise its trunk in salute. "Sheriff, can I see that print out? The report from the DNA search?" He paused, thinking. "How'd you do that. I thought state crime labs could only compare two sets. Pat gave you mine. What about hers?"

"A warrant. Another option you guys at the papers don't have. We dropped by the house the other day to serve it. No one home. Easy enough to go into the bathroom. It's amazing the number of places DNA gets dropped in your own home. Hair, toothbrush."

"You can do that?"

"Yes, and we did."

"No, I mean do relative tracing." His mind was off on another track, somewhere between the current problem and his work in progress. "You can check for family relations? I thought it was only good for checking identity, like who did it. Sample matches for forensic evidence."

"It's good for that, and if your State Lab's new guru is one of the bright bulbs that used to work for 123 and Me, then you can go a little further, check for the places where families leave their footprints." He steepled his hands over his desk calendar. "We found you, indicated as a parent."

Saylor still didn't have all the pieces. "But Sandra Hardin, I heard she died in childbirth — Oh, shit!" He doubled over tried to put his hands over his head and winced as he touched the bandage. "Oh, fucking shit. She should have told me." Something broke. He started heaving with sobs. He didn't want this to happen in the Sheriff's office, the fucking Sheriff of all people. When he looked up, tear tracks ran down his cheeks. "You have no idea how much my first wife would have wanted to raise a girl." He wiped his cheeks with the backs of his hands. "You're sure. There's no room for error?"

"I can get you that report."

"Thanks, I'd like that." *Loose threads. A lot more loose threads.* "Uhm, did you track down the connection between Sandra Hardin having a baby and the Lawrences?"

"Well, there was nothing in the DOH database. Department of Health."

"Thanks, I figured that."

"Or DVS."

"OK, got me."

"Division of Vital Statistics." Saylor nodded. Pierson continued. "But it turns out that our Mrs. Lawrence was pretty high up at Sacred Heart. It's a Catholic Hospital in—"

"Pensacola, I know."

Click.

"Oh, so it remained in house, adoption records sealed." The connection was falling in line. Eleanor Lawrence had had a still-born child. A lot of those are accompanied with hysterectomies. "She wanted a baby, got herself on some sort of list? And shortly afterward, they show up in Apalach with a brand-new baby, and the adoption records are sealed by the Department of Children and Families. Welcome to the funny house." He began to shake. His body was visibly vibrating.

"You going to be all right?" The Sheriff's agitation grew as Saylor's shaking grew. Saylor started to laugh, a hard gasping laugh. He cried out. "*Jeeesus, fucking H, fucking Christ.*" He took a deep full breath to try to stop the shaking. "Who the fuck could come up with that?" He glared at Pierson. "You know, today started out as a pretty decent day. One of the cardinal days of my life that I'd never hope to forget. And *this* happens."

"Well," Pierson began slowly, his southern drawl adding syllables to the word. "I don't think you'll be forgetting it. And you now have the solution to your problem."

Saylor stiffened. "What? What kind of a solution is this to anything?" His voice dropped into the range of a growl. "I find out the girl I've been looking for is my daughter I never knew I had? That for all you or I know, she is either in captivity somewhere or dead. *THAT*'s a solution?"

Pierson's arms crossed over his chest. "Do you know what NOK means? In police jargon?"

"Yeah, I read murder books, I read case files. Next of Kin."

"You would be surprised how many times a violent act can be traced back to next of kin. You remember JonBenet Ramsey?"

"Yes."

"Ever hear of Andrea Yeats?"

"Yes, that was in Houston, before I was there. But yeah." The chill began again. He started to breath harder. He wasn't going to feint again. He tried for long deep breathing. "You think I tracked down my long-lost daughter, and snuffed her for a fortune I didn't know she was worth?"

"How do I *know* you didn't *know* the she was your daughter; didn't *know* what she was worth?"

Saylor was getting angry now. Pierson kept pushing. "How do we know you didn't find out about the properties by doing an online records search at the courthouse. They've been digital for the past five years, going back to the 1920s and getting further back every year."

"But I was just there—"

"And knew exactly where to look." Pierson shook his head in the negative. "Marlene? The older one? She said your search was pretty impressive. You knew exactly how to search for which properties."

"Because I did my homework first. Ever hear of Zillow? Ever hear of the Property Appraiser?" He was getting loud, *need to calm down*. He found he'd gotten to the edge of the couch, leaning forward, an aggressive, muscle-wound stance. A lineman waiting for the hut-hut. *Breathe dammit!* He leaned back on the couch cushion. Calmer, anger squelched. "I did my homework. Property Appraiser. Search by name. The properties are still listed as the original LLC. And the report only gives taxable value, with current tax laws market value can be considerably higher. So, the search on Zillow provides better estimate of actual market value."

Pierson began to close his case. "And here we are. There's one person in the world who has a contestable right to challenge a probate court for control of the Lawrence assets. Next of Kin." Pierson's face looked almost smug.

"You...I called you. Yesterday, trying to see if there was some way I could help you. So, I come in being helpful, and now I'm your prime suspect? What about this other guy? The broken hearts club guy. Where's he?"

"That's uncertain, we're on the lookout. Guys like him, hard to tell, could be out on a trawler. He might be back with the tide or tomorrow's. Could be up the river."

"Up the river?"

"It's tupelo season. Bee keepers will be wanting help getting their boxes up on dry land in the tupelo stands. He's a day labor kind of guy. No steady work and not much of a residence."

"How about fled the state after kidnapping and murder."

"That's not off the table." Pierson leaned forward again. Pointed a finger at Saylor. "You just be sure you don't leave the state of Florida. Ya hear?"

"Sheriff, I'm not going anywhere. I've got a book to finish, another one half-born."

"Good to see you aren't wasting your time down here."

"You can't get all possessive with your 'down here'. Shit, you forget I *am* from here." He stood up. "There anything else about me you'd like to reveal?"

"I think we've covered it."

"I haven't heard you singing Miranda. Am I free to go?"

Pierson nodded at the doorway. "Free to stay comfortably buttoned up in Eastpoint."

"You may find that I need to get to town every now and then. Don't worry, you can pass me off to your auxiliary, Patrick Wills."

With little need to add anything further to the conversation. Saylor stood, and with a bare nod at Sheriff Pierson, left for his mobile refuge and a soul-cleansing swim in the bay.

18

This Isn't Telephone News

His head still hurt, throbbing, dizzying pain. Not disabling physically, but he knew writing was shot for the afternoon. He'd driven down to the gas station at the point for a pint of gizzards and found them sold out for the day. Saylor settled on chicken fingers and potato wedges from the in-house fry cook and added a pint of Ben and Jerry's. He figured he had as much comfort food as his heart would stand for the day. *Should I call a cardiologist? The EMT said maybe I should call a cardiologist?*

It was early afternoon, but getting hotter. For the first time, he decided to unroll the eight by sixteen cloth canopy attached to the upper edge of the camper. Broad red and white stripes to go with the only decoration on the white slab of aluminum siding. But shade! Saylor brought out a folding tray that reminded him of the stamped aluminum TV trays his family would use when dinner time conflicted with the seven o'clock sitcoms. Settling in with his Styrofoam packaged dinner and diet coke, he looked out across the bay in its full-sun glory. Seabirds dove and dined while he licked deep fry fats from his fingertips. *Life! Ain't life grand.*

His thoughts had been running to the morose. Sheriff Pierson was still short of reading him Miranda rights, and what? *Had the sheriff actually learned anything other than to check for his reaction?* He'd want to call his legal contact back in Texas. Probably Margaret Campbell would know. Miranda's a federal law. Rules are rules. He'd like to find out from her if he had any future leverage on that point.

And there was Belle. Ah, the day really had started out great. Waking up next to a warm body in bed had become a fading memory. The master suite in his camper, a double bed-sized mattress with a small hanging closet, separable from the rest of the unit by a cloth

114

curtain, ensured that you could tell if you were sleeping alone or not. After his wee hours' typing had run dry, he'd managed a half-hour of near sleep before Belle began to move. He discovered that she had restless leg syndrome, and she snored lightly. More cute than bothersome.

Discovery stage. Margaret had once told him that court cases are like relationships. The discovery stage is exciting, invigorating, as new information comes in every day. His relationship with Melina was case closed status, now only professional. Their fling between his two marriages was brief, but they'd parted by mutual consent and still had uses for each other's professional skills. He'd need legal advice from time to time. She'd need case publicity, from time to time.

A breeze caught the awning causing it to flap. He looked up at the red stripes and smiled at the thought of Belle showing up with a sixer of Red Stripe. He wondered whether to call, share the latest. *No, this isn't telephone news.* He then realized he didn't have her cell number. A quick search for the store brought up the landline number. She picked up on the sixth ring, breathless.

"Hey, how's the day going?" *Keep it light.*

"Fine, I just have a customer in here who doesn't seem to mind that I needed to get the phone. How's your's been?"

"I've been thinking about you." *No lie there.* "I've also been thinking about dinner." He looked over at his unfinished lunch. "Something local, seafoodish. On the better side of not very expensive. Can you recommend something?"

"Sure. But my treat this time. I have some news for you."

"Oh, can you talk?"

"No, and I really want to hear what the sheriff had to say, but there's people out in the front room. I need to go try to sell something expensive." He could hear her humor coming through.

"You go, girl. I have news too, but it isn't telephone news. I'll come by about quitting time. Six, right?"

"See ya." And the connection went silent.

Disappointed that the conversation had been so brief, he decided on one more potato log, finished off the coke, and tossed the rest.

Dinner was served at a venerable establishment overlooking the river. Brown paper table cloths, plastic trays, and plastic set-ups. Twenty years prior, when he was still locally famous, one of the Friday Night Football notables, he and a date would have been bumped to the front of most restaurant lines. Tonight, a new generation of servers looked at them with the benign but meaningless smiles of the overworked, footsore, underpaid, and under-appreciated. They were eventually seated at a table overlooking the finger piers below. Most of the slips were empty, reserved for customers who would boat in for dinner. The fried oyster basket was as delicious as he remembered. A single beer with dinner helped with the slight throbbing in his temple. He'd removed the bandage and sponged off any fresh scab crusts. On questioning, he deferred to later. Long story. Etc.

From their outdoor patio seating, he watched an older couple, he with age-appropriate white hair, she with a freshly touched-up shade of brunette, as they boarded a pontoon boat and proceeded upriver against the evening tide. That might be nice to do some evening with Belle. His mind popped back to the present.

Belle had been talking, he hadn't been listening. "I'm sorry? Posters?"

"I've been all over the county today putting up posters." She handed over a black and white handbill she'd printed with tear-off phone tabs at the bottom. Lindsey's picture, a blow-up of one of the recent ones at the house was centered between 'Missing' and 'Please call if you've seen Lindsey Lawrence.' A reward of $2,000 was offered for any meaningful tips.

"You've been busy."

"Yeah, I closed early drove over to the Island, out to Two Mile, even over past your digs to Carabelle. I finally ran out of staples." Her smile of triumph faded into what was becoming a perpetual worried look.

"That's great, Belle. I should have thought of that."

"Well, no one seemed to want to buy anything this afternoon. Two bottles of honey, a poster, this morning. A block of coral at lunch, then nada. I began to feel useless."

"I hope the posters do some good. Can I keep this one?"

"Sure."

He folded it into a quarter of the original and tucked it in his back pocket. Looking up, he saw the pontoon boat was now almost out of sight upriver. The idea of a river cruise reinserted itself. "Belle, it seems you've forestalled any immediate action that would evict you. Do you think it would be alright to tie my boat up at the dock? At the river house? It would save me some hassle whenever I wanted to go out. There's fresh seafood in it for you if my hooks get lucky."

"Just a second, I'll call the property manager." She mimed a phone call. Then, "Don't see why not. Might be fun to go for a ride up the river too."

"I think I can arrange that." He began to mentally list some of the places he and Patrick had explored in their days on the river. Fishing, drinking a little. Smoking a little. Sunbathing and trying to get lucky with the girls. He told Belle he knew Patrick had taken at least one of their friends to one of the hidden landings off the main river for "sunbathing" and a picnic. The following Monday, the girl walked into their little crowd, landed a sucker punch to his gut, and stormed off. It didn't take much of a stretch for everyone to figure things out.

As the story wound to its end, he asked. "So, you have news?"

She scanned the open-air deck and appeared to think better of saying much more in public. "Let's go to my place. I can show you there what I can't show you here."

They parked their cars under the house, and as she headed for the stairs, he looked toward the river. "If you don't mind, I'd like to check out the dock before I bring the boat over."

"Sure, I haven't been out there in weeks."

Saylor liked her "Sure." It was bird-like, musical. Or at least music to him. Walking through the unkempt grass, he thought he might like the workout of mowing the lawn, at least maybe the area immediate to the driveway, house, and a good wide path to the dock.

The dock was sturdy enough. In the dimming rays of twilight, he could tell that the two-by-six decking was sound, screwed down against wave action on a surge tide. The pilings were heavy six by sixes rather than the pole wood often used. Good money well spent, he concluded. The dock sported a floating wing downstream side that could rise and fall with the tidal range. That would make tying off with bumpers easy. The tie-off cleats were heavy-duty galvanized steel. He stood, concluding that it was more than strong enough for his lightweight aluminum runabout. Probably strong enough to have tied up their thirty-something-foot sailboat. Looking at the cleat layout, he confirmed his guesstimate. Heavy duty cleats for a weighted keel sailboat were located on the deeper river side. Lighter duty cleats on the bank side of the finger pier for a light-weight runabout.

"Jase? Come here."

He turned to see Belle on one knee peering at the deck planking. From his vantage near the end of the deck, he saw what she'd been examining close up. Bending close beside her, he saw, unmistakable on the weathered gray wood planks, signs that something had been recently drug along the planks. The thin veneer of mold growing for years had been scuffed clean. The lines of disturbed or scraped mold extended from the grassy end of the dock to a few feet beyond the first cleat, where a boat would have been tied up.

"This wasn't here the last time I was out here with her. Oh, Jason!" She stood, emotions wringing her face through the initial stages of shock. Here was evidence of some sort that did not bode well.

He took her in her arms, held her close. He could feel her fighting the urge to break down.

She continued in a near whisper, rushing it out. "It was such a beautiful spring day. Absolutely cloudless sky. It must have been about a month after El died. Lindsey was coming to grips with her new status as an orphan. I'd never thought of it that way, before then, but she was. The last time I was in the boat, she drove me over to Lake Wimico just for the hell of it. Way out there, no other humans around for miles, she let out this scream. This god-awful, gut-wrenching scream." She stopped. The shuddering in her chest had stopped. "We were going flat out down the Intercoastal, and that scream. I screamed too, it felt great. And it felt awful. She let the boat slow to a stop and we both cried for Eleanor."

She looked up into Saylor's eyes. "But for her, it was way worse. Both parents gone way too soon." She snuggled her head into his shoulder. "Should we call Pierson."

"The sheriff?" He studied it out for a moment, then agreed with his first inclination. "No, not now. We uh, we have an understanding of sorts."

"You never told me about this morning, how that went."

He glanced up to the upper-level deck extending out from Eleanor's bedroom. "Let's go to the house."

19

Top of the Fold

They decided on the lower deck off the living room. They'd considered going upstairs but hoped to retain any crime scene integrity in the upper bedroom. If there was anything to be learned there by a forensics team, *if* the sheriff ever sent one, it would need to be kept as pristine as possible. And besides, the lower deck had pretty much the same view as the upper deck. They settled into the white PVC Adirondack chairs.

The sun was setting behind them, lighting up the line of cypress trees across the river. They had lost all of their deep winter russet and literally glowed in the bright greens of early summer in the lowering sun's light. Beyond, a rack of four thunderheads over Tate's Hell Swamp shone in brilliant hues of amber and gold against darker cerulean shadows. Sparks flashed between the cloud tops and from cloud to ground in silence. Low distant grumbles arrived in time delay as afterthoughts.

Despite the River House's humbler location, Saylor thought, it's a nicer setting than any of the family's beach houses on the island. It had privacy that none of the tiny lots on the island could boast. It had permanent neighbors that looked out for each other, and it had a lot to offer besides sand and surf. Then he slapped at a mosquito. He understood why a small wicker basket was screwed to the outside porch wall containing various concoctions of sun oils and bug juice. He got up, put a squirt on both forearms, lathered up, and then handed her the bottle.

"I guess we both have news," she started. "You want to go first?"

"Why don't you. Mine might be upsetting—it's top of the fold kind of news and this view is too gorgeous to spoil with reality."

She added, "If I do, then we're going to have to get up and leave the view."

He chuckled silently at the problem. "OK, I'll go first, but put on your seatbelt." He proceeded to recount the semi-interrogation, semi-conversation he'd had with Sheriff Pierson. When he got to the revelation that he, Jason Saylor, was the biological father of Lindsey Lawrence, she gasped, wide-eyed.

"Oh My God! Jason! That's so freaking weird!" Then, "Oh, I'm so sorry! Did he send you the file? The report from the State DNA lab?" The multiple responses burst out in staccato cadence before he could respond to any of them.

"I don't know, I haven't looked at my email since about four. I showered to get the smell of the bay off me before I came to meet you for dinner. I haven't checked." He met her worried stare. "I don't have any reason to think he'd lie about that. And it's true that her birth mother, Sandra Jane Hardin, and I were actively intimate for about the last ten days of that summer. Summer's last fling, you know."

She nodded. "Oh shit! Jase!" Eyes wide in shock, her head wobbled back and forth. He saw her lower lip tremble before she clamped her lips tight.

He thought he read her reaction as to be that he might actually be involved. He shifted his weight in the chair to face her more directly. "Look, Belle. I swear to any of the Gods in Heaven, or Olympus, or wherever. I did not have anything to do with Lindsey's disappearance. It was top-of-the-fold breaking news to me that she might be my, er, is my child." Her distorted face changed a tick toward normal but continued to slowly say no by wagging slowly back and forth.

He continued to defend himself. "And the sheriff's assertion that I could do such a horrible thing to my own child just to get control of her estate is crazy! That would be the act of a mentally unstable person, a psychopath."

She seemed as emotionally distraught as he had been. She stood abruptly and moved to face him. She was a silhouette now, in the shade of the house, dark against the brilliant canvas of yellows and oranges behind her. At first, he didn't see her hand reach out. He flinched at her touch, unaware of her intent.

Belle stooped to grasp his hand. "Come here, I need to show you," she faltered, "show you something."

He followed her into the main downstairs room. She sat on the couch and pulled at a piece of wood on the face of the coffee table, revealing a small drawer under its centerpiece. The top of the table had a beveled glass insert over a display area that showed off a variety of shells. The shells, usually covered by a circular doily and a table lamp, came to light as she pulled the drawer out. His eye went to the largest cowrie shell he'd ever seen, a branch of white coral, a perfect two-inch cube of red coral, a six-inch-long but narrow spiral shell he'd never seen on a Franklin County beach, and a large bivalve common to almost everywhere, but rare for one that large to be still mated at the hinge.

Belle picked up the bivalve. Its purple and white stripes beautiful in their randomness. Who could guess at the environment that had caused those random colorations? She held it up but didn't offer it over. "I was sitting here this morning before going in to the shop. Just watching the sun over the river. I like it when there's a light breeze on the water, it turns the mud-brown river sky blue. Well, my eye caught the shells under that doily and wondered how they were put there. Just random curiosity, you know."

He nodded, looked down at the shell, and back up. There was an intensity about her face as if something was about to burst out of her chest, but she had to tell it just right.

"So, I found this drawer and looked the shells over, played with them. I tried to blow through that spiral thing. The last one I picked up was this kind of ordinary-looking clam. I know it's not common to find one this big, still attached," she paused, "and it rattled." She shook it, and he heard the light ceramic-sounding rattle. She shook it again, gently—another light tinkling.

"I turned on the table lamp and slowly pried the shell apart." She repeated the action, her fingertips on the ragged edge, her palms grasping the rounded hinge side carefully, then turned the slight crack in the shell down, and a small key fell out.

Saylor looked at the key, not wanting to break her story-telling spell but also restraining his urge to pick it up. "Do you know what it goes to?"

"Yes, I do."

Her look was hard to decipher. She seemed undecided, hesitant. "I think you need to see this." She held up the silvered key by its flat round finger pad and looked at its profile in end view. She then handed it over to him, and he repeated the pose with the little key.

Saylor noted the squared side and the double-s curve of the blade. "I'd seen that shape before. I thought it was peculiar."

"You know what it goes to?"

She put her hand out for the key again. He gave it up. She stood and walked toward the stairs. He followed as they went upstairs to the back of the master suite and into what had been Jeremy's old closet before it became household storage. She knelt before the line of linen curtains on their hangers and tugged at the fire-proof vault. It was heavy, but she only needed to bring it out into the light. She tilted it up, so the single ceiling fixture lit its face. Along the front band of metal that contained the two tumbler locks was a thin decorative line. A row of curving s-shapes traced a line between the two tumblers. Belle slipped the key into a recess that was virtually invisible in the line of printed esses. He heard the snap-click of the lock release. The spring-loaded top popped up about a quarter inch. He found he was holding his breath and exhaled audibly.

From her position on her knees, she looked up and grinned. "It had the same effect on me this morning."

"For Christ's sake, Belle, what did you find?" He was amazed that she'd been sitting on this new information all day!

She got up in a squat, hauling the safe out from the wall, and with a grunt, lifted it. "Let's go downstairs."

The fire safe was, at most, sixteen inches by just short of two feet, he guessed, and a little over seven, maybe eight inches high, and weighed at least thirty-five pounds. Its clamshell design with a metal band around the edge of the top side would probably have been extremely tamper-resistant if they had to try. He had no idea what it was made of, but the sticker on the bottom claimed it was resistant to three thousand degrees for two hours. Saylor wondered how long it took a typical house to burn to the ground.

The key was still in its slot. Opening it, they found several envelopes, some with legal return addresses, one plain and unmarked. Beneath these, a short stack of manila envelopes of varying thickness with simple handwritten numbered labels. Belle began to pull at the pile. Saylor put a hand out to stop her. "We don't have rubber gloves. Where's that box from before."

"Just a sec." He heard her bounce up the stairs, dangerously fast, then her break-neck return. She sat down beside him, tossed him the bag, and pulled on a pair of gloves. Fingers inserted in blue, she began again to sort through the contents of the safe. Lifting the stack of envelopes from an uneven bottom layer, she gasped. The lumps at the bottom of the stack were uncovered to be five bank-wrapped packets of twenties. The purple striped labels on each said each one was worth $2,000.

"Well," Belle said, "looks like there was adequate walking around money set aside for emergencies."

"They do say that in case of a storm, pack light and pack fast. I guess Mr. or Mrs. thought this would do it."

She said, "Let's start with the letters." She opened lawyer envelope number 1.

"Last Will and Testament of Eleanor Sands Lawrence." They read together out loud. Heads together, they skim read through the opening paragraph and its attests. In the case of Eleanor's death, all material, liquid, and invested assets were to be transferred to her daughter, Lindsey Hardin Lawrence. After the two brief pages of the will, there followed several pages of assets, and their locations: several banks in Florida and one in the Caymans. The short pile of paper proved Sheriff Pierson's statements of a family fortune approaching ten million dollars.

He reread the name aloud, Lindsey Hardin Lawrence. Eleanor had retained Lindsey's birth mother's family name as Lindsey's middle name. *Sandra Jane Hardin's lineage lives on in Lindsey. God, I only hope she's still alive.*

The next envelope was on the same par. Lightly yellowed with age, they found the earlier version of the Last Will and Testament of Eleanor Lawrence and Jeremy Aikens Lawrence. Reading it, in the case of the death or certified mental incapacitation of either, all assets were to be transferred to the other. In the case of the death of both, all assets went to Lindsey. Further language spoke of the condition for an establishment of power of attorney to Lindsey in the case of the death of either and mental incapacity of the other. "That's strange," Saylor said, "but not too usual."

Belle gave him a hard look, full of unknown meaning. She picked up the unmarked letter envelope. Its folded contents were less formal and included a cover page over the "Last Will and Testament of Lindsey Hardin Lawrence." The cover page, in a combination of cursive and block handwriting, read, "To the finders of this document, I've left a copy with our family attorney, Sheldon Hargreaves Esquire, for filing. Please seek his assistance. To my knowledge, except for the following, I know of no other relations to my parents to pass on their considerable assets.

"On hearing of her foreshortened life expectancy, my mother, Eleanor Sands Lawrence, explained to me that I was adopted almost immediately upon my birth to a young woman who had the terrible misfortune of dying from complications of childbirth. I only know that she was a student at the University of West Florida before she could no longer attend classes. She refused to tell the hospital staff any information leading to the baby's father. It is my understanding that he is ignorant of my existence.

"I will seek to discover his identity, however, should an accident occur, and I cannot reunite with my birth father. I direct Mr. Hargreaves to act on my behalf to direct inquiries, such as may be possible after the passing of time, to locate my birth father. Having no ill will toward an individual who, in all probability was not told of my birth, I hope he is found to be in good health. I, therefore, direct Mr. Hargreaves to seek this person's identity, and if he is found, to transfer four-fifths of my estate to him. The remaining estate shall be bequeathed to the Sacred Heart Hospital's endowment trust in Pensacola Florida. In the event that after a minimum of two year's due diligence search, no such trace should be found, then one hundred percent of these assets should be bequeathed to the Endowment Fund of Sacred Heart Hospital of Pensacola. Therefore..." and the remaining was the 'sound mind and body' formatted text usually found in an Internet-generated simple will. Attachments appeared to be copied lists of assets from her mother's will.

Belle had been holding the papers as they read together. She said, "I wonder if this is what their lawyer almost said but didn't." She set them down when his eyes lifted from the page, focusing on nothing. "I don't know what to think." She said, sotto voce.

"I don't know what to say." They shared a glance, looked down at the paper again. Saylor leaned back into the couch cushions. Hands behind his head, he closed his eyes.

"A. I show this pile of paper to the sheriff? Rise to suspect Number 1, or: B. I don't show it to the sheriff, find out that Hargreaves has already provided it to him and rise to suspect Number 1." He let the choices distill in the air, then. "Or. C. Let this stuff be discovered, by Pierson's crew or the FBI when they show up and we're the innocent recipient of the news."

Belle just stared. "But Jason, don't you get it? You might own all this." She waved a loose arm around to signify the house. But the meaning was all-inclusive of the Lawrence assets."

He took that in, eyes pained. "That, my dear, is a worst-case scenario. That would mean that somewhere out there, her body is waiting to be found. That sweet young girl has been used horribly and thrown away." He looked up, met her eyes. "Belle, I would not want to do anything with these papers except ignore them for now. I can't predict how Pierson would react. If I'm in jail, I can't continue to search. I could probably post bail. But the papers from here to Saskatchewan would crucify me."

He thought of the morning's discussion with the sheriff. "You remember the case of JonBenét Ramsey?"

"Yes. The kid."

"Yes, the kid. From the crime of the century. Do you think the parents did it? Or were materially connected to a cover-up?"

"Yeah, so does the rest of the country."

"Right. The network talking heads do what talking heads do. They hint, they drop innuendo, they suppose, they do everything but convict. I'd be the most hated man in the United States before the next news cycle dropped. JonBenét was killed on Christmas day, 1996. The Ramseys, in the following years, claimed innocence, defended their son from conjectured implication, and finally avoided prosecution for negligence. I don't know the State Attorney here, but I'm sure he wouldn't shy away from a podium that had six network microphones attached." He pressed the balls of his thumbs into his eye sockets. "I'm screwed six ways from Sunday if this becomes public knowledge."

"Jason?" She placed her hand on his knee.

He took a long inhale and exhale, then. "Yes?"

"Whatever you want to do, I want to help. I only knew her for a few months. Maybe three whole months if I checked, and she was a good kid that life handed a pile of problems. If she's in trouble somewhere, we need to help." His eyes were still closed, but he heard and felt a shudder from Belle. "If she's not, we still need to find her and put her to rest." She looked toward the glass wall and the thousand acres of swamp and wetland beyond. "I just can't think of her being out there, either way."

She had been sitting on the edge of her seat. He reached for her waist and pulled her close. "Thanks, just having someone to talk it through with is a help."

"You got it, Mister." She attempted a smile.

"I came over tonight, with the intention, the hope, of spending another wonderful night. Belle, I don't think I can. I don't ever think I will ever forget last night. But today has been one for the record books, not sure I can separate my head from all that's happened." He pulled her head in, kissed the top of her head. Nuzzled her, sniffed, taking in her scent. "Tap water? Really? Tap water?"

She pulled back, kissed him on the forehead, just ahead of the still swollen bruise. "Then, my friend, you'd better get moving."

20

Oil on the Water

The following morning, Jason Saylor, a possible heir to a small fortune and one of two people most likely to be charged with abduction with intent, found he could not write a coherent paragraph. He started several, tossed them into the magnetic ink dust pile. The nice thing about computers, you never saw the wastebasket full of pages with three of four lines on them. Or the ones with a chapter full of crap writing.

He pulled his Prius over to the backline of the RV park where he'd been told to stash his boat and trailer and hooked it up. Driving over the bay toward Apalachicola, he watched as a squadron of pelicans in single-file formation headed the opposite direction. They used the wind deflected from the concrete sidewalls of the bridge for lift. They got a free ride for most of the several-mile trip from Apalachicola to Eastpoint. He wished for that freedom, for a life so simple that his biggest issue was breakfast. At the end of Bluff Road, he launched at the 'new' Abercrombie boat landing, having no idea who the city or county father was for whom it had been named. Twenty years gone leaves a lot of holes in your sense of place. It only took a few minutes to get downriver to the Lawrence dock. Tying up, he resisted a few guilty thoughts that the house and land might go to him via some labyrinthine path.

He called out to Sugar at least three times before the animal ceased its objection. He saw the wag, the smiling eyes. Sugar was probably a good dog. Although he knew that most German Shepherds were softies, he wasn't going to test her right now. He stood on the dock, enjoying the sun on his head and shoulders. Not hot yet. With April moving toward May, that would not last long. Only a hint of wind ruffled the water on the far side of the river. Brown glass slid under the dock so smoothly he couldn't detect any ripple. Lost in a reverie, an internal discussion of the multiple outcomes possible. Their branching paths. The lawyer, a longtime friend of the family, manager of the family trust. Hmm, trust? Or not to trust?

Ah, The Trust. A lawyer could make a lot of money managing a trust. Manage one-third of ten million dollars right into his personal bank account. It might be a good idea to hand the locked safe over to the sheriff claiming no knowledge at all of its locked-away contents.

He didn't realize he'd been noticing them again, but at fairly regular intervals, thin circles of petroleum-stained water slid under the dock as the river passed by on the way to the Gulf. It made him angry. The estuary, he knew, was the breeding ground for millions of shrimp, mullet, trout, grouper, reds, cobia, crab, sea bass, even sturgeon. None of them would benefit from oil pollution. He looked upstream, remembering the oil stains from a few days ago. Other than a few of the neighbor's docks, he couldn't see any source. The slicks were small, five to eight inches in diameter. Those that meandered near one of the square dock posts beneath him were shredded by the eddies. Others continued to thin out in an effervescent display in a myriad of rainbows. He reconnected the gas line, cast off, and followed the line of shimmering dots upstream. Moving slowly against the river, he found himself back at the boat ramp. Someone had offended Mr. Abercrombie's memory. Something down there was leaking oil.

The land on either side of the river was bond paper flat. Generally, in this part of the estuary, only dredge piles left behind by the Corps of Engineers rose more than a few feet above the river. The 'bluff' at the end of Bluff road was an exception and rose to maybe four feet above the river's normal level at high tide.

But the river had been hauling sand to the estuary and beyond for eons. He had no idea how deep it might be. Could he dive and find an oil can in this brown stew? Could he feel for it with his toes? How far upstream would it be from the spot they popped to the surface. He decided to cut the offender some slack. An oil can might have been left on a trailer as someone went to retrieve their boat or rolled off a boat. But what if it was something bigger, a lost engine off a transom? Inspiration grew from his thoughts. He remembered the fish finder transponder installed on the transom. All he had to do was plug the unit in. The display unit was still in its box in the trunk of the Prius, just downriver. This was good, he had a diversion from the larger problems of his day. A simple problem to solve, and he had the means to solve it.

In less than fifteen minutes, he'd been back down to the house, shared a few thoughts with Sugar, and was back up the river watching the bottom profile. It was simple to line up with the dotted line of oil drops, and he began his run. He watched the trace line closely as he moved at less than a mile an hour against a two-mile-per-hour current that was slowing in response to an incoming tide in the bay. The depths tracked out in an orange bottom line: twelve feet, eleven, twelve, a sharp edge at eleven, must be the end of the dredged area, then abruptly, six and a half, a few feet later, back to eleven. He tried the run again, drifting down on an idled throttle and got the same result with the apparent bump at seven-foot depth. Upstream again on his first track. Lining up his bow cleat on a leaning sweetgum upstream, he again recorded a bump at a depth of five and a half. Drifting back over it again, he got a different result, about six. By this fourth pass, he'd glanced ashore and lined the apparent center of the blip to be on a line with a stained spot on the boat ramp's concrete. Easy to track and remember. That stain was maybe two car lengths from the downstream launching pier.

He made his next pass over the anomalous lump parallel to the finger pier. Again, the orange trace appeared on the small color screen. "Holy Sweet Mother of God." Ten years of Catholic Sunday school, most of them with catechism training, and all he had left of his faith was profanity. It had served him well in times of stress. He set the fish finder to record mode. He'd be able to plug the unit into a USB on his laptop and print out the result. He guided himself slowly and canting against the current, as straight as he could on the alignment of the stained apron. "Jesus, no! Please no." The trace, presenting the squiggled deviations common to the machines, still clearly outlined the profile of a car, most likely a small compact.

He'd let his throttle loose and drifted below the Lawrence dock before he bothered to look up. Tapping a few menu buttons saved the trace to memory. He unplugged the unit and stowed it away. Motor off and tied up, he looked upstream again. The small oil slick stains continued to drift under the dock. *No choice, I have to call the sheriff.*

21

9-1-1

But Saylor was conflicted. Call 911? Call anonymously? Send an email? Leave a note on the tip line? They could have an IT guy there clever enough to track IP addresses. His would lead to Houston, and Pierson's minions would be knocking on his door in five minutes. Thinking about it, even his flip-phone's Austin area code would lead back to him. How many Texans were in Apalachicola?

He was still at Belle's, or Lindsey's, or maybe he should think of it as 'the Lawrence House,' or maybe the 'river house.' He couldn't decide what to do next. He was convinced a car was just beyond the two launching piers that flanked the generously wide boat ramp. Fact: Lindsey's boat and car were both missing. Fact: she couldn't have relocated both without help. If someone else did, they would have needed help to get rid of both car and boat.

Conjecture: if the car in the river was hers, would she be found, or would her corpse be found? Would the boat have been used to remove her from wherever she'd been taken? His eyes moved back out over the placid ochre waters of the Apalachicola. There were a hundred little feeder creeks between the landing and the Georgia line and probably twenty more good hidey-holes in the estuary's feeder channels.

He walked back over to the dock. A quick glance upriver said whatever was down there was still leaching oil. He bent to look at the weathered planks again. It would be evident that the dock had seen little use for several years. But Lindsey must have used it, or the trailer wouldn't be sitting in overgrown grass. The scrape marks on the moldy dock clearly told that something, some package, or other large object had been dragged toward the river. Maybe Lindsey's limp body had been dragged across these boards. He stood, head back but with his eyes closed to the sun, hands on the back of his head. "Dammit all!"

He pulled out his phone and dialed 911 dispatch. Briefly and matter-of-factly, he related his finding. He suggested that a dive team be dispatched and added, probably a wrecker service. Swallowing resignation, he drove up to the boat ramp. First to arrive on scene were two green and white patrol cars. Three officers in total. He approached, holding a fixed neutral smile. At least, that was what he hoped he presented. He recognized Officer One from the traffic stop. Officer One recognized him. This time, Jason could read the name tag. Burgraff, Officer Burgraff.

"Morning, Officer."

"Are you the one that called in to dispatch?"

"Yessir."

"You wanna explain what you found? Why you called?"

Saylor went over the sequence, wishing they were standing in the shade. He hadn't put on sunglasses earlier, the morning had morphed into afternoon, and it was hot on the asphalt. He closed with, "It has a recording feature from the transducer that lets you store the plot. I can print it out for you if you'd like."

"We can get to that if needed. For now—" Officer Burgraff looked over his shoulder at the sound of an approaching wrecker. He turned back to Saylor. "For now. Where'd you say you think this vehicle is?"

"Follow me." Saylor walked over to the oil stain he'd seen on the ramp, sighted parallel to the launching pier, and pointed. "It's out there, maybe twenty feet beyond the end of the pier."

"You mind hanging around?"

"No."

"The sheriff will be here in a bit. I'm sure he'll be wanting to talk to you."

"I'm sure he will." Saylor looked longingly at a shaded portion of the pier. "Mind if I sit over there, out of the way?" He got a nod and removed himself from the center of attention. The wrecker was told to turn off his lights and stand by. While they all waited for a dive crew to appear, he considered calling Belle at the store, but thought better of it. Sooner than he'd expected, a little over an hour since his first call, a yellow crew truck with a boat rescue logo drove up. Their grill flashed pulsing yellow. The light turned off, and two men in swim trunks and neon yellow long-sleeve BoaT RescuE shirts discussed the location.

He needed to touch base, to communicate with Belle. He sent a text, hoping it wouldn't put too great a kink in her afternoon. [Q? Remind me what color car did Lindsey have?] A few minutes later, his phone buzzed, [honda, civic, silver], then [everthing OK?]. He sent back two thumbs up. Then, [I'm good], and a kissy face.

One of the divers put on a thin neoprene wetsuit jacket, grabbed a pair of fins, and came over to sit beside Saylor. It was a convenient location because the ramp to deck height was comfortable. With the incoming tide beginning to back the river, the water level had risen to just beyond Saylor's position. He spoke to one of the divers, "Good for you, the river's slacking."

The diver looked up, nodded, grunting as he pulled on his flippers. "Yeah, glad it's not full low tide. This ramp can be a bitch when there's a four-mile-an-hour cross current."

"You've done this before?"

The diver just grimaced. "Too many times." He spit into his mask, wetting down the glass, and fitted it over his face. No snorkel. It was a shallow water dive.

Saylor pointed again for the diver's benefit. "Should be about there just beyond the pier. With the river slowing, you might be able to see oil spots on the surface."

"Got it, thanks." The diver backed into the water, heels first, his flippers slapping the concrete. Then, thigh deep, he flopped backward and swam. He was nearly dragged under the pier before he countered the current. He turned, took his bearings, and dove again, trailing bubbles. The diver's head bobbed to the surface about twenty yards farther out. Facing the small crowd on the ramp, he flashed a thumbs up. "Yep," he shouted, "There's a car here." He ducked his head under and began to pull for shore.

The afternoon wore on. The tow cable was pulled out and prepared. The two divers suited for SCUBA and pulled the hook into the brown current. Saylor's official duty was restricted to wait here for the sheriff, but he was fascinated to watch the divers and wrecker driver quickly jell into a recovery team. They'd done this before. At the same time, he dreaded what they might pull out of the river. The two patrol cars had been moved to block the driveway to the frustration of a few would-be afternoon fishermen. Yellow crime scene tape was strung across the gap they couldn't block. By early afternoon, the tow truck's winch began to whine. The cable tightened, snapped taut, and the take-up reel started to move whatever was at the other end. Something shifted on the reel and the cable crackled, sounding like the snap of two lightsabers.

Across the river, movement. An osprey swooped down, skimming. Its wings gaining lift from ground effect. Talons forward, then down. A furious down swoop of wings and it was off, a shining fish body fighting its last fight. Back at the landing, everything stopped moving except the cable. Deputies stood staring. The incrementally gathered crowd at the yellow tape barrier stopped their head bobbing. A row of head high cell phones recorded the proceedings. The winch ground on, the dripping cable inched out of the water. A surface boil, an eddy, not there before grew on the river surface. A small v-wave grew, spreading downstream from the disturbance. A lump rose, sparkling wet in the midday sun, and moved toward the shoreline with the menace of a beast from the deep. He remembered to breathe.

The emerging monster appeared to shift its approach in jerks as its wheels resisted the angle of the cable. A now recognizable roofline of a car grew. A small bow wave tumbled on the upstream side. Brown water spilled from the downstream side window. Silt had little purchase on sheet metal and glass, and as soon as the trunk emerged, he knew. Silver. The wheels wanted to guide the car in a circle to the left, the cable corrected in jerks toward the center. What had probably taken less than three minutes overall felt like thirty. He wished he could have been anywhere else, to simply get the news delivered. Driver's seat, trunk? Was she in there at all? Why would someone be so stupid as to stash a car here? They weren't going to be telling him. He'd know if they called for the Medical Examiner that there was a body in the car. If Lindsey was in the car.

Pierson arrived, no siren. The response command vehicle had arrived moments earlier. A big, military bearing vehicle that said, by its shape and massive construction, that whoever was in charge was nearby. Sheriff Pierson walked up, casually interested in the drama playing out on the boat ramp, startling Saylor at his approach.

He'd been keyed up, expectant. Without prompting, Saylor described the entire sequence. Oil spots on the water. The depth runs with the fish finder—the long, soul-twisting wait for the preparations and the emergence of the silver Honda from the river. They stood, shoulder to shoulder, watching the slow-moving drama.

Opening the doors required a Slim Jim. The electric door lock mechanism had shorted out. A mullet flopped in the footwell of the back seat. Some tension-relieving laughter among the crew. Nothing to see but brown water. Her purse, with keys and wallet, was found in the console. A soggy sweater, leftover from cooler weather, was pulled from the back seat, tagged, and bagged. They were sitting now on the back tailgate of the command vehicle. The harsh grinding noise of the metal saw working at the trunk was too distracting. He found Pierson to be a good listener. As a reporter, he could appreciate that.

Officer Mallory approached. "Sir, there's no body in the car." He'd said no body with no inflection, hard to distinguish nobody from no body. Something tight in Saylor's neck released. His ribs seemed to lack the ability to hold up his frame. His relief was palpable, observable. He and Pierson shared a look. He thought, he understood, that Pierson understood, that it was genuine relief, that maybe Pierson needed to go look for the jilted wannabe boyfriend. He left as the Honda was being loaded onto the flatbed wrecker, wrung dry, but relieved.

22

Fully Involved

Later, at a slightly upscale upstairs restaurant, Saylor described the entire sequence: oil spots on the water, depth runs with the fish finder, the long, terrible wait for the preparations, and the emergence of the silver Honda from the river. Since the door mechanisms were locked or ruined, opening the doors required a Slim Jim, a standard burglar tool and indispensable tool for law enforcement. Nothing to see but brown water. Her purse with keys and wallet, a gooey mess in the console, and a soggy mass in the back seat that turned out to be a sweater.

He continued, reliving his personal terror. Doors opened, one by one with careful forensic determination not to spill or spoil evidence, the flopping mullet. The meticulous photography of every detail, anything more important than errant candy wrappers was labeled and bagged. The trunk took a while. He described it carefully. Not jumping to the end. "They brought out this huge saw. Like a Skilsaw only its bigger and meaner cousin. Sparks flying, the shriek of that blade on metal. And me sitting there parboiling in the afternoon sun. Not allowed to leave, not wanting to leave."

She urged him on. He was a writer. He liked words and storytelling. "And? They got it open."

"Yes, of course. Sorry, I got caught up in it. They opened up this square hole and as the last bit of metal fell away, the trunk just popped open a few inches."

"And Jesus, Jason. What?"

"Nothing. A spare tire, tire changing tools. All of us, the sheriff, his deputies, one of the boys in blue from Apalach, the EMTs, all of us felt this wave of relief. NO one wanted to find her in there. Too many movies."

"What did the Sheriff say?"

"Pierson had a lot to say. I went over the chronology again. How did I happen to find the car, from beginning to end? He wanted to know why I was on the dock in the first place. So, he knows about us. He disapproves. I think he disapproves of everything." Saylor took a sip of iced tea. "I told him we were getting to know each other. Kind of hinting the obvious without saying the obvious."

"You embarrassed about me?"

"No! It's a guy thing. A new relationship, his suspicion about every damned thing. No, Belle, I am not embarrassed by or about you." He held up the nearly empty tea glass in a toast. "If anything, lucky. I'm damned lucky."

"Lucky, huh?" Her ear-to-ear smile lit up her face, dimpled chin to arched eyebrows. "I'll take that."

They made tentative plans, weather permitting, to go to the beach. Act like tourists, safe enough to be seen together anymore, she'd said. Anyone who knew her from before would have shared her business with anyone else from the old days. He realized he really didn't know her history. Little more than that of her family—estranged mother and disgusting stepfather.

"That S-O-B had porn fantasies of step-dad, step-daughter fun and games."

He grimaced at the image. His own family had been on the margins of dysfunctional but hadn't lowered itself that low. "I can't imagine Belle. Sorry."

She twirled a deep-fried golden shrimp on her fork in a lazy circle. "Hey, you got nothing to be sorry about. He, he who shall remain nameless, is a real piece of shit and he'll never put a shine on that in my eyes."

"He ever try anything? Beside staring?"

She went still, blinked. "At this point, I'll just say if he ever does again, he'll be dead within a week, and I know he knows that."

He was on the verge of saying I'm sorry again, caught himself. He did feel sorry for the loneliness that the loss of family can bring. He couldn't remember the last time his mother had called from Austin. Maybe Christmas. He'd called to check in when he got situated at the campground. For Belle to have a home here in town that she couldn't or wouldn't go to seemed worse. "What about your friends, your gal pals?"

She had just popped another shrimp in. Ill-timed for a response. She smiled through the chew. "When you stay single, when you don't have kids, when you don't go to church, it's amazing how much those people fade away. Or," fast eye roll, "I faded off their lists. I—" She waited for the words to formulate in the proper order. The right ones. "I sometimes tend to piss people off."

"What's your main talent at pissing people off."

"Hmm, you know, just being honest, candid, maaaaybeee just a little too candid?" She said it as a question. "It's probably gotten me checked off a list or two." She shrugged a who-cares shrug, grinned, and took a bite of hush puppy dipped in tartar sauce.

"And this makes you a good candidate for a shopkeeper? Retail sales?" He caught himself smiling, perhaps at her expense, and tried to stop the slow spread of a smile.

"Those are strangers. I get some repeat customers who love the place. Folks who actually own those beach houses and want the art or shell collections, the corals. Shit, all the crap we sell to create some kind of beach resort or down-home atmosphere in those rentals. But mostly my customers are strangers, the weeklies that want some trinkets to remember the vacation before their two-day drive back to Michigan." A wave of her free hand swept in the small downtown area's few city blocks. "This town would not be sustainable if it didn't have all those weeklies." After a pause for reflection, "and I don't have to be friends with them, just friendly."

Saylor knew the distinction. Nodded understanding. "No boyfriends from the past haunting you? One that got away?"

"Come on, Jason. Can we just enjoy dinner?"

It came out a little too hard. He could see the regret for the harsh response in her down-turned eyes. He had interviewed far too many sources for stories not to have become a reader of emotional facial response. "Forgive me. I shouldn't be digging up your past."

"Diggin? You brought out the backhoe." Something had changed there, just at that moment. Her head tilted slightly to the left, mouth pursed. Then, "But I need to tell you." Her breathing sped up to short puffs. She'd set her fork down, both hands were in her lap. In the pause, he became intensely aware of the buzzing of a bug-light zapping the season's first mosquitoes near the end of the restaurant's open-air deck. "There was a guy. Almost *the* guy. But he left." She seemed on the edge of letting something out that should be kept in.

"You can save it, save it for some safe time. It's OK." He reached across the table, a symbolic gesture at least.

She pulled a hand from her lap and grasped his thumb. Before she spoke, she was squeezing it with unconscious intensity. "I had an abortion." Her eyes were rimming with emotion. Sadness, regret, shame?

"God, that must have been a hard choice." He couldn't imagine. "And I'm not judging, right? Totally your choice."

"At the time, it was the only choice, for me. This town doesn't see it that way. Between the half that's Catholic and the other half that's Baptist or Methodist, most of them are Saturday night assholes and Sunday morning Christians. You don't get much slack cut around here." Her small hand lightened up on the pressure on his thumb. "Brent was a good guy, I did love him then, still hope he and his have a good life." She rolled her eyes to the ceiling fan. "Another batch of friends stayed with him and checked me off their lists."

She peered at him like she was re-appraising. Mapping his features, reading his eyes for content. "I've known you for a week. I feel I can trust you. I don't feel that about a whole lot of people and not many in this town. To them, I'm a cast out. Cast off. Yeah, she's from here, but not quite right, not quite good enough, or doesn't come to our church so, so..." A short breath. "Jason, can I trust you? I felt like I could when I called you back into the store last week. I did need help and I was drawing a blank on who I could trust."

He reached across and took her hand in both of his. "Belle, there's nothing you've said, shared, that makes me think anything less of you. I know it's early for us. But I like us. If you don't mind being with someone ten years older..." He didn't know why he dropped the time bomb. "Well, I like being with you. I'll leave room for some time in the future when we have more than dinner each night." He didn't want to say a lot more just yet, and life was just complicated right now.

"And there's a thing. I need to see if I can find out what's happened to Lindsey, so I don't go to jail for one thing, and—" He swallowed hard, felt the emotional block seal off his throat before he could get the next word to form. He waited a breath. "—to have found out that I have a daughter. That she may be dead. That she might be held somewhere for someone's perverted pleasure." He closed his eyes, felt the pressure of her other hand on his. "Belle, I'm extremely happy to promise you at least dinner, every night, maybe popcorn, maybe more. But at least that."

Jason Saylor did not sleep well. His dinner date with Belle had gone well. He'd been invited to the River House, they'd begun to call it that, but he knew he needed to write. To at least act like he was writing. Their goodnight kiss in the restaurant's oyster-shell parking lot had come close to changing his mind. There were times he felt like a kid again. That first rush of emotion on becoming emotionally connected.

But that rush of elation, good cheer, and plain horny-minded attraction wasn't the cause of his sleepless turning and discomfort. The terrors of the day imposed on the night. He imagined a sodden, fish-abused corpse in the driver's seat or worse. Lindsey. Tied, gagged, and rotten in the trunk. Too many crime series directors had been successful at horrifying their audiences. It wasn't hard to imagine. It was hard to turn off the thoughts. Had she been fed to the gators upriver? Was she still alive in some hell on earth?

At dawn, he found himself at his dinette, laptop cracked open. Coffee fresh and hot, a toasted and buttered bagel at hand. He looked beyond the laptop at the brightening grays of an overcast morning across the highway. He considered a morning swim. No, stop distracting yourself. Andie Jackson has got to move toward getting close to her next assigned kill. He opened a file, and gave it a toss-away title, Coffee Shop. It would get deleted, replaced with a number, but it helped him keep track.

Coffee Shop - 4th rewrite

Jackson looked up from her laptop's keyboard, hoping her glance through the coffee shop's window would be mistaken for a writer's pause. At least a third of the patrons were students or others with laptops, coffee, and pastry. She was, she assumed, the only professional killer among them. Her current assignment sat facing her direction at an outside cafe table. The scalloped edges of a green and white striped table umbrella shifted occasionally, listless in a light afternoon breeze. The Louisiana sky beyond was discolored by the bronze-tinted storefront. Just a bit of the blue bridge's upper works poked unexpectedly above the line of two-story storefronts across the street. The bridge, she thought, is a movie director's godsend. Gives instant place recognition if the shabby French Colonial storefronts don't do it.

The young woman looked to be having a good afternoon, flipping through a package of photographs. Jackson smiled to herself. Everyone's last afternoon on the planet should be a good one. Pleasant memories, taking a second look at some past time with friends or family. What was she thinking? Who had she shared those moments with? A lover, friends, family? Would that family grieve? Probably. Would they grieve, even with the knowledge of what she had done and what she intended to do? If they knew of the horrors she had planned for the evening, and the agony inflicted on the eighty thousand fans at the football game?

From her seat in the coffee shop, Jackson couldn't see the insect that caused her target du jour to wave at the air, flipping her long straight ebony hair in a swish. Really an elegant neck, she mused. Jackson caught the flash of a gold earring before the hair settled. Margot was now packing the photographs into a neat rectangle. She'd straightened, flexed her spine—time to go.

Jackson casually closed her laptop, took a sip of the cold coffee, and slipped the laptop into her shoulder bag. She didn't have enough time to do the right thing: put away the uneaten bagel, toss the cup. Her target was on the move, so she moved. Jackson was outside now and following. Margot's yellow silk blouse and skin-tight jeans were hard to miss. The hips, five car lengths ahead, wiggled just so as she walked on low-rise heels. Under different circumstances, she'd be happy to get to know the owner of those hips much better. Too bad it had to go down this way. Her burner phone buzzed twice, incoming. She ignored it. She had, at minimum, to ID the vehicle, and, if possible, play the final hand. Yellow blouse turned at the corner and moved toward a silver Honda parked beside the street., Attached in the next space back, a Boston Whaler on its trailer.

She stopped as if to look at an email or text message. Looking over the phone, she took in as many details as she could. Silver Civic, at least ten years old, appears to be heavy on its rear axles. Loaded with what? The tires on the trailer looked like they were struggling with their load. She sauntered casually foreword, pecking uselessly at the phone. Bundled and secured in front of the center console, were six silver canisters. Diving tanks, plus two five-gallon metal gas cans. A row of four more diving tanks was strapped in a line across the back seat. Looked like the materials for an extended SCUBA outing. Inside the tanks, she knew, was enough gas to infect eighty thousand fans, Saints and Patriots, with the deadly virus. Were the team names part of the message? Or was the venue just convenient?

Not today, missy, not tomorrow. Her eyes narrowed with solemn purpose. She slipped the phone back in her purse and stepped in front of the Honda, looking left and right, confusion on her face. She appeared to notice yellow blouse sitting in the driver's seat. Oh, happy day! She twirled a hand in a rotating motion, asking to lower the window. A flash of frustration crossed Margot's truly beautiful Eurasian features.

Jackson leaned in. "Excuse me, can you help me out?" Her left hand came out of the purse, now holding her favorite neutralizer. The pistol was poised over yellow blouse's neck before her target had a chance to look surprised. When Margot looked up into Jackson's eyes in rising panic, Jackson just smiled and said quietly, Tough shit, bitch, happy trails." and fired the silenced 9mm into her left jugular. Too bad about the yellow blouse, those stains were never coming out. Straightening, appearing to thank the driver, Jackson stepped out and across the street as her partner pulled up in a black Suburban. She called out to the front seat. "It's done, Javier. It's over. Tell the janitors to be careful. There are nine canisters of gas in the boat and probably a lot more in the trunk." She leaned forward, catching his eye in the rear-view mirror. "Can you find us a bar? I need a drink."

Javier held her glance in the mirror. "Are you kidding? This is New Orleans."

◇ ◇ ◇ ◇ ◇

Saylor scrolled up, no red squiggles pointing out misspellings. He scanned for dropped hyphens. He was not a perfect typist. Not even close. But he had a habit of correcting as he went. He had the honesty to know there would still be typos even if he went back two, maybe three times in the rewrites. Typical first run clean-ups included a visual at least a few days after writing a scene or chapter. Then run it through one or two grammar checkers, then the first manuscript hard copy for a read-through. Somehow, final editing on-screen just didn't work. And he kept adding things that eventually would need those other editing stages. That's why he paid an editor to clean up. He reread it. Something was standing out that he'd missed. Was that Javier or Xavier in the earlier chapter? He noted that he'd gratuitously made yellow blouse's car a silver Honda, a Civic no less. *What's with that?* Boston Whaler? He punched up Belle's contact and tapped the phone icon.

"Belle, remind me what kind of boat Lindsey had?"

Groggy with sleep, "And good morning to you too!"

"Oh man, it's still early. Sorry."

"No, that's not it. I've showered and had coffee. Not in that order. It's just that, well, I enjoyed our night last night and was having happy thoughts. Then you call up, all Mr. Business, about a boat."

"Sorry to be a Debbie Downer. I was up early writing, and something occurred to me. I was using a scene, a scenario that I was actually in, as the basis for a scene in the book. The first time I saw Lindsey sitting outside a coffee shop, I remember walking past her as she was looking at pictures. On the way to my car, I noticed a boat on a trailer in the parking lot. Noticed only because it's a very congested parking lot. The cars park on a diagonal, so if the driver with a trailer in tow found a space with an open one in front of it, they'd fit. But it would be hell to pay to get out because you'd be going the wrong way if you pulled forward, and it would be virtually impossible to back out of a space like that."

"You remember all that?"

"Well, it came back to me as I was typing. I'm not saying it was *her* car and trailer. But it got me thinking about the boat. It was a Boston Whaler. I remember that because we used to cruise the river on an old beat-up one when we were kids. They never seem to wear out." He caught that he had just used the 'we' pronoun. An image flashed of Patrick Wills' beaming face in the sunshine, his longish hair flying in the wind. Saylor had been in the bow, for ballast, the boat bouncing lightly on full plane at their Evinrude's top speed as they wound through the many finger channels at the mouth of the river. He came back to the present. "Both her car and truck went missing, the car's been found. The boat is still missing. Do you by any chance remember what kind?"

"Heck if I know. I think it was a Whaler. Yeah wait, there's a thin red line around the top below the rub rail. It said Boston Whaler right about the middle. Before that last trip with Lindsey, El used to take short sundown cruises. She took me a coupla times. Sometimes up the river. One afternoon, a slow day at the shop, we went all the way around the Johnson Creek loop. Twice we went downriver for seafood at the Oyster Bar." She paused, real pain evident in her eyes. "I miss that lady. Real good people."

"I know, Belle. It's tough to lose quality people."

"If you need the hull number, I think the registration for it and the trailer are in one of those manila envelopes in the safe."

"Great, might not come to that."

"Hey, I got to be going. Things to do at the shop before I open."

"See you tonight."

He almost tossed a 'love you' into the closing. "See ya." He wasn't sure what he thought, too soon for love? Not too soon for infatuation, surely. Not too soon to feel...*what's that fireman's phrase for a house afire?* Fully involved. *Yeah, I'm fully involved.*

23

Loose Threads

Gotta tie up the loose threads. What else? Friends. She had to have friends. Saylor gave himself a mental head slap. Homer Simpson's "Doh!" played itself out. He'd been gone nearly twenty years. He'd forgotten to focus on Lindsey's friend network. Belle had, for all intents, disenfranchised herself, but even with a few casual contacts remaining, she would have had few contacts ten years her junior. But as far as he knew from the papers, Lindsey was a popular girl and would have a friend group, possibly a clique of besties, frantic for her condition. Time to play the reporter card.

Facebook, he thought, that's for the older-than-dirts. Snapchat and MeWe were out there. He'd gotten a few invites to join. Those had been from thirty- and forty-somethings, so probably not a platform for high schoolers. Although there might be something newer, he knew some kids still used Snapchat. He signed up for it and logged in, using his own persona, but not his personal phone. He used the old flip phone the Chronicle had issued years ago. Gonna act like a reporter, be a reporter. He immediately found that there was not a Lindsey Lawrence. *Crap! How do you find people?* Do I have to find a YouTube video to figure out how to work Snapchat? He told himself, *"Go old school 'till you can't."*

His subscription to yearbooks.com was still active, so he pulled up their website. As soon as he'd zeroed in on the yearbook, named the *Echo,* he realized. No need! There was a yearbook in Lindsey's room at the River House. He'd seen the spine and the year and Franklin County High School in a collection of larger format books on her shelf. Belle had done the search for signs of the reason for her disappearance. This hadn't seemed pertinent then. But it could surely find her friends. He stopped for lunch and a diet coke at the gas station on the point. The community was called Eastpoint. The *'point'* was the intersection of Hwy 98 and Patton Drive, a small feeder road that many used to shortcut the distance to Hwy 300, the road to the St. George Island bridge. As usual, his get-it-and-go lunch was finger-licking good, and his car was freshly bathed in the aromas of deep-fried chicken fingers and potato wedges. He crossed the Gorrie Bridge into Apalachicola, noting for the first time that the huge bird roost power line stanchions had been replaced by towering monopoles as the line crossed the river and turned north through town. *What else has changed since I've been gone?*

He pulled up in front of the History House and parked. Out of habit and a reasonable case of paranoia, he checked in all directions for patrol cars. *Am I still being watched, surveilled?* The overhead silver bell announced his entry. Belle looked up from the counter. She was helping a sunburned woman in a sleeveless, tailored top and shorts that would have retained the designer's intended chic if the wearer could lose forty-five pounds. He had to wonder about these people. They've already toasted themselves to a ruddy bronze or beyond, and they still tempt the sun god, aka, cancer, to eat their flesh. He slid down a side aisle that boasted a collection of exquisite injection molded and painted copies of small salamanders, newts, and frogs. As he took in the entire display, he realized it was a themed section. Everything reptile was here except snakes. If salamander was to be your motif, the History House, Decor and More had you covered. He looked up as the door ringer peeled the exit of the sun-worshiper.

Belle called to him as he turned. "Hey, mister. What can I do for you?"

"Depends on whether you lock the door or not."

Both hands on her hips, she adopted a Mae West come-on pose. "Hmm. Let me think about that." One finger went to her lips. She licked it, slow and wet. "Mr. I'm sorry, but I don't close for lunch for another thirty minutes.

"You tempt me, madam." He made a show of looking at his watch, looked up, rueful. "You truly do."

"So, why are you here? Aren't you deep-diving into the history of Lindsey Lawrence?"

"Yes, but I need to research her yearbook. I was going to do that online, scan for pictures of her and friends, then I realized there's one in her bedroom. I noticed it the other night when we were first crossing the line into serious 'who done it' mode. So, I need the keys to the house."

She tossed the keys to him, sniffed, furrowed her brows together. "You're eating that deep-fried crap at the point again?"

"Guilty as charged, your honor."

Minutes later, he pulled into the shade of the elevated River House. His eyes fell on the empty trailer by the shed. No loose threads. He walked over to the shed and found a rusted lock hanging loose on the hasp. The shank was lined up with the lock but not pushed home. Opening the door, nothing of interest. The usual lawn tools. A riding mower, two red plastic gas cans. One had its OSHA safety valve sawed off. *Good job*, he thought, *a usable gas can.* He closed the door and walked through tall grass over to the trailer. Current registration on the tag. He hadn't paid any attention really to the one in the coffee shop parking lot. This one was about the right size. The lawn area looked as if it had not been mowed since growing season took off in late February. This was late April. Split centipede seed tops were already forming. He looked down at a tire and spotting a bare spot near the far side tire, then looked over the frame at the tire closest. A tire print, easily identifiable by a curve-sided rectangle with dead grass stems. New shoots were invading the brown zone where it had been parked previously.

The trailer tongue wasn't bolted to anything, although a hitch coupler lock was fastened to it. Smart again. He lifted the tongue and pulled. The trailer moved forward about two feet. Beneath the most recent imprint, blanched yellow grass stems. Not dead brown. Conclusion: it had been moved at least once since winter. It could have been Lindsey's in the Tallahassee parking lot. *Significant?* He blew out a puff of exasperation. This *could* have been the trailer under the boat in the parking lot. It wasn't an imagined scene. It was a memory he'd used to concoct the Andie Jackson scenario. That was easily six weeks ago or so. At that time, Lindsey was in Apalachicola, learning the ropes at the family store. *Why were the boat and trailer towed two hours away? Was that important?*

He looked out across the river, noted a dark gray bottom on a rack of boiling cumulus clouds. He climbed the stairs to the first floor and headed to Lindsey's room. The annual was there, actually, two of them; junior and senior yearbooks of the Echo. He flipped through the senior yearbook first and found her staged, coiffed photo. She was beautiful beyond her years. But the innocence in her face told him that, as an actress, she could have played someone aging through fourteen to twenty-four. No doubt, more than one of her classmates had lost his heart over this one.

Looking at her picture, he had a temporal life-shock. Lindsey could have passed as a double for Sandra Hardin, her mother. Saylor's good friend in high school, also a graduate of Franklin County High, could have had her picture pasted in here with the only difference being the shape of the collar and the hairdo. He looked up at the miles of sawgrass beyond. "God Almighty," he said aloud, "I don't talk to you much anymore. IF she's alive, look out for her while I track her down." His fingertips tracked to his chin, but he stopped short of signing the cross on his chest. That habit had died a long time ago.

He took the book out to the porch and settled into one of the deck chairs. He stared with some humor at the inside cover. It was plastered with scrawled good wishes from a dozen friends. He pulled his phone and began taking pictures of each page. Cloud shadow passed overhead, making it easier to see his screen. Good enough shots for examining on his laptop later. He continued to flip through the pages. Nothing familiar except the closeups. The school was new to him. Saylor had gone to the old white concrete two-story building in Apalach. This new structure had been built on dredged fill to avoid storm surges. It had no character. Maybe, he thought, it would develop, but the thing was a collection of pods attached by covered walkways. Gone were the echoes of leather on linoleum after a late afternoon session on the practice field. He felt a sense of loss of time and history irretrievable.

He kept turning pages and taking pictures. Many of the entries were freehand scrawls, inane shout-outs from the class clowns. Some ended with the writer's Instagram or Snapchat tag or email. *Tags, that's it. People don't use names on Snapchat, they use tags, or is it handles?* People who wanted to stay in touch provided their handles. One inscription caught his eye. It was scrawled in a barely legible cursive in the open sky background to a group of four girls clustered together, arms intertwined behind each other's shoulders. Lindsey, grinning in profile, looking at the other three. The three dead-eye focused on the camera lens—*four very attractive kids. The pretty girls always hang together!* He closed in on the inscription and snapped its picture.

"Lindsey, be sweet. I know you'll be the center of whatever crowd you find up at FSU. Stay smart, stay cool, stay loose. (not that loose! Ha hah!) Love ya forever. #JenJen0303." That, he supposed, was the tag or handle, or whatever they were called now on the social platforms, of one of the four names in the photograph, that would be Jennifer Stovell. He opened his phone, did a White Pages name search for Jennifer Stovell, Apalachicola. "No entry found." He tried again, Jennifer Stovell, Florida. Two hits, one in Lady Lake, Florida, 74. The other Gainesville, Florida, 19. Bingo. Miss Jennifer Stovell is at the University of Florida.

No point in stopping with one success. He looked at the phone's capture of the picture to see that he also had the other two girls' names. Marcie Helms and Aida Granger. Backtrack. He went back to the Senior photos section. These two were on the same page, same row. Next to Aida's in blue ink, a pair of linked hearts and "Class of '20 Rocks! Aida." At the end of the row, Marcie's name had more white space. In a tiny block print, he had to lean in to read, a cartoon text cloud surrounded, "Betcha Robbie Cee ain't gonna walk straight for weeks. See you in Tallytown my dear." So, Marcie was at FSU too.

There was no Robbie Cee. Searching the C's, he found Robert Caine. Maybe he'd forgotten it was picture day. Most of the seniors had gotten the memo and come to photo day in a white shirt and a tie. Robbie wore a T-shirt. Only the top of the printed text on the shirt was visible, but it appeared to be the stylized Metallica logo. Robbie was not particularly ugly, but this was not his best presentation. No one, except his mother, would call him handsome.

A splat of rain hit his head, another the corner of the book. He was up and out of the chair and under the overhang in seconds. He'd been studying and not noticed the blackening of the sky. The shimmering silver curtain of the oncoming rain had turned the river a rough gunmetal gray. Every color beyond the curtain was muted by the gray overwash of the downpour. The sound reached him before the mist. When the wall of rain from the deluge crossed the river, enveloping the house, he slipped in the sliding door and just watched.

Bruce Ballister

The swamp waters beyond the estuary had finally warmed enough to begin producing the kinds of summer rains that would wash over the city for the next six months. He knew well that a high nineties, muggy miserable afternoon could get a cooling wash from seemingly nowhere on two minutes warning. Afterward, the steam would rise from the pavements creating a steam bath that trapped tourists would complain about or brag on as they described their interrupted shopping trips.

Situation normal here, part of the fun, part of the atmosphere. Saylor chuckled to himself; atmosphere is right—one hundred percent humidity with a seventy percent chance of an afternoon shower. Sometimes a deluge, sometimes just enough to really steam the place up. Home sweet home. It did feel good to be home. He turned to set the yearbook down on the coffee table and looked around the River House's great room overcome with melancholy. If the worst happened, if Lindsey had been killed, there were papers upstairs that could eventually be filed to make this house his home. He shuddered with a chill that came from a coupling of the damp rinse he'd been blasted with and the thought that Lindsey, a daughter he'd never known to exist, the girl he'd met only by sheer happenstance, might be forever out of his reach.

24

Chasing Threads

There was no Robbie Caine. Robert Aaron, according to his mother, was gone to the four winds. She "hadn't seen his useless hide 'round here for a coupla weeks now."

He persisted in the face of futility. "Ma'am, we really do need to find him if it's at all possible. Do you know of any job he may have taken? I'd heard something about he occasionally crews on the shrimp boats."

"That boy take a real job on one of them big boats? Only if he'd fell drunk and been Shanghaied. Tell you what mister. If you do find him? Tell him to come on home. Me and daddy are all right now. We got things settled. Tell him to come on home."

"Yes, ma'am. If I do, I will, and thanks for your time." He hung up. Over the years, his accent had become malleable, situational. Going to FSU had removed quite a bit of his Franklin County native drawl. His few years in Austin put an east Texas lilt to it. The decade and in Houston had removed most of the native-son Southernese. Houston and Harris County had swelled so much with new thirty-somethings from everywhere that most offices sounded like any large urban center anywhere in the US. He called it NBC English. Talking with Maybelle Caine had just ripped twenty years off his dialect's migrations and recalling the sound of his own voice on the phone made him laugh. "GAWley, boy! Whaat has happenet to yur voice?"

He called up the screen capture he'd taken of the White Pages report on Marcie Helms. There was a phone listing, and it had the 653 phone exchange of a Franklin County landline. White Pages was an unreliable source for cell phone numbers. But just maybe, maybe the honesty-is-the-best-policy route will work out. Semi-honest anyway. He dialed what he assumed was the family phone line in Apalachicola. Another female voice, from deep in the South, answered.

"Mrs. Helms?"

"Yes, can I help you?" The voice was cultured Southernese. The light lilt, a noticeable trace of breeding or practiced imitation.

"Hello, I'm Jason Saylor calling from the Houston Chronicle. We've heard about the disappearance, perhaps an abduction, of a Miss Lindsey Lawrence. We understand your daughter is a friend of hers."

"Yes, yes, they were...I'm sorry are good friends. All through school since kindergarten and Sunday school." There was a short pause. "And, if you don't mind me asking, how did you know this way out there in Texas?"

"The yearbook, ma'am. From the high school yearbook. They appeared to be pretty close. The story, the wire services have picked up on her story and it's making national news."

"Ah huh. Bad news is good news in your business, I guess. How exactly can I help you? Mr. Sailor was it?"

"Yes ma'am, Saylor with a Y. We'd really like to talk with your daughter Marcie but need the best phone number for her. Do you think she'd mind? We're trying to paint a complete picture of Lindsey, human interest kind of thing."

"Well, you're speaking to someone who helped raise that girl up. I almost feel as proud of her as I do my own daughter, she was over here so much. You probably know her mother was a shopkeeper, worked all day. So, after school, the two of them were thick as thieves up in Marcie's room. I can tell you that Lindsey was...is a very bright and talented girl. She had," there was a short pause, a sound like a swallowed sob, "*has* so much to offer when her terrible ordeal is over. I *DO* so hope they find her soon."

"We all do ma'am. May I ask what kind of activities she involved in?"

"Oh, well, there were so many things they were into. Cheer squad, tennis, Lindsey was on the school golf team, but you probably know that if you got to look at the yearbook. She was an excellent singer. I so wish she had kept coming to choir practice." Mrs. Helms' voice dropped to a lower volume as if transmitting more sensitive information. "Her mother stopped bringing her to church after her husband passed away. Such a terrible tragedy. *THAT* was hard on Lindsey. I can't imagine, but I suppose it happens all the time..." and almost to herself, "with his kind of people."

What did that little innuendo drop imply? Gossip, insider knowledge? Distrust of an absentee husband? Saylor had the feeling that he might be on the phone with Mrs. Helms longer than he'd wished. "Thank you so much, Mrs. Helms, you are being extremely helpful. Would you be so kind as to share her cell number? I'm trying to get an article to the editor for the evening edition."

"Well, surely. You sound like a nice young man. And that's Marjorie Helms. Do you need me to spell that?"

"No ma'am, I have it from the listing." Saylor smiled to himself as he jotted down the number. Nice young man. She probably pictured a young reporter sitting in a vast newsroom, not a contemporary of hers, sitting in his smallish RV just down the highway.

If he closed his eyes, he could fill in the view from his former Chronicle office chair, clutter, file cabinets, post-it notes in five colors. Deep research stories made up one pile, daily news coverage in another, long lead ideas in another. He spoke to the world at large on a black hardwired desk phone with the twin rows of department line buttons, the paper-issued flip phone, and his own on their charger cables. The two monitors on the workstation connected him to the world. If he swiveled his chair, his back was to the glass wall on a hallway. No visible sign of the outside world. He hoped that when or if he returned to the job, the new Chronicle building on Texas Street might be completed maybe as soon as the summer or fall of next year, but there had been slowdowns. Even with a view to a window, or a window wall office of his own, it would still be a view of another wall of windows across the street, or that old brick pile, the Rice Hotel. There was no hope of getting a view as soul-centering as his view across the bay, or better, the deck's view of the Apalachicola estuary from the River House.

He stepped out of the camper and walked across the highway. Low tide. Exposed sand flats stretched two hundred yards to the water's edge. The grassy bottom began not much further out. Easy walking for sand dollars. He thought he'd like to get at least one really good-sized one. Let the rest go about their bottom scrubbing lives. A low line of B-52s in Vee formation, for some reason, he'd always thought of brown pelicans as B-52s, worked their way upwind to the southwest. A kingfisher cried out from a pine on the property next door that still had a scatter of tall pines. He gave a second thought to a barefoot walk on the exposed sand flats. But not today. The sea air smelled great, but there were still threads to pull. No loose threads. He'd leave the door open and a window opposite for the breeze to pass through. He needed to call Marcie.

He got an answer on the sixth ring. "Hello, Marcie Helms?" He used his friendliest voice.

"Sorry, uh, yes. I don't usually pick up out of area code calls. Who is this?"

"Hi, Marcie, I'm Jason Saylor, I just spoke with your mother who gave me your phone number. Is this a good time to talk?"

"Yes, is she alright?"

"Oh, yes. Your mother's fine. I'm a reporter with the Houston Chronicle. I'm trying to get some background for the Lindsey Lawrence story. I've taken a personal interest in this, and I hope you can help me get to know more about Lindsey. I understand from your mother that you were both close."

"Oh, my God. Poor Lindsey. I pray for her every time I think about it. About her." In the background, a music soundtrack, one of the new female pop leaders he knew he didn't know, was turned down to silence. "Gosh, I'm glad I picked up. I usually let unknown numbers go. They keep trying to sell me car insurance or Medicare. I'm not even twenty years old yet and Medicare?"

"I understand completely. I wish there was a law, but we have to deal right?"

"I suppose."

"Listen, Marcie. Is there any reason you can think of anything, any reason all, that Lindsey might have gone off on her own? I need to check that off first, just so we know what we're talking about. Great new love of her life. Eloped to a Vegas wedding? Or perhaps, off to a state with safe abortion clinics? Somewhere she'd have complete privacy. I'm grasping here, trying to think of some reason she might have gone off and is not in some very serious trouble."

Marcie was silent for only a breath. "No, there had been a sort-of boyfriend here. Kappa Alpha. Turned out to be a complete jerk. He thought a third date was reason enough to get to third base. So, no."

A short bark of a laugh. "No Vegas wedding. And as for the other, she wouldn't. I don't think she would. But it's beside the point."

"Why would you say that?"

"Because, she had her, uh...visitor two weeks ago. You know? So, she couldn't be pregnant."

"You're sure?"

"Absolutely. She was up here a few weeks ago, checking out officially from the university. She stopped by to catch up, we had a Frap together and, well she needed to borrow..."

"I get it. So, no pregnancy. No elopement. She was in otherwise good spirits?"

"No! She wasn't in good spirits at all! She was crying on my sleeve. Literally, I was hugging her while she sobbed in my arms." A pause. "I don't know what Mom might have said, but Lin and me? We're like sisters from another mister. Close as you can get 'cause neither of us had sibs. She was talking about her mom and the cancer, and suddenly she just broke up. Like there wasn't anyone else in the world to talk to." Saylor listened to light rapid breathing on the other end. Then in a voice raspy with emotion, "Because there wasn't anyone else, and now she's gone too."

He felt like a voyeur. Witness to a moment that shouldn't have to have been exposed and rubbed raw. Personal loss rips open the heart like few other events. He let Marcie collect herself and quietly asked. "Marcie, please, I know this is tough for you. Just one more question?"

Sniff, and snuffle. "I'm sorry. I think I'm OK now. It's..."

He waited a moment, listening to a girl in emotional distress, then, "I know, Marcie. I hope keeping a light shining on her case can help. Listen, I don't know if you know this, you might from crime shows, but in the large majority of cases, when a person goes missing, it's often because of someone close to them, next of kin, an acquaintance, like that. Back in Apalachicola, is there anyone she knows, maybe someone from high school, anyone who might have some grievance. An old boyfriend. Someone with a perceived grievance?"

"I can't think of any right now. If I do, should I call you back?"

"Marcie, one of my sources mentioned a Robbie, Robbie Caine."

"Oh, oh hell. I hope the hell not. That retard!"

"What are you saying, Marcie? What happened between Lindsey and Robbie?"

"Well, it wasn't her specifically. It's been a while, Spring Break. This time last year. A carload of us girls from school went over to Destin. That's a beach town on the other side of Panama City from here. Well, we saw him there. He seemed to be alone, on the beach, walking by, and came up to us like we were all good friends from school, 'fancy meeting y'all here, what's going down?' So, he's a creep, right? And the four of us, we probably weren't real nice. Told him 'you might know us, but if you knew us, you'd know we wouldn't be hanging with you.' You know? We crushed him."

"We threw some major shade. There were a lot of people standing around on the beach. A bunch of them started laughing. He was pretty much humiliated. He threw a drink at us. A cherry something that stained half our towels."

"Sounds like that might have made him pretty mad."

"I suppose, but we were all having this great party, right. And this creep from home who was basically a downer wanted to join up with us."

"That was the end of it?"

"No, we saw him at the hotel two nights later. He was sitting, alone still, at a table for four across the restaurant from us. Just staring. If looks could kill, there would have been mass murder in the place."

"What did happen?"

"Nothing. We got our check and left. Never saw him again that week. Didn't see much of him the rest of the year at school. You know? Thinking about it? I'm not even sure he finished. Not like I checked up on him or anything. Robbie just wasn't one of those people you paid attention to."

He knew there was more. *If* he'd interpreted it right, according to the scribbled note in the yearbook, someone in their group had seriously wounded Robbie's masculinity with a kick or some other punch to the nuts.

"If you think back to that time at the beach, or later at the restaurant, was he particularly focused on Lindsey?"

"No, not at the time. "I think they might have been friends in like, pre-K or early grade school, but hey, that was a very long time ago."

"I understand. I'll follow up on him. So, there's no one else you can think of?"

"No. Usually Lindsey was the kind of person who said hi and hello to everybody. Was everyone's friend. Said no to being nominated for prom queen because Jennie, one of our friends, had been nominated, and she didn't want to compete. She was on the student council, worked on the school paper, cheer squad, shot a ninety at golf."

"Yes, I did research some of that, but you don't get the personal side. So, thank you, Marcie. This is terrific background. And I'm sorry for getting you upset. You've been a great help. Oh, wait. Something just occurred to me. Do you happen to know if Robbie Caine was ever arrested? Did he have any trouble with the law you know of?"

"Yes, matter of fact. But he got off, as a juvenile."

"What was that about, when?"

"He was caught busting into some of those fish houses up the river."

He knew what she was talking about, but he was supposedly in Houston. "Fish houses?"

"Up the river from Apalach. There's probly, eighty, a hundred or so. Scattered around. Boathouses, no houseboats. But they're mostly ricky-ticky things. Most are built on oil drums or big ole slabs of Styrofoam. People go up the river to fish." A laugh slipped out, overcoming the sorrow. "Or to drink and have crazy sex. Who knows? No one's looking and no one can hear you. Private as you'd want to be."

"And he was stealing from these houseboats?"

"Some of 'em are real nice. Solar panels, refrigerators, TVs. All the comforts. Except you have to bring your own water. Can't drink the river."

"I see." He did see. He knew very well there were about that many, probably more, home-built houseboats tied off to trees on the banks or deadfall, loosely anchored in the river with enough leader rope to allow them to rise and fall with the various flood stages. "Marcie, Thanks. Like I said, you've been a great help."

"Yes Sir." There was a pause. The line didn't go dead. "And thanks for helping keep her story alive. Thanks for listening. Bye."

Nice girl, he thought. A good friend. He could imagine the group, though. A little bit high on whatever at the beach. Dancing to something in their bikinis and feeling grown-up for the first time. Poor Robbie, either there by accident or design, was humiliated. Well, Mr. Caine? I think you must be suspect number two on the sheriff's list.

25

Beach Trip

Belle's store was closed on Sundays, and it was time to deliver on a promised trip to the beach. He brought up his idea carefully because he was actually more interested in visiting some of his old haunts up the river. "Belle, you've been to St. George how many times in your life?"

Belle was tending a pan of popping and sizzling bacon. "My life? Uh, something less than a thousand, and something more than several hundred." She flipped over the four strips of bacon. "Does this mean you're going to weasel out of going to the beach?"

"No," Saylor stood and stretched. His bones weren't at all old at thirty-eight. But some mornings, the years seemed to be telling him that more sleep was a necessity. "No, I'm just offering an alternative to thirty minutes and two bridges to a beach full or snowbirds."

"You do realize most of 'em are from Georgia and Alabama, right?"

"Doesn't matter. I was thinking of a private beach. Just in case you wanted to fill in those little white triangles." His grin, boyish, sly, suggestive, adulterous, played across his face in variations of a lifted eyebrow, tilted head.

Smiling back, she pointed the spatula at him. "Momma should have warned me about horny sailors."

He objected, "Wrong spelling."

She insisted, "Same horns!"

"Same Saylor." He thought about it. "So, you're still wanting St. George? What about little St. George? Only locals, but still company."

She looked up at the ceiling, thinking. "Little St. George would do. The triangles might have to wait to get tanned another day. But it's possible over there."

He looked disappointed. But when he considered the choices, the island vs. one of the riverside beaches upstream. It was supposed to be a calm day with light winds from the east. He'd checked. Any winds from the east would build swells that could break on an outgoing tide as three-footers with almost no separation between them—a challenge for his little boat. But Little St. George was to the west. Tidal flows would cut down any surf near the cut. The cut, dredged decades ago to give the city's trawler fleet easy access to deep water, split the barrier island in two. One side with all its beach rentals and tourism and a popular state park was accessible by bridge. Little St. George, as natural as God could build an island, was accessible only by boat. It had a few wild hogs, fewer wild goats, and deer. Some talked of feral cats, but he'd never seen any.

Thinking about it more, the idea grew on him. "Might be some good shells over there. You like long walks on the beach?"

"And piña coladas, too." The toaster popped. "Come here, butter your bagel. This bacon is about done."

They ate, watching a little news over breakfast. The Panama City station had a short clip featuring the Missing Teen Still Subject of Search in Franklin County. Lindsey's face appeared on one side of the screen while a public information officer asked for any information on the missing girl. As the story progressed, the pictures changed from a yearbook pose to smiling photographs in different settings. Belle looked over at him when the news moved on. She tapped the volume down several notches. "The sheriff still leaving you alone?"

"I don't know if I'm paranoid, or just noticing patrol cars more than I used to." He washed down a bite with coffee. "You know, they are ubiquitous, unseen background. Then they tell you that you're one of two people being investigated. You start noticing them all the time."

"No calls?"

"Nope." He was thankful, "No news from the sheriff."

"What's next? Any loose threads to tie off?"

"That's the problem." He leaned back, sighed, let his gaze wander across the tree line in Spring's glory on the opposite shoreline. The river flowed on, uncaring, inexorable. Fated to die as it gave life to the estuary and the bay. With its brown water laden with Georgia silt, oxygen, and nutrients, the river meant so many things to the city and county and the water life that had been here eons before man. It fed the swamps with nutrients in flood stage. The wetlands stored that water and gave it back when the Corps of Engineers reduced flows up at the state line. His mind drifted back to the present. "I can only think of one thread, and I don't even know how to grab it. What color it is, how long, or what fiber."

"Huh?"

"Robbie. If I could lay money on it, I'd bet that Robbie Caine, Robert Aaron Caine, is suspect number two on the sheriff's list. Hopefully by now, number one on the list. His momma doesn't know anything, or more likely, won't say anything."

"You could stake out the house." Then she reconsidered. "Nah, you couldn't. Everybody in this town knows everybody's business. You'd have to be the invisible man to watch his house."

He nodded. Knew it to be true. "Screw it, it's Sunday. Let's just go enjoy some Florida sunshine, have some fun."

"I need to pack some things, beachy stuff."

"I'll grab my tackle."

"Fishing? Cool, I'll get mine."

As he walked down the stairs to get his things together and prepare the boat, he thought, *Cool, she likes to fish.*

In forty-five minutes, they had thrown together needed supplies and were passing under the high bridge into the broad expanse of Apalachicola Bay. In another two minutes, they were bouncing off two-foot swells with white caps. Farther into the main body of the bay, whitecaps looked like they might be even larger. He slowed the boat to a crawl and turned the lightweight boat into the waves. "I'm not sure we want to do this today. This is not a light and variable from the east. He pointed straight up. This is twelve to fifteen knots, could get higher, and we've got over five miles to go to the cut." He was already butt sore, and she had the worst of it in the bow where spray would splash over after every second or third roller was crossed.

She was huddled into a small, curled ball with wet hair. "I was hoping you'd say that. I didn't want to poop on your party. But it's pretty wet up here."

"Let's go upriver."

"I'm good with that."

Fifteen minutes later, the lightweight v-hull was on a plane, buzzing over smooth, wind-kissed ripples. Not enough fetch on the river for the wind to do much more than that. There were already boats pulled up on the dredge beach just upriver across from the Abercrombie landing, so he left the main Intercoastal channel and took the right turn into the river proper. He made another tight turn to the right and a slower one to the left before a remembered sand pile came into sight. A product of the Army Corps of Engineer's work when the river was still being 'managed' for navigation, the long dune-shaped pile was out of place with the low wetlands around them. But it had a sort of a beach, and they had first dibs on it.

Fishing was slow. Belle pulled in a decent river cat on a small piece of pork, but it flipped off her hook as it came out of the water. She rebaited her hook and set the rod in her rod holder. Their mobile encampment included a tarp, a blanket, beach towels, two folding chairs, and an umbrella. It was a Sunday, so any hopes of absolute privacy were shattered by the realization that boats and even jet skis were going to be zipping by at high speed or pontoon boats and cabin cruisers would be gliding by much slower. The customary waves and 'how's the fishing' were exchanged. Belle was more relaxed than he'd ever seen her. A loose blouse, two lower buttons fastened over a bikini top. Below, she wore cutoff jeans with pockets peeking out over her bikini bottoms. She looked good enough to eat! Early still, but bonds were forming that he did not want to break.

The Chronicle entered his thoughts. The newspaper's office was as different a setting as could be imagined. Only a rare location would provide any vista outside of the bronzed and blued glass canyons of downtown Houston. There had to be a way out of that fate. *Could there be a way for a newspaperman to carve a living in the wilderness? What about roving reporter? Maybe a stringer for the networks?*

While trying to look as if he wasn't staring, he watched a thirty-foot plus motor cruiser with at least two families' worth of passengers come up the river so slowly that its passage was marked by little more than turbulence astern and ripples spreading from the bow. Two on the bow were looking through binoculars and pointing. He followed the glance to a bald eagle atop a giant dead cypress. Its giant nest incongruous on the weather-thinned support. Others were talking, laughing, or sharing a drink or a hot dog from the stern-mounted grill.

A hole in his chest, forgotten for a few weeks, throbbed. The bitterness of the divorce had washed a black patina over some difficult years. Life in the suburbs. The inbound commute on the Katy Freeway had been daily torture, but the weekends roaming state parks, the Galveston beaches, sailing on the bay. They'd had fun. He'd thought they were both in love. She'd been pretty good at faking it. Or at least, it just hadn't been enough. As the cruiser rounded the turn a quarter-mile upstream, his gaze fell on Belle, apparently asleep behind her sunglasses. Could this be just a bounce? A rebound fling? Or a good thing, something to build on? She was slim, athletic, but acerbic enough apparently to have alienated a lot of her former friends. Yet competent as a shopkeeper. Ambitious? Hard to tell after what, nine or ten days? He'd lost track.

She turned her head toward him. "You're staring."

"Just thinking is all."

"Admit it, you were staring."

"OK, you're the best-looking scenery I've seen in years. Why not?"

She beamed a hundred-watt smile back at him. "What were you thinking?"

"That I wish we had that private beach."

"Men! One track. Always the one track." She lowered the sunglasses and looked over the rim. Her eyes were still shaded by a green banker's visor.

Where do you get those anymore? He said, "See, the view just improved."

"Seriously, what's got you so—contemplative?"

Ah, the perfect word. "When I left Houston, there were several reasons for leaving." He fell silent, thinking about what order to list them.

"You going to share them?" The sunglasses were back on her nose. The tilt of her head indicated she was listening with interest.

"Alright. The biggest and most immediate. I'd been working an investigation into some financial dealings, or misdealings, involving two very powerful commissioners, a judge, and an officer of the Texas State Bank. It hadn't gone to print yet, but the fact that I was asking questions, and the kind of questions I was asking got people nervous. Those people are social friends of two on the Chronicle's board and I was told to back off." The professional part of him still stung. "Some of these folks were dealing with people on the dark side. People who were known to be involved with human trafficking for everything from farm labor to sex shops." He raised his hands in open-handed frustration. "To know that these supposed community leaders were profiteering on misery of that sort had me on their case almost full time. They were scared. I was told to go away for a while or expect to be downsized. The phrase my editor used was, 'Either that or go back to Whoville.'" He'd been staring vacantly at the shoreline opposite and turned back to return her gaze, smiled. "I kind of like it back here in Whoville."

"That's one."

"Two, I'm a little over four months out from settling a divorce. What I thought had been a good marriage, wasn't." A sigh of regret. "She found that she needed to get some experimentation out of her system. I first thought it was just that she'd been screwing my neighbor, a former good friend. We'd shared barbecues on Sundays and argued over football games. He was a Cowboys fan. I've always been a Falcons fan. He was also my wife's good friend. In some of our final arguments when things got down and dirty, she admitted to much more than I'd be willing to forgive as her mid-life crisis."

"In that arguing stage, I woke one night to an empty bed. Checking out the house, I looked out and saw her coming out of the neighbor's garage. Something like 3:00 a.m. It just wasn't going to work out. We decided to sell the house, split our assets down the middle and move on. I certainly wasn't going to stay in that neighborhood." He fell silent. His blank stare still roamed the shadows and deep greens on the other side of the river. His mind relived the last of the heated arguments and the small peck on the cheek that had been her parting gesture.

"Jase?"

He looked back at her. Sunglasses in her lap now.

"Some people suck. You just have to be able to admit it. Some people just don't know how to be good people."

"Yeah, I keep re-learning that."

"The trick is to remember that it isn't always about you."

"True. You know, there was this thing about the talk yesterday with Lindsey's friend Marcie. And for that matter, with her mother. They were helpful and all. Really, helpful. But I had the feeling I wouldn't like them. She and her mom seemed to have this casual sense of superiority. The kind of people that I never liked back in college. Like they and their kind were the rightful heirs to the best of everything." His mini-rant ran out of steam. "They, I don't know. It was just a feeling. Marcie is just a kid and she has a lot of life lessons to learn. Her mom is my age, probably. She's gonna be set in her ways for life."

"It's a small town, and there are some small minds." Her mouth pursed, brows furrowed then brightened. "But you know, some of the folks around here are decent in their hearts. They just don't realize how they come off. I've stayed on here because I don't really know what else to do right now." She got up and stretched, took off the visor and the sunglasses, and opened her face to the sun with eyes shut. She opened her arms wide and sucked in a lungful of clean air. "Oh, but it can be blissful here."

His heart expanded a size, watching her enjoy the moment, the setting.

She turned back to him, grinning. "OK, I think we're up to three."

"Got me. Number three. I'm looking at her."

"I'm a reason for leaving Houston?"

"Definitely, you're one of my good reasons for not going back."

She took two steps and straddled his legs, facing him. She opened the remaining bottom two buttons and opened her shirt in invitation. He noted a few small beads of sweat on the tiny hairs just above her cleavage. His eyes took in the movable feast and rose to meet hers. "Belle, there's gonna be another boat by here any minute now."

"We're not catching anything here but rays and mosquitoes. Whad'ya say we head back down to the house?"

They had broken camp. Saylor sat at the console, his hand on the throttle. He called to her over the low idling putter of the motor. "Wait for this boat to pass by before you shove off." A small runabout on a fast plane was heading down the center of the channel from upstream. Although the river was close to a hundred yards wide, it seemed prudent. The boat sped by. A young man in a reversed baseball cap stared as he passed by. He noted a rock band T-shirt on a camo background. Belle pushed off and hopped onto the narrow seat at the bow and pulled in the small throw anchor they'd half-buried in the sand. They both turned their heads when they noticed the drop in engine noise. The speeding boat had slowed and was turning around.

With no apparent reservation on his invasion of their privacy, the young man came back upriver to a point even with them, staring hard. Something approaching a grin spread across his face, but his eyes were unreadable behind sunglasses. Saylor wondered if it was just an impossibly rude kid ogling Belle's obviously attractive body. Or, what? The boat turned, the kid gunned the motor, and it was off and speeding downriver in a few seconds. The entire encounter hadn't taken a minute and a half. Belle, from her perch in the front, said. "Well, THAT was pretty damn rude."

Before he throttled up to head home, he said, "I hope that was all that was." He'd made out the boat's make as it came back for the slow pass. It was a Boston Whaler. He hit the throttle and turned the boat downriver.

26

Sex and Surveillance

They'd left the beach with clear intentions of becoming 'fully involved,' the shorthand he'd suggested. The weird, disturbing behavior of the kid on the runabout hadn't damped that urge, and the few minutes it took to get back down to the River House only increased their urgency. Their fishing gear and picnic supplies lay in a heap under the house at the door of the one-room bungalow. The immediate need to couple, to connect, lay groundwork for any as yet unspoken future lay spent on their glistened foreheads, blushed skin, sweated backs. The few clothes they'd worn fishing were strewn in a path leading from the door to her bed. It had been a glorious and mutually satisfying release of tensions, building over the last few days. They were still entangled when he shifted a leg to help her ease one of hers out of the pile. "Whew!"

"I second that." Her voice, still ragged from exertion, was just above a whisper.

He bent to kiss her before rising. "Going to shower, back in a jiff."

"Hold up, I'll join you."

Both of them enjoyed the hot needling spray, helped each other with unnecessary back rubs, equally unnecessary front rubs, and remembered how hard it was to maintain a fully engaged kiss with a shower aimed at their heads. Laughs, giggles, and a towel pop or two ensued before they found themselves back in the kitchen, clothed but ravenous. She opened a cabinet and stared.

He spotted a familiar box second shelf up. "I see noodles. What kind of cheese do you have?"

"Cheddar, and gouda probably." She rummaged in the refrigerator and came up with two blocks of cheese. She turned to face him. "But what to go with it."

Saylor thought of one of his favorite childhood meals. "You have any hot dogs?"

"Polish turkey sausage, is the closest I've got."

"Even better. My skill set includes that challenge. How 'bout you work up a small salad."

They set about making their simple feast. Belle asked, "What about that dude in the boat? The guy who turned back to check us out?"

"I was just thinking about him. Bothers me, maybe too much." He asked, "He's no one you know?"

"Hard to tell from the distance. I couldn't tell hair color, but it looked medium dark in the back. Skinny as a rail. Needed a shave. That's about all I'd be able to give a cop. Well, he did have on white fishhouse work boots. So, could be he works or did work at one of the packing houses."

"That's good, I didn't notice the Franklin County wingtips." He smirked at his own joke. Fishhouse workers were required to wear white rubber boots in the processing houses. They got worn to and from work and on lunch breaks. The boots were the mark of an employee of one of several seafood packing houses on the waterfront. "What I did notice was that he was driving a Boston Whaler."

"Damn, I thought that thing looked familiar!"

"Would you swear to it? It being Lindsey's missing boat?"

"No, they're peas from a pod." After a pause, "And it was Eleanor's boat, and I only rode in it a few times I told you about. I didn't really pay that much attention."

"Well, it made me think of something. Something Marcie said. I didn't think about it at the time. But it came back to me while we were sunning on the riverbank." He tried to reconstruct the sentences. Then remembered he might have had his phone on record mode. He'd been thinking about it possibly too long.

She broke his reverie. "You gonna share?"

"Yeah, just a sec. We somehow got to talking about those boathouses, the fishing shacks up the river. She aptly described them as ricky-ticky. She thought I was a reporter in Houston calling on background and might have thought that I imagined eighty-thousand-dollar houseboats."

"Houseboats?" She speared a roll of sausage on a fork already half full of dripping sunflower gold macaroni and took the mouthful.

"Yeah, she had a phrase, a description about the loneliness out there that struck me at the time." He pulled out his cell phone and pulled up the recording of the conversation. He fast-forwarded through most of the recording and found the clip. Marcie's voice, tinned by the small speaker, said, "People go upriver to fish, or drink, have crazy sex. Who'd know? No one's looking and no one can hear you. Private as you'd want to be." He watched her chewing thoughtfully, taking it in. He said, "At the time, I thought of you, us." He gave a one-shouldered shrug. "Being as private as we'd want to be."

She managed to smile while chewing. Then her left eyebrow raised in objection. "True, but a lot of those boathouses are packed in like neighborhoods. Packed a little too close."

Serious now, he retorted, an upside-down fork pointed across the table and generally in the direction of the river. "I haven't been upriver in twenty years, but I know for a fact that some of those little swamp channels could hide a boat." *Hell, Seal Team 6 could hide a small navy.* He let the point of the fork sag. "It would take weeks to check them out."

"So, you're busy?"

He wanted to laugh, but it came out as a puff of air. "I'm supposed to be finishing a rough draft of the book. I was hoping to get it to Lisa, my editor, for a content read, checking for inconsistencies, plot suggestions, by the end of the week."

"So, what are you going to do?" Her eyebrows raised in question. "Go sleuthing or became a famous novelist?"

They finished eating, half watching the news, half talking about anything else but their own current events. Table cleared, dishes stacked, they went out onto the deck and settled into the high-backed chairs. The longer days were adding daylight, stealing large hunks of nighttime as the sun moved farther from the equator. Belle settled into her chair, diminished by its size relative to hers and her posture. She'd tucked her heels up and closed her arms around her knees, settled her chin down on their shiny tops, and took in the view across the river.

He looked at her, her comfort level with him, and likewise. This felt comfortable. He too, was at ease. Could be more at ease if he ignored the book, ignored his quest to find Lindsey, if he ignored the troubling incident on the river. It seemed like a lot to ignore.

The sun was still an hour above the tree line behind them, but its shadows extended out over the river. A flash and something white flashed again to the south. Perhaps a quarter mile away near the old railroad bridge, a fisherman was working the other bank. A trolling motor silently moved it slowly upstream. He saw the flash again and his gut tightened. A reflection from a reel wouldn't be head high. A reflection off glasses would be a pinpoint from that far away. A reflection off binoculars would be bright enough.

Belle was gazing toward infinity, absorbed in the circling hunt of the local Osprey. He said, "I'll be right back. Stay put."

Lazily, "OK, don't have anywhere to be."

He casually got up, took his empty glass and hers, and went inside. Just inside the door stood the gun cabinet. He pulled out one of the two long guns that had scopes attached. Resting on the only chair that had a view of the southern reach of the river, he sat, raised a knee for a prop, and sighted the rifle downriver. He found the boat out of focus. Found the knurled focusing knob on top of the scope and turned. The figure on the boat leaped into focus. The young man in the camo shirt, hat still backward, was staring at the house through binoculars. He was staring right back at him. He knew, logically, that the guy couldn't see behind the plate glass. It would be reflecting the colors of the evening sky. For just a moment, the kid on the boat lowered his binocs to wipe sweat from his forehead. He lowered his hand and wiped a lens on the bottom hem of the T-shirt. The shirt's background was camo, but the pattern on it in silver was a Lynyrd Skynyrd concert tour logo. His camera, with a decent telephoto lens, was in Eastpoint. But he wouldn't need the camera's optics to remember the face. The boy in the boat was Robert Aaron Caine.

"Hello Robbie." He replaced the rifle in the cabinet and leaned his head through the opening in the sliding glass door. "Belle, can you come in here a minute." He felt like any further exposure amounted to reckless endangerment.

"Sure, getting buggy anyway." She closed the door on the certainty that with the approach of darkness, and the spring season, biting bugs of all sizes were going to proliferate by the millions. Every single one of them happy to feast on a human. "What's up?"

Saylor told her, pulling her further into the room, out of the voyeur's line of sight. They sat on kitchen stools, far enough into the house that even if the boat moved directly across the river, an observer wouldn't be able to see that far into the structure. "I'm going to go back to Eastpoint. I'd feel better if you came with me."

27

Suzanne

Saylor sat in one of his webbed patio chairs, considering his recent lack of attention to his book project. He needed to get back on track with his editor/agent. It was a touchy relationship, at best. He pulled his phone out and tapped in a message. [Lisa, if you liked book two's rough draft and are going to spend some time with it, I've got a basic concept for book three.]

The message was meant to be short. Lisa was a busy person. With only one book in their history column, he wasn't yet *that* good a client. No need to tie up your editor/agent with BS. He had more in jell form in his mental filing cabinet, but he kept it short unless she asked for more.

The sun emerged from clouds making it hard to see his screen. He got up and stepped into the air-conditioned camper. He typed on in two thumb mode: [The Agency sends Andie Jackson and her new partner, now a growing love/hate interest, to Columbia. A girl there has been found dead. Not unusual in mega-city Cali, but this girl was rico. Muy rico from her dress and styling, a gringa rica, a rich white girl from physical appearance. The local Policia send fingerprints to the US and INTERPOL. Turns out she's been reported missing from school at Harvard or Yale. Maybe only Princeton, but a blue blood with state department connections. When the FBI collects a pile of PMPs (prominent missing persons), it's discovered that there are at least five girls, eighteen to twenty-two, missing from the military-industrial leadership, Northrup, Boeing, etc. Tbd. Narco vs. Cartel. What do you think?]

Saylor scanned it before hitting send. *Always scan before hitting send.* The tapping on his door came simultaneously with his tap on the send button. He hadn't heard the crunch of gravel behind him, the announcement anytime someone cruised the RV park's crushed rock drives. Half expecting his 'good old friend' Patrick, he was surprised to see Patrick's wife, Suzanne, smiling up at him in a straw hat and Jackie O sunglasses. An elegant yet not ostentatious sundress beneath. From his angle, her cleavage was deeper than he remembered and lightly peppered with freckles and one inviting beauty mark. *Best not to think about that.* "Hi," he turned to glance quickly inside, then, "I wasn't expecting company."

The smile flashed on unabated. "Do you need a moment, to stash the stash?"

He laughed, "No, no stash, it's just that I've still got breakfast spread around. What the hell. I think I'll get over the shame."

Suzanne stepped up and into the two-foot by two-foot space that doubled as a hallway and foyer. Saylor began to put away the residue from the toasted bagel and coffee he'd had for breakfast. The silver-wrapped cream cheese was still out tempting one of Florida's five billion flying insects. He welcomed the company, but this was Suzanne. Former girlfriend, Suzanne, and Patrick Wills' wife. Wills. The sheriff's auxiliary willing to sell out a former best friend, Wills.

He'd just tossed the cream cheese back into the micro-fridge. Straightening up, he turned to find her a half step away. He took a half step back. "Fancy meeting you here."

"Jason, I wanted to come by, maybe talk a little, catch up."

There was something about her smile, not strained. Pained. Like something tender inside was hurt. "Suz, are you alright?"

The smile returned to its former brightness. "Yeah, yeah. I'm good, I just thought about you out here, and..." she raised both shoulders and an eyebrow in a shrug.

"Good, good to hear." *Man, that is lame, and what the hell did she mean by that?* She was lovely. She'd been treated kindly by father time. But getting on into the sun season and Suzanne's skin was still only a shade darker than a cheesehead's in February. "Listen, Suz, I'd love to talk, but maybe we want to move your car into like the third or fourth row back, to the other side of the community room and pool area. He looked over at her ride. "Your bright red Audi might not have too many doubles around here. People do and will talk." He wondered how much to say. "Based on Pat's last visit, it might not be good for people to see you visiting me."

She opened her mouth to object. He just put an index finger to her lips—*nice shade of lipstick. Stop thinking about it.* "Please, humor me."

Five minutes later, her car was as far back as it could get, in line with the boat trailers and off-season camper storage. They settled into chairs under a patio umbrella by the pool. This is good, he thought, no one around here but tourists. "Is this OK?" If anything, her face registered disappointment. *What had she expected? Hoped for?*

Suzanne looked across the pool area, took in the newly installed community activity room. "This is nice, Jase. I've never looked in here driving by. Seems like it might get comfy."

"Actually," he said with no sense of untruth, "this is a sight nicer than the old homestead's neighborhood." His family's neighborhood, a few blocks north of the former county high school, boasted small lots, modest homes: most clad in fiberglass shingles or plywood paneling, single-pane windows, and patched roofs. Many of them sagged on piers that had been settling into sandy soil for sixty years or more. A little new construction replaced vacant lots and rebuilds, but the area was aging out and wasn't nearly as attractive a location to build as any of his old neighbors would like. There on the backside of Apalachicola, one of the northern Gulf's quaintest, oldest cities, property values were not rising. "I was just through there, driving around, yesterday." He didn't really want to mention that he'd been at the River House, up Bluff Road, the main artery in the neighborhood.

She tilted her head, putting her head in full shade. "I was too, thinking about the old days." A smile on the rueful side formed, faded. "I miss when the four of us were kicking around, trips out to the island, up the river, football trips on Friday nights."

She was pushing his buttons. Good ones. His smile was genuine. He nodded yes. "Suz, I do too. I remember those days with some regret sometimes. The, what do they call them, 'the halcyon days of youth?' And we had a lot of good times."

"What kinds of regrets? I thought the two of you, you and Pat, were like brothers in arms, brothers from other mothers."

"We were. Yes we were close, and at the time, Suz, and don't get me wrong. At the time, I kind of thought that you and me−" He stopped, he shouldn't say anything here.

174

She simply said, "—would be together. Me too. I did too." She went there on automatic. Filled in the blank.

He thought about her home back then, one of the ancient gingerbread-covered homes with a direct view of the bay, a rarity in Apalachicola. "So, where are you now? Out on the Island?

She chuffed a laugh. "No, I'm in mom's old place. She and dad moved up to Tallahassee, semi-gated retirement community. She said, as far away from storm surge as she could think and not be too far away from my kids." She rolled her eyes. "She didn't say, 'not too far away from me.'"

"And Patrick?"

"He's got a condo over in Carrabelle. He's got a boat in the water over there."

She moved a hand to her cheek, brushed back an errant curl. The movement was so *her!* Casual, understated, the hint of glamourous, looking good right now.

How many nights had he laid awake, thinking about her through the years, wondering about the tall skinny kid who'd bloomed into a fairly gorgeous young woman in that last year before graduation? He matched her stare, histories, memories, certain secrets flowed both ways.

They'd both shifted their glances to a kid paddling around the pool on bright yellow floaties. He broke the growing quiet. "I used to imagine the four of us married, you and me. Pat and Sandra. I had no idea what we'd all be doing, whatever it was, it wasn't here. But that we'd be together, still a foursome for cards or whatever." He laughed, embarrassed at his own candor, the color rising in his temples. He filled his cheeks and blew. "Whoof, didn't go down that way did it?"

"Jason, I'm sorry. Maybe I shouldn't have come over. I—"

"No, I'm glad you did. At this point, I'm at loose ends, professionally that is. I'm not exactly fired, but it wouldn't take much for that to be real. For the leave of absence to turn into absent without leave."

"You mean you'd stay here after the book?" Her eyes brightened, lost some of their latent melancholy.

"I don't have any idea. I really don't. I know North Florida pretty well. I know East Texas pretty well." He waved a hand encompassing the wide world. "There's a lot I don't know anything at all about.

175

Sometimes I wish the Army had sent me somewhere interesting. More interesting than suburban Virginia. Ick. Hell, in Texas, most of our vacations were five or six hours away, and we hardly ever left Texas."

"That marriage is really over? What was her name?"

"Caroline. And it is so over. Irreparable."

"Sorry that you had to do that. Go through that." Her eyes turned down, her fingers curled into loose fists.

"It's alright, Suzanne. Don't be sorry for me. It's an American rite of passage. Get through that first marriage, then get on with your life. In my case it was a second marriage, but..." Both of her fists clenched. "OH shit! I'm sorry, I didn't mean to imply. Crap. Color me Mr. Stupid." A tear track shone out of the shade of the straw sun hat. The rim momentarily dipped as she wiped at it with her wrist.

"You said second marriage?"

He swallowed hard, recalling. "Yeah, I met a girl in school, Penny, for Penelope. She was a dancer, a magician of souls, a budding Buddhist, and I completely fell off the rails for her. We married the week after graduation. She had a gig with a dance school in Austin and we moved out there." He pulled at a split nail. "We uh, we had plans, our whole lives planned out. Cancer had other plans." He winced as the piece of nail came loose. "We had six great years, and one that really sucked."

"I'm so sorry Jason," her voice soft, barely audible, "no kids?"

"No, no kids. I used to wonder what it would have been like... raising kids." He looked up again, met her eyes.

"At least you didn't have to do the single dad thing." She said it as if it was a consolation.

Then he realized she'd been doing the single mom thing. "How are you doing, with Pat, or without," his words were becoming clumsy, "parenting?"

"He's actually been great. We go to her school things together. Have some family meal times occasionally. He's a great dad." She opened her mouth to add something, waited. "He's just not a great husband."

"Christ, Suz. I heard you and Pat were going through some bad times? We really didn't talk that much about you guys when he was here."

Because Pat wasn't really here to talk. He was here to collect a DNA sample, maybe some prints. He said, "When he was here last week. Two weeks ago? I don't think catching up was really on his mind."

"I know," a sniffle, "he told me. I thought he was awful for doing what he did. I mean, if he said, 'Look, Jason, the sheriff asked me to do something, knows we're old friends. It's just a matter of checking you off a list.' That might not have seemed like betraying an old friend."

"Or ensuring that I'm on the list." That's precisely what it did feel like when I found out. He wondered how much she and Pat really talked. "What else did he tell you? About the DNA, the sheriff?"

"Not too much. I guess you're cleared, you're not arrested." Her smile was weak but hopeful.

"No," he said, "but I'd raise a lot of suspicious questions if I decided to leave the State of Florida."

"Jase, when he told me about it, I was furious, but I let it drop. We argue enough as it is. But he did tell me he felt like a real shit head for doing what he did. He could have told you straight up what he was doing, that Sheriff Pierson had asked him to collect a sample just to clear you, if nothing else." When he didn't respond, she added an opening. "So..."

He leaned forward on the table. Waited. Suzanne looked, if anything, expectant, shifted her weight, and leaned forward, elbows on the table. "Suzanne, twenty years is a long time. A long time to carry guilt around. When I came home from school late that summer. You were off in the Carolinas, but I checked in at your house first to see if you were back. That was before I even went to see mom."

He put up a shield, elbows on the table, he covered his eyes with his hands. Shame hurts. "I ran into Sandra, we had a few beers, she had a joint. A warm summer night ran its course. We enjoyed each other as old friends and very awkward lovers. I don't think either of us felt like it was love, just lovemaking. She was eighteen, I was nineteen. Grown up kids, but kids just the same." He swallowed the lump threatening to stop him from continuing. "I wish it had been you, Suzanne." His voice broke. He had to stop. He looked up. She was facing him, hat brim up. Tear tracks were flowing. He wanted more than anything to hug this good, good person. His old heartbreak. His

177

friend. But this was Patrick's wife. "Suzanne, everything is so different now. You are married to Pat. I'm...I'm in a relationship. Not a long one, but it's good, rewarding, comfortable. It might have a future if she wants it to."

She was shaking in her seat, vibrating. He stopped. *Fuck me, I'm a dumbass.* "I didn't think all of that was going to come out like that. I don't mean to hurt you. I'd never want to hurt you."

She took a breath, calmed herself. "Just a minute." He watched as she bit her lip, upper teeth giving her lower lip as much pain as she could stand. Her chin dimpled, something, possibly bile, swallowed. She blew out. "I was...it was a long time ago, like you said. Both of you left town, in different directions. Pat and I were the leftovers. We made the best of it."

"And now we know that it's not all good."

She looked up at him. Hard. Piercing. "Jase? Is it ever all good? Does anyone ever get that?"

"No, I suppose a lot don't."

Her head dropped but rose again, an off-center smile trying to re-establish itself.

She's strong, had to be, I guess. He realized he didn't know anything really, about her new life, about the last twenty years. "You look like you're doing OK, here. Staying here seems to have agreed with you."

The smile was back—the ten-million-dollar smile. "I've done OK, yeah. I worked my butt off, but I'm doing all right."

"Doing what?"

"Started in real estate. Managing rentals. I was the fresh young face that handed out keys, tried to tell people on the phone that no, their perfect week in that perfect house was already booked. But the real money is in commissions. I worked for one of the established companies for a while, then a friend and I started our own little company. She and I are doing pretty well." She held up two hands showing crossed fingers. "As long as the hurricanes go everywhere else."

He thought about the sixty-thousand-dollar Audi parked in the back row, her up-scale wardrobe. "I'm glad for you, Suzanne. I really am." Then as if to qualify the praise, "I'm glad you're doing well here."

"Thanks, and it gives me time to spend with Hannah. I get to set my work schedule. I ... we can afford to enjoy life's little pleasures."

He nodded, appreciating that a good life could be had here. Knowing too that their parents had come from different strata in a stratified town. He'd left, she'd stayed. Divergence, convergence. It brought him back to the present.

"Suz? Not sure I should ask."

"Ask. We're down to the bones here aren't we."

She'd summed it up. Things left unspoken for so many years had been cut open and laid bare, and they weren't going to change anything. "Why'd you come over today. Looking like ten million bucks."

She looked up from under the brim of her hat. "Why darling, I always do look like ten million bucks." Her smile was back, masking, but it was back. "Well, some days, only five million." She smiled through pursed lips. "I wanted to tell you something you don't know. You were gone, and it never made the papers, but it made the rounds if you know what I mean."

He nodded. "I do, yes I do know what you mean. What happened?"

"It's about Lindsey's family."

He drew in a breath. "OK. Shoot."

She looked up into the ribs of the umbrella, forming the paragraph that would have to unravel. "About eight years ago, there was a big sting operation on the offshore fleet. The Feds, ATF, FBI, Narcs, the Coast Guard, etc. Lots of jackets with big yellow letters on their backs. That made the news. But what didn't make the news came a little later. Wax-dipped and cellophane-wrapped kilos of pot started washing up. Several more of heroin a few days later were drug up in a net. At first, it was kind of a joke. Square mullet. There was some primo pot around for a while."

He smiled, imagining. "I can see that."

"Pat was on the force by then. Helped as liaison to the Fibbies." She stopped, "Sorry, that's what he called the FBI."

"Yeah, got it. So?"

"So, I shouldn't be telling you this at all. Dining room conversation in the privacy of our home. You don't know this. Two of the big trawler captains went down right away, two more were under investigation, lots of fingers pointing and talking about connections with the Columbian cartels. This is about when the Columbian government began to lower the boom back home and the cartel bosses were running scared."

"I remember." And he did, the biggest story to have ever erupted from his home county, and he was over seven hundred miles away.

"It turns out that Mr. Lawrence's boat was off sailing the deep blue sea on two of the occasions that the Coast Guard was making their calls on the fisherman. At first, he'd been called in as a witness. Then, one of the investigators began to really hound him. Nothing came of it. Jeremy's name never came up in the paper. But they had some successes. Pat said the rendezvous locations were over fifty miles out and Lawrence's phone could be tracked going toward those areas. But nothing could be pinpointed because of the distance from cell towers.

The Lawrences never made any secrets about their cruises. They'd casually say they were planning a cruise down to Tampa to take in a concert, come back the following week. So, they 'just happened' to be in the wrong place and at the wrong time. At least twice."

"You said Columbia?"

"Yeah, serious exporters by any and all means."

"Yes, they were, and probably still are."

"The investigation left town. We were just a staging area for some of the fieldwork, but Pat had made a friend in the ATF that he'd call from time to time, reporting comings and goings of the big boats. And he heard some things. Occasionally, I'd just happen to be standing on the other side of a bathroom door while he was talking. Curious, you know?"

He just nodded. Something had just clicked. "Sure, I understand."

"Lawrence's name came up. I checked the marina, their boat was gone. I happened to see it at the fuel dock three days later, and that night, Pat's on the phone in the bathroom again."

"So, he was reporting on Mr. Lawrence's whereabouts?"

"Yes, well, both of them would usually go out, both of the Lawrences, Lindsey stayed with a friend." Her brows knit tight. "That's what was so unusual."

He thought he'd been following. "What was unusual?"

"A year later when Mr. Lawrence went missing. Lost at sea. His wife had not gone on that cruise. She just said that he needed some alone time. We all learned that he got in trouble in a squall. The boat was found a couple of weeks later. The main mast was broken just above the boom. We saw it when it was towed in docked up at the city marina. Yellow crime tape all over the place."

"Had he ever been charged with anything, anything like formal charges?"

"No, he had a good lawyer, one of our best."

"You remember his name?"

"No, but I can check the listings. I'll text it to you."

"Please, do." She fidgeted, he sensed a bird getting ready for flight. She wore minimal make-up. Approaching forty, she was still stunning. "Suzanne, I truly hope you and Pat find a place, that place, where you can both be happy."

Her chin dimpled hard. She pushed her chair back to stand, he followed suit. He walked her to the car and walking beside her, their pinkies brushed. Their hands caught hold. She twirled, pivoting on her toes, and rose to plant a dry kiss on his cheek. "You be careful, ya hear?"

"Will do."

"Two flavors of cops have told you to back off, so just be careful. I know you're going to do whatever you want. But please—"

She was a half-head shorter than he was. He pulled her to him, arm around her back, lifted the straw hat, kissed her forehead. "Suz, if this were a different world, this could have been a different morning." He felt something in her deflate. "But it's not. Maybe in a different time, or different place. This is neither." Her head snuggled into his neck. The straw hat hung from one hand. He felt her head nod acknowledgment. "So, before we get really stupid, crazy stupid, you'd better leave."

He stood watching, so still he might have been cast in bronze. Watching as she backed, turned, and drove off. When she'd passed out of sight, a speeding red flash behind the neighbor's pines, he exhaled and slowly walked back to his camper. Something had clicked in their talk. He replayed their conversations, listening to the gravel crunching under his sandals. Something about Jeremy Lawrence's two-sided deal with the Feds and the Columbians. "Columbia, huh." He murmured. "That was what clicked." He remembered the tucked away honorarium from the Columbian Air Force, and he remembered exactly how crooked and double dealing their air force was back in the day. "Shit."

28

Hargreaves

Jason Saylor and Belle Tellefson had promised each other to get together for at least dinner each night. The pattern felt like grounding. Sharing their days' activities was real bonding. He shared his 'catching up' with Suzanne over a linen tablecloth on a corner two-top in the upscale Owl Cafe with some humility. Filling in some backstory, painting his life in short, colorful strokes. The greens and yellows, and the blues. Eventually, he got around to telling her about Suzanne's visit. That there had been depth to that high school relationship, but like so many other things, that it had drifted into the past. And based on that visit, there were still friendly ties that could be trusted.

He also shared the possible intrigue over Jeremy Lawrence's involvement with illicit import/export business. As the tables at the Owl Cafe began to empty around them, they noticed they were almost the last to leave. The spying creep on the river was now a known factor of unknown but possible danger. Even here, though, paranoia held sway, and she parked toward the back. They opted for the privacy of the campground pool enclosure. Sometimes, privacy is a good thing.

The pool wasn't quite warm yet, but they dipped anyway. Taking long pulls underwater, he could easily swim the length of the pool, do a roll-tuck-push and get halfway back. Belle could do better, two pool lengths without coming up. Tired and invigorated, they cuddled in the shallows. Caressing each other's gooseflesh, she straddled his crossed legs, hers locked behind him, her arms around his neck. They giggled like kids when the water proved too cold for him to perform. From out of the darkness, a voice called, "Get a room."

That broke them up. Through their own laughter, they heard chuckles from the darkness beyond the fenced pool enclosure. They decided to retire to his camper, 'to get a room.' On the counter, his phone's message screen indicated that messages had come in. His editor Lisa liked the idea for book three, [Topical, weave it into current post-covid geopolitical context]. *I can do that*, he thought. The next was from Suzanne. [enjoyed our chat, in spite of it all. I do still care. LLs atty is Sheldon Hargreaves be careful ♥♥].

"Belle?" Her name rose in question.

"Yes." Her arms were around his waist from behind. One hand, then two working at a button on his Hawaiian print shirt.

He felt the pressure of her breasts on his back. Knew from the pressure that there was nothing between them and the shirt. No bikini top, nothing. "Uhmm." Her fingers loosened the button, lowered to the next one. He closed his eyes, clasped his hands soft on her forearms. The last button came free, together they removed his shirt. Still behind him, her hands stroked the fine hair that formed a dark line down the center of his chest, rose, and tweaked a nipple each. He felt nibbles at the base of his neck, felt one of her hands lower, searching, diving under the waistband of his trunks. He turned, pulled her head to his, felt her lips open, felt her tongue dance.

Afterward, they lay on the not quite twin-sized bed at the back of the camper, something bigger than a cot, less than a real double bed. Campers were intended to cuddle. A white shaft of moonlight fell across the line of her hip and thigh. Saylor thought the profile, the curves of a woman's body, in almost any position was the source of more beauty in the world than perhaps any other single set of images. Belle's breathing was quiet beside his. She was curled facing the back wall. He tried to remember if she had mentioned which attorney she'd consulted to ensure the continuity of the store and protect the Lawrence's house. He thought back to Suzanne's text. Be careful and the hearts. That was after the bit about the attorney. Was that a warning? Or afterthought?

He rose to relieve himself. That was happening more and more as he pushed past thirty-five. Is this too soon? Do I need to get a checkup? Might want to do it while I still have insurance. He stepped back to the bed and saw moonlight shining off Belle's eyes.

"You're awake."

Sleepy sigh, "Yeah," a yawn. She shifted to cover her mouth as a second deeper yawn took hold. "Barely. Everything OK?"

"Yup," he slipped back under the sheet. "Just had to get up to pee." He rolled toward her, rested a hand on her hip. "Get some sleep, it's only three something."

"Before we came to bed, you were going to ask me something."

"I did? Uh, I was?"

"Seemed like it, maybe you were going to shatter my dreams with bad news."

"You have dreams?"

She kneed him softly. "You rat. You've burrowed into where I haven't let anyone be for a while now."

He kissed her forehead. "Sorry."

Silence and soft breathing. "I could have been wrong." She said, again sleepy, drowsy overtones slurring her speech. "Probably trivial."

He said, "Oh, I remember now."

"Fine, you almost let me get back to sleep, and now you remember."

"I had a message on my phone when we got back from the pool." He didn't want to get back into the Suzanne discussion, but the question remained. "Jeremy Lawrence's attorney, back when he was in possible trouble with the feds. It was Sheldon Hargreaves. Is that who you're working with now? With the estate?"

"Yes, that's the guy. Is that a problem?" She rolled back over to face the wall, scootched her butt into his curves.

He shifted a little closer, spooning. "Maybe not," he kissed the top of her head, rested a hand on her waist. "Get some sleep."

"Um, hmm." The only answer.

For just a moment, he notched himself up on an elbow. In the monochromatic light of the half-moon, his eyes traced the curves of her shoulder, hip, and thigh under the single-layer folds of the sheet. *Oh Christ!*

He woke early to find his mini-fridge nearly barren. Enough half and half for a cup of coffee each but only one yogurt, one stale English muffin, little else in the way of breakfast fixings. Belle opted to go to the River House to eat, shower, and prepare for work. Dawn's earliest light brightened the eastern horizon across the bay as he watched her pull out and drive off. He remembered his laptop was in the Prius and turned to get it. At his camper door, Saylor was reaching into a pocket for his keys when the starburst shell exploded at the base of his neck. He was aware of crashing to the paver block patio and then nothing.

29

All Will Be Revealed

Movement. Boat-like movement. Dreaming? Vertigo. Nausea. Headache. *Can't move my feet in the sheets. I Can't move anything!* He tried to roll over. Something hot blazed across his head. "Jeesus!" Hot sheets of pain flashed down the length of his spine.

"I think he's coming to." A voice, soft unfamiliar, female.

He opened his eyes, closed them. *I'm blindfolded?* He tried to move again, *and I'm bound?* The over-riding smells were plywood and human sweat. *Think! The laptop is in the car. You just said goodbye to Belle.*

He called out, "Belle!" Then, "Belle?" as a question. You said goodbye to Belle, a swish of air, pop, and a flash of light. The crack against the base of his neck with something heavy, hard. He couldn't move his hands to check the spot, but the base of his neck was the source of the stabbing pain.

"Are you OK?" The voice again. Not Belle, for sure. Lower timbre.

"No," slowly enunciating, "I am not O K." Movement again, *footsteps on plywood*? But the movement of a deck *or a boat at anchor?*

"Careful there, mister, all will be revealed," a second breathy, deeply southern female voice chuckled much closer, overhead. He tried to move back.

"Hold still now." The second voice, smoker's overtones and sounding very local, but still not Belle. Fingers pulled at the blindfold, lifted. It didn't get much brighter with the cloth removed. He blinked. A piece of lint hung in his left eyelid. She brushed at it with dirty fingertips. He wriggled but couldn't get upright.

"Easy now," the first voice said, "you were pretty beat up. Let her get you loose."

Taking stock, he'd been bound at ankles and wrists. A single low wattage light bulb hung on a wire strung over a nail near the middle of a blank plywood wall. The room seemed to be about right to be a truck trailer or a shipping container—long, narrow, not much taller than maybe eight feet wide. Two women, one was kneeling over him, working at his wrist bindings. Another young woman sat on a stool near the bulb.

The closer one, smoker's voice, pulled at his bound wrists. He shifted to sit up, saw that he was sitting on an old army blanket. As much as he could tell in the dim light, she had pale skin, medium brown hair, one of those designer blends, almost blond, but shading into the reds, at the tips. Not red hair red. That neon red that defied nature. She reached to flatten his tousled hair. Seeing him flinch, she backed up, stood. "I'm just going to turn you loose, be still."

"Careful, Mur." The other one said. The other, tanned, auburn hair shading toward a dark brunette at the roots. "We don't know why they tossed him in here."

He thought about the pronunciation, not Mar as in Mary, but Mur as in murder.

The one identified as Mur said. "You going to behave? We're small but mighty." The other one laughed without a hint of humor—a short huff at the back of her throat.

He nodded yes, shook his head at the cobwebs, blinked, then. "Yes, I'm going to behave. He held his wrists up to be released from the five or six wraps of duct tape. Mur smiled down at him through pursed lips. Both intent on her work and wary, not trusting, as she unwrapped the layers of tape, she asked, "You look like you're wide awake now. You hurt anywhere?" She pulled the last bit of tape off his left wrist. "Ouch!" White bands of flesh ringed the wrist, pale from contact with the tape, and now free of any hair. "Anywhere besides there." The smile widened. "That bump on your head looks harsh."

He felt the scar on his forehead from the sheriff's desk, then the really painful muscle trauma at the base of his neck. She pulled at the last strip of tape on his right wrist.

"Oww, damn!" He grimaced at the last pull of the tape. "Yes, back of my head feels like I got hammered." He thought about his word choice. "With a hammer, not drunk." Mur knelt down on one knee to help with the tape at his ankles. As she pulled at the outer layer's frayed edge, he pulled away from her reach. "I'll take the tape off, thanks though."

"Did I hear you say, Belle?" The one still sitting under the bulb asked. "You know Belle?" The brunette was pretty, even in the dim light and despite the smudges of dirt. Good lines. She'd clean up good. Appraising them, he thought that considering their conditions, they were both excellent candidates for trafficking, but not destined for the tomato-picking trade.

He remembered he'd just been asked a question. "Yes, the last person I remember seeing was Belle Tellefson."

"Who are you?" This from Mur, now standing. Below a loose over-large pullover, she wore tan cargo shorts. She went back to her stool and sat, then leaned sideways against the wall. The shifting weight made the room move. He had the same incipient vertigo sensation that he was afloat. That the room was floating. He chalked it up to concussion. Maybe another incident of syncope. He started to work with still feeble fingers at his taped ankles.

"I'm Jason, Jason Saylor." He spelled it. He looked from one to another. Introduction time. He focused on Mur. "Mur is short for what? Merlin?"

"Nah, Mercy, Mercy Brynn Johnston." She puffed a short laugh. "Mom was a super Christian. She had a hard time getting pregnant. Must o' thought it was God's mercy to give me to her." She flashed a hint of a smile. "God has a sense of humor."

"So, Mercy B?"

"You catch on fast."

He looked at the other girl. She seemed the younger of the two, more reserved but showing signs of exhaustion, maybe as scared as he was. She wore full-length stretch jeans and a formerly bright blue scoop-neck T with a fish logo over the heart in white. Not the idealized Christian fish logo, something closer to a sea bass. Both young women were scuffed, dirty, and were apparently in the clothes they arrived in. Who was asking who questions here?

He was afraid of knowing the answer, but he had to ask. The fish logo was too familiar. "And you are?"

The girl blew sideways at a curl of hair that kept flopping over her left eye. "I'm Lindsey, Lindsey Lawrence." A hint of a shrug. "Nothing cute to do with that. Usually, just Lin." Her face was blank, an emotional zero. She screwed her lips into an 'O' then pushed them to the side, considering him. Deadpan, she said, "If you've been downtown to meet Belle. That's my store."

He leaned back into the corner of the cell. His first thought, *Oh Shit!* There under a 25-watt bulb was his unacquainted daughter. She was in neutral mode because of shock or exhaustion. Saylor had to hold back his own surprise. He didn't want to lay what he knew on her just yet. Her face had been in partial shadow of the bulb almost vertical overhead. Its shadows distorted her features. She lifted her chin to blow again at the tuft of hair, and he saw it. The girl from the coffee shop. The girl from the restaurant. The girl on the beach in the seafood restaurant T-shirt. His daughter.

With a grudging smile trying to emerge, Lindsey said, "I'd say welcome to our abode. But really, we haven't had time to fix it up." She swiveled on her stool. "Let's see, this is the living room. I guess you're sitting in the foyer. Please watch your step next time you come in. That entry was a little rough." She pointed a thumb over her shoulder to the far end of the long rectangle. "Back there you'll find the bedroom," she waved at two thin mattress pads, "and our bathroom, restroom actually. No bath's possible." A porcelain toilet sat in the far corner.

Mur looked at Lindsey, "I guess it's now a unisex restroom." She frowned, "Is that the right word?"

Lindsey shrugged an I-don't-know. She leaned closer toward Saylor, peering in the low-wattage light. "Do I know you? Have we met?"

What to say? As little as possible for now. "Yes, I recognize you. We talked one night while you were fixing setups at the Fish House. I'd had an early dinner, it wasn't busy yet, we chatted."

"Right, then you were on the beach later. Shnockered on your ass."

Saylor felt his ears reddening. "I, uhm, yeah. And not since. Don't know if you remember me saying. I'd just been divorced. She used to tell me when to quit. She's no longer there."

Mur asked, "you on the wagon?"

"Not totally, but that's not really important."

Mur was right back at him. "So, what is important, Mr. Jayson the sailor?" She seemed to have a weird way of talking. A little arrogant. Aggressive? Yeah, aggressive, but a put-on, practiced self-defense aggression.

He raised his hands, palms up. "What's important? What the royal fuck? Why are you here? Why am I here? Why does this plywood box feel like it's floating?" His voice had been rising. Anger at having been ambushed. Anger at not knowing what happened to Belle. Anger at the apparent equanimity of these two girls. "And where the hell is Belle? I'd like to know what happened to her?"

Lindsey asked, "How do you know Belle?"

He looked at them. Lindsey, he knew to be nineteen, just past that birthday. Mur, Mercy, was hard to gauge. She might be a year or two older. Backwater country accent. More of the country musicality than Lindsey's. "First things first. I'm the new guy who doesn't know what the hell's going on. What is this thing." He looked side to side at his, their prison.

Mur said, "Dude, all we know is it's a floating plywood box."

He realized a faint hum had been background white noise for most of the time he'd been awake, the mechanical-electric buzz vibrated through the plywood walls. An AC unit? The questions just started piling up. "OK, let me give you my short story, then ya'll can give me what might be a longer story."

He began with the BOLO.

"What's a BOLO?" Mercy asked.

"Uhm, cop talk for Be On the Look Out"

Mercy nodded. He continued, "About two weeks ago, I got pulled over by the sheriff and put in a line-up because I fit a description. Blue compact car, middle-aged male, dark hair. So, I stood there with four other guys while someone behind the mirrored glass checked us out. It was because you, Lindsey, had been reported missing by Belle. The Belle from your shop. The Belle I'm worried about."

"That was a couple of days after Lindsey went missing. Two days later, I was called in again for a second interview. So, the sheriff and I got to know each other a lot better. According to him, I'm on his list of persons who should not leave town. There's at least one other still on his list."

"Wait a minute." Lindsey looked surprised and hopeful. "Sheriff Pierson *is* looking for us?"

Bruce Ballister

"Yes, he is. Because Belle registered a missing person's report. You live in the county, her address is your address, so jurisdiction went to the sheriff. There are pictures of you on half the telephone poles in Apalach, out on the Island, and I've seen a few in Eastpoint."

If anything, a small tight smile grew on Lindsey's face. He offered the last tidbit he'd heard on the news. As local efforts to locate her had been failing, the FBI had been asked to provide assistance. "Maybe they'll help. They are supposed to be here tomorrow or the next day. I forget."

She looked grim. "Mr. Saylor, what can—"

"I'm just Jason, or just Jase. No mister needed." And anticipating her question. "Who knows, the Feds might help with the other suspects? They can be pretty persistent. I've met a few of their field types."

Mercy seemed to brighten up. "You have? What do you do?"

"I'm a reporter. I work, used to work, for the Houston Chronicle. But I was back here to take some time off the job." *No need to get into another long story here.* "I came back to write a book or two. Relax a bit, kick back. Then this happened, and—" He leaned back into the plywood paneling, sighed in exasperation. "—I got involuntarily involved." He gestured at Lindsey, then looked at Mercy. "What about you?"

"Me?" She puffed, "Pffft. Me, I'm just the original occupant of this plywood hotel." She affected an air. "I really wish we'd known to expect you, we'd have tidied up."

He'd seen it before, humor to mask terror. "Mercy, how long have you been here.?"

"A little over three weeks, I think. I'd been scratching on the walls like they do in the prison movies, but I'd go to sleep, wake up to the same god-damned light bulb and not know if it was the same day or not." She looked to Lindsey. "Then she showed up with a watch that tells the date. She's been here two weeks."

Saylor nodded. That seemed about right. He'd lost track of days of the week. His only measure had been when Belle had Sundays off. This was, he thought, a Tuesday.

He looked at Lindsey, "What time is it, what day?"

"Tuesday, twentieth, 12:30."

"PM?"

"Yes, you were only here about, I guess about two hours before you woke up."

"So, somebody whacked me, bundled me up in broad daylight, and brought me here?"

Lindsey pointed at the blanket he was sitting on. "That's what you were wrapped in when they tossed you in here. We weren't sure if you were alive or not. We unwrapped you, tried to make you a little more comfortable."

"They took you in daylight?" Mur asked.

"It was pre-dawn; just getting light. I think I was going to get something from the car—my laptop." He patted his pants pockets, no phone, and remembered it was on the counter inside the camper. He looked down at the blanket, didn't recognize it. At least, he knew he didn't own it, and it didn't look like something from the Lawrence's house. He thought about it. "Whoever did it, was ballsy enough to take me in plain sight of a well-traveled highway."

"Day-um." Mur's speech had more added notes than most.

"Yeah, dammit all to hell." He rubbed gingerly at the throbbing lump at the base of his neck. He thought, there's going to be some severe bruising there. His eyes focused on the ragged edges of the olive drab army blanket. Its color dating it back to the previous century's Korean or Vietnamese wars. "Lindsey? Does this blanket look like it might have come from your house?"

"Never seen it before."

Good, not from there. Belle may be OK still. He took in the plywood walls, the floating sensation. The theory that he'd been moving closer to for a few days had come to life with him in a walk-on role.

"This is a houseboat, somewhere up the river?"

Lindsey answered. "Yes, only not *on* the river. The only time we hear any motors is when Robbie or Shirk comes by to deliver food and water. I think we're up one of the tidal creeks. They probably put up a 'Trespassers Will Be Shot' sign or something."

Saylor thought about that, probably true. He looked back at the incongruous toilet. A roll of toilet paper hung on a length of string from another nail. He noticed a grill in the far corner of the ceiling. "I'm guessing that's a boat or RV air conditioner running on solar-powered batteries?"

Mercy responded. "Pretty sharp cookie. Got us all figured out. Even the plumbing?"

"Hole in the floor?" A small craft manual bailing pump in the corner was attached to a PVC pipe through the floor. He nodded toward it. "That pump fills the tank." He smiled at Mercy, who looked to be about to put on another show of fawning over his intellect. "I was an investigative reporter. I figure stuff out real well." He found his childhood accent becoming more accentuated. The speech of his youth, before the amalgam of east Texas, before college. "Where are you from, Mercy?"

She looked back toward Lindsey. Something was exchanged, eye language. Lindsey nodded yes. Mercy turned back to Saylor. "I was sitting outside a bus stop in Marianna, waiting for the eight o'clock bus to Montgomery. Marianna's up the road. You know where that is?"

"I am from here, Mur. I'm a local boy. I know exactly where. North side of town or south?" It made a difference.

"Nowhere actually, open land northwest of Marianna, south of Cottondale. 'Bout as country as you can get without raising pigs. My folks were decent folks." Her voice had a shade of challenge to it.

He held up his hand in mock surrender. "Not saying a thing. Just..." *Get back on track.* "So, someone stopped to see if you needed a ride? How'd that go?" Saylor saw the slump in Mercy's posture. *Dammit, idiot!*

She looked down between her knees. The silence drew out. He saw the changes in Mercy's face. The jaunty, I can take on the world act was gone. A little girl in pain looked back. Lindsey said softly to her. "Mur, you don't have to tell him. It's not important."

Mercy rocked her head back and forth slowly, still focused on her shoes. He noticed them for the first time, tread worn thin, scuffed. They needed a pass through a washing machine. She looked at Lindsey, sidelong, mouthed something that looked like 'fuck you too,' then straightened to match his expectant stare. "What if we just say they had their way with me, coupla times, and leave it at that."

"Jesus, I'm sorry. Who...?"

"Shirk first, then Robbie, then...both." Mercy's face melted, she got up from the stool and walked toward the far end of the box. He then noticed the bruising on the back of her legs.

He didn't know what to say. "Lindsey, did they mess with you?"

"Robbie tried, I kneed him where it counts. Took his mind off me for a while." She flashed a grin. "Not the first time, I don't think he likes me anymore."

The silence drew on. He'd scratched at a very raw wound. "Mercy, a day or two ago, I lost track, there was a news item on the Panama City station about Lindsey's disappearance. Nothing about you. To my knowledge, no one knows you're missing."

"Figures." She shook her head. Disgust? Disappointment? "They thought I was gone off to Montgomery. I guess they think I'm up there, having a grand old time."

He wondered how many other girls simply go missing; not missed until it's far too late. He looked beyond them past the dim bulb into the dark recesses beyond. "I don't suppose you two have figured out any way out of here. Banged on the walls, looked for loose flooring? That kind of thing?"

Lindsey looked over her shoulder toward Mercy, then back to Saylor. She said, "If you were going to go to the trouble to store a couple of kidnapped girls, wouldn't you first go to the trouble of making it hard for them to get out?" She looked at him like he was a simpleton. "Duh!"

Mercy turned around, wiping her cheek dry. Spoke up. "I'm not the first one to get to spend their holidays here either. When I got here it still smelled of disinfectant, like it had been hosed down with bleach or something. And there was that scratching on the door and around the hole in the floor at the toilet. Someone was in here and probly as scared as I was."

He shook his head. "This sucks. I'm guessing this machine has been operating for a while." He glanced up at the thin line of light coming in around the door frame, noticed the pathetic scratch marks. *With what? Fingernails? Plastic knives?* He asked. "How often does Robbie or Shirk or someone bring food, water, resupplies?"

Mercy answered, "About every two days. I had asked for a clock those first few weeks, to keep track of time, to know when to eat, sleep. Shirk just laughed and said to eat when I got hungry, sleep when I got tired. That he'd try to get here every two days."

"How old is Shirk?"

They both shrugged. Mercy spoke up. "I don't know, 'bout forty or so. He's real rough and strong." She wrinkled her nose. "And he stinks like he doesn't like showers."

Saylor just nodded. "When they come, do you they always come alone? If you only see one, does that one talk to anyone else in the boat?"

Lindsey answered this time. "This morning when you dropped in, there were two of them. Robbie and Shirk."

Mercy added. "First time there's been two in a while. Most of the time now, it's just Robbie." She looked over her shoulder at Lindsey, who'd stood, stretching. "She showed up at gunpoint. Mr. H and Robbie came then." Lindsey nodded her agreement, scowled.

"Mr. H? He have a name?"

"Hargreaves." Lindsey looked like she could spit nails. "Sheldon fucking Hargreaves.

"Holy shit." Saylor muttered softly, "Hargreaves?"

"Yes, Holy shit. My fucking lawyer."

30

Fucked-Up World

"Sheldon Hargreaves?"

"The one and only, total piece of crap Sheldon Hargreaves." Lindsey moved back to her stool, sat.

"That's beginning to make sense." He looked up at her. "Would you mind moving that stool to the opposite wall? That light may not be much but it's right above your head. Makes it hard to look straight at you."

"Sure." She grabbed the stool top between her legs and moved six feet to the left. "In what universe does Mr. H. being involved make any sense?"

He puffed and blew out. *How to condense two weeks of research and effort? How much to tell her before anything else happens?* "Remember? The sheriff considers me one of his favorites for your abduction?"

"Yeah, that's not going so well is it?" Mercy smirked, sharing a look with Lindsey.

Saylor tried to remain sanguine. "No, not for him. Looking on the bright side, this is a boost to my case. Why would I conspire to have my ass tossed in here with the person I'm supposed to have kidnapped?"

Mur said, "Hell of an alibi!"

"Alright, granted." Lindsey acknowledged, "Still don't know how my lawyer doing this makes sense."

Saylor had been sitting up, leaning into the same corner he'd been dumped. Testing his legs, he stood. The space was even smaller than he'd thought when he was lying down. He could easily reach and press against the plywood sheathed ceiling. He looked up and pushed. It didn't give.

Back to the question. "A week or so ago, I ran into Belle when I was trying to figure out who would gain from your disappearance." He indicated Lindsey with a nod. She actually asked me to help."

"Get anywhere?" Lindsey asked.

"I'd really only come up with two scenarios." He held up an index finger. "In plan A, you've been kidnapped, come into harm's way: rape, imprisonment for resale on the trafficking market, or a simple rape and murder by some psychopath."

"A simple rape and murder." Lindsey's face contorted in disgust. "What fucked-up world do you live in?"

He shrugged. "It's a fucked-up world in a lot of places." He paused. "Human trafficking for sexnyrf is too common."

Mercy held up her index finger. "Just a minute. Your Plan A has two scenarios. Sell her as goods, or murder." She tilted her head, looking for agreement.

"Well, yeah. But either way, it's just to get rid of her. Nothing to do with her estate." He extended a second finger on his right hand. "Plan B has someone looking to get their hands on Lindsey's estate. You have no known next of kin, right?"

She didn't respond immediately. He waited, remembering the letter in the safe. She said, "It's possible, but that's a long shot story, not relevant."

He nodded. "Look, with no next of kin, probate would be a bitch, but someone could eventually get their fingers in that pie." He made sure he had eye contact with Lindsey. "It's a big pie!"

She stared back at him with slowly widening eyes. "The store, a house or two? What?"

"According to the property appraiser, and some realty sites, a handful of beach houses and the River House add up to almost four and a half million. According to the actual market prices, closer to five and a half million. I'm trying to remember now if the store property was in that mix, but then too, there's the stock. That's probably worth a hundred thou wholesale. If liquidated, it could bring someone another couple of years' worth of spending money. Then there's the trust money set aside for your school. If you aren't around to use it for that purpose, it will go somewhere."

Her eyebrows knit in question. "Where?"

He continued. "Most likely a lot of it would go to the trust attorney who handled the liquidation, Mr. H, as you call him. Not the best friend of the family I could think of. And actually, according to the sheriff's digging, your real net worth is closer to ten million."

He waited for the reaction. The girls did an almost comic double-take. Looking at him, drop-mouthed, then each other, then back to him. "There are papers in your parent's fireproof vault that hint at a lot more wealth, at least one off-shore account. I never got time to look at them, but there are a couple of envelopes in that stack from the Alexandria Bancorp, in the Caymans. Lindsey, I don't know how a lot of that was accumulated? Some of it may have been good investments at the right time. Your folks possibly had good business sense. But there are hints in what Belle and I found out that point to something going on under the table."

Lindsey's questions tumbled out. "You and Belle? Ya'll got into dad's safe? She's helping?"

"Yes, we did a bit of research on your holdings, and she got limited power of attorney to maintain the business." He added, "So you don't get foreclosed on by anyone in your absence. She's a good friend, Lindsey, to both of us. She's been helpful in finding out tidbits of information. She's worried about you." Lindsey just nodded at first, digesting.

Saylor shifted his glance to Mercy. She'd been following the exchange like a spectator at a tennis match. "Mur? Do you know if you or your family have any assets? Anything of value that a third of it could be worth a lot to Hargreaves?"

"Why a third?"

"That's a lawyer's typical take, subject to a lot of conditions, but that's typical for settlements."

Mur shook her head, side to side. "All daddy's got is a doublewide, and some ancient tools in a pole barn on two quarter sections of pine trees."

He had to think back to Florida surveying. It had been a long time since he'd taken Florida geography in high school. "Two quarter sections make three hundred and twenty acres. Half a square mile. If most of that is pine trees, that's a lot of money standing there." Then he remembered Hurricane Michael. The storm had come ashore near Panama City and cut a swath of destruction up the west side of the

Apalachicola River and onward deep into South Georgia's ag lands. "Did those trees get destroyed in Michael?"

"Some did, some were young and just blew around a bit, and the big ones did alright. I drove the burn roads with him. Only the post pines were bent over, some broken. We were mostly on the west side of the storm. So the ones that got blowed down were pointing south. Weird looking!"

"Where exactly was this property?

"Up near Cottondale. Up the road from that new sawmill."

"And your parents are alive and well?"

"Momma's sick, but I think most of it is her gin. She's a ginny. Daddy's got heart problems. But he does alright."

"Do you have any brothers? Sisters?"

"Did. My older brother drove his truck into a tree on I-10. Two years ago."

Saylor didn't respond, just nodded.

Mercy asked, "So, does that mean anything?"

He was thinking out loud. "Both of your families have property assets. Somebody with the appropriate legal skill set could make a lot of money managing estates in probate.

He looked back up at Mercy. "You ever hear your folks talk about selling?"

"Well, yeah. There's a big push to turn that area into some kind of industrial development. A Korean car company or something." She pronounced it 'Ko-Rean.' "They've been asked to sell. Daddy was waiting for the price to go up." She shrugged. "They'll probably just get someone else's property. It's split in two by a railroad."

"Serious? There's railroad access?"

"CSX runs through twiced a day."

"Mercy, that property is probably worth a whole lot of money. Your dad has what others don't. Industrial development loves a railroad."

"Oh, Day-umm, didn't think of that." She looked to Lindsey with round questioning eyes.

Lindsey asked, "what do you think any of this means?"

He leaned back into the corner of the plywood walls. "Just guessing at motive here. But both of you are, if you don't mind me saying, very attractive young women. It could mean..." He stopped himself. Did he want to say it out loud? What had been worrying him for weeks about Lindsey?

"Could mean what? For crying out loud." Mercy had come back to her stool. She was poised to sit but stood motionless.

"It could mean that you are going to be sold. Trafficked." He sighed heavily. "Both of you." Now that it was out there, he added. "Or you would both be dead by now."

Mercy muttered a soft, "well fuck me," and sat down.

"My guess is that Mr. H, attorney Hargreaves, is waiting on a connection to get you two west to New Orleans or Corpus Christi, or south to Miami. Then you'd disappear."

Lindsey whistled softly. "Been thinking about that." She exchanged a look with Mercy. "We both have." She waved an overly expansive hand at the small quarters, two stools, a light bulb, an old trash can, and the toilet. "What else do we have to talk about?"

Mercy asked. "So, why are you alive? Why aren't you gator food?"

He pursed his lips, frowned. "My best guess is they want to find out how much I know. Maybe... I don't know."

"Maybe what?" From Lindsey.

"Maybe they know I've been getting close to finding out what's going on and need to know how much I've shared with the sheriff."

Lindsey said, "As soon as they get a chance to talk to you, you're not worth much more to them. Right?"

Saylor nodded. He'd come to the same conclusion. He knew there weren't going to be many chances to get it right, to maximize any opportunity. "We need to make sure that if Robbie or Shirk comes alone next time, that we are on the offensive. If Hargreaves comes, then, I don't know. Play it by ear?"

Lindsey asked, "You have something in mind?"

"Let me think on it." He had been thinking about what to do next off and on during the conversations. Question and answer with the two girls helped fill gaps and close off some ideas. There was no metal in the room. They were given plastic cutlery with the food deliveries, or nothing at all. The trash can was plastic. Trash was taken every few days. The only holes in the enclosure were the vent for the solar-powered AC unit and the hole under the toilet. Both were far too small for even Mercy, the thinner of the two, to squeeze through. A simple glance at the wall showed the plywood walls were screwed down. A sixteen-inch pattern in all directions. More than a match for plastic knives. The door hinge and locks were on the outside, and he could see the rounded end of carriage bolts that fastened them to the outside. Not easy to break out through the door. And there would be no boat to leave wherever they were.

He offered. "The best thing I can come up with: "Plan A, a bum's rush. We charge Robbie or Shirk at the door."

Mercy said. "They're armed and know you're in here now. Not as easy with them pointing a gun at us."

He addressed both of them. "You said that normally it's just one person making supply runs?"

Lindsey said, "Yes, most of the time it's just been Robbie." She huffed, "Squirrelly little shit."

"We might need to draw him in. Maybe, hmm. I think I have an idea." He put his fingers to his chin, thinking.

31

Exceptionalities

They finally figured out how to tell if it was daylight or not. By lifting an edge of the toilet off the floor, an easy feat because the plywood was rotting around the base, they could tell if the water below was mud-brown or night-black. That evening, the water below seemed brown, murky brown. Gator-friendly brown. Creatures that can navigate in the dark and hunt by their prey's vibrations have an enormous advantage in murky brown waters. The next morning, at 6:30 by Lindsay's watch, the water was clear but stained tannic brown by cypress. A shaft of sunlight lit the circle of visible bottom, possibly four or five feet down. Putting the porcelain throne back in place was the only difficulty. It was in all their interests to make sure it still flushed to the river and not seep inside their plywood holding cell.

The knowledge they gained was verification that their floating prison was up a tidal creek. Tidal action meant they were still much closer to Apalachicola than Wewahitchka, the next nearest town fifty miles upstream. Their creek was flushed by silt-brown river water on the rising tide, back-flushed by tannic, tea-colored, clear-ish water on the ebb tide. Whether this knowledge would be helpful was anybody's guess. The girls' earlier assertion that they were up a seldom-visited side creek seemed to be borne out. Saylor's first day in the box had passed in conversation with Lindsey and Mercy; exploration of any possible means of escape, and brief histories. They were astonished that he really was a local boy, but only completely convinced when he turned on his high school version of his home boy accent.

On his second afternoon in the box, the hours bore on, tension growing with the anticipation of a food run or an in-force visitation by their captors or their captor's bosses to deal with Saylor and any information he might have, or...who could guess? They discussed it until no one wanted to discuss it anymore. The overhead air conditioner hummed on but began to drop behind the demands of late April. Saylor felt sweat forming on his forehead. He'd already soaked through his shirt at his pits. His funk joined the general funk of the plywood and nervous-anxiety-fear sweat that had been the resident perfume of their prison since he'd come to. He wondered absently, and for the third time in he didn't know how many few minutes what time it was. A low distant rumble bespoke an afternoon thunder cloud reaching maturity.

"Lindsey, what time is it?"

She appeared to wake from some reverie. "Uhm, 4:30," she dropped her wrist, "ish."

"Ish?"

She raised her wrist again, tapped the dial, "4:32." She flashed him a brief disinterested smile. "Better?"

"Thanks."

"You have someplace you were supposed to be?" Mercy asked with almost no sincerity.

He huffed a laugh, "Any place but here would do fine." He looked up, matching Mercy's glazed stare. "Mercy, how old are you?"

"Twenty-two, twenty-three in July." Her brow wrinkled in question. "Why?"

"Just curious, you know. It's my reporter's genes kicking in." He didn't say he was wondering what her approximate market value would be in the Central and South American flesh markets.

Mercy sat up, straightening her spine. She tilted her head. "Well, Mr. Reporter Man. Turn on your mental tape recorder." She shot him an enigmatic grin. He couldn't tell if it was wit or bravado. "I'm Mercy Brynn Johnston, twenty-two, female, coulda been a blonde but washed out as a brunette. Been 'experienced' for going on eight years now. Graduate of WAVE, class of '16. And now, if I wasn't looking to a career in the international meat market, I'd be looking for a job." When she registered the usual confusion, "she spelled out, "W-A-V-E, Washington Academy of Varying Exceptionalities." She winked, "I'm exceptional."

"I can see that." He flashed her a grin and a nod.

"Means they thought I was too stupid to care and didn't want me to drop through any more cracks. Then they tested me, and I was a grade or two above the other eighth-graders in English and could do algebra backwards and forwards. I was more of a behavior problem than they wanted to deal with. So, I got STEM-ed." She eyed him for recognition. "You know about S-T-E-M?"

"Yeah, and I guess that's a good thing?"

"Yup, overall, but remember that 'varying exceptionalities' part? Some of my short bus classmates were really doing all they could do to clap hands and not miss." She sighed, looked down between her feet, then looked up again. "I guess that's not fair. I'm just glad that I got born with brains and not fetal alcohol syndrome. I'm glad someone saw something in me and got me out of my spiral, and no one hit the flush handle. I did end up learning a few things."

"Good for you." He nodded in recognition of his own preconceptions. He knew in his head that accents mask intelligence. He'd let her thick panhandle accent and her decision to travel by interstate bus paint his assessment of her into too many stereotypical corners, many of which he'd fled from. Although the speech of rural Panhandle Floridians is distinct to a trained ear from that of eastern Texans, he'd managed to fit in as a local to most. Then he'd done his damnedest to wash the accent away. He absorbed the new understanding. "So, did you take anything in particular? College prep?"

"No, nothing like that. Not planning on going either. Systems programming, coding, web services, website services. That sort of thing is good pay now, better pay later. If I ever get the urge to bone up on the medieval wars of western Europe, I can buy the book."

"Your parents must be proud."

"Shit, momma was pissed that she had to drive me to a school the buses didn't go to. Cottondale is clear across the county from the W-A-V-E" She paused, as if considering whether to go deeper. "Mom was a fan of gin and Jesus, worked part-time waitressing a breakfast and lunch buffet in Marianna. Dad worked his trees, harvested pine straw in winter, liked his two or three Natural Lights before dinner. He did some carpentry around the county and took what he called his heart pills when he remembered them."

Decent, hard-working country folk, he summed. Possibly no connection with the estate angle he thought Hargreaves was working. Hargreaves or his people would have to engineer the deaths of an alcoholic and a heart patient. Maybe that was not too hard. It could be that Hargreaves was working the long shot, or perhaps it was just that Mercy was a target as she was. Worth good cash in the flesh markets.

The next thunder crash made them all jump. The plywood walls actually reverberated with the blast. With no hope of seeing anything, all looked up at the wooden ceiling as if it could give a clue. And on cue, the already underpowered bulb dimmed. Saylor saw that both girls noticed the dimming bulb. Lindsey pointed up. It was the gesture of a Christian point to the heavens, but her target was the now silent air conditioner. She said, "Oh crap!"

Saylor knew it to be true. The unit's vibration had been the background white noise, omnipresent, so constant that it became unnoticed; until it stopped. Whatever wiring had been on the roof had been too close to the lightning strike and fried. Perhaps, he thought, a capacitor blew. He tried to inject a hopeful note. "Well, it's probably cloudy out there, chances are the sun will have gone behind clouds."

"Not the point, mister." Lindsey pointed up again. "That thing is our fresh air supply." She saw his eyes shift to the noticeably dimmer bulb. "That's on battery until there's no more battery. Could be the solar panel is dead too. Don't suppose you have a flashlight on you, do you? Or a fan, or a saw?" Her wisecracking humor was on point. They'd soon be needing a way to exchange air with the outside world, and it would soon be pitch dark in their box. Their present options were the hole in the ceiling blocked by the AC unit, the hole in the floor blocked by a toilet, and a thin crack at the door sill.

For at least the fourteenth time, he made the pat-down pocket inventory. "I got nothin'" His eyes again surveyed their cell. "So, essentially, we're in a cave. This is all the air we're going to get until someone comes." He got up from his corner perch. He could reach the ceiling, but only just. Saylor figured they'd used two by four studs, but instead of resting the ceiling rafters on a capping course, the builders had cheaped out and nailed the rafters into the sides of the studs. Easy weekend construction where building codes were non-existent.

He walked to the back of their cell and examined the sixteen-inch square grill. He hooked fingers between the blades of the draft deflectors and pulled. He nearly pulled his weight off the floor before the grill came loose. He stumbled back with fingers still stuck in the metal slats and fell on and then off the toilet. Coming to rest against the wall, hands and arms outstretched with the grill still held aloft, he began to laugh at his clumsy efforts.

The girls' faces transformed from shocked concern to humor at his own embarrassment, then morphed into outright giggles. Mercy said, "That would have been easier with a screwdriver."

"No lie, sweetheart." He was in a careless heap beside the toilet.

"Are you OK?" Lindsey asked?

He carefully extricated his fingers from the blades of the grill and stood. He felt at the back of his neck. It was still sore, but not as bad as when he'd come to. He then felt places in his back and butt that would be exhibiting bruises the next day. If, he remembered, he was to have a next day. Moving back to the exposed underside of the AC unit, he saw that it was the type that flush-mounted to a camper's roof. Its intake and exhaust ports shared a much smaller opening. It was a twelve-inch square opening that no one could hope to squeeze through. He also saw that he would need to get closer to see if the unit could be removed to allow free air circulation with the outside world.

Using one of the stools, he could get his head into the air space between the ceiling rafters. He was feeling for whatever fasteners might be holding the air conditioner in place when another electric crash and boom of thunder rolled overhead. He'd pulled back and cringed as automatic impulses pulled his hands and head away from the dangers outside. As he stood again, gentle shushes of rain on the roof deck began and, in a few moments, changed pitch into the steady roar of a heavy downpour.

He stepped down, looking back up into the hole in the ceiling. "Well shit." He moved back to his blanket and curled into a cross-legged pose in the corner.

"Well shit, what?" Lindsey asked.

"Well, the oxygen in here will probably last longer than this downpour." He hoped it would be true. He knew the rains would probably lighten in ten to fifteen minutes and might be gone in thirty. He also knew they could last all night. He explained that if he could dislodge the AC housing and it continued to rain, their relatively safe and already uncomfortable cell would become a wet, dank misery. Rain would pour through the opening. They could move away from that end of the box, but their weight would create a slope in their floating cell that would cause the rain to run toward them.

"So," he finished, "we should decide by vote. Do we breathe what we've got till we can't stand it or go ahead and open this box up to the weather."

Lindsey raised a meek hand. "I vote for waiting a bit. If we have to break that open to breathe, let's see if we can miss getting soaked in the process."

"Yeah, sounds good to me." Mercy agreed, giving a princess wave with her left hand.

He nodded, "Agreed." Then looked up at the roof, which still rumbled under the heavy downpour.

An hour later, the air was distinctly stale. A forebrain headache was forming distinct from the pain at the base of his skull. Saylor recognized that this incipient headache was probably due to oxygen deprivation. They would need fresh air soon. If they waited much longer, he or they might not have the strength to break the air conditioner off its mounting screws. They agreed, by common reckoning, that the occasional light patter on the roof might only be drips from overhanging branches and not the trailing effects of the storm. No thunder had been heard for a while. All hoped they could avoid whatever rainfall that might be lingering.

Saylor found himself again balancing on one of the stools, his head inside the cut-out in the ceiling. He ducked and asked, "Can one of you unwrap the wire on that light and see if I can get some light up in here?"

Lindsey unwrapped the wire on the nail that secured the light and brought the bulb on a wire to him. The added light confirmed what he could tell from feeling around in the dark. The outer layer of roof decking was another simple layer of plywood over framing. The edges of the hole were lined with roofing felt and sheet metal. In one or two places around the bottom of the roof's cut-out opening, he could see small bumps in the plywood or even a few screw tips. And the decking was barely a half-inch thick. Depending on what was used as waterproofing around the edges, maybe, just maybe, he'd be able to bash and beat against the unit and knock it loose.

Mercy was at his side, holding her stool. "Here, have at it. It's the only hammer in town."

He stepped off his stool and noticed the difference. One had three legs. Mercy's stool had four. The beginning of an idea began bubbling: an augmentation to their Plan A. But the immediate problem was at hand. He took the stool by two legs and bashed upwards. Looking into the hole, he saw he'd only dented some of the sheet metal around the intake and exhaust ports. He took a deeper breath of the thinning air and pushed the stool up into the hole again.

"Don't be shy with that thing," Lindsey called to him.

"All right ladies, here we go." He took another deep breath, feeling that the air was no longer giving all the energy it should.

Bang, bang, bang, crack.

A thin line of daylight glowed from one corner of the AC. He turned to the girls, raised an eyebrow in victory, and positioned the stool again. Pushing up against the weight of the unit, he pushed with his remaining strength. Crack, creak, and release. He felt the movement of the heavy air conditioner. He figured it to weigh only sixty to seventy pounds, but it was a straight-up push, and he was winded and working with the oxygen depleted air in the box.

Panting, he motioned the girls to come over. "You two grab two legs each and shove when I say shove." He pulled his stool to the side and made room for them directly under the opening. With effort, he positioned himself with his arms extending up into the hole and his head among the legs of their stool. He found an area of the AC's frame that was flat metal and got ready.

"Ready?"

"Yes," in unison.

"On three—one, two, three. Push."

They all did, the last screws pulled free and the thing moved. But it had to go sideways to let air in. Briefly, a bright flash of light reflecting off the machine blinded him before it fell back onto its original position. Without looking down, he said, "It has to move sideways. I think to my left it's still hanging on to some weather stripping or something or maybe a final screw. I don't know. The next push should be easy but try to move it to my front. I'll be pushing it that way."

In response, he felt the next shove from below and he pushed again. This time, with a bit of side English, it slid forward. When it fell back, a thin triangle of sky was visible. The lumpy side of a dark gray thunderhead filled the narrow view. Wonderfully sweet-smelling rain-swept air eddied into his confined bit of airspace between the rafters.

"Woo hoo!" and "Hot damn! We did it!" from below.

"Sorry ladies, we're gonna need more than that." He filled his lungs with the freshening air. "Ok, again, give me two or three more pushes. I'll be trying to shove it to the side each time." Another deep breath, and he felt the headache subsiding. "Ok, give me push, two, three, four, push."

Saylor counted the cadence and in four push cycles, they had moved it to the side and almost clear of the entire opening. He stepped down and away, letting the girls breathe in the freshening air under the opening.

"That, my young friends, showed your exceptionalities to a T. "He winked at Mercy.

He looked back up at the new opening as a low distant grumble echoed from the departing storm. He squinted into what appeared to be the fading light of evening, trying to understand what direction the thunder had come from, decided it didn't matter, and then noticed a thin whining overtone.

An outboard!

"Quick, someone's coming. I hear a motor." He stepped quickly over to his corner. The stools were back in place with one minor modification. "Get ready for Plan A. Adlib the deal with the AC." As he got into position, he saw with satisfaction that Lindsey was restoring the bulb to its nail on the wall.

32

DON'T!

At 6:20 p.m. by Lindsey's watch, they listened with mounting tension as the approach of an outboard became more apparent. The motor throttled down as it drew close. Saylor asked, "Does that sound like Robbie?"

Mercy answered, "Couldn't say, but that's his boat." They made final preparations for Plan A. The two girls had wrapped his wrists and ankles in tape, but not together. Using pieces of the tape he'd taken off they applied a single strip of tape over the top of his wrists and also incompletely around his ankles. These bindings could be pulled apart quickly but gave the appearance that he was still bound. They guided him into the approximate curled position he'd been in when dropped off. Perfecting the scene, they draped the bit of army blanket over him that had partially covered his body.

The approaching boat slowed to an idle, then stopped as it bumped against the raft. The box shifted with the extra weight of someone stepped onto its deck. They listened to the rattle of metal on metal and the unlocking of the hasp lock. Then a shout. "Ya'll get back from the door now. Ya hear? I don't want no funny business." The door cracked open. A thin shaft of early evening light tripled the brightness inside the box.

Lindsey called out. "Hey, Robbie, did you bring something cold this time? Hot Coke is not worth drinkin' on."

"You just shut your smart mouth, y'hear?"

Saylor could see through squinting eyes that Caine's shadow on the wall had him in the doorway. He'd have to wait.

The girls squinted against the glare and appeared to be cowed into submission. Mercy called out to Robbie, his skinny profile dark against the light. "Hey, I think you killed that dude. No matter what your mama tells you, you're a fucking idiot."

Still outside, Robbie took the bait. Stepped into the doorway. "You shut the fuck up, bitch. You want me to show you who's boss here?" He set down a tangle of plastic grocery bags to look at the blanket-wrapped body on the floor. His other hand held an automatic pistol.

Mercy taunted back. "That Glock is the only boss, without it, you're just another do-nothin' hick."

"We'll see about that in a minute." He noticed the light coming in from the hole in the ceiling. "Hey, wha'd ya'll do the air conditioner. You know Mr. H. ain't gonna fix it for you two. Maybe the next batch, but especially not you two."

Lindsey answered, "Had to, the lightning storm knocked out its power."

"So, why'd you have to break it. You trying to escape?" He laughed, "You cain't get outta that hole, and where'd you go if you could? Ten miles of swamp and gators in all directions." He spit, "Shit for brains, both of ya."

"Air, idiot." Mercy taunted, "Air. Without that thing blowing, there's no air in here. Lest we laid on the floor and sucked at the bottom of the door." She shrugged a nod toward Saylor's curled body. "Wasn't going to touch him to make room. He's fuckin' dead."

Lindsey added, "What your boss would say is a habeas corpus."

Robbie looked down at the bundled form at his feet. Saylor was still in the blanket, unmoving. "He hasn't moved?"

Lindsey said, "Not a twitch." Her laugh, full of derision. "Add murder one to your resume, Robbie Caine. Quite the up-and-comer, aren't cha? Kidnapping, molestation, attempted rape, and now, tah-dah! Murder one!"

Mercy looked aside to Lindsey. "Maybe he can get it reduced to unintentional homicide. Isn't that what they call it when you didn't *mean* to kill them?"

Lindsey met her glance with a smile. "I don't know, he hit him while committing a felony. Basically, kidnap, so I think it's murder in the first."

Mercy added to the insult with a snicker and a sneer.

The pistol dangled from his right hand, but he raised it in menace, pointing it at Lindsey. "You listen here, you two shut your damn mouths." He took a step and a half inside the box.

She pushed back harder, "You ain't got it in you to do it on purpose. Whacking a guy in the head is one thing when you want to knock him out. You wouldn't have had the balls to kill him outright."

He took one step closer to the girls entering the box and another to the side. He was standing near Saylor's curled body. Mercy stood, backed up to stand behind her stool. His attention shifted to her. "You stay put and set your skinny ass down." Caine looked down at Saylor's quiet form. In the shadows, Saylor's shallow breathing was undetectable. Their faked taping on his wrists was just visible from the edge of the blanket. Robbie kicked tentatively at Saylor's knees. No reaction. He kicked a little harder.

"Kick a dead man when he's down." Lindsey maintained her mocking tone, transferred his attention away from Saylor. Robbie took another step toward her. She stood up, defiant, sidling to the middle of the box from her stool's spot against the wall and took a half step backward. "You are a real piece of work, Robbie Caine. First-class piece of crap."

Caine took another step closer to the girls, another step away from Saylor. He raised the gun again, holding it flat, gangland-style, and motioned it toward Lindsey. "You just shut your stupid mouth, or..."

"Or what?" Mercy jeered. Then hocked a spit toward Caine's shoes.

Both girls stepped back a step, out of reach of the swinging gun. Caine stepped closer again, raised the pistol as if to hit her with the barrel.

"DON'T!" Lindsey cried out, stepping back, arms raised over her face. Caine stepped once more, closer to the girls, as they retreated again toward the back of the box. The floating prison's motion from their activity partially masked Saylor's move. The shout of 'don't' was his cue. His faux taping came apart with a sharp ripping sound, but Saylor was up, one leg of Lindsey's stool in his hand. It came down hard on Robbie's gun hand as the kid turned on him. The Glock fell to the floor, and Robbie screamed out in pain. He bent in agony, clutching his right wrist. "You mother-fu..." was all he got out before the second blow with the stool leg whacked him across the temple.

Robbie went down, deflated, unconscious.

"Jesus Christ!" Mercy's arms were up, hands covered her mouth. She leaned into the sidewall of the box.

Lindsey steadied herself against the raft's motion, looked down at their fallen captor. "Did you kill him?"

Saylor knelt beside Robbie's body. "I don't think so, hope not. I'd like to see him do serious time at Raiford." He stood above Robbie's fallen body and looked at the girls. "It's time to go. It's getting dark soon and we're literally up a creek." He realized he was starving and grabbed the bundle of grocery bags on the way out. They quickly loaded into the fiberglass boat tied up to a cleat. The motor was warm and started on the first pull.

Mercy shouted out, "Woo Hoo!"

Lindsey followed with a shout of her own. Both were grinning in victory.

He gave them a thumbs up. "Great job of acting ladies."

As they motored cautiously out of the narrow tree-lined passage, the low angle of yellowing light hinted at a scant hour of sunlight remaining. But even with an hour, he had no idea how far up or down the river he was. Or even if he was on the river. They could have been up one of the many tidal channels that feed the bay. "We'll be in darkness soon, so we better get moving. Get down in the bow and get as comfy as you can in case I hit a snag."

The way out was obvious. A narrow channel, five, ten, or fifteen feet wide at most, wound through dense vegetation. He could see where overhanging branches had been sawed clear to permit passage of the holding cell, their plywood prison. Looking back, he noted its sheet metal siding and slightly bowed roof. Galvanized sheet metal was bent over the slight curve. Either some real thought had gone into the box, or they'd simply stolen someone's raft from its mooring and retrofitted it with insulation, the interior plywood sheathing, and the cooling system. He slowly backed until he could turn around and moved toward the only exit from the heavily vegetated wetland. Dense greenery, the bright, fresh greens of the new season were darkening fast in the gathering shadows of dusk.

Lindsey raised her voice over the motor noise, "Hey, this is my boat!"

He called up to her, "I figured it probably was as soon as I saw the Boston Whaler sticker on the dash." It had a typical layout for a small center console runabout. A row of seats across the back over a small storage compartment. An elevated seat at the console, passageway on both sides of the console. Most boats outfitted for fishing would have removable swivel seats forward. This boat didn't, and the two girls curled into the open padded seating forward, providing ballast to keep the nose down.

He navigated a few tight turns, passed a double stack of bee boxes. Looking behind, he read the posted sign. "Stay away, Tupelo bees at work." That would have kept away pretty much anyone who played on, fished on, or otherwise used the river. The region was famous for its Tupelo honey. Not only was the honey well-loved for its particular taste, but it wouldn't turn to sugar for several years and didn't need refrigeration. Locals would obey the simple sign out of courtesy.

They disturbed one small gator that slipped into the water on their approach and uncounted box turtles. Time for them to start their night rounds anyway, he thought. The sun's angle would no longer warm their backs. In less than ten minutes, they came to the river proper. South, downstream. He knew they were closer to Apalachicola than Wewahitchka, the community situated halfway to the dam at the Georgia line, because of the tidal response on their creek. But how far would they have to go to get to the River House? He'd want to stop immediately at the River House to see if Belle was all right.

He looked back and saw how quickly the hole in the tree-lined bank disappeared. He called out, "I'm going to mark this spot." He throttled down and turned back toward the narrow entrance to the feeder channel. There was a shallow bank on both sides, and from the current joining the main river flow, it appeared to feed a good size area of swampland. Rummaging in the storage compartment, he found a red shop towel crumpled in a rack for oil storage. Using the two corners of the rag, he tied it from an overhanging sweet gum branch. Letting go, he pushed the throttle lever forward, and the boat rapidly found its plane angle.

In a little over five minutes, the river opened up as another channel joined from the right. He knew where he was, finally about ten minutes from home. As they rounded a bend, another boat approached from downstream. He maneuvered to the west bank. It was a normal navigational move to keep to the right. It also kept them in the blue shades of the approaching dusk. "Ladies, stay down up there."

As it passed, the other boat dropped from its high-speed plane and rolled forward, turned, and sped up to follow them. A bull horn called out, "Robbie, it's me. I told you to stay there."

"Dammit!" Lindsey and Mercy were heads-up looking around the console at the following boat. "Girls, please, down in front. I don't want him to see you."

"Who is it?" Both asked, nearly simultaneously.

"I don't know, but I'd guess it's your favorite attorney at law." He looked over his shoulder. The other boat, larger, an inboard, and probably powered by GM was faster and gaining. "And stay down! Lay flat on the damned deck. He's got a gun out." He cursed himself. He hadn't wanted to fingerprint the pistol Robbie dropped but wished very much he had it now. If nothing else, it might keep the other boat at a distance. A shot rang out from the other boat. "Fuck!" He lowered himself so he was sighting forward around the right side of the console, thinking small. *How small can I be? Jesus!"*

The other boat was back on a plane and gaining, inexorably gaining. Another shot fired and a spray of Plexiglas blew away from the windshield, mere inches from his head. A ragged hole punched through it at about shoulder blade high if he'd been standing. He began to zig-zag, it would slow him down, but the other boat wouldn't be able to get a steady bead as it bounced across his wake. *Son-of-a-bitch, there's usually a half dozen boats in these two or three miles of river.* Then it came to him. *Tuesday.* Not prime time for fisherman going home, and sundown is not the best time for tending trot-lines. He noticed for the first time that Lindsey wasn't in the bow with Mercy. A quick glance to his left, and he saw her creeping toward the rear seats with the Glock in her right hand.

He pressed down on her shoulder. "Hey, stay down. You want to get shot?"

Lindsey looked back up at him, stoned serious. "Stop zigging. Keep her straight and narrow as fast as she'll go for the house." She moved to just behind the console and cautiously peered over the back seats with the gun held in a two-handed grip.

He looked back at her, by her grip on the pistol she seemed to know what she was doing. "Lindsey, you know how to use that thing?"

She looked up, smiling. "This is my gun!"

The trailing boat seemed to be forty or fifty yards back, still gaining. Its white hull throwing sheets of horizontal spray and its bow was bouncing making aim difficult. Another shot from behind. Nothing seemed to be hit. He looked down. Lindsey now had a two-handed firing range grip on the gun. She raised her head over the rear seat cushion as her index finger slid into the trigger guard.

The Glock barked beside him, startling him. There was no apparent change from behind. It barked again. The following boat swerved hard to the left, toward the center of the river, nearly throwing its driver out of control. They gained fifty yards before the larger boat recovered, sped back up, and followed in their wake. Saylor used the extra distance to put long S-turn waves behind him. With satisfaction, he noted the boat stayed straight on but lost both speed and stability, bouncing off his wake.

Saylor knew from relative boat speeds that they could not keep up the dance, just to end up at the Abercrombie Landing in a running gun battle. It was several more miles down to the city proper, where only a complete idiot would pursue a homicidal chase, with at least two waterfront restaurants full of witnesses. He saw a sandbar approaching on the right, the one he and Belle had sunned themselves on only two days ago. He back throttled, dropping the nose just a bit, but it gave Lindsey a little more cover. "Aim for the center of that boat. If the bullet isn't deflected by fiberglass, he's standing behind that console." He saw her nod.

She turned her head toward him so he could hear, "Slow it down a tad more. Let me get my best shot in. His head is down. That last shot freaked him."

"Good girl. I'm going to drop to half throttle, take your best shot at the centerline of that hull." He pulled back the throttle, letting the bow drop to almost level. The trailing boat came on, straight at them. After a quick glance back, he thought, *any time now would be good.* The Glock fired three more times, the bam, bam, bam, incredibly loud in the cockpit. Another salvo! Bam, bam, bam. The gunfire announced to the world that dire events were going down on the river. The trailing boat pressed on. Saylor pushed the throttle forward to full, and their little boat leaped forward.

Just upstream from the Apalachicola's junction with the Intercoastal Waterway, the meandering river makes a hard turn to the right and a harder turn to the left. The following boat would have a good shot at his crouched position while they were in either turn if it could get a stable firing position. He hunkered down, trying to think small, and tugged the wheel to the right for the first turn. Looking back, the larger boat was leaning on its chine, hard into the turn as well.

Saylor looked forward, just in time to make the hard left, skirting under some overhanging branches, taking a few leaves onboard. He glanced left and right as they sped into the larger expanse of the Intercoastal channel. Ahead, two boats were queued up at the landing. *Witnesses, what would that S O B do?* He looked over his shoulder to see if their pursuer would maintain his murderous intent in public. To his surprise, the following boat plowed at full speed into the river's west bank and disappeared into a wall of green foliage.

He pulled the throttle back to idle, the Whaler rocked forward as its following stern wave passed under them. "Lindsey, I think you got him."

33

Got Him

Lindsey raised from her crouch to stand beside Saylor. They could both see that the line of waves spreading out from the pursuit boat's wake pointed at the line of trees. They hadn't heard a crash due to their outboard's flat-out whine, but it was apparent that the other boat wasn't going to be coming out of there on its own. Saylor checked the sun angle, slanted rays still made it through the western tree line, but those would not last long. If Hargreaves was in there, if he was alive, Saylor wanted to talk to him before the lawyer became a night snack for the several good-sized gators that would be smelling blood any minute now. Time for help. He sped down to the landing, slowed to a crawl, and shouted at two fishermen who were about to load an idling flats boat onto its trailer. "Hey, we have a boater just up the river's gonna need some medical help. Call 911, then give us a hand. He's in the first bend of the Apalach, just out of sight."

The two fishermen looked at each other, then back at them. Saylor called out again. "9-1-1! Sheriff! Now!" He then throttled hard, pivoted on his stern wave, and sped back upriver. They entered the Apalachicola cautiously. He crouched again, uncertain of the condition of the other boat's driver, and whispered down to Lindsey. "Hand me the pistol."

"No, you drive the boat, I'll keep you covered. My boat, my gun."

He couldn't argue with the logic. Any sign of the boat's passage had dissipated in the current. But soon enough, they found the white stern labeled "Recess" with shredded fiberglass around the mounting ring for the inboard-outboard drive unit. The vee-hull had hiked the boat up across a two-foot-high bank. Saylor thought the shock must have been damned hard. First, the bow would have kicked nearly straight up, then the prop would have hit the bank and stopped him cold—a vicious ride followed by a hard landing for the driver.

He dropped the throttle back to an idle. Looking forward, Mercy was huddled in a small ball, crying. *Oh damn.* "Mercy, I think it's over. But just stay there for now."

Lindsey said. "I think I must have got him or winged him good." As he guided the boat closer, she went forward and used a bowline to tie off to the grounded boat's power unit. Saylor killed the throttle. In the sudden calm, he felt blood still pounding in his ears. After the noise and adrenaline of the chase, it was quiet, eerily quiet. Creepy quiet in the thickening dark. He looked, listened for any sign of life on the larger boat. All he could hear was the buzzing of evening insects. He couldn't remember where the phrase came from, but it came, ridiculous considering. *Is you is? Or is you ain't?*

From their vantage, they couldn't see over the stern of the other craft. "Lin, I'm going to see what's what. Would you *please* hand me that gun?" With a look that said, I'd rather not, she did. He hooked the barrel into his pants pocket. The boat, the *Recess* by the gilded name on its stern, was wedged between a young sweet gum and a centuries older cypress. What used to be a chromed sunroof support system was now a twisted mess of tubing. He had to worm his way through the sweet gum's limbs and the wrecked superstructure but was able to use them as a ladder to get over the rail of the larger boat. He crawled through the twisted tubing and found their pursuer's body forward of the cockpit. He was on his back, laying among pieces of a shattered windscreen, his face contorted in agony. Saylor imagined the guy's body flying through the windscreen on impact with the bank. A trickle of blood oozed with the pulse of his still-beating heart from a hole in the man's lower rib cage. As he approached, he heard the sound of the fisherman approaching and dropping to an idle. He called over his shoulder.

"Did you guys call 911?"

"Yeah, dispatch mustered the sea rescue people."

"Tell them if they have a chopper and a sling, to send it! Or...," his voice dropped in indecision.

"Damn." *What to actually do?* He called back to the girls. "Hey? Does Shirk have a Z-Z Top beard and mustache?"

"No, he doesn't, unless he's wearing a disguise." He heard her voice, questioning. He'd thought the pursuer was the attorney or the other accomplice, Shirk. Saylor crept forward. "See if those guys have a flashlight, it's getting dark in here."

Besides the hole in the man's chest, a horrid bone-deep gash on his left cheek was beginning to ooze. Taking further stock of the injured man, it appeared his left arm was dislocated, its angle uncomfortably impossible. *It must have hurt like hell to get thrown around like that.* Looking at the dislocated arm made Saylor's temporarily forgotten neck hurt again. He crawled forward. The bearded man's eyes opened to slits. He groaned, tried to move, failed. His eyes tracked left and right, then found Saylor's and locked on. His eyelids opened wide as his body arched in a rack of pain.

"Take it easy. Medics are on the way. And so is the sheriff, so just be good and know that help is coming." Saylor took off his shirt, folded it into a wad, and pressed it on the wound.

"Ahhh! Fuck that hurts."

"I need to press on the wound to keep you from losing more blood." He registered the pain in the wounded man's eyes. "Sorry, best I can do before the EMTs get here." Saylor didn't know if the bullet wound plus internal injuries from the crash were going to turn the guy's lights out. The eyelids closed again. Saylor tapped him lightly on the forehead. "Hey, buddy, stay with me. Don't let yourself go into shock." The man's eyes closed again. Not clenched shut, but as if they had lost the will to stay open. "Stay with me. What's your name?" Nothing. "Hey, listen up, do they call you Shirk?"

The man's eyes opened to a little wider than slits. He inhaled, groaned at the pain. Under the lids, the man's eyes rolled back and forth, seemed to see, then focused again on Saylor. "Jer..." came out in a puff.

"Jer? Like Jerry?"

He coughed, and a trickle of blood came up with it and dribbled down the ragged beard. In a ragged whisper, "Jeremy."

Oh shit! Saylor hadn't expected to hear that. He had expected something closer to Shirk. He leaned in to hear better, "OK, Jeremy, your last name, so I can tell the medics when they get here." An early-season mosquito landed on Jeremy's forehead. Saylor flicked it away, then noticed one on his forearm, swatted it.

"Lorass, haaah, no," he huffed through another painful cough. Then, clearly, "Lawrence. I'm Jeremy Lawrence."

Holy shit, risen from the dead. "Well, Jeremy, you just try to stay with me. Help is on the way. You took a really hard hit when you jumped the riverbank." He thought he heard a choking cough, which could have almost been a laugh, but this wasn't the time for humor. "You trying to talk? I didn't catch it."

"The bullet didn't feel that good either." He may have been trying for a grin, but his mouth condensed into a rictus, dribbling bloody bubbles.

Saylor felt dampness under his palm. He lifted his hand off the wadded-up shirt and saw that it had been bled through. *Damn this mother fucker!* Lawrence's eyes were closing again. Night was closing in, and it had become truly dark under the canopy.

Someone crawled through the branches and onto the boat and came up beside him. The newcomer flashed the light on the bloody mess under Saylor's hand and then up to the bearded face. A man's voice asked softly. "You know this guy?"

"Only by reputation. Thanks for the light."

"Happy to help." The voice was smoker's gruff, sounded like a two-pack-a-day guy.

"Did you get an idea of when the Sea Rescue crew might get here?" He remembered the wait. Was it only a few days ago? At the landing, a few hundred yards downstream.

"We told 'em you said there was a hell-bent emergency up here, dispatch said they'd do what they could."

"Good as it gets, I guess." He thought about Lindsey in the boat. *Damn this mother fucker.* He looked over at the other boater. "Say, could you check on those two girls. They've had a rough time of it up the river. See if they need to eat? Do you have space blankets?" The thoughts came tumbling out, his mind on overdrive. "See if they can eat? Maybe a bottle of water? See if you can convince them to not come looking?"

"One of 'em said this guy had been shooting at you? That true?"

"Wish it wasn't so. Man, I wish it wasn't so." He looked back over his shoulder, indicated a handoff for the flashlight, took it. He pointed it at an expanse of white fiberglass to light the area and returned his attention to Lawrence. "Hey, Jeremy! You still with me?" He felt and heard the gruff-voiced fisherman clambering back over the stern of the boat. Heard him tell the girls and his fishing partner they probably didn't want to go look.

Jeremy Lawrence was still in the world but seemed to be fading. Saylor's eye caught the glint of a plastic water bottle on the deck a few feet away. He grabbed at it, twisted it open, and splashed some cool water on Lawrence's face. "Hey, come back to me. Don't let yourself go to sleep. You with me?" A nod. A cough produced another dribble of carmine bubbles. "Listen, it looks like the bullet just creased your lung or you'd be in much worse shape. Your arm is hurting like a bitch right now, but they can fix all that. Do you understand? Nod if you understand?"

Lawrence nodded.

"I need you to hear me. To understand me. We good?"

Another nod.

He bent close to Lawrence's ear, whispered quietly but clearly. "Your daughter is here. She is in the other boat. Do you understand? Lindsey is just behind me in the other boat. Understand?"

Another nod. A wince.

Saylor wasn't sure if it was pain or regret. "Do you want to say anything to her?"

Lawrence's eyes, they had been opening wider, looking almost human normal, closed again, pressed closed. His right shoulder tried to move, remembered it was broken. The left arm came up, covering his face with his hand.

Yeah, the shame of it all. "Jeremy. You may make it, you may not. Do you have anything to say to her?"

His hand came down to rest on Saylor's over the gunshot wound. With increasing pressure, Lawrence tried to push against the wad of blood-soaked shirt that was trying to save his bodily fluids, to dislodge it. Lawrence's eyes searched upward, found Saylor's. Holding that stare, Lawrence shook his head slowly and pushed harder against the bandage.

The message was clear. Saylor let Jeremy's hand move his. He looked down in the dim light that filtered back down on the scene from the flash-lit boat hull and the backscattered light into the green sweet gum's leaves above. The heart pulse was now barely visible, but the darkened red steam still rhythmically oozed out of the wound. "I understand. Anything you want me to say?" He looked into

Lawrence's eyes to see if anyone was looking back. The eyes didn't focus, but the lips moved. Saylor lowered his head to Lawrence's ear, whispered hard. "Anything you want me to tell Lindsey?"

"Sorra...tell her, sorra."

As he watched, the dying man's eyes shifted once. Over the stomach wound, a bloody index finger twitched, and Jeremy Lawrence left this world.

Saylor pulled back, sighed. Little had changed. Lawrence hadn't moved since he'd boarded the *Recess*. He looked up through the dense canopy. Above the few leaves lit from the flashlight, the deep indigo of the evening sky had turned to black, seeming to brighten the light green of new growth around them from the flashlight's glow. In the distance, the high whine of an engine approaching at top speed grew from around the bend in the river. Soon the trees around him were pulsing with the red and blue flashers of an official visit. Saylor extended two fingers and shut Jeremy Lawrence's eyes. From the little he'd learned about Lindsey from their two days in the box, he didn't think 'sorry' was going to cut it.

34

The House Dealer

The sheriff didn't release them until nearly 9:30. They weren't even allowed to eat the 'evidence' in the two bags of food that Robbie Caine had brought to the floating prison cell. He did allow Saylor to make a phone call to Belle to let her know he was alive. He was not surprised then, when he tied the boat off at the dock. Belle ran a furious sprint from the house and leaped the last three feet into his arms. Her arms around his neck, legs around his waist. Her squeal of delight squelched only by his backward step into the river. The thick tension of the evening lifted in laughter. The dark mood of recent death had dampened even the joy of escape and their survival of attempted murder. The laughter that followed the dunking released a layer of funk that had threatened to dampen the celebration of still being alive.

The delay by the sheriff's crew, and then the High Sheriff himself, had postponed a much overdue dinner. It wasn't until 10:30 that the four of them were seated around the River House's five-foot diameter dining room table, eating buttered noodles and parmesan with rotisserie chicken from the local IGA.

Lindsey had been dropping into a post-adrenaline-high depression, absorbing the reality that she had killed a human being. "Lindsey, there's no effing way you could have known." Mercy was doing her best to mollify her cellmate. She had tried to joke on the short river trip down to the family dock, should they call each other cellies, for old cellmates, or besties. Lindsey had proved to be hard to cheer up. "Look on the bright side, Cellie, we aren't going to be sold to God-knows-who into God-knows-what."

Lindsey just looked back at her and glared. But Mercy's elation at being freed was irrepressible. A slight tight grin was working its way onto Lindsey's face. "I do think about that. I thought about it a lot for two weeks. No one raped us, well, Robbie tried."

"But you kicked him in the balls." Mercy's voice was victorious.

"Not for the first time, either." Her glance at Mercy had the beginning of a smile.

Belle looked over to Saylor, who was chewing quietly, watching, smiling, relieved. Getting to know his daughter in a way that he could never do if she knew what he did.

Belle picked up her long-stemmed glass and tapped it with the back of her knife. Ding, ding, ding. "I'd like to propose a toast." They found their glasses and raised them. "Here's to beating the bad guys." Three of the four of them took sips. Mercy downed hers in two gulps.

Saylor said, "I recognize that there's one among us who is not yet of legal drinking age..." He said it with a smile and a glance toward Lindsey.

Mercy interrupted his train, "Hey, special circumstances, adult supervision, et cetera."

"Regardless," he continued, "or be that as it may, or whatever. Isn't that what you young'uns are saying now? And whatever...I think the moment needs a proper celebration, and Lindsey's mother had excellent taste in red wines. Would you all agree?"

Here, heres answered.

Lindsey offered' "Here's to Mercy, a truly merciful friend in time of need. You probably kept me from going bonkers in that plywood hell. I can't imagine your week in there with no idea of day or night." She waited for her breathing to overcome the lump in her throat. "Misery and shame to men like Hargreaves."

Saylor poured another half glass for Mercy. It appeared they were not through with toasting yet. She and Lindsey held a shared look of admiration and friendship. With rimming eyes, Mercy offered a soft, "True dat."

True dats echoed around the table.

"And here's to Lindsey," Saylor continued the toast, "for your resolve and bravery under fire. You must always remember, no matter what else happens, *you* were being fired upon. You did the honorable thing when our fates were uncertain. When our lives were at a testing point. You passed the test. You are a braveheart, in the truest sense of the word."

More here, heres followed. He turned to Belle, "And to Belle, who kept the home fires burning. I'm so glad that you did not have the opportunity to join us." Again, the chorus of here, heres. She reached over to him across the edge of the table, palm up. He took her hand in his and squeezed. He tossed her a quick wink. She raised an eyebrow, and with a quick flick of her eyes indicated upstairs.

Lindsey laughed, "Oh My God! They are already into secret eyeball sign language and have only been together two weeks?"

Belle blushed. A red bloom crept across her cheeks, fanned across the edges of her ears.

Mercy pointed. "Guilty as charged."

Lindsey stood and attended to the wine glasses that could no longer properly toast with the remainder of the wine. She then stood with her glass out. "And I'd like to propose a toast to Jason Saylor, Mr. Nick of Time." The other two stood, glasses out. Feeling the pressure, Saylor stood, and they tapped glasses at center table.

When seated again, Lindsey asked, "I wonder when the sheriff will let us know who the guy in the boat is, er, was."

Saylor blinked. Jeremy Lawrence's wallet was in his pocket. In the fading light of that terrible night, he had not wanted Lindsey to learn the man she'd killed was the man she knew as her father. Besides, whether the shot alone would have killed him was academic. The boat crashing into the river bank at speed certainly added to his internal traumas. He could think of countless cases where a stomach wound alone, even one that clipped a lung, was survivable. If not for the crash, Lawrence might have survived. Saylor had elected to leave his identity to the forensics for now.

Saylor decided on deflection, said, "The driver's license said he was Phillip Jones. I may find who Phillip Jones is in the morning. Sheriff Pierson wants me to come by at ten for a formal follow-up. The scene on the river wasn't appropriate, especially with the EMTs giving you two the once over. Plus, they still had to go up the river to find and capture Robbie."

"You think he'd still be there?" Belle asked.

Mercy laughed. "That little chicken snot wouldn't dare try to get across that swamp at night."

Saylor followed up. "I think she's right. No flashlight, and no gun. Only a fool would try to cross that swamp to get where? Flag down a boat, and hope that weekday traffic, none, by the way, would come by to save him? No, if I didn't knock him into the hereafter, he was still there. By now he's probably in cuffs in a sheriff's boat, trying to think about pleading out and who he can throw under the bus to get time off."

Lindsey added. "That sounds just like that weasel. I'll try to get his prison address and send him a tube of K-Y jelly." They all took in the implications, grins spread, and they all burst into laughter. She added, eyebrows raised in jest, hands out and looking at the other three. "He always hated being the butt of someone's jokes." Mercy howled at that with tears running down her face while holding her gut laughing.

"Good one," Saylor laughed. "Glad there's some humor to be had at this hour." When the belly laughs subsided, he added, "And on a more serious note, hopefully in the morning, Pierson can provide an update on Hargreaves."

Lindsey agreed. "We've got to hope he didn't get a warning and leave. He's the key to figuring out what was going to happen. I really don't think either Robbie or Shirk was let in on master planning. Neither of them ever let on that there was any boss other than Mr. H., meaning Sheldon Hargreaves. They were 'H. said so and so,' or 'I'll have to ask H.' Robbie let it out once or twice, the whole name, Hargreaves. He was supposed to just say the H but sometimes slipped up."

Saylor had heard Shirk's name come up before too often. "Who was this guy you've been calling Shirk?"

Mercy filled him in. "He's the one who helped Robbie dump you in the box with us. He's a low-life who lives in a little trailer up by the prison at Sneads. Couldn't even make it as a guard. Now that's a low life!"

"He'd been working timber off and on since then, mostly off. Did some cuttin-out work and straw bailing for my dad a few years back when I was too young for him to be looking at me like he did. So daddy fired him." She huffed a silent humorless laugh. "Be poetic for him to end up in his neighborhood prison. Isn't kidnap Federal?"

Lindsey said, "I think so," and looked to Saylor.

"Yes, it is a federal offense." He opened both palms out.

From nowhere, an unexpected thread pulled loose. *Would Lawrence have been trying to disguise himself?* He thought about the

ID in Jeremy's wallet. "Wait, a minute," Saylor said, "did anyone ever mention a Phillip Jones?"

"Uh, no," from Mercy.

"OK, anyone know if Phillip Jones is Shirk's real name? You said Shirk doesn't have a big beard?"

Mercy and Lindsey shared a glance. Mercy said, "No, he looks— kinda like you—only dirty."

Saylor was taken aback. "Well, that could explain me being pulled over." He stroked the three-day growth on his chin.

Lindsey added, "a week's stubble maybe, usually he only shaves when he showers and that's not real often. Sorry, but you kinda look like him, height, weight and hair color..." She nodded, appraising the similarities. "If you slept in a gutter for a week, slopped some hogs, then hitch-hiked across Alabama, you'd be a fair twin."

Saylor couldn't help it; he started to laugh and was soon joined by the rest.

Lindsey and Mercy looked at each other, remembering his question about a beard as he'd crawled into the ruined boat. Lindsey looked back, "So, who was the bearded guy in the boat?"

Saylor felt and suppressed everything but a slight knitting of his eyebrows. The only tell of a reaction. *Not the time. This is not the time.* He said, "The sheriff said it was Hargreaves' boat, makes sense, judging by its name. Have to be one of his working associates." He had to build on the lie for now. "Maybe it was the time for the pick-up, and the bearded guy was the connection."

Saylor thought about connections. *What was Papa Lawrence's intent? Fiend or friend. Was he selling her or saving her? Talk about loose threads! Soon the FBI will be involved.*

He addressed the three women at the table. "Pierson told me tonight that the FBI agent is due in tomorrow. So, maybe by the time I talk with him, the guy will be here. With the beard on the boat dead, they'll have to get Federals' help to track down Hargreaves. Based on the name of that boat, I'm fairly sure that it was his. So, tracking his car and his purchases will be easier with interstate federal warrants helping. And if that guy's fingerprints are on record? Well, we or they would know within a few hours."

Belle asked, "What about Robbie Caine?"

Mercy huffed. "Drop him in a hole and nail down the lid." Mercy clearly did not like Robbie Caine.

Saylor wagged his head, not certain but taking the lead. "I'm thinking that he's going to plead out at the first possible chance to help nail Hargreaves, maybe even help locate Shirk."

Lindsey asked, "Do you think they really intended to sell us for sex slaves? Didn't you say that?"

"I think I said trafficking. But, yeah, that's pretty much what that means." He could have elaborated, based on his experience with the complex organization he'd helped to uncover operating in Harris County, Texas. But he didn't want to add to their nightmares for the immediate future with that kind of detail. He closed with. "That's also a federal statute. If they catch up with either of them, they are going down for a long time."

The table's mood had grown somber. The reality of the girls' alternate future had sobered the earlier levity.

Lindsey said quietly. "Still, I'd really like to know what the plan was. I mean, I kind of do, but..."

"Maybe you don't," Belle answered just as softly, putting her hand on Lindsey's. "Maybe it would be good to figure out what to do next and move on. There's so much bad and evil in this world. You could lose a lot of sleep thinking about the could-of, would-of possibilities."

In bits and pieces, the girls filled Belle in on their ordeal. Mercy had been picked up at the bus station, her plan to work at one of the Alabama casinos waylaid by being snatched, tied, and gagged for the trip down the river.

Lindsey had been drugged with a spiked glass of coke at Hargreaves office. She'd left Jason on the beach that last night and gone to meet Hargreaves at her house to sign assignment documents putting the parent's properties in her name. "I had another document I said I was going to bring him the next day or so. It still needed some work. Never got the chance, did I?"

"What was that about Lindsey, you had unfinished estate business?" Saylor was a trusted entity now. He felt he could ask, reasonably sure of the answer.

She looked back, appraising, sensing a mutual trust bond. His help in the escape, his acceptance by Belle. "I haven't told anyone yet,

230

not even you Belle." She shifted in her chair to take them both in. "My dad isn't my dad." She flustered, waved a frustrated hand to clear the air. "No, what I mean is as mom was facing her last couple of days, the doctors at Shands Hospital were finally telling her to get her affairs in order. She told me something she'd intended to tell me before I left for FSU and never got around to it." Her glance took in everyone, ensuring attention. "She and Jeremy adopted me. They aren't my parents."

"Holy Christ!" Mercy muttered. "That's a load of crap to take on."

Belle just stared, knowing the lie, apparently letting Saylor take his time with that truth.

"Yeah," Lindsey agreed, "but there wasn't ever going to be another convenient time was there? The doctors didn't give her much more than a week, two at tops. As it turned out she died a few days later. Anyway, as she told it, before she took the assistant manager spot here at Weems hospital and started playing with rental properties, she had been the HR administrator at the big Sacred Heart Hospital in Pensacola. She and Jeremy had been trying for years but she couldn't get pregnant. His sperm count was low to non-existent." She rolled her eyes, "Figures." She paused to collect her thoughts, took a sip of wine. "So, I was born to an unwed mother. My mother died in childbirth, or maybe a day later, I think mom said it was sepsis. All that was shortly before their move here to Apalach. So, all my life I thought that mom and dad were my parents. I could never figure out how mom's strawberry blond, and dad's rusty brown hair, gave me this light brown mouse hair."

Belle said, "I always thought your hair was gorgeous."

"Miracles of Garnier, my sweet Belle!" She smiled back at Belle, ran her fingers through her hair, recreating a few dozen TV commercials. "It's not me. And I've got grey-blue eyes depending on the light. Mom and Dad's eyes were both brown. Possible, not probable. I tan just by looking at the sun. Mom burnt, then freckled. It finally explained a lot of wondering."

Mercy asked. "Damn gurl. Why'd you even wonder about it? Your eyes and skin?"

"No, I mean, that contributed to it. But Dad? Dad was..." Never mind. He's long dead, and I won't..."

To Saylor, she seemed to shrink. A real sadness possessed her face for an instant. Something painful passed behind her eyes and was shut away immediately. There was obviously something off between her and her dad in the past. Seven years prior? It could have been typical pre-teen angst and rebellion up against a military-bred disciplinarian's demand for order. Despite that, never having a chance to say goodbye.

He noted the green decimal clock on the microwave. "Ladies, I won't say it's all been fun. But a lot has happened since my breakfast with Belle yesterday. My head still hurts. A real live bed awaits. I at least would like to get some sleep. I need to process some of this before my chat with the High Sheriff tomorrow morning." Saylor stood, rubbed at the back of his neck and shoulders. Winced. He looked at Mercy and Lindsey. "I imagine he'll be calling you ladies too, for additional statements. We're lucky he didn't want them tonight." He puffed out a gasp that proved his exhaustion. "Good night all."

The hot shower felt great, the funk, the adrenalin rush of pursuit, the fear of death, Jeremy's death, washed clean. He lay sprawled across Belle's bed, thinking about the day. *What a fucking day!* His final sigh let all the tensions go. Downstairs earlier, the laughter, the banter had helped.

Even the grudging acknowledgment from Pierson, when he'd finally arrived, felt good. The sheriff had made the comment that some people are born victims. They'll hope for the best until the end comes, not having put up resistance that counts until it's too late. Others, he'd nodded towards Saylor, take up the fight at the first opportunity, and often end up being witnesses for the prosecution rather than the poor dumb bastard in the ME's report.

That thought gave him pause. The poor dumb bastard in this case was Lindsey's adopted dad. *What was it about her dad that she'd been unable, at least too uncomfortable, to share?* Perhaps Eleanor had just taught her well, don't speak ill of the dead or your dad. Bum deal.

He was reminded of a saying by one of his favorite co-workers in Houston. Back at the Chronicle newsroom, his desk faced the desk of his best friend at the paper, separated by only a four-foot-high cubicle wall. Emmanuelle Salazar, nicked Sally since middle school, was Costa Rican Hispanic. They often tag-teamed when going into the Latin neighborhoods. Sally's accent wasn't spot-on Mexican or even Texican, but she at least had fluent vocabulary if not appropriate street patois.

And Sally had a thing for casinos. Sally liked to say that life is like the house dealer. The house dealer expected you to lose. You were not supposed to win. Only by paying attention to all the players, and especially to the house dealer, could you expect to win. When they were working on a story, she'd call up her metaphor again. She'd say something like, "See, you need to know all the players. Figure out what's in their hands, recalculate the odds." Crouched in the boat, he figured Jeremy Lawrence for a player. But what was his role in the game? Saylor had no idea what cards he'd held before he folded, cards unseen.

How had he been planning to retake control of the properties, the holdings? After all, he'd been declared dead. After a year's absence, Eleanor had taken exclusive control of their shared assets and written an ironclad will that transferred it all to Lindsey. *And her attorney had been Hargreaves! Hard to figure. And Jeremy Lawrence? What was his angle? Where had he been for six or seven years? Why was he there and planning to do what? How was it that he was in Hargreaves' boat?*

He heard the shower sounds stop with a squeak of the faucet handle. He consciously slid over, rolling to the side, freeing half the mattress. He just wanted to sleep, to put the day away. Literally, put it all to bed.

He felt the mattress shift with her weight. Then her breath on his ear. Then the tip of her tongue, then gently, teeth. Her kisses followed down his chin line, found his mouth. She was delicious, *or was that just her mouthwash?* Umm. "I was going to sleep."

"I was going to make slow passionate love to you. Let you know I've been worried out of my mind for two days." Kiss, nibble. "Let you know how happy I am you're safe." I heard those gunshots from the deck. Scared me to death." Nibble a little lower. "Then there were all those emergency sirens and flashers. Any idea how worried I was?" She kissed an eyebrow, the bridge of his nose, the still-red scar from the sheriff's desk. "You still want to go to sleep?" Kisses moved from

233

chin to collar bone, to nipple. Her hand shifted under the sheet, found him responding. "I didn't think so." Nibble.

She purred, "sleep is over-rated."

"That's what I've heard." He leaned back and relaxed, enjoying the slow journey of her lips and tongue on their way south. He muttered a silent thank you to the house dealer for his current hand.

35

Last Interview

Officer Mallory, officer number three from his first encounter with the Franklin County Sheriff's Department, was on desk duty. Saylor approached his desk, this time without any fear of not being able to walk out again. "Good Morning, Officer Mallory, good to see you again."

"Mr. Saylor, I'd say it's good to see you back, but I spent a double shift last night bagging a shithead in a shit hole." If there was a smile on Mallory's face, it was unreadable as such. "I think you've met the young man."

"Sure did, we traded blows, but that's about the depth of our relationship. Mine still hurts, how's he doing?"

"He'll survive." A brief trace of humor tried and failed to alter Mallory's face. "I'll say this, he was glad to see us."

"I imagine. The little creep was OK with sticking young girls in that box, listening to gators bark at night, but him? I bet he was about ready to mess his drawers."

"Nope, sorry to disappoint. Wish you'd a been there, though. I never saw someone so happy to be cuffed." Mallory checked his watch. "You go on back, I think you'll remember the way." His right fist stifled a yawn. "Last door on the left."

Saylor tapped on the door, got the nod, and entered. Pierson's red-rimmed eyes told of an all-nighter. "Morning Sheriff, I don't suppose you got much sleep."

Pierson swallowed a yawn, closed-mouthed. "Got a few hours, maybe two. How are the young ladies?"

"Resilient, strong I'd say. Considering what they were probably facing, pretty amazing."

The sheriff nodded, taking it in. "Have you told your daughter yet?"

"That she's my daughter? No, last night was about celebrating life, to the extent possible, and trying to convince her that she wasn't responsible for that guy's death." He eyed Pierson, this time as a citizen, and a father, not as a suspect. "When will you call her in, for her version?"

"It'll be a few days, I suspect. From what I saw and heard at the scene, our talk last night. It can wait till the Feds want to talk, take care of it all at once." Pierson turned his head slightly, squinted. "She is one very lucky young lady. Mercy too. From what your buddy in the FBI told me of Hargreaves' connections, those two were probably destined for the Saudis." He shook his head, his face a sneering picture of disgust. "Those guys are evil."

Saylor nodded, imagining life of a prostitute even as a consort, in a culture that still considered women to be chattel. He came back to the moment. He'd been having waffling thoughts all morning about whether, or actually when, to admit that he'd pulled Jeremy's wallet. He asked, "Do you have an ID on him yet?"

Pierson's left eyebrow twitched. He said, "The boat was registered to Sheldon Hargreaves. But oddly, the address on the registration is in Pensacola."

Saylor pursed his lips, nodded.

Pierson asked, "The Lawrences were from Pensacola, right? That's where they adopted Lindsey."

"Yeah, that all seems to check out." He paused, sheepish. "Sorry, there was a bit of wine going around last night. The Lawrences moved here shortly after she was born."

"That all?"

"No, what she shared was that she had been adopted. Correlates with what you learned. A young woman had died in childbirth, at the same hospital Eleanor Lawrence worked. Senior staff position, so they smoothed out the adoption process. Adoption records sealed by Children and Family Services. Worked out well for Lindsey."

"But she doesn't know about you?"

"No. Not yet. Sheriff, have you been able to run down Sheldon Hargreaves? Robbie Caine implicated him as his direct—"

"—contact." Pierson interrupted. "Mr. Caine was more than willing to talk to us. Couldn't shut him up on the boat long enough.

We had to read him Miranda on that little porch at the end of the houseboat."

"Houseboat? Heck of a houseboat."

"Well, it used to be one. Underneath all that Styrofoam and plywood, there's someone's former river cabin. There are still hull numbers on the pontoon boat. We're running down the owner. You might not have taken the time to look back as you left, but it still appeared to have windows if you looked at it from the outside."

Saylor thought back to their fast exit. "Can't say that I looked back for that long, I was more concerned with finding the main channel before dark fell." He fell silent for a moment, remembering.

Pierson asked, "Do you remember seeing who attacked you?"

"No, I had just said goodbye to a friend–"

"Belle Tellefson?"

Saylor sighed, he should never underestimate this sheriff. "Yes, it was early dawn, half-light. I had just said goodbye, she was driving off and I was watching. I must not have heard anyone approaching over the noise of her tires on the gravel drive. Then wham, bright lights exploded, and I woke up in the box."

"So you didn't see anything?"

"No, the girls, Lindsey and Mercy, said I'd been unloaded by two guys. Robbie Caine and another much older guy, forty-something they guessed, goes by Shirk."

"They tell you anything about him?"

"Just that he was a loser, couldn't make it as a prison guard. Mercy had known him because he'd done some day-labor for her dad. I think she said he had a trailer up by Sneads."

"She said Sneads?"

Saylor thought back to the conversations. "No, she said up by the prison near Sneads. Thinking about it, I don't know if she meant the trailer was near Sneads or the prison was. I guess I assumed Sneads or Chattahoochee, but it could be anywhere out in those woods."

"OK, thanks, that matches what Caine said this morning." Pierson sat back, pushed back from the desk, and crossed a leg. "Anything else you can remember at all?"

Saylor rubbed at the base of his neck. "My neck still hurts like a bitch." Then he remembered the loose thread. "But what about Hargreaves? You talk to him yet? Has he gone?"

"Let's stay on the guy in the boat for now. His prints came back as someone we know to be close to the Lawrences." Pierson let that hang in the air, studying Saylor's reaction.

Saylor knew that Pierson knew. He shifted to the side to get to his front pants pocket. "Sheriff, last night—" He paused, struggling to reach into his jeans. "—last night was pretty awful. Lindsey was horrified that she had just killed a man. Even though that guy was shooting at us. She put a shot group on the centerline of the boat, hoping to penetrate the engine block, or maybe wound the driver in the leg. But the guy had crouched behind his console, and both boats were in motion. I tried to tell her over and over last night that his flat-out crash into the riverbank did tremendous damage internally, certain aggravation of anything the bullet might have done." He set the wallet down on his side of the desk.

"When did you find out?" One side of Pierson's face twitched to the right.

Saylor took a breath, sighed. "He told me. I saw that he was fading. I kept working at him to not go into shock, to stay with us, to stay alive. He didn't know me from Adam. I point-blank asked him who he was. He told me."

"You were surprised?"

"Hell, yes! The man was supposed to be dead for six or seven years. And that beard, I thought I was talking to some tough guy named Shirk."

"But it was Jeremy Lawrence." Pierson glanced down at the wallet. "You know the background there?"

"Only that he had been suspected of having dealings with the Columbian drug cartels."

"Mr. Saylor, I know you are a reporter, and you're working on a book. I can share some info on him that probably only she should know. Just so she knows. No one else, understand?"

Oh boy, here it comes. Finally. "Sure thing. Completely off record. Never heard it. And the book has nothing to do with anything going on here. It's a euro spy vs. our spy thing."

"Lawrence was a US Navy flyboy out of Pensacola. Twenty years, rated in transports, fast movers, and rotary wing. All-purpose kind of pilot. Turns out he could drop a DC-3 or a C-130 into a jungle with the best of them. Did some undercover for ATF and later, for DEA as a bush pilot and got to know some big players down there." Pierson took a breath, waited for Saylor's mouth to close again. "Those big players found out about the double identity and gave him an option. Either he went to work as a for-real pilot, or his family back here would be killed. Wife and daughter tied, raped, and slaughtered like sheep."

"Christ, that's a motivation."

"No one should ever have that choice to make." Pierson gave the slightest nod. "He convinced them that to do that, he would have to disappear. Fake his death. That much you're figuring out as I go, right?"

"Yeah," he said slowly, "pieces are falling into place." Saylor closed his eyes, rubbed thumb and forefinger at the bits of morning crust, still hanging onto his eyelids. "So, his disappearance was part of an honorable act to save his wife and daughter?"

"That's the story I've got."

"Just between you and me?"

"Yes."

"It doesn't sound completely right. Something Lindsey said, no, hinted at, last night."

"What was that?"

"Not so much what she said. I got the impression that there was little love lost. My building impression of the man wasn't good in the first place and her, well, her attitude toward the memory of her father wasn't shining in the least. Like there was something bad there. Or maybe, shit. Maybe it was just having been left fatherless, she held a grudge. She was what, eleven or twelve?"

"You'd have to ask her. Maybe when you have that heart to heart."

"Sure." He noticed there hadn't been any offering of coffee or even a cigarette this time. Maybe those were only for interrogations. He opened the wallet, turned it toward Pierson' and pushed it across the desk.

"Phillip Jones?"

Saylor shrugged one half-hearted shoulder. "That's the name, but the eyes and cheeks look just like the pictures of dad back at the house."

Pierson examined the picture intently, then set it down.

Saylor asked, "Now can I ask you about Hargreaves? Are you able to share anything?"

"Not a damn thing. He's in the wind."

"So, a person of interest?" Saylor asked.

"Right now, he's my primary focus."

Saylor canted his head to the side, let a one-sided smile form, linger. "I'm just happy it isn't me anymore."

Pierson looked up toward his door and nodded. A young officer came in with two cups of coffee. Saylor took his, saw it had creamer, blew on it, and took a sip. He shared a glance with Pierson who had just done the same. "Thanks." He glanced at the wallet which was still open to the driver's license pocket. "That's Jeremy Lawrence. I checked in the house and online for his pictures. That much is a match, but not the identity in there. The address may give you clues as to where he's been, and what he's been up to lately."

"And it could be completely bogus."

"Absolutely, in fact, probably." Pierson looked at him closely. Saylor didn't know what the next question might be, waited.

"Saylor? I think not telling Lindsey last night was a good move from an ethical, 'right thing to do' consideration. But you do know withholding evidence in a murder investigation is a felony crime. Right?"

"You're calling Lawrence's death a homicide?" Saylor chuffed a disbelieving "Hah. Even Hargreaves could get her off that charge. Anything to do with his death was purely self-defense. Case closed your honor."

"No, just checking. Seeing if you are on your toes this morning." A real smile appeared. "Coupla weeks ago, I told you to stay out of it. Not go messing around."

"I believe your phrasing was, 'I don't want you mucking around in my investigation.'"

"That sounds like me. So, here's where I apologize." He slid his contact card across the desk. "You've helped us in ways we might not have expected, and the girls are safe because of your 'mucking around.' So, if you do find something out, maybe get close to Hargreaves and need help in a hurry, here's my number."

Saylor picked up the card. The front was a standard black and green print for a sheriff. Gold star in a green field imprinted in the corner. He flipped it and saw in large block numbers, 9-1-1. Below those, in much smaller hand-printed numbers, ten digits in standard phone format. He looked up to see an unexpected nod from Pierson. "Your cell?

"My cell." Pierson bit at his lip, seeming to consider what to say next. "Hargreaves has either gone for good or is going to be back. We have a warrant to search his offices. The forensics crew and the Feds are over there now. He may have some documents or materials he'd need to retrieve before disappearing entirely. But, if he's smart about how deep is the shit that he's in already, he needs to eliminate a material witness or two. If his previous accomplices were only Lawrence, Caine, and whoever Shirk is, then he's down to acting on his own. I don't think he'll be linking up with someone as useless as Shirk." Pierson leaned forward. "You be careful...and you be extra careful about Lindsey and Mercy."

Saylor pulled his phone from his pocket and took a quick snap of the back of the card. He caught Pierson's look of irritation and said, "Sorry, I lose cards all the time. Phones, not so much." Saylor blew a silent whistle through pursed lips. A thought just came to him that hadn't bubbled to the top since he was pulled over. "Sheriff, that BOLO, when I was first pulled over. Who called in a description that got me pulled into the line-up? I was thinking if it had been one of the waitresses at the Fish House, I would have been ID'd back then."

"It was one of their waitresses. She reported that a drunk had approached Lindsey on the beach. She came down to see if Lindsey was going to be OK. But Lindsey got up and walked off to the parking lot, leaving you asleep on the beach. Meryl said you looked like someone who lived under the bridge. Dark hair with a bald spot, middle-age."

"Dark car? Wasn't that part of the BOLO?"

"It was the only car in the parking lot in the morning."

"But she didn't identify me that morning."

"Yes, she did. But we didn't have anything else to go on at the time." Pierson's hand pulled at his chin. A shrewd grin flashed across his standard neutral face. Then, "Anything else?"

Saylor took that as permission to go. "No Sir." He stood, slipping the card into his shirt pocket.

"And Saylor?"

He stopped at the door. "Yes?"

"Be expecting a call from the FBI. Atlanta area code, 770."

Saylor had half expected to be shown down to an interview room. Glad it wasn't going to happen yet. "I can't wait."

36

Gun of Choice

Hargreaves was on Saylor's mind as he left the sheriff's compound. He was heartened to know that Robbie Caine was behind him in an eight by ten, rooming with several of Franklin County's least enterprising citizens. The Feds would be talking with him for the next few days, but Hargreaves would be on the move and in increasing desperation. The attorney was on the wrong side of the law now and likely knew he couldn't return to his office or his home on the island.

Then there was the unknown quantity of the low life known only as Shirk. Caine might know more than a nickname for the man. He would probably have the address or location up in Washington County where the man was supposed to have a trailer. The fact that Mercy had called it a trailer and not a mobile home said something. It was one of those older things, probably still on wheels, with highway styling, not something more up to date meant to look at least just a little like a site-built house. In his forties and still a roust-a-bout, Shirk could be dangerous. A lot more dangerous than Robbie Caine.

He sat in his Prius, dialed up Oyster Radio, and filled his cheeks with air. Charlie Daniels' *The Devil Went Down to Georgia* filled his car with energy. He puffed out the air out in exasperation. *What next? I need to get back to the River House.* First, he needed to get a change of clothes or two and pick up his shaving kit, then check on the ladies. Maybe this evening, get back to the book.

As he pulled into his parking space, a fifty-ish woman with a purple dye strip in her hair exited the fifth wheel next to his. In almost a month, there hadn't been anyone actually in residence. She waved. He tossed an automatic wave back. He tapped the power button on the Prius and got out.

The woman approached with apparent urgency. "Mister? Hi, I'm your neighbor Eileen, Eileen Atkins. She jutted a hand forward, demanding to be met.

He took it, the required deed done. "Ms. Atkins, glad to meet you, but I'm kind of in a hurry. Maybe we can get to know you later." He took her accent for Michigan or maybe Wisconsin. Somewhere in the frozen north.

"Oh, is it a we?" She gushed, "Wonderful maybe we can chat later today, that would be nice. We're just in from Chicago."

"I'm sorry, I don't know if I'll be back today, but—if you see anyone lurking around, would you call this number please?" He pulled the sheriff's card from his pocket and handed it over.

"OH! The sheriff!" She looked up wide-eyed. "Are you a deputy? I never met a deputy socially before." She seemed positively pleased.

"No ma'am. I'm not. But I really do need to be moving if you'll excuse me."

"Before you go, there was a car here earlier. Came by and looked in your windows. Terribly rude, you know. People ought to respect boundaries. That's what I say."

She caught her breath and was about to continue. Saylor put up a hand palm out to stop her, open-mouthed. "Eileen, can I call you that?" She gulped, nodded yes. "Eileen, do you remember what kind of car it was? Anything about the man?"

"Well yes, I do. I'm usually very observant. It was a white Land Rover. The license plate said defender, she spelled out D-F-N-D-E-R. Pretty car. Pretty expensive if you ask me."

"Uh, huh. What about the driver, did you get a look at him?"

She put her index finger to the side of her nose fixed a stare at the Prius' fender. "Let me see. He was maybe mid-forties to fifties. Losing some hair in the back. Brown hair going to gray in the temples." She looked back up at him. "Probably be a lot better looking if he didn't look so worried. That's why I came over to tell you. It looked like he really wanted to find you home. He knocked on your door at least three different times as he walked around your home."

"Thank you, Eileen. I think I know who that was. I really do have to go now."

"The thing is, after he figured you were probably not home, he tried to get in. Your door wasn't locked. Whoever that was went in.

"What?"

"Yep, the guy went in, we heard some doors and drawers being slammed, but he came out..."

She was still talking as he left. The Prius tossed gravel as he made the turn to the exit. *Land Rover, huh? Who has that kind of money in this County? Gotta be Hargreaves.* Impatiently tailgating a contractor's pickup, he reached absently for his phone. I should call Pierson. No phone. Not on the dash, not in the passenger seat, not in pants. "Shit and damn, it's on the Sheriff's desk."

He crossed the long bridge toward Apalachicola in considerable excess of the posted limits, wishing that, for once, he'd spot a patrol. Cresting the high bridge over the river, the city spread out below him. He wondered if he could call it home again. Then he dropped down the other side of the bridge onto Market Street. Three older women in sundresses, sunglasses, and scarf-wrapped hats took their time crossing the street to the Gibson Inn. *Tourists! Well, the city needs 'em.* They looked up surprised by the silent approach of the Prius and made a show of speeding up without actually gaining any speed.

He swerved around them and pulled up to a left turn at the caution light. Ahead, only one light to go, a right on red onto 12th Street, which would become Bluff Road. He was speeding again, sixty-five miles per hour in a forty-five zone, then seventy, and breathless. He slowed as he crossed the tracks and pulled up to the security gate at Big Oaks circle. Newly installed, the chain-driven opener took its time sliding the wrought iron gate out of the way. Waiting, he noticed tire tracks in the grass, bypassing the gates. *Shit! As* soon as there was clearance at the gate, he pressed the Prius for all it could give on the sandy potholed road.

From a hundred yards out, he saw the outline of a white Land Rover under the house. Its position blocked Belle's Subaru from moving. *Shit!* For once, he was thankful for the Prius' silent drive. He let it roll to a stop short of the gravel parking area. *Where were they?* The question of the moment determined how to approach, how to enter.

He glanced left, whispered a 'hey, good boy' to Sugar, thankful that he and his car were now recognized as neighbors. From ground level, looking upstairs, voices were audible but not close. *Second floor?* He took extreme care to open the handle on the mudroom door.

No sound. No one in sight. *Take it slow, let their conversation drown my approach.* At the kitchen door, he peeked out across the great room. No one was visible. The sounds came from above.

Saylor heard Lindsey's voice, loud and clear enough to understand its plaintiff tone. "I don't have any idea where the key is. It was Mom and Dad's safe."

Hargreaves' deeper demanding tone. "Don't give me that shit! She must have told you when she knew she was dying."

Lindsey's reply, "I don't know." A slap. "I don't KNOW!" Crying now. "I really don't know!"

Saylor slipped off his shoes and stepped/slid across to the gun cabinet. The voices had stilled, but he kept moving. *No stopping now.*

His hand was over the smaller shotgun, the 410, when, BAM! The first shot passed by his head. The pfft of its passing was unheard over the splintering of cypress paneling behind him. He ducked, grabbing the twelve-gauge as he dropped. It wouldn't have been his gun of choice. It was what was at hand when the shot shattered the silence. He shuffled quickly to his stomach behind the back of the two-person settee. *Did Hargreaves know the guns in the cabinet were unloaded?* Crashing and yelling from the top of the stairs. Male and female voices shouting, someone had tackled him. Gunshots flew wild across the ceiling. Bam, bam! Then three more and upholstery stuffing exploded in a cloud of white motes from the back of the couch bare inches above his prone body.

Six shots down. Hargreaves has at least nine more. Saylor heard yells and sounds of a struggle from the balcony. He couldn't reach the ammo drawers from cover. *Now or never.* He slid a few feet on his belly and reached for the second drawer from the bottom. *Need ammo!* He raised his head, knowing that if Hargreaves got control of his gun hand, he was in the line of fire. He was also over thirty feet away. *Was Hargreaves actually any good with a pistol?* He spotted the 12-gauge #3 buckshot he was looking for.

Hands shaking, Saylor ripped the box apart, racking the slide back to open the breech, and loaded a shell. He repeated the action, put one more in the tube, and pushed the slide forward. No time for a full load. He popped his head over the edge of the settee. In split seconds, he took in the moving scene.

Mercy was lying on top of Hargreaves, who was trying hard not to be pushed over the top of the stairs on his back while also trying to get at his gun. Mercy had it by the barrel, playing a very dangerous game of keep away while she pushed with her legs to shove his torso over the edge of the top stair. He saw Belle and Lindsey peering from the doorway of the jack and jill bath. He yelled. "Belle, Lindsey, get back! Get in the closet!"

He rose, snapped the safety off, and ran for the base of the stairs. "Mur! Let go of him. Get back!" His bellowing voice got her attention. She let go and rolled off. Hargreaves shifted the pistol from his left hand on the barrel to his right hand on the grip, rolled toward Saylor, and lowered it. Saylor's shotgun rose. Both guns fired. Saylor heard the ceiling wood splinter behind him as Hargreaves' leg twitched unnaturally.

The pistol dropped, clattered down the steps, and came to rest. A scream, born of agony and surprise, filled the room. Saylor looked up first at Mercy. She was tucked into a ball clear of his firing angle. No sign of the other two. They'd ducked. He'd arrived at the top of the stairs by now.

Hargreaves looked beaten. He lay back in agony. His left hand moved gingerly toward the ragged hole just above his knee.

"Hold still, if that's clipped your femoral artery, you'll bleed out in minutes."

Hargreaves let the weight of his legs pull him partially over the edge of the stairs and wedged himself up on the first stair down with an elbow. Examining his damaged leg, he cried out again, a wounded animal in pain. The howl morphed into a yell of blatant fury. He leaned forward, making a grab for the barrel of Saylor's shotgun. They struggled for just a second before it came to rest on Hargreaves' chest. Saylor leaned into it and racked the next round into the chamber. Nothing in his eyes told Hargreaves there was any mercy in them.

Hargreaves looked up at him with murderous intent but now without the means. "You! You meddling son of a bitch. You've ruined everything!" His eyes dropped to his leg. It was bent backward just above the knee, the bone beneath clearly shattered. With no choke on the shotgun, the pellet's damage was spread across the width of his leg. A bright red stain spread across the fabric around a ruined hole two inches wide. "Oh FUCK! That hurts." He leaned forward to touch it and drew back.

"Sheldon Hargreaves. Glad to finally meet you." Saylor felt like spitting. "You are one sick bastard." When he looked back up for the girls, they were carefully nosing around the corner of the bathroom doorway. "It's OK, I think it's over. We're gonna need a belt. Can one of you get a leather belt from somewhere?" Neither of them moved. Mercy relaxed her fetal position and rolled over to look at him. He yelled this time. "Belt! Now!" The heads disappeared.

Lindsey came out with a thin pink leather belt with Calvin Klein's initials on the brass buckle. He took it, looked down at Hargreaves. "Hold still. I'm going to put a tourniquet on. It's going to hurt like a bitch."

Hargreaves was going gray, breathing hard now. "It already hurts like a bitch."

"Good," Saylor said, "glad to hear that." He lifted the wounded leg a few inches to get the belt under it, smiled as Hargreaves cried out again. "Glad because you would have been just as happy to have killed me on the spot." He pulled the belt tight. "Right?"

Hargreaves swore again, "Oww! Fuck you! Does it have to be that tight?" He glared up at Saylor. "You don't have to be so rough. You won, all right?"

Saylor reached down and slapped Hargreaves hard across the side of the head. "And Fuck YOU! I won? This isn't chess or checkers. Are you kidding? You just about killed me. What deviant shit did you have planned for Lindsey? For Mercy?" He reached back to slap him again. Hargreaves rolled to the side. Saylor let his arm drop. The three girls were now at the top of the stair immediately behind Hargreaves, who had slid carefully into a sitting position on the second to the top stair. "Ladies, you have anything you'd like to say?"

Mercy was closest. She boxed his other ear with a cupped hand.

"Ow!" Hargreaves hadn't seen it coming and cowered away from any further blows, protected his head with both arms.

"Eloquent! A well-chosen comment." Saylor said with a little humor in his voice. "Lindsey, Belle?"

Belle said, "You wanna hand me that shotgun? I'll be glad to have an unfortunate accident. Slip maybe while I'm walking past."

Hargreaves shifted away from her. Pressed his weight against the banisters. Saylor looked at him he'd deflated. Saylor thought about how long it would take for the EMTs and Apalachicola Police to arrive. "Hargreaves, you're going to survive. Long enough to become a well-liked cell block lawyer. Plenty of new clients are going to love you filing their appeals."

"We'll see about that." Hargreaves was defiant.

"Really? Two witnesses to abduction, kidnapping." He looked at Mercy, "Probable attempted rape? Intent to traffic? When the sheriff gets through with Robbie Caine, the rest of it will unfold. He's one of the sheriff's most cooperative witnesses. And by later today, the FBI will be scheduling interviews. Counselor, when we're all done, you're done. It's over. Finito!"

Hargreaves looked up. His forehead and cheeks were ashen, sweating. "Would you just call 911 please? Stop with your running on?"

"Really, do you think you need medical attention?" Saylor scanned the faces of the three girls. "Waddya think, ladies? Ya'll think it might wait just a minute or two?"

Saylor got a chorus of: "I'm in no hurry, not going anywhere, whatever." He leaned over the wounded leg. *The thigh is not meant to bend at that angle.* He resisted an urge to gag, balled a fist over his mouth, and swallowed the bile rising in his throat. The tourniquet was working, the wet blood oozing on his pants was turning dark, no oxygen. Old blood, he'd stopped the blood loss. He pointed a thumb over one of the ragged holes. "Counselor? What do you think would happen if I pushed right here?" His thumb brushed the red-stained fabric edge just above the entry point, above the shattered femur.

"Oh! Christ no!" Hargreaves stiffened, pushed harder into the banister.

"Well, then. I have a few questions before anyone calls 911. You're alert, conscious, the only thing you might lose by us taking too long is maybe, this leg. They might have to cut off any part of it that's been deprived of oxygen."

"You can't do that! I have legal rights."

"Really? You're looking at the judge, behind you there, our jury. We're not feeling really lenient right now."

"Fuck man." He winced, tried to reposition the lower leg. It didn't budge. "I'll sue."

"Sue? You're not going to sue! I don't have anything. My wife, that's ex-wife, has it all. I'm sure you know how that goes. Me? I have a twenty-five-year-old camper. You've seen it, you were there this morning engaged in a B and E, and I have a witness who just loves to talk."

"What do you want? Quit screwing around and call 911."

"First I need you to stop talking like a lawyer and start talking like the piece of shit we all know you to be."

Hargreaves looked over his shoulder caught the stares of Lindsey and Belle. Mercy was behind him, just out of sight. He shut his eyes, waited.

Saylor moved the thumb back and forth across the top of the wound. "I can push right here." He depressed the thumb just enough to make it known he could go harder. "I just need you to tell us all what you had planned. What was your master plan?"

"All right, all right." Hargreaves was sweating now; his body was expelling fear fluids. He turned his head to see Lindsey. "Your dad had planned for a long time to try to get the properties, his properties back in his name. He had some unfinished business in Cali, that's Cali, Columbia, not California."

"Go on. What kind of business. We're all ears." Saylor urged.

"He started out years ago, working for the feds, deep cover for the good guys. A bush pilot, he moved goods and money back and forth between the Columbian bush and Haiti." He stopped panting for air. "His identity got busted by the cartel. They found out he was a fed. He began working for them, on threat of death." He took a deep breath. Winced as a wave of pain passed.

"What about Jeremy's accidental death."

"That? He and Eleanor were almost quits anyway. He was gone most of any given year. She was running a couple of businesses and raising a kid. He thought if he disappeared, he could somehow come back here, take care of her, and get a hundred percent of the assets."

Lindsey spoke up. "For real? He planned to kill mom?"

"Listen, kid. Absence definitely does not make the heart grow fonder. Your mom started seeing casual friends in a more than casual way. And I'm sure he had access to some Latin honeys on the job. The cartels are good at making life good as long as everything is going their way."

"I don't believe mom was sleeping around." Lindsey was defiant.

"You want me to prepare a list?"

She was silent, then. "I don't think I want to know."

Saylor pushed him to continue. "The accidental death?"

"Yeah, right." His breathing was getting heavy, labored. "Shortly after he flipped, went to actual work for the Cali Cartel, he arranged for a pickup outside the two-hundred-mile limit. He set the auto-sailer to point his boat into the path of a storm and left it. He didn't expect for it to be found. But no biggy, the lie worked." Hargreaves looked up, more haggard now. "Can I have some water?"

Saylor nodded to Belle, "Go ahead and call 911, no wait, he recited the number from Sheriff Pierson's card. Let him know we have a GSW to the leg above the knee. There's a tourniquet in place but a lot of blood loss. EMT's will be here in less than ten minutes." To Hargreaves, "Please counselor, what was the plan of the day? Why were Mercy and Lindsey in that plywood box?"

He closed his eyes, licked at dry lips. "I can't say. I can't incriminate myself. No court would make me."

Saylor pressed down, his thumbnail half disappearing into the pellet hole. Hargreaves screamed. "Christ!"

"Christ is about the only help you're going to get around here if you don't start talking. You still want that water?"

"Yes, yes, please get me a drink."

Mercy appeared with a mouthwash cup full. Saylor held it for Hargreaves to sip. "OK, here's some water, there might be more. Start talking."

37

No Mister Nice Guy

Sheldon Hargreaves winced, closing his eyes tight against the pain. He leaned back into the banister and began talking. "It only took a year to get Jeremy declared dead. I helped her with the paperwork. At the time, I didn't know he wasn't dead. She couldn't get it transferred fast enough. Lindsey became a problem for Jeremy when Eleanor died." He winced, looked up into Saylor's eyes with pure hatred.

"Please continue, Counselor."

Hargreaves head leaned back, resting on a banister. "The estate is still in their corporate name, JEL LLC, but she had the officer's names changed so Jeremy was no longer named. She used the death certificate I'd managed to get for her to have his name removed from the corporation." He stopped, breathing hard.

"And?" Saylor's fist with thumb extended reached close to the open wound.

Wide-eyed, Hargreaves said. "Don't, please. Don't do that." He took a hard breath in, held it against the pain. "...and, I'm on the paper now, as Secretary to the LLC."

"My, my, that is convenient."

In defeat now, Hargreaves added, "but I never turned those papers over to Eleanor, or to Lindsey."

"Son of a bitch, so you've been planning this for a while?" Then he thought *that version hasn't been recorded yet.*

"No, it was just insurance. In case Eleanor's cancer—shit. In case Eleanor died. I'd have an angle."

"Isn't there some sort of oath you people take? Something to keep you from becoming such assholes?"

Hargreaves glare was malevolent. "Fuck you!"

Saylor asked, "OK, when was the will recorded?"

"Same time. We, Eleanor and I, did a complete update on the Estate, added the offshore accounts, new appraisals, etc. She made Lindsey sole beneficiary, except for a decent bequest to Sacred Heart. That hospital in Pensacola."

Saylor looked up at Lindsey. Her round eyes stared back. "You want to ask him anything?"

She edged closer, asked, "When did you learn that dad was alive? And—when did the two of you start working out this, this fucked-up plan?"

Hargreaves didn't look well. His face had lost color, his breathing was becoming shallow. Saylor gave a light tap to his head to get his eyes to open. "Focus. Did you hear the question?"

"Yes, about a year ago, I got this call from Port au Prince. I had to look up the international calling codes to figure that out. It was a message. Jerry, that's what he was calling himself then, left this long message. Called in some loyalty debts from years back. Said he was alive and well, working for the Feds." He raised a hand as if weighing something. "I don't know, he could have been still working both sides. He was making good money, but he was pissed that Eleanor's little side jobs, that's what he called her real estate gaming, was doing so well. He may not be a sterling character, but he's not stupid."

"Then he found out she was dying and how fast she was fading. He needed to get control of her assets." Hargreaves coughed, cleared his throat. "He had some decent money of his own set aside, the feds had been paying him by sending funds to a Cayman account. It was the same bank they had used as a couple to shelter some assets from the IRS. Some banking glitch or other, he found as a dead man he couldn't get at his own assets. That was the original call." He looked up at Saylor. "You guys called 911?"

Belle answered. "They should be here in a few minutes. Lindsey went down to open the gate."

Saylor knew time was short. "Fine, what was the plan for the girls? Why the plywood prison?"

"Jeremy had gone over. I mean. He was no longer Mr. Nice Guy. He ran with bad people who did bad things."

"Your kind of people?" Belle asked, anger turning the question into an accusation.

Hargreaves bit at his lip and closed his eyes for a moment. Saylor tapped him again. "Wake up. Stay with us. Help will be here shortly. What about the box? It didn't look to me like it was brand new. Like Mercy wasn't the first."

"Right, right. She wasn't, there were some others before. Robbie and his friends would pick them up at a bus station or a bar. You know, 'You need a ride?' or 'You want to party?' There are girls out there that will say yes. They hit upon a plan to sell them. To send them out with Robbie's uncle on a long-lines charter boat. The first time, two years ago, two girls went to Spring Break in Destin, never came home. Next year, same thing in Panama City. They would meet up with one of the fast boats moving drugs and do the exchange."

"And you helped them with this how?"

"Identities, initial funding. And better connections in New Orleans."

"Quite the enabler, aren't you?" Saylor's opinion of the legal profession was dropping to a new low. "When did Jeremy Lawrence know about this. Did he know about Lindsey?"

"Yes, he knew all about it. We talked about it. I had to tell him, with her as sole beneficiary, she had to disappear. Even if it was only for a few years. She had to be elsewhere.

"As a companion, or a whore?"

"He never said."

"And Mercy?"

"Outright sale, usual channels. She's young, cleans up nice. Good body. Not as good as some, but the light skin. Gets top dollar I was told."

"You are a piece of shit to even talk like that. Like she's USDA grade A." Saylor considered another head slap. Decided against it. Sirens could be heard approaching the gate on Bluff Road. He spared a glance up to see that Mercy had turned to the wall, her head buried in her arms.

"One last question, Counselor. Why was Jeremy Lawrence on the river yesterday? Why was he even there?"

Hargreaves looked him squarely in the eye. "Beats the shit out of me. Total surprise to me. Pissed me off that he destroyed my boat!"

Saylor huffed a laugh. "Counselor, you're not going to be needing that boat."

When he looked up again, Belle was holding Mercy in her arms. Looking down, Hargreaves had passed out. *Bastard!* "Come on ladies, lets leave this thing for the EMTs. We don't want to be in the way.

38

Mr. Right Time

Hargreaves was gone. Loaded into the back of an EMS van and given a police escort to the hospital. Mercy helped Belle clean up the mess after the sheriff's lab had photographed bloodstains, bullet holes, and the general layout of the scene.

Saylor sought out some privacy with his newfound daughter by mentioning to Belle, with a raised eyebrow, that he had to follow some loose threads. He and Lindsey settled into the lower deck's Adirondack chairs. The sun was high overhead and had gotten hot. Early afternoon, late April. Even with the relatively mild spring, temperatures hit the high eighties. Saylor hoped the moment was right for his revelation. Hoped for, he wasn't sure what. Acceptance?

"Lindsey, you really don't know me. For all we've been through in the last what, a little over two days. We really haven't had a chance to talk. You and Mercy have been through a living hell. I'm concerned for both of you."

Lindsey looked at him with an expression that said, that's sweet but looked back out across the river. He continued. "Are you going to be alright? Besides getting a new lawyer to make sure that Hargreaves hasn't done any long-term damage. According to Belle, the store's doing fine." When he paused, she looked back at him. He added. "I've really gotten to like Belle a lot. In a short time, we've gotten close. I'm concerned for her too."

She tugged at her overshirt, loosened it, and set her sunglasses on the arm of the chair. She leaned her head back and faced the sun, her eyes squinting against its glare. After a silent moment when he thought she wasn't going to respond, she said simply. "I think I'll probably go back to school. Maybe take a couple of classes summer session, then go full time in the fall."

He nodded agreement but realized she couldn't see him. "Sounds like a plan. Take it slow, you've been through a lot. What were you majoring in?"

"Nothing. I was floundering, taking this and that, whatever sounded interesting. Mom was OK with it, as long as I figured out something before registering for Junior level classes."

"Anything standing out?"

"Business maybe. It turns out I have a small business enterprise to run. But lately? I've considered women's studies. Nothing like being slotted for some sultan's harem to turn your head around."

"Lindsey, I'm so sorry all of that happened."

"Not your fault. You're Mr. Right Time at the Right Place."

"I was almost Mr. Dead in the Water."

She turned her head, then as that strained her neck, raised up to support herself on an elbow. She looked at him more intently now. A sly smile crept across her face. "You know? That was scary as hell, but I'd never been so excited. It was like...I don't know, wow! Totally awesome."

"Hah, yeah. Nothing like getting shot at to get your mind working at top speed."

"It also occurred to me, like just this morning. Dad was into secret ops. Spy games. I mean, only for the druggies. Not like the Russians or something, but Damn! I wondered if there was a path into one of the agencies."

"Lindsey, all of that's possible. You've only completed one semester. You can focus on anything. Business sounds good. Criminology with a specialty in forensics sounds good. Women's studies, probably wouldn't pay as well, but could be a particularly good fit too."

"Lots to think about." She settled back into the slats of the chair.

"You just turned nineteen. Plenty of time." He watched the neighborhood osprey swoop long and low over the river. It snagged at something and missed. It wheeled around, saw nothing but a small boil in the water, and flapped for altitude.

She said, "Did you see that? There's a fish down there, just got a new lease on the rest of the day. That's kind of what I feel like."

He smiled. "I did see that. Pretty cool for that fish, huh."

She turned to look at him again. "You and Belle getting serious?"

His eyebrows raised in surprise at the question. But it was a good question. "I think we are very much interested in finding out more about each other. She doesn't want to move too fast. I've been married twice. She wants to figure out if it was me or them. That takes time." He watched as the osprey took up its perch on a bare cypress branch. "...and I want to take time. She has a prickly side herself, but I think she is worth me taking that time, to see where this goes."

She nodded in agreement. "She's been great, taking over, teaching me how to run my own store." She put the sunglasses back on, turned to face him again. "What about you?"

"That book I mentioned? It's got a few bites at two publishers. My agent is talking to them about a multi-book contract. Series. It would keep me from having to go back to the newsroom in Houston. Not even sure they want me back. Papers are shrinking, going to become the victim of digital news." He stared out across the ancient river. "I'd stay here and continue to write if the book, or maybe books, get picked up." He paused, considering that course. "If that happens, there will be book tours, and I have a camper. I can be mobile to support a book tour. But Belle. Damn, I really like Belle."

"Mr. Saylor? I don't want you to hurt Belle. She's brassy, a fast mover, bit of a potty mouth. She likes what she likes, and I can see that she likes you. But she's vulnerable. She's been hurt before, by a lot of her old friends to boot."

"Yeah, I've gotten part of the story. But I get it. I'll do my damnedest to not hurt her."

Lindsey settled into the chair again. "Good, she's good people. Without her, I'd probably have closed the store down. Sold it."

Change of subject. Now is as good a time as any. "Lindsey, when Belle and I were going through the papers in the fireproof safe, we found an interesting document." *Dive in.* "You had a will drawn up. It may have been the reason that Hargreaves had you taken to the box."

"My will? It put everything in a trust." She turned to look at him again. "So, you read it? You know there's a guy out there somewhere that doesn't know I exist. If something happened to me, you know, like a Mack truck, I get hit by a bus. Something totally not expected, then all of their holdings that went to me go to him, and to Sacred Heart Hospital." She paused, taking in the most recent developments.

"I guess in hindsight, Sheldon Hargreaves knew he'd never really be looking for the mystery man. He'd just suck on admin fees forever."

"I know. That's one of the reasons I wanted to talk to you out here, alone."

She looked apprehensive if anything, but he had her attention. She pivoted in her chair, leaned toward him.

Go for it. "You know that Pierson considered me to be one of his prime suspects, right?"

"Yeah."

"He got one of my old friends to come by my place to get some DNA materials. Hair, my toothbrush, and a fingerprint off a beer bottle. I didn't even know he was doing it."

Lindsey looked confused; the discussion of his DNA was a non-sequitur.

He continued, "The sheriff was just pursuing due diligence on what he considered a prime suspect to check my DNA based on hair and residues found here. Based on the BOLO, I'd been ID'd, but that wasn't enough evidence to charge me. Look where that led."

"Yeah, who'd a guessed."

He nodded, he wondered about her abduction. He'd been hit really hard, and it still hurt. "Do you remember much about how you were taken?"

She moved her sunglasses to the top of her head. "Wasn't much of a struggle. Hargreaves suggested some tea or coffee while we were finalizing some updates to my school trust fund. We settled on some diet cokes. We were sitting inside, here at the house. I'd just put down a couple of glasses, but I had to go to the bathroom before I sat down. I was about two sips into my coke when I began to get dizzy, confused. I couldn't seem to find a word in mid-sentence. Before I could get a third breath, I was out. Woke up in the box, just like you. Taped fore and aft."

He nodded and smiled, appreciating her nautical metaphor. "I told you about the line-up right, back when we were in the box?"

"Yeah, yeah, but..."

"Well, the sheriff called me in when the results came back."

"And how did that make any connection?" Her look changed from puzzled to worried. She sto4od and backed toward the railing. "You weren't here. How—?"

259

"I hadn't been here. I haven't been here for a long time."

"Huh, you're not making sense," she said, confusion wrinkling the top of her nose. "What are you trying to tell me?"

"I'm sorry, I haven't been able to figure out how to tell you. He called me back in for further questioning because he had great motivation to do so. One of the prime suspects in almost any domestic case is a next of kin with a vested interest."

Her confusion was total. Nothing made sense. Her back was up against the deck's upper railing.

"Whoa! Don't be afraid. I, I've known since that talk with the sheriff." He rose but did not move closer. "Lindsey, I'm your real biological father. I was a good friend of your mother's in high school..."

Her hands moved to her mouth. Her eyelids lifted in wonder, shock as her head shook in disbelief. "How, how did...?"

"I came home for a school break when I was just about your age now. I had just finished my freshman year at FSU. She had just finished high school and was about to go to UWF for her freshman year. We hooked up." He sent a facial shrug. "I'm sorry I couldn't tell you earlier. There was simply too much going on at the time, at each time. This is the first real opportunity—"

She stared at him. Seeing for the first time that her eye color matched his eyes. Her mouth slowly gaped open, then closed. "So, I'm a Saylor, with a Y?"

"You are whoever you want to be. Stay a Lawrence in honor of the two people who raised you. Pick a name from your ancestry that you like. Take your birth mother's name, Hardin. Her name was Sandra Jane Hardin. A really beautiful person, inside and out."

"This is going to take more than a moment to digest."

He began to smile as she started a thinking/speaking trick that both he and Belle used in reciting lists. She began to tick off the tips of her fingers. "So, you knew about me, about you and me, by the time you were dumped in the box." Index finger. "You knew the whole time we sat around in there talking about our mini-histories." Middle finger. "You knew while we were racing down the river getting shot at and shooting back. Ring finger. "You knew all along that the Phillip-whose-it in the boat was actually my dad, Jeremy Lawrence." Pinky finger. "And that I shot, and probably killed Phillip-whose-it." Thumb.

"Son of a bitch!" She stared. Her head slowly shook back and forth in disbelief.

All he could do was nod slowly. Accepting and admitting it all. "Although I had suspicions, I didn't know you were who you are until we made introductions in the box. Can you think of a good time in there for me to have told you who I am, who *we* are?"

No answer.

"I didn't know it was your father when he was shooting at us, but I found out in the boat. That didn't seem like the best time to tell you that the ZZ-Top guy, AKA Phillip Jones, was your long-lost and presumed dead father."

She turned a quarter turn away, parked her elbows on the rail, and searched for the osprey. "No, but somehow, I'm still a little mad." Her mouth opened again and closed. "This changes everything, doesn't it?"

"I understand, if..." He didn't finish because he didn't know if he did understand. He reached a hand foreword, palm up, an invitation.

They both started moving at the same time. He enveloped her in a hug and felt her shuddering. Understood that there was plenty of reason to be crying. Emotions have to be aired, let out, shared, expressed.

He put his hand to the back of her head. It was the first time he'd ever hugged a child, with this much emotion. It slowly dawned on him, maybe it was a hiccup mixed in with the shuddering, that maybe she was not crying. *Was she laughing?* He pulled away, a fraction of an inch, as much relaxation of the hug as her arms would permit. "You alright down there?"

"Yes, and here I thought since mom died, I'm an orphan. I almost get back a dad I don't really know, lose him, and get another one I never knew existed. And he's you! Mr. Right Time."

"You're OK with this?"

"It's just, well, you can't make this shit up." Perhaps for the first time they'd been together, she must have realized she was with a parent. She apologized for her language. "Sorry, can't make this stuff up."

"Hey, listen, I'm a writer and I couldn't make this shit up." He felt her snork a small inner laugh. "And don't worry about the language around me. Language is a buffet; it needs salt and pepper."

"Who said that, a Chinese philosopher?"

"No, I just did." He caught movement in the plate glass windows. Dark except for the foreground lit from the sunlight on the deck. Mercy and Belle were nose-smearing close at the glass. Both were grinning ear to ear. Belle gave him two thumbs up. "Look Lindsey, look at the ladies. I think we're going to be all right."

39

The World Says Hello

Saylor was all about loose threads. Even after a press deadline had closed, he'd make follow-up calls to check on witnesses and sources to see if they were alright. Sometimes he'd give fair warning that they would be in the morning or evening edition, back when there were two editions. Or he'd check, simply to satisfy a nagging suspicion to see if there was more to a story than the deadline would permit.

There was a huge loose end hanging on his personal story that he couldn't ignore. And it had life-changing implications for any future with his newfound daughter. Granted, Jeremy Lawrence was a dirtbag. He'd done a lot of dirtbag things in the employ of the Cali Cartel. None of those things, none of the fancy piloting, and none of the God only knows what else he'd done in the dual relationships with the US Agencies or the Columbian Federales could explain his serving up his daughter to the Cartel. He opened his laptop to list possibilities:

JL's Motives
- Jeremy had a plan to get her to Columbia, elsewhere? and keep her under wraps, maybe even as his daughter, until he could get legal control of his properties,
- He wanted to intimidate her into signing over the properties,
- Attorney Hargreaves had undertaken her kidnapping on his own, hoping to profit from her sale on the skin market,
- Did JL know that H had written him out of the LLC?
- Had JL found out about her abduction by H and was actually on his way to rescue her when he found an unknown man motoring away with the two girls,
- He'd actually been trying to rescue his daughter?

Bruce Ballister

- ????

Looking up from the screen, he could see the arc of a rising sun working through the distant tree line. He got up to refill his coffee mug. Refortified, he opened the sliding glass door to the lower deck and walked out to watch the sunrise over the estuary. He allowed its brilliance to burn circles into his retinas before he looked away. He took a long pull of his favorite stimulant and set the cup down. He closed his eyes to let the bright circle of the sun's imprint on his retinas fade as he listened to the world wake up. A dog two or three houses downriver barked at some nuisance. Next door, Sugar answered the call, passing on the alarm. Somewhere, out in the sawgrass swamp expanse beyond the river, a hawk cried out. Below him, a wren worked its way through the tall unmowed grass, looking for breakfast. Absently, he watched it stand on a seed stalk of centipede grass, push it to the ground, and patiently strip it of fresh green seeds. He ran back over the list he'd made. None of the scenarios he'd come up with were good.

He was startled as a hand landed softly on his shoulder. "None of the above?"

He turned to see Lindsey standing beside him in a robe with a towel wrapped around shower-wet hair. "Good morning, starshine." He offered a good morning smile, raised his cup to her in a toast.

"The world says hello." She smiled back down at him.

"That's pretty good! I wouldn't expect your generation to know the lyrics from *Hair*."

"Mom was a fan. She had gramma's old collection from the sixties. The vinyl. I tossed it all out, but I've still got the re-release on Apple music."

"You tossed the album?" His face showed mock horror.

"It was scratched beyond listening pleasure, and the disc was cracked. Besides, on the download, you don't have to turn it over after each side."

He sighed, "True." He stood, joining her at the deck rail, and looked out across the river, remembering. "My copy was stolen. A B&E by some local kids. Never able to press charges."

"Sorry, in good shape it's worth some money these days."

264

"Yup." He turned to face her, elbow on the deck rail. She turned to face him, a miniature of himself crossed with the mirror of her mother.

"I guess it was a little weird, not looking anything like either parent." He wanted to say more. "At some point, you must have noticed that you look nothing like Eleanor?"

"I had my suspicions, you know. You look in the mirror, wondering. I would have expected something, like, around the eyes or something, like—" Lindsey leaned in, peering up into his eyes, "—like yours."

He couldn't help the smile forming. "Yeah, but I'm probably the first to say you are the spitting image of your mother but with my eyes. Sandra was a great person. I was really upset to hear about what happened to her."

She looked down and out across the river, her face wrinkled in sadness for a moment. When she looked up, she'd replaced the look with a smile—one of those put-up smiles when you have to have one. "I guess I have to settle for just being lucky. Lucky that she decided not to do the coat hanger thing; to have me. I'm sorry I never got to know her."

He nodded, holding her gaze.

She continued, "I hope someday we can sit, and you'll tell me all you know about her."

"You bet. I've got some bridges to repair with one of my old friends. His wife and Sandra were best friends, as close and you and Marcie. We should all get together and let us introduce you to your other mother."

"That would be great."

"Say, when you came out, you started with 'none of the above.' What was that about?"

"Your list."

He drew a temporary blank. "Oh, the list!"

"On your laptop." She glanced toward the window wall, the depths beyond nearly impenetrable in the reflected bright glare of dawn.

"I should have shut that, sorry. I was just trying to figure out the angle. Why you were on that holding barge? Why would your dad have been involved? Why would he have been there then, and doing or intending what?"

With both elbows on the deck rail, she turned her head a quarter-turn away from his. "I don't know if you've heard different. What Sheldon, or Marcie's mom, or anyone might have said is probably nothing close to the truth."

He didn't respond, feeling she might be close to letting something out. From the side angle, he could see she was sucking on the inside of her cheek. Her voice came out soft, too soft for anyone five feet away to hear. When at last she let sound out, it was flat, emotionally barren.

"We didn't really get along. Some of it may have been his former military hard-ass attitude all the time. But he was always gone too. Mom and I got to be really close. I felt like the only child of a single mom once I got older and could see for myself what was going on."

He waited, wanting to ask her to elaborate. After a long pause, he heard her blow out with force as if reaching for resolve. "I often heard them fighting upstairs. Sometimes it got loud and ugly, and that seemed to be what to expect when he was home. He drank whisky, she drank gin. It wasn't pretty. The next morning, or the rest of the weekend, he'd be all friendly to her. I get that people get mad and make up, but it was like a war zone sometimes. I just tried to stay away. If I knew he was coming home from Pensacola, I'd try my damnedest to stay at Marcie's house. But it got better."

"That's good. Did things work out for them?"

She turned to look at him. "Not that I could tell. It was better when he was working for the NARCs. When he was gone on assignment, he just wasn't there to be trouble." She huffed a silent laugh. "I just never felt like he was interested in being a dad. And from what I overheard when they yelled, he wasn't much of a husband either."

"That can be tough to live through. When I was a kid, dad would be out on some out-of-town construction job and only come home weekends. And he liked to drink hard whisky."

She shared a glance and nodded, then looked back out across the river. "Up until I was three or four, he was only home on weekends. He was still active duty out of Pensacola, but I guess somewhere in there, the narco work started up because he was gone for months at a time."

"I get it. Hargreaves did say that absence does not make the heart grow fonder."

"Yeah." The word came out as an indictment.

"Sorry for what he said about your mother."

She turned to him. "I don't know if there was anything to it. She had friends, and I spent a lot of sleepovers at Marcie's house. It might have happened. I just hate that Sheldon slipped that image of her into my memories."

"I imagine losing your mom was hard." He shook his head. "No, no I can't. My mother is still alive, remarried. I haven't had that 'I'm an orphan' moment yet."

She continued, "When dad went missing...when Jeremy went missing. I was eleven. I was a little wiser than when I was a little kid. I wasn't afraid of him anymore, but...I sometimes wished he wouldn't come back. Then I heard that dad was missing at sea. I felt guilty as hell when the boat was found wrecked. Like somehow, my wishing had helped it be so." She paused, lost in the past.

She continued, again facing out across the river into an infinity that only she could see. "I'm not sure I could honestly say I grieved. I just felt hollow for a while and, well, I moved on. Mom and I moved on. But when mom died, I fell apart. She came up to Tallahassee, took me out to dinner. On the way back to campus, she pulled over for the heart-to-heart discussion. She told me about her diagnosis, the prognosis." Her voice began to waver. "I think I started packing the next morning. I didn't even tell her I was coming home. I knew I wanted to spend as much time with her as I could." A sniff, she wiped her nose on the back of her wrist. "All that going on and dealing with the news that I wasn't even her kid, their kid. Eleanor needed to fill a hole in their marriage, and I showed up."

Saylor had heard of it before. Eleanor had lost a child, baby Janet, but she still wanted to be a mother. She'd been the driving force for the adoption. Jeremy put his career first and never really bonded with the adopted child. Saylor felt the hurt in her tone. She was reliving some hard times, so he'd know.

She turned back to face Saylor, eyes red, cheeks flushed. "Mom just said to be strong, that it's one of the risks in a military family. And that confused me, because I didn't connect the boat accident with anything to do with his military career. I thought he was working for the feds."

"Oh, Lindsey. I don't know what to say."

"Shortly before that last trip out in the boat, they'd had another one of their big blow-ups. I thought he was going to hurt her. Mom came downstairs and told me to go over to my friend Marcie's house and wait. It's about a mile or so down the road. I took my bike. I was talking to her in the yard when I saw him blast by in his car. That was the last time I ever saw him."

"Damn, Lindsey. I'm so sorry."

"Some days really suck, you know?"

"Yeah, they do. I think that chapter is over and gone. So, you never saw him again until the river, that chase on the river?"

"No, he never came by the barge, the box, our cell; whatever you'd call it."

"Do you think you might want to get some counseling?" You now know that he wasn't your father, but still, for some people, the idea of having killed a person can work on them...and you two had a history, good or bad."

She turned to face him. "I've been thinking that's probably a good idea, for before I go back to school." She blew at a hair that had blown across her face. "I wish, at least I think I wish, that I knew why he was there, on the river. What he was doing."

"I guess we'll never know."

"I'm not sure I would want to. He's gone. And Sheldon's arrested and gone, and good riddance." She breathed in hard, blew out hard. Purged. "But look at it this way. I found you, er, you found me."

Resilience, this girl is strong, resilient. "I'm glad we found each other."

He started to reach toward her, an opening. She curled into an embrace. "Glad to meet you, Lindsey." He pulled back, "Listen, I've got to go in to talk with the feds this morning at ten. We can talk more later."

40

Up the Creek

Saylor left the sheriff's compound in time to make a lunch date with Belle. He thought he'd have time to get to his camper and make some notes, but he barely had time to get to downtown Apalachicola to pick her up. The interview had gone from precisely ten o'clock to almost noon. He ducked when the silver bell rang out overhead as he entered the shop. It still surprised him. "It's me."

"Come on back, I'm wrapping." Belle called out.

He found her elbow-deep in brown craft paper as she bundled a three-foot-long plastic red snapper into the heavy brown paper. Three short lengths of packing tape dangled from her left forearm, ready to secure loose ends. With the snapper bound in brown paper, she gave the initial wrap two layers of bubble wrap before setting it into its shipping box. "This load of fish is heading for Wisconsin." She looked up and grinned. "Guess why?"

"They don't have enough red snapper in Wisconsin?"

"Close. The owner is an avid ice fisherman. On the rare occasions that he stays in the frozen north for more than a week, he spends at least three days tending a hole in some lake I'd never be able to pronounce."

Saylor looked confused. "And that's for his ice cabin?"

"No, it's for his lakefront cabin. He wants if for over his fireplace."

His confused look deepened. "I still don't get it."

"He's gonna get his buddies to guess what kind of fish it is. They've never been further south than Tennessee. So, he's hoping to win some bets."

"A sale is a sale, I guess."

"It was my idea. I could see he was dawdling, not quite ready to walk out and leave it on my wall. So, I got him talking." She finished with a beaming smile that had more candle power than the overhead lights.

"Cha-ching." He returned the smile and felt the pressures of the last few hours disappear.

"Exactly, cha-ching, and I have three more of those in stock, at a hundred-fifty apiece."

"Whew! You ever think of going into sales?"

She blew him a Bronx cheer.

"Come on, close up and let's go get some lunch. We can talk over crab cakes."

They met Lindsey and Mercy for lunch at the Up-the-Creek Raw Bar and took a second-floor balcony set-up for four overlooking Scipio Creek and the river beyond. Occasional passing clouds kept the heat down, and the weather was springtime gorgeous with a light breeze from the bay indicating that the coastal thermals were kicking in for the day. The mood was upbeat but with a foundation of expectation. Saylor had just finished with the FBI.

"So, you gonna keep us in the dark?" Belle asked, almost bouncing with anticipation. "Spill it."

Saylor had been trying to collect his thoughts, to spell it all out in sequence if possible. "Well, first of all, I knew the guy. That helped."

Mercy almost spit out the iced tea she just sipped. "You really do know people in the FBI?"

"Yes, Mur. I do. Joe Mollinado and I met on a story I was doing last year. Actually, that story is one of the reasons I left Houston." He shrugged. "Unconnected longer story. Let's just say, we knew each other from work uncovering a trafficking ring in Texas." He decided to just dive in.

"For starters, Sheldon Hargreaves was no surprise to the FBI. He'd been a person of interest for almost a year based on his contacts with watch list bad guys in New Orleans. There are three major locations on the Gulf for the movement of girls to the south and undocumented workers to the north. Some of these, the ones I was investigating, were for the sex trade all over the US. You've got Miami, no surprise, New Orleans, and Houston. All are major shipping centers and literally, boatloads of empty containers move south in any given month to ports across South and Central America or back across the Pacific to Asia. Any one of these might be used to transport captives in the flesh trade."

He had their attention. It was a grim subject, and two of the three would almost certainly have become victims of the system. "Hargreaves only had to collect his victims and deliver them to a holding house in New Orleans." He grimaced. "That was scheduled for last weekend, but Robbie's connections had been arrested." He looked over to Mercy. "That's why you stayed there so long."

Lindsey asked, "Did you find out about dad?" She frowned. "About Jeremy?" She was already recasting the roles of fatherhood in her life.

"Lindsey, we may never know, unless Hargreaves is cooperative enough to share more with the FBI. For the time being, pending arraignment or his turning state's witness, he's not saying anything. He's not going to defend himself, but he's lawyered up and his new attorney is due in tomorrow. So, we don't know. And Jeremy can no longer tell us what he was doing. We may not know for some time until the feds and the sheriff compare notes." He reconsidered. "Maybe something will come out of testimony from Hargreaves. For the time being, think the best."

Lindsey looked down at her untouched combo basket of broiled catfish and oysters, remained quiet, and poked with no apparent interest at her food.

He pressed on. "My best advice is to assume the best. Assume he heard what Hargreaves was planning and had come back to get you out of there. You saw my list of scenarios. It's probably not complete, but it's fifty-fifty he was trying to get you out of there versus he's complicit in you being there. For now, for the sake of your memories, put him on the high side of that."

Lindsey nodded. "I guess that's best. If I spend the next six months trying to hate the man and find out he was trying to rescue me, that would be weird."

Belle reached over and put a hand on her shoulder. "Sweetie, I think he's right there. You have too much to do, to repair, to keep hate in your heart that might not need to be there."

Lindsey shared a look with Belle. "Thanks, you're probably right." She pivoted back to Saylor. "What about Robbie and Shirk?"

Bruce Ballister

"I don't think we have anything to worry about. Robert Aaron Caine is facing federal charges: kidnap, intent to traffic, and attempted rape. Even with cooperation and pleading no contest, he's facing a minimum of twenty years in lock up." He took a sip of his tea and leaned back in his chair. "Shirk is William Don Taggart, AKA Billie Don Taggart, AKA Shirk, and a few others I don't remember. He has a state and federal rap sheet—"

Mercy interrupted. "Do they know where he is?"

Saylor nodded. "Yup, he's in the Washington County morgue." This brought varied reactions from around the table, from Mercy's 'Hell yes!' to Belle's dropped jaw. "He was found in his trailer with a bullet through his neck. Probably dead before he hit the floor. Initial reports link the caliber of the bullet to the 9mm that Hargreaves brought to the house last night. Forensics will have to make the confirmation, but it looks like Sheldon Hargreaves, your Mister H, was cleaning up some details. No one will ever know what his intentions were after he secured the papers in that vault. No telling whether he intended to kill or transport you all. Belle would have been an unexpected bonus if he'd somehow managed to get all three of you to New Orleans."

Belle's hands flew to cover her mouth. "Oh My God! That never occurred to me."

"Well, it occurred to Joe Mollinado. Your name is being added to Hargreaves' charges." Saylor raised his hands palms up. "He's never getting out. Between the kidnapping, human trafficking, attempted murder, and actual probable murder one charges, he's looking at life without the possibility of parole." He looked over to Lindsey. "You're going to need a new lawyer."

"Yeah, no shit." She stopped, round-eyed. "I mean, yeah, I will."

He laughed, "It's all right! Let's not worry about the role of father-daughter just yet. Deal?"

"Deal."

He looked at her untouched plate. "You know, those are a lot better warm."

She looked down, stabbed a battered and deep-fried oyster with her fork, and began to catch up with the others.

Saylor looked over to Mercy. "Mur, you have any plans? Are you still thinking about moving on to Montgomery? The casinos?"

272

"Nah, Belle and I got to talking this morning. I'm going to give her some help at the store so it doesn't have to close in the middle of the day for lunch or she doesn't have to just eat a sandwich in the back room while juggling sales."

Belle piped in excitedly, "And she's going to set up a website for the store." El talked about that as she was getting sick. Said it was one of the things she had always intended to do. But bless her heart, Eleanor had trouble finding where to plug in a USB. I finally showed her how to attach pictures to emails, but the woman was technically challenged." She waved a hand over to Mercy. "Mur, on the other hand," she flourished her hand in mid-air, "is fluent in three website platforms, Adobe Illustrator, and general geek speak."

Mercy flushed in embarrassment. "That's what I was going to be doing in Montgomery, but I like the present company better."

Saylor was surprised. He had made assumptions about her going to work for the casinos, which were several social ladder steps below website designer. He nodded approval. Looking back to Lindsey. "College?"

"I called this morning to set up some counseling sessions. I'm going up to Tallahassee next week. I think I need to ... uh, resolve some issues." Her head bobbed as her mind went elsewhere for a moment. She glanced back up at him. "But yeah, I'm going to chill for a bit. My old friend, Marcie Helms invited me up for the week. Then, I don't know, I'll move back up to Tallahassee and get ready for school this summer. It's only a little over a month off."

"Sounds good." He was pleased to see her resilience, her confidence. Eleanor had been a good mother to her. "Say, Lindsey, the reporter in me still has questions, unresolved loose threads."

Belle rolled her eyes. "Yeah, look where looking for loose threads got you."

"Hey, might be it was a good thing for these guys." He waved a fork at Lindsey and Mercy.

Lindsey said, "Give it your best shot."

"Back in Tallahassee, when I first saw you, a perfect stranger, you were looking at pictures of something. I was wondering if those had any bearing on anything, if it would have been some kind of clue as to where you were."

"Nah, nothing fancy. Just some pictures Mom and I took on our last trip over to Little St. George. She did some shelling. I took some pictures. We both knew her days were numbered. It was fantastic and melancholy at the same time."

Saylor nodded, understanding the mix. "Did you by any chance have your boat with you in Tallahassee?"

She looked at him like he was a defrocked psychic. "How? What made you—"

"I remembered the detail but wasn't sure if it was something I'd put in a scene I was writing or if it was from real life."

"Yeah, I used it as my personal u-haul to get stuff moved back down here from school. They were hounding me to clear out my dorm room." She looked around at their bemused faces. "What, you never used a boat and trailer to move furniture before?"

Saylor said, "Fair enough. No more loose ends, for now."

Lindsey, having finished her second oyster, asked. "And what about you, Dad? What are you going to do?"

He looked at Belle, saw her openly expectant face was as curious as Lindsey's. Looking out across the river at the bay he'd grown up on, he said. "I think Houston has a lot less to offer, current circumstances considered, than right here. I have at least two books in the pipeline, and I pay cheap rent at the RV park." His glance fell back on Belle. "And you never know, something else might come up where I'd just want to get more settled."

41

Settled

Jayson Saylor sat at his laptop. His mind was split in too many directions to work, but he felt he had to keep working. It would be a distinct understatement to say that the last few days had been a distraction from the progress he needed to make on the first outline draft of novel two. His editor had asked for it a few days earlier, before the bump on the head. *Man, that was only four days ago?*

He took a breath and began typing:

Andie Jackson ducked involuntarily. She knew, factually, that by the time you hear the bullet, it's already missed, but still. She stole a glance back at Amos. He was braced at the wheel of their Zodiac and attempting to maintain a zig-zagging target for the asshole ahead who was trying to kill him, or Andie, or both. He had no cover and risked it all to keep a steady course. Andie was crouched in the bow of the boat, both for ballast, to help keep the nose down for less wind drag, and for the scant amount of cover. Neither the sniper rifle nor the Sig Sauer P228 was a good choice, but that's all she had.

Conzuaga was ahead and losing ground, but not fast enough. If he made it into the mangrove swamps ahead, he was as good as lost. In the failing light of the evening, finding him and his human cargo in that maze would be all but hopeless. Andie raised her head above the tubular frame of the rigid inflatable's hull. Conzuega's boat was still a hundred yards ahead. She yelled back to Amos, "Stop zigging. Just haul ass. We need to catch up *now!*" The little boat stabilized almost immediately. Amos kept his line just to the side of the lead boat's line of cavitation bubbles. On this track, there were lower cross swells and minimal loss of bite due to aerated water. Conzuaga's boat drew closer to the line of mangroves, only a thousand yards to go. His jet drive would allow him to skim along in places that would have their stern drive chewing mud.

"Shit! He's going to make it." Ahead, she saw a dark opening in the line of foliage.

"Bastard!" She drew the handgun forward and stabilized it as well as she could in a two-handed grip. Her only advantage? The lead boat was having to deal with low white caps and was a less stable firing platform. She lowered the foresight to a point that completely covered the dark silhouette that was firing back at them. Three shots. Bam, bam, bam, in quick succession. Then three more. The head of the gunman who'd been firing at her disappeared. The boat ahead jerked slightly but kept flying toward the opening in the mangroves. A sense of hopeless resignation began to settle in. They weren't going to catch him in time. Conzuaga's speeder had a small V8 pushing a Jacuzzi jet. In the calmer water near the tree line, she could see that they were no longer closing on the lead boat.

One last chance, she reached back and jerked the sniper rifle from its case. She quickly spun the knurled knobs that locked the scope down and set the scope aside. She drew the bi-pod legs down and let them rest on the forward curve of the inflatable hull. She yelled back again. "Straight at him. Best you can do, Amos. Keep 'er straight!" Scopeless, the Barrett M82 did have a tiny sighting tick at the top of the barrel. It would have to do. She flicked off the safety and leaned her cheek in on the smooth steel barrel. She lined up the sighting lug and took aim. Boom! Unsilenced, the powerful rifle told the world that someone was in danger or dead. Birds of all kinds lifted out of the swamp ahead. She looked forward. Conzuaga's Hawaiian print shirt was still there, centered behind the console. "Fuck!" His boat was now less than two hundred yards from the line of foliage.

But wait! She now saw that he was slumped over the console. As the most wanted trafficker of souls in El Salvador slid off to the right of the driver's console the wheel slowly turned to the right as well. The boat began to turn into an ever-tightening curve.

The shooter was down, apparently, and Conzuega seemed to be out of it as well. As she watched, the boat had missed the approaching tree line and would soon be turning in an increasingly narrower arc back toward them. She raised a fist, signaling Amos to slow, then stop.

He stopped typing. As his fingers tried to keep up with his mental commands, he'd realized he couldn't let Conzuaga's boat crash into the tree line and recreate the intensity of damage at the scene he'd lived through only a few days ago because he'd endanger Conzuega's female human cargo. *Hmm, how am I going to get Andy aboard a speeding boat that's driving in circles. Ah, shoot out the engine without hitting any of the girls.*

He looked up at a knock on the door. He quickly looked around. His RV/home/office still had the distraction of a fantastic water view, but he'd been spending fewer hours here than at the River House. He tended to get a little messy when he was working. He thought, *pretty well cleaned up.* "Come in." Turning, he saw Belle climbing up and in. "Hey beautiful."

"Hey handsome." She looked at the laptop, recognized his writing application's screen. "You keeping Andie Jackson safe?"

"Heck no, she's in a gunfight on a fast boat nearing the mangrove swamps of El Salvador."

"Jeez, I wonder where you got that idea." She hoisted a package onto his countertop. He recognized the bag as being from the Easy Mart station at the point. She added. "I figured you'd type through lunch. Thought you might want something."

He raised eyebrows in anticipation. "Whatcha got in there?"

"Your usual. Nothing fancy." She pulled at the contents and revealed a grease-stained tray of chicken fingers with four tater logs laying on top. Next, she found the sixteen-ounce Diet Coke, and the pint of Ben and Jerry's. She grinned at his smile. "I'm not going to let you do this all the time, you know."

"I was just going to ask if you were trying to spoil me."

"No, and I don't want to kill you with cholesterol either. This is dinner for two."

"So, you're saying you have long-term concerns for my heart?"

Belle was standing beside and behind him. She leaned over and planted a wet kiss on his ear. She whispered, "I'm saying my heart has concerns for your heart." She planted another kiss at the edge of his eye. "Why don't you hit the save button on that thing and clear the table."

A few minutes later, facing each other across the tiny table, she said. "Lindsey and I were just talking."

"Yeah, about what?"

"About you."

"And...?"

She licked at some potato spice residue on her fingertips. "She and I have been sleeping in those two downstairs bedrooms. Eleanor's space upstairs has been pretty much untouched, right?"

He thought maybe he knew where this was going, but stayed quiet, except for, "right."

"Well, what if you and I were to take that upper suite. You wouldn't have to live in this tiny house. You wouldn't have to work in your kitchen, or shave sitting on your toilet."

He smiled at her, "You're saying you want to shack up with me? That moving to the River House is OK with Lindsey?"

She tossed the remainder of a potato log at him. He ducked.

"Yes, Mr. Jason Saylor, novelist, rescuer of young women, and occasional jerk. I'm saying I want to give that a try." She adopted a pout, "Mostly 'cause it's eating into my gas budget to keep driving over here." She tilted her head to the left in a pose, raised one eyebrow in question. "So...?"

"So, it's about your gas bill, is it?"

"No, you idiot, I think I'm falling for you."

He dodged another piece of potato log. He slid out of his seat, reached to help her out of hers, and pulled her close. "One good thing about sharing a meal for two."

"What's that?"

"Nobody has bad breath." He leaned down and kissed her. "I think I like that idea."

"That nobody has bad breath?" She pulled back a little, smiling up at him.

"No, that we shack up together." He pulled her close. "Umm," he murmured, "you taste like potato logs," and kissed her again.

End

If you enjoyed this book, please, leave a review on Amazon.com, or Goodreads.com or anywhere you discuss books with friends. Indie authors depend on the gracious responses of our readers on these and other public platforms to expand our readership.

Please check my website; **www.ballisterbooks.com** for other books you may enjoy. Will Jason Saylor's saga grow? Who knows? I'm working on it...

If you'd like to join my growing mailing list, drop me a note at: **bruce@ballister.com** subject reading list

I promise not to spam your inbox!

Made in the USA
Columbia, SC
26 January 2022

54264312R00159